ELECTRIC TRAIN

DAVID BEATY

Electric Train

SECKER & WARBURG · LONDON

For B, as always

First published in England 1975 by
Martin Secker & Warburg Limited
14 Carlisle Street, London W1V 6NN

Copyright © 1975 by David Beaty

SBN 436 03912 5

Printed in Great Britain by
Cox & Wyman Limited
London, Fakenham and Reading

PROLOGUE

HERE LIES the soft south-east of England. Here are smooth hills and water meadows, apple orchards and hop fields, sluggish rivers, bluebell woods, cherry-blossom and green pastures. Here are Georgian houses, Tudor manors, Norman churches. Here are two bishoprics – Rochester and Canterbury – old inns and coaching houses, ancient monasteries, fertile farms, prosperous breweries, oasthouses, papermills, brickworks and smugglers' lairs. Here is chalk on the hills, clay in the valleys. Here the coastline is rimmed with holiday towns. No mountains, no high rocks, no industrial smoke, no shanty towns, no slums.

The Green Belt is what the planners call it, London's lung, and in shape not unlike one. Stockbroker and wine-merchant country is what Socialists call it. Tour operators call it the Garden of England. Politicians call it the jumping-off ground for the European Economic Community. Metropolitan planners call it the "overspill area". Officially, it is designated the County of Kent, its crest a prancing white horse on a red ground above the motto *Invicta*.

Unconquered is hardly accurate – the Angles, the Saxons, the Danes, the Celts, the Romans and the Normans all in turn came here, raped and pillaged, left their blood, coins, houses, roads, place names, customs, sons and daughters. But at least it is true for nearly a thousand years. The Spanish and the Dutch tried to conquer. So did Napoleon, the Kaiser and Hitler – all failed.

Soft is not quite right either. The Battle of Britain was fought above these fields. Under the clay, there are skeletons of British and German aircraft, as well as the ironstone from which the early Britons made spears and swords as well as ploughshares. The grandfathers of these enormous oaks were fashioned into Nelson's battleships. And in the winter, the east wind from Siberia freezes the ponds and covers this same green countryside

5

with a white mantle of snow as it has done for around ten million years.

This hill we are standing on now has also been here for ten million years. Made of chalk veined with clay, it is 770 feet high and is covered in heath and pastureland. Blackwater Hill forms part of a chain called the North Downs, a natural bulwark that stems Greater London from invading the fields of Kent. Here on the top are birch trees, beeches and a scattering of pines. No houses. Footpaths, but few people. There is a certain desolation here, a loneliness, out of the way, forgotten. In any case it is Parkfield and the sea thirty miles south that the Londoners want, and on a fine Saturday morning on the roads you can see them nose to tail like so many elvers. Horses graze here. Peewits nest. Skylarks fly in. Lovers come to lie in the depths, concealed by kindly clumps of bramble and bracken, but they are far too preoccupied with themselves to appreciate or care that these hollows in which they lie are bomb holes.

At 2.15 p.m. on 18 August 1940, a Dornier 17 on a daylight raid to London was intercepted by Spitfires and jettisoned its bombs here. Six five-hundred pounders exploded, five of them apparently harmlessly on the hillside. The last of the six fell into the Weald Valley down below, hitting the village school of Marlcliff and killing nineteen children.

You can't see yet – it is still too dark, and the sun does not rise for another half hour. But they are all buried down there in the churchyard by the side of three navvies killed making the tunnel nearly seventy-four years before. By a coincidence, not so odd in the circumstances, the same hymn was sung at both gravesides – "Cover my defenceless head with the shadow of thy wings". The navvies were Irishmen, far from home, their names – Hugh Killick, Shaughn O'Hennessy, Michael Diamond – are carved on the gravestones, above the terse announcement that they died from a fall in the Blackwater Tunnel on 11 December 1866. Three and a quarter miles long, ventilated by tower-shaped shafts opening on to the hill, the tunnel was a major engineering feat in its day and cost four hundred and fifty thousand pounds. Ten tons of gunpowder were used in the blasting operations, and five hundred men worked for four years and a half to complete it.

There was every sort of trouble – the clay was too greasy and the chalk was too soft. There were engineering problems in introducing an upward gradient on the northbound track. There was discontent among the men, strikes, lay-offs, fighting, warring, drunkenness. On the day of the fall, Killick, O'Hennessy and Diamond were standing on raised platforms a mile and a half from the southern entrance, laying bricks up the curved sides – skilled and painstaking work in the darkness illuminated only by the flickering candles stuck in their hats, for which they were paid piecework rates averaging three pence an hour. They complained of a flow of water that was putting out the candles and shifting the bricks from the roof of the tunnel arch. They said it was coming from an underground lake above the tunnel, just as Amos Boaks had said. This Boaks was a hanger-on doing errands for farthings, not regarded as one of the company, but subject to strange sayings and doings, such as water-divining from the top of the hill, using a Y-shaped hazel twig that would bend like a snake in his fingers – particularly just here where we are standing amongst the green humps and dumps of the bomb craters.

Since little progress had been made with bricklaying that day, the foreman started to curse and swear as foremen have done, do and will do. The water he declared to be just a trickle seeping through the chalk, a product of the wet autumn, and to believe Boaks was to be simply daft yourself. The men continued to work on the tunnel roof. At a quarter to seven, they were just packing up for the day when without any warning – beside, above and behind them – the tunnel collapsed under a river of water that streamed out of the inside of the hill.

For months after the accident, no work was done on the tunnel. There were arguments, prophecies from Boaks, fights over pay. The project was on the point of being abandoned, with very great loss to the speculators, when a consortium of Threadneedle Street bankers stepped in. That winter the weather was cold and dry and the water problem receded. The pay of the men was increased by a penny an hour, the work was resumed with a will and the tunnel was completed in time for Queen Victoria to open it on 24 May 1869, her fiftieth birthday.

Few records of these people now exist. Till the start of the

Second World War, there was an old farm labourer in Marlcliff who spoke of the fall, remembered Boaks, had seen Queen Victoria driving through in state. After which, millions had followed her northwards and southwards on their way to the sea and back again. Nourished by the railway, villages began to grow into towns. As London spilled all over south-east England, more and more people working in the city began to live in the Weald. Improvements were made. And five years ago, to the commuters' satisfaction, the line was electrified.

More, heavier and longer services were scheduled. To and fro, to and fro, to and fro went the trains into the tunnel and out again, in again, out again, in again, out again.

The southern entrance is just underneath us. Now in the morning twilight, you can see the two brick buttresses, once red but now green with moss and grey with lichen, stretching on either side of the twin track like wide-open arms. Those dark shapes at the base are beech trees and the black blobs are brambles. The tunnel mouth itself is rounder and darker and blacker than any of them. Though you cannot see it, you can feel through the soles of your feet the southbound going through. You can hear its regular metallic heart-beat and the click of the wheels on the joins of the rails. You can smell its acrid breath, warm and dry and smoky. It is as though just for this fraction of time, the hill has come alive and then out into the beginnings of day, its square windows still blazing, like a phosphorescent snake, goes the train to streak down the straight track south – and Blackwater Hill goes back to sleep again.

That halo in the sky to the north is not a pink aurora borealis nor is it the dawn, but the lights of London. Gradually, it fades as the eastern horizon begins to crack and brighten. And now comes the sun – burnishing the cock on the spire of the Marcliff church, glittering on the slates of the school roof, making the red tiles on the sides of the houses blaze. They are still here, but the people who built them have gone. The fields are here, but there is no sign of those who enclosed them. Roads remain and the railway, but the navvies have disappeared. Gone without trace, thousands and thousands of men and women. In the six hundred square miles of the Weald Valley, now slowly materialising out of darkness, they breathed, worked, fought, worshipped, gambled, made money, lost money, ate, drank, slept, dreamed, loved and hated. There were births, weddings, deaths. Soldiers from twenty wars came and went. Squires governed, parsons preached, girls flirted, doctors healed. Again, lost without trace – thousands of people, millions of stories – draining away without trace like water drops into the river in the valley.

Only scraps remain. Odd people here and there have tried to catch the drops as they fell, and to preserve them. A poet lived at the turn of the century on Blackwater Hill, caught bits of life, pickled them in poems. There are ancient letters fading in some attics, old reports and newspaper files, stained photographs, bald statements of births, marriages and deaths.

That glint of grey and gold down there is the dome and columns of an old house, the home of the Mannering family for the last four hundred years. You can just make out the maze and the high topiary hedges of the formal garden leading down to the lake, and beyond, the curious high Tudor chimneys of the lodge. Along that lane outside the gates, at the end of the eighteenth century, close on midnight Lady Elizabeth Mannering used to drive a coach and six at frantic speed to her lover at Southover, until she broke her neck at that hairpin bend by the bridge over the river.

A woman left her husband on that bridge a hundred years later, and he drowned himself in the shallow water. If you look very carefully at the bark of that big elm tree on the bank, you can just see the scar of a bullet that murdered a young girl sixty years ago. The gap in that hawthorn hedge marks where a boy on a motor bicycle without a crash helmet went through it at eighty miles an hour and killed himself. In that chestnut wood to the right, in the snow just after Christmas only last year, a tramp froze to death, and you will find the cold charred stumps of his fire that went out.

Do you see that red light coming out of the morning twilight, changing to red and yellow, now to green? Those are the traffic lights at Gallows Cross Roads – the only traffic lights in the area. The residents pressed the authorities for fifteen years to put those lights up, but it was only after two buses collided there that the

Council spent a penny rate to erect them. Two hundred years before at that same spot was hanged a man who had cheated another out of his farm.

A helmet and a broken sword were found beside the Roman road that runs beside the railway. Not far away on that unguarded level crossing, six months ago, a man in a car stalled on the line. The granite chips between the wooden sleepers are faintly discoloured, and the grains of sand which were thrown down to cover the blood have still not quite been washed away. On that granite rock that juts out of the cutting is carved *Mary and Alan 1885*. How did they meet? What was his job? Was she pretty? Did they marry? Were they happy? And in that cave in the hillside close by can just be seen the beginnings of a beautiful woman's face, crudely carved by an unknown artist two thousand years ago.

Follow the straight railway lines three miles further and that dark smudge is the beginnings of Ocklington, population 9045. When the railway was first brought here, the population was only six hundred and two. There was all the same a tremendous uproar against the railway being brought here – public meetings, demonstrations, fights and even sabotage. All that died away when the railway brought prosperity. Now there are twelve farms, a rash of small factories, an old mill, a ragstone church, a long intestine of a main street, a triangular square, ninety-eight shops, two thousand and twelve houses through which flows a dirty stream called the Nene, a trickle in summer and liable to flood in winter.

On the north bank of this river and to the east of the town is Terrible Down. The name is too much in keeping with prevailing practice, handed down for centuries, of disguising fat Kent farms under woeful names – Wildwood, Gravelacres Starvecrow, Beggarman's – in an effort to keep the poor and the tax collector at bay, to arouse much comment except by strangers. But in fact, unlike the others, Terrible Down lives up to its name. Thistles grow here, thorns and nettles, and now in the autumn the place is wild with purple loosestrife, convolvulus, clumps of gorse and brambles. The thick clay is littered with broken tiles and bricks, which once were made here. Cinders from the gasworks, tins and rubbish are dumped here. Boys

10

come here to play war, digging shallow trenches and hurling pieces of brick at each other. The Girl Guides once tried to turn the drier north end into an allotment to grow Brussels sprouts and cabbages for the old people. Peterson Brothers, the Development Company, tried to buy the land from the Council to build flats, but this has been refused. Its only use is on the Fifth of November when, after the solemn procession through the High Street, the Bonfire Society burn Guy Fawkes here. At the north end, a witch once lived in the thatched cottage now called Blakeneys. From there she worked evil spells, till the townspeople drove her out on to the down where she vanished. All that could be seen was a hare which they shot dead – and the witch was never seen again.

Little can be seen on Terrible Down today. A mist has come in from the river. Nobody stirs. No animal moves.

And then suddenly, a muzzy light comes on in the end terrace house of a row called Railway Cottages. The front door opens. A young man comes out, wearing a brilliant yellow plastic jacket.

This is Tom Armitage, the youngest son – a gandy dancer or tracker on the railway, like his father and grandfather before him. The watery early-morning sun plays on his face as he walks towards the station – red cheeks, dark brown eyes, black hair cut unfashionably short, but with Edwardian sideburns level with the lobes of his ears, perhaps as compensation. He is tall and lean and he walks on the front of his feet with something of the easy grace of a greyhound.

The roads are almost deserted. There is nobody in Station Approach. He goes through the gate of Number 6, walks up the garden path and slips something under the door. It is a letter addressed to the only child of the house, Sheila Tate, inquiring why she had not turned up for their date last night. Then he continues down to the station where a motorised Wickham's trolley takes him and ten other trackmen to start work on various parts of the line reported in need of inspection or repair. He is dropped off with four other men in the middle of the Blackwater Tunnel.

Bright electric lights illuminate the line and the dark cave over them. As he walks northwards, he is suddenly aware that he

11

is sloshing through water, and his shoes and socks are soaked. Looking up, he sees a diamond-coloured film of moisture seeping through the brickwork. He calls out to his foreman, who curses and swears and tells him to fix it, even if it takes him all day.

The date is the sixteenth of September. The time is 7.05 a.m.

Kra – na – na – k . . .

A horrid noise, brassy and insistent, a cross between a corn-
crake and a tin drum, sounded out the alarm in the front bedroom of 19 Arlington Avenue. The little white-faced clock on
the bedside table danced with irritation that no one was taking
any notice.

Edward Blake heard it through muffled wads of sleep. The
sound was an invader, hammering at the door of comfort, a
disturber of the peace. He did not want to wake just yet. Just a
few more minutes in this warm bed. Just a fraction longer of this
mindless, formless dream. He put out his left hand blindly
groping for the clock to stop the alarm, failed to find it, and then
simply waited for the mechanism to run down, since all things
went away of their own accord if you waited long enough

Far from lazy, energetic and active once he was up, always
he had difficulty waking. He lay still for a moment, as if movement would disturb the last of his dream. Often these days he had
this strange certainty that he had dreamed. Yet no fragment
remained. The dream was totally beyond recapture or recall. In
the night, some cobweb had touched his submerged self, and left
no trace other than the knowledge that it had been there.

"Edward!"

His wife was back from the shower. She pulled off the plastic
cap with a crackling noise like the breaking of a wax seal. Her
voice was affectionately sharp. The practical loving voice of duty
and the day. Still unrecalled, he watched her pull on her slacks.
There were droplets of water on her pinkened thighs. A small
soft floured roll of flesh at her waist that he averted his eyes from
lest he hurt her by noticing.

"Edward!" Daphne spoke to him again through the wool of
her jumper as she dragged it over her head. "Come *on*! The
progeny won't get up if you don't."

She patted his toes as she walked round the foot of the bed, brisk again and affectionate, her neat slightly long-nosed profile cameoed in the morning window light. Over the past fifteen years it had hardly changed. Perhaps, he found himself wondering, it ought to have changed more. The good strong chin very gently doubled. A light line, like some artist's rough, joining the nose and mouth. The small forehead gently furrowed in an expression of surprise more than irritation. But the brown eyes, bolder than the rest of the face led you to expect, hadn't changed at all. They were the first thing he had noticed about her. Large, full and sparkling – gay even. He remembered them looking at him all those years ago across the floor of the dance hall. It had been, Daphne sometimes said with a kind of coy and prancing gaiety, love at first sight. In a sense quite correctly, he believed. Except that, exact and meticulous in his thought processes, he totally disbelieved in such a state of being. "In love" had a dated 1930s ring.

Their marriage had been the natural culmination of long years of companionship and courtship. Daphne had finished her domestic science course at the same time as he had got his degree. A First. Surprising to his contemporaries and friends, less surprising but none the less gratifying to himself. He had gone on to postgraduate work, but not being an academic, choice of a job had been fairly inevitable. He disliked the thought of industry. There was no family connection or family business to offer a niche. His mother, on the point of a second marriage, had written voluminous letters, pointing out that now the world was his oyster, but suggesting no guidelines as to where to find the pearl. Daphne's father, a retired major, had been helpful. Mindful that he advised for his only daughter as well as a widow's only son, he strongly supported Blake's inclination towards the Administrative Civil Service.

They became engaged a year after Blake was appointed Assistant Principal, married when he was promoted. They had not lived together before they were married, nor had he been, if that were the right word, tempted so to do. He respected Daphne too much, he told himself. The marriage had happened, taken its course. Like justice.

A white wedding. Uniforms or morning suits. Daphne's

14

father had given her away. He had actually wept at the wedding poor old chap. When he died, they moved away from Wimbledon down into the country, and had bought this modern detached house. Daphne had furnished it with a slightly dated taste. Done some of the painting, all the hard work really. Required only of him that he assume his role of loving husband and father. Not that she was a managing woman. Just the wife of a certain type of man. "You," she had once shrieked at him during one of their very rare rows, "are the sort of man things happen to!"

She had shrieked it with the special sour-lipped venom of a deeply held grudge. The remark and her manner of delivering it had strangely disturbed him.

Outside the window, the cold crisped leaves of the silver birch trembled like Siamese temple bells against a pale pink sky, but he was too immersed in his thoughts to notice them as he pulled back the bedclothes. He got out of bed slowly, ran some hot water, dipped a shaving-brush into the soap and reached for his razor. His own grey eyes regarded him hopefully and searchingly. Like the undreamed dream, his reflection sought something that it was never quick enough to catch – perhaps because it wasn't there.

The eyes were intelligent and steady enough. There were smile-lines at the corners – crow's feet as Daphne more correctly called them. His brows were neat, his forehead wide but furrowed. His hair had not greyed or thinned over the years – a source of secret and unadmitted pride to him. But it was an indeterminate colour, like an old burberry. And over the years his pale large-featured face had acquired a life look of hounded but benign frustration. He now shaved that face – unenthusiastically but with precision – scrubbed his still excellent teeth, dressed in a dark grey worsted suit, white shirt and blue tie with just the faintest spot of red in it, and went downstairs.

Daphne over by the Aga, lifting eggs from a boiling pan, warned him to see the toast didn't burn. Peter was packing his satchel. He could just see the burnished top of Sarah's head through the kitchen window, an outstretched uplifted arm as she broke off a twig of beech. Like a chord lightly

15

touched, the unknown dream reverberated in an inexpressible sadness.

Daphne followed his eyes. "Nature table. Sarah's one point ahead. Reverend Mother's giving a prize."

"Bribery," he smiled.

"Life," she said and popped an egg in its cup. "You haven't forgotten the Parent–Teachers' meeting tomorrow? I think we should go. Show the flag at least."

He nodded. Hopeful agnostic as he privately called himself, nominally C. of E., he was always slightly ashamed of sending his daughter to this Catholic convent. But it was cheap, less crowded than the secondary school, had good buildings and nice food and always gave him the feeling that he was doing something for Sarah.

"You've not forgotten it's Peter's birthday next Monday?"

He tried to shunt his mind on to presents. "No."

"Can we go to Warborough to look for something on Saturday?"

"Yes."

"Sarah needs a new pair of shoes."

"We can get those at the same time."

"And I'm going to look for a new winter coat . . . if that's all right?"

"Of course it's all right."

"You're watching the toast?"

The toaster no longer popped up. There was a pane of glass cracked in the window over the sink. He had promised Daphne that he would paint the ceiling which was peeling but he had not yet had time to get around to it. That shelf by the breakfast bar still needed two screws in it.

"If you've finished, d'you mind giving Sarah's shoes a rub over?"

He rummaged in the cupboard for the shoe-cleaning box.

"There's a button off my blazer, Mum."

"Peter . . . what a time to tell me!"

"Dad . . . can I have 5p for tuck?"

"Edward, it's seven thirty-five."

He collected his coat and briefcase, said goodbye to the children. A quick kiss from Daphne in the hall. " 'Bye, Edward."

16

"'Bye."

"Be careful!"

"I will."

"Don't work too hard."

"I won't."

"And you'll be back on the 5.55?"

"I'll be back on the 5.55," he repeated, "but don't worry if it's late."

"What is the matter with the trains these days?"

It was a rhetorical question which he did not trouble to answer. He waved at the garden gate. Daphne disappeared. The front door of his home closed. He began his mile and a quarter walk to the station.

Scattered detached houses like his own at first, fields, a small chestnut wood. Then the terraced houses by the gasworks at Bridgend, the triangular square and the shops in the High Street. Finally, sharp right down Station Approach.

Like a water drop merging with a stream, now he was surrounded by others. Men in mackintoshes and black bowler hats, carrying briefcases and umbrellas. Girls in high heels and bright coloured miniskirts, waterfalls of hair – red, blonde, brunette – teetering round the puddles on the pavement left by yesterday's torrential rain. Bare-headed young men in flannel suits, walking together. Middle-aged women in woolly coats. White-haired men, bald men, long-haired youths were flooding towards the station, interspersed with cars driven by wives who deposited their husbands with a peck on the cheek and were off.

Just as Edward Blake was entering the tiny booking hall, a plumpish man with red cheeks and bright black eyes in a short cavalry-style overcoat was pinning a beautifully typed notice on the green baize board.

I am in communication with British Rail, Blake read, *regarding the continued overcrowding and lateness of the trains. They regret the inconvenience but state that the line is suffering from old rolling stock, under-manning, a track planned over a hundred years ago, and inadequate repair and replacement. Since a substantial government grant is required for the line to run at all, in*

17

the present economic climate British Rail can only say that they will do everything they can to improve the situation.

> Gordon Cunliffe (*Chairman, Rail Passengers' Consultative Committee*).

Other commuters, reading it beside him, muttered that this was the same old story. Used to late trains and trained to be patient and long-suffering, Blake simply shrugged his shoulders, went over to the barrier, showed his season ticket and walked on to the platform.

He turned left to the north. Others turned right to the south. Like himself, the commuters were creatures of habit. Those who took up their positions at the south end of the platform remained to him indistinct, simply different-coloured blobs as in an Impressionist painting. The turners to the left were more recognizable. The closer they came to the second Victorian iron lamp standard, where he always took his stance as the most likely to get a seat in the second carriage of the train, the more their characteristics impinged.

Round owlish glasses covering bright birdy eyes, jutting underlip, thin, sprightly, fifty-fivish – Miss Edna Price who lived with her old father in a house he passed every weekday on his walk to the station. She nodded to a young girl with curly brown hair and a face that could have come straight off a chocolate box if there had not been so much horror-film mascara round her big blue eyes. Her name and address was advertised for all the world to see – "Sheila Tate, 6, Station Approach" written in the paperboy's scrawl on the copy of *Woman's Own* she was reading.

Blake nodded to no one, spoke to no one, looked at no book, no newspaper. Already he had entered into the limbo between the problems of his home and the problems of his work. It was a vegetable sort of existence almost as restful as sleep. For an hour and a half in the morning, and an hour and a half in the evening, nobody could get at him, nobody could interrupt him. He was neither a husband-and-father nor a Civil Service Principal. He had no role and no responsibilities. Though it might be considered an anonymous sort of existence, at least for this period of time he was free. His life was divided into three compartments – 19 Arlington Avenue, his office at the Treasury and the electric train – each self-contained and separate. It was quite impossible to do any work on these late overcrowded trains. So he sat (when he could get a seat), his guards down, giving his mind a rest before the hectic business of the day, half in a dream, idly watching the countryside go by.

He stood quite still under the unlit lamp standard. Around him others talked and shuffled. Every now and then one or other would walk to the very edge of the platform and look south along the three silent rails – two cleaned aluminium-bright by the friction of the wheels, the live rail for the electric current duller and spotted with soot – as though sighting along a rifle, and then loudly speculate on how late the 8.01 would be *today*.

Lady Marjorie Mannering last saw Ocklington's vision of herself in the gleaming bonnet of the plum-coloured Rolls Royce. Perhaps the reflection was what did it. Looking down from that angle, she could see all of her forty-two years plucking at that once smooth clean jawline, the little puffs under the blue-grey eyes, the thickening waistline below the handsome, motherly, but barren bosom. She was a handsome enough woman still. Tall, well-made (hideous expression) with pretty fair hair framing a pretty plumpish face, pink and white once, now deepening (even more hideous word) to red.

Her skin was carefully powdered and well made-up. As this was her "London" day she was dressed in her "Committee" clothes. A smart (but not too smart) blue suit, a little blue mink hat that her hair curled quite naturally and rather prettily around, and very high-heeled hand-made shoes that showed off her exquisitely turned ankles and minimised her strong horse-woman's calves.

"I'm hoping to come back on the 5.55, Robbins."

"I shall be waiting, m'lady."

"If I'm delayed, I'll 'phone."

She swept past a poster announcing that Lady Marjorie Mannering would be opening the church bazaar on the eighth of November, and dismissed Robbins and the poster's other self with a smile and a wave of her well-shaped hand.

This was for her the relief of travelling by train. Just for an

19

hour or so, she saw a collection of totally different faces from the church people, the Committee, the associations, the charities, the political clubs, the landed families, with whom she normally mixed. A relief from the endless talking, the deferences, the enthusiasms, the misbegotten enterprises she had to lead, the empty speeches she had to make, the things she had to pretend she didn't see.

In each a pious role for her to play. Lady Marjories don't have fights, don't make trouble, they turn blind eyes, smile, leave a sweet scent wherever they go. That's what Lady Marjories are for.

But here, she thought, queuing for a ticket, she was herself alone. No one knew her, or if they did they weren't interested. No one asked her to sit on their silly committees or give a donation or write a letter, or even listen to them. They were a quiet lot. Silenced by early morning and hastily swallowed breakfasts, the daunting prospect of a day in the city and the endless frustrations of coming to and fro on the train. They didn't want to talk any more than she did. They wanted nothing from her. They erected their tents of privacy around them – their *Telegraphs* and *Times,* their *Expresses* and *Mirrors.* She bought her ticket, went on to the platform, turned left, moved north, cleaving her way like a swan in a grey millpond.

She smelled the dank railway air, sweeter at this moment than any flower bed at Ocklington Park, and read on the hoarding the evangelist message for this week, *Thou shalt love thy crooked neighbour with all thy crooked heart* with a smile curving her full and pretty mouth.

She had still that same smile on her face when she saw Cunliffe, beastly man. Crooked neighbour was right, if his thatched cottage, Blakeneys, was near enough to Ocklington Park to be called neighbour at all.

Cunliffe had recently been coming to see Ralph, her husband, more frequently than ever on business. He was, she was sure (reverting as she frequently did these lonely days to schoolgirlish conversation with herself) a nasty bit of work.

Immediately, of course, he hailed her in so far as that type of person could hail anyone. He raised his bowler hat and gave her what he imagined to be a gentlemanly bow.

20

"Ah, Lady Marjorie, a very good morning to you."

He advanced towards her, hand outstretched. Would claim her for the entire journey. She saw her seventy-five minutes of freedom vanishing like water through the sand.

She threw him a cool good morning in return, consulting her wristwatch with astonished alarm as if it had spoken some hitherto forgotten message. She spun round without looking, cannoning into a bulky body on the crowded platform.

She felt one of her high heels make contact with someone's foot. Heard a quick impatient exclamation. A hand grabbed her arm to steady her, but none too gently. Her powdered face brushed a rough tweed shoulder.

She looked up. For once, *far* up. Into a half scowling, half ruefully wincing face.

"Hey, watch out where you're going, lady!"

"I'm frightfully sorry."

The scowl became mockingly raised eyebrows. The man stood for a second, looking her up and down. Then he smiled at her, rather as she had smiled at the evangelist message a moment ago, as if he found something about her genuinely amusing. He had a black moustache and very white teeth, and the smile had a quality which was simultaneously hateful and delightful. His eyes were very light and very blue and the whites were faintly bloodshot.

Those eyes remained on her face while facetiously he dusted powder from his shoulder.

"I hope I didn't hurt your foot," she said, flushing.

"You tread pretty hard, lady. I wouldn't want you to make a habit of it." His smile deepened the lines down his cheeks. There was a mocking light in the cool blue eyes.

"And you grab pretty hard," she heard a voice quite unlike Lady Marjorie's reply as she touched her arm. She could still feel the grip of his fingers.

Some remark hovered on those mocking lips. But it was never said. Suddenly *tee-who* – the klaxon sounded. Round the bend and into the straight came the electric train. There was a collective groan as an engine with only three carriages appeared.

"No Firsts *again*," the man Cunliffe hissed behind her, as if he wanted her to do something about it.

21

Lady Marjorie was swept forward, pushed and once even grabbed until she found herself in the non-smokers' section of the second carriage, middle seat facing the engine, with the hefty black-haired man in the tweed jacket standing uncomfortably close to her.

A haven, one would think, anonymous again. But with the sixth sense of those who are for ever beset for favours and requests, as though he had actually touched her, Lady Marjorie could feel the hungry eyes of a young man with jazzy hair who had sat himself down on her right.

Diffidently, Blake had waited on the outskirts. Last into the non-smoking half of the carriage, he had given up hope of a seat when suddenly he became conscious that there was a small space on the side facing the engine. A woman in a fawn raincoat squeezed herself up against the window. He murmured "Thank you" without looking at her, aware only that she was sufficiently slight to make his seat comfortable.

The whistle sounded. The iron wheels began, slowly at first, then quite fast, tapping like a hypnotic metronome speeding him into his queer suspended limbo-land.

Ocklington's many houses, ugly shops and uglier small factories flickered on the square screen of the dirty carriage window. He could, had he chosen to, have identified the corn chandler's, the brickworks, the brewery, the Square, the doctor's, the dentist's. But he looked out at them with a glazed and inward-turning eye.

Like the half-remembered dream, he had the feeling that at some unspecified time at some unspecified part of the journey, he would discover what he believed himself to be. Daphne, of course, would have laughed at him. So would his colleagues at the other end of the line. So would everyone, come to that. But he had a queer sort of feeling that here, untrammelled at the home end by his role of husband, father and householder, and at the office end by the red-tape trappings of the Treasury, he would find, like the television programme, the real Edward Blake.

He glanced around the compartment, wondering if any of the others had the same secret yearnings. Did Chairman Cunliffe over on the right, the big chap standing in the aisle with the bold bloodshot eyes, Sheila Tate sitting opposite with Miss Price beside her ask, no, *search* blindly in the muffled tunnel of their own being. Who am I? Where am I going? Why am I going there? What in hell is it all about? Why do I make this godforsaken journey twice every weekday? Why do I suffocate on stale air? Crouch in this filthy compartment? Immolate myself in the vast mindless hive of the Treasury? For what reason? To support the family. But to support them to do what? The same up and down merry-go-round. Lemmings who never even get a sniff of the sea.

Outside, the labyrinth council estate gave way to water-meadows glimmering a wet green. Cunliffe cleared his throat and began holding forth about further complaints he intended to make to British Rail. The heavy man with the bold bloodshot eyes whistled through his teeth. Sheila Tate turned to the Problem Page in *Woman's Own*.

A herd of Friesian cows was reflected in the cloud-dappled rain ponds of this wet autumn. A brown pheasant flew out of the brambles of the rising ground. There was the harsh heraldic sound like the clash of cymbals as they entered the Blackwater Tunnel.

Edward Blake noticed none of these. He had reached a familiar point in his self-examination. Were he free to do exactly what he had wanted with his life, what would he have done? Were he free now, what would he do? Supposing he had discovered that he had only X number of weeks to live, how would he use those weeks?

The echo of the wheels reached a crescendo of exultation, died down again, rose again. The stuffy air in the compartment was pierced by the high vibrations. The dust on the floor danced all round his clean black shoes, an old chocolate wrapper flicked the brown court shoes of the thin woman next to him. They were going fast, trying to make up time. The lights from the windows flickered furiously on the brickwork.

And then suddenly, with no warning at all, the lights went out. The scream of the wheels turned into the banging of the buffers, the screech of air brakes. The tunnel echoed to the racket of urgency and alarm.

23

Then they stopped dead.

The darkness was thick and contained. Blacker than the blackest night. Palpable and menacing like dense unclean fur. Nothing could be seen, *nothing*. In the compartment there was a combined in-drawing of breath. Then silence – not even the rustle of paper or the shuffle of feet.

They waited for the lights to come on, the train to start up again. Darkness and silence seemed somehow to go hand in hand with eternity.

Nothing happened.

"What the hell is British Rail up to now?" Cunliffe's voice, curiously welcome. "Anybody got a light?"

Nobody had – a non-smoking compartment. Nobody had a torch, nobody had anything. Only the tiny phosphorescent hands on his watch glowed like fireflies on Blake's wrist.

It was then that he became conscious that the woman on his left was trembling. Pressed tight as they were, it was impossible not to be aware of her distress. He turned his head in her direction and said quietly, "It's all right. Don't worry."

"Yes, I know. Thank you." A quiet controlled voice speaking with audible effort from between clenched teeth. A woman's voice rather than a girl's.

He tried to remember anything he'd noticed about her when he got in, but there was nothing except that she was new.

"You've possibly just started using this line."

"A week ago."

"Ah, that accounts for it! You're just a new recruit. Us veterans get used to it."

Other people had begun talking now. Angry voices fumed. Somewhere at the far end of the carriage a child screamed – a fearful nerve-twanging sound. He heard the woman catch her breath. She must have clasped her hands to stop them trembling, and he could hear the faint sound as she thumped them on her knee, like someone in great pain. He stretched out his own hand, found them and held them tightly.

"Does it happen often then?" she asked, making an effort.

"Every autumn. Especially a wet one. Always the same. Wet leaves get on the line. So the wheels can't grip."

"Is that all it is?"

24

"Probably."

Someone down the compartment began shouting about a power failure.

"Could it be that?" she whispered, turning so close to him and so urgently that he could feel the warm fan of her breath on his cheek.

"They might have switched off temporarily, that's all. Sensible thing to do really."

"You don't think the engine's broken down?"

He had been thinking that was probably what it was. But he said immediately, "Oh, no!"

"I'm sorry to be so silly." She drew in a deep tremulous breath. "I'm not usually like this. Blood, illness, anything like that, I'm all right. It's just tunnels. Since I was a child . . ." a small self-conscious laugh, a severe self-chiding tone, "which is a very long time ago, I've had this dread of tunnels . . ."

The shoulder pressed against his shook at the word. Quite unselfconsciously, he put his free arm round it. The woman's hair brushed under his nose. It smelled clean and sweet as if she washed it every day. It hadn't had time to acquire the railway smell like his own clothes had.

"Everyone hates tunnels," he pronounced as authoritatively as Cunliffe. Authoritative, he felt. A new Edward Blake, more purposeful and more capable, struggled upwards.

"It's the birth trauma, my husband says." Her teeth chattered.

"Does he travel up to town?"

He felt her shake her head. "Oh no, hardly ever. He's an artist."

"Good? Successful?" Wishing afterwards that he hadn't put those two words together.

"Very good. But not recognised yet." Despite her nervousness she spoke the words with dogmatic firmness.

"So he works at home?"

"Yes."

"Which is where?"

"Fordbridge. We have a small cottage by the river. The light is very good in the valley there. And he likes painting water."

"Plenty of it for him at the moment."

25

She laughed politely. They talked of the wet summer, the flooded fields. Then they lapsed into silence. Blake drew in a deep breath. There was a new smell in the compartment now mingling with the dirt, the old musty smell of the upholstery and the acrid smoke of the tunnel. A smell of human sweat and fear seeping through the city clothes and the smart suits and dresses. An animal smell like the feel of the darkness. There was an animal shuffling sound too, and only half-intelligible mutterings. I wouldn't like, Blake thought, to struggle out of a doomed craft with this lot.

"It's as if one is being slowly suffocated," the woman whispered.

"I know. But don't think about it."

"Has it ever happened before?"

"We-ell, not quite as bad as this. Usually the lights stay on."

"That makes it better."

"But already I'm seeing a bit. Aren't you? I can see your profile. And I can see a little outside the window beyond."

"So can I. There's a light I can just see far down the tunnel. And there's something shiny on the brickwork."

"Water," he smiled. "Everywhere water."

"And water and electricity don't go well together."

"I suppose not."

"We'll be very late."

"You'll get used to delays on this line. You'll learn to grin and bear it."

"How long now d'you think it will be?"

"A couple of minutes. Not much more."

But the minutes ticked by and there was no movement. Were the signalmen reliable these days? One never knew. Never stopped to think really. One had to put trust in other people. But could one? A darkened train, the signals failing. A smash-up in the tunnel. The dreaded nightmare – for himself, never mind the woman on his left.

The small glow on his wrist told him twenty minutes had gone by. He began to wonder what was going to happen when the fast 8.45 came thundering up the line.

. . . . .

26

Lady Marjorie Mannering was not afraid of the dark nor of tunnels. She couldn't think of anything physical she feared.

Dark tunnels were anonymous places. People didn't ask in tunnels, or talk in them for that matter. It was as if they were afraid that the sound of their voices would crack the darkness around them.

So she sat with her smart shoes pressed together, holding her handbag between her gloved hands. She smelled the cheap after-shave of the young man next to her, the foul air of the tunnel drifting in through the slightly open window, and a fouler smell that didn't drift in from outside – fear.

Once she heard the big tweed-jacketed man she'd bumped into whistle some tune through his teeth, and she turned her head towards him, staring at the place where he stood in the darkness. She felt rather bold and girlish doing that. And the thought of him standing there was ridiculously pleasing.

Someone in a matter-of-fact way asked, "Anyone got a match?"

There was a relieved shuffling of feet, a rustling through pockets, and she half expected her acquaintance to come up with a light of some sort, but he didn't.

Sporadic conversation started up. Nervous. Demanding. Ah, how well Lady Marjorie knew the timbre! People seeking what comfort was to be had from one another.

Time passed. Already they had been stuck here twenty minutes. At the far end of the dark compartment, a child started crying. Beside her, the young man with the awful-smelling after-shave hammered silently on her conscience and consciousness. She turned herself to his dark place. A faint pale movement in the black glass. "Have you ever been stuck like this before?" she asked in her best and most ridiculous Lady Marjorie Mannering voice.

But the young man didn't reply. She felt the tweed-jacketed man smile.

And then suddenly the young man was on his feet. He seemed to leap from her side like a little twisting animal.

"I'm getting out of here!"

A thin nasal voice, high with an odd panicky excitement. She put out a hand to catch him, comfort and steady him. But he

27

wriggled away like a child, fended her off with little peevish sharp-nailed fingers.

An authoritative voice from the other cubicle, middle-aged and nice, called, "Stay where you are! There's a down train due!"

Then it was all darkness and nightmare and confusion. She heard the young man's excited gulping breath. Felt his clumsy movements. Knew she had to stop him, but was not sure from what.

She said urgently, to no one in particular, "Quickly! He's –"

The sound of the door being opened. There was a breathy gasping-in of that acrid hell's-mouth air. A fluster of water drops. Grunts. A leg brushing hers. Heavy breathing.

The young man squealed, "Let me go!" The tweed-jacketed man drawled, "Shut up, you stupid little bastard! Don't try that again or I'll sit on your face!"

"Shall I get up?" Lady Marjorie was looking up again at him though she couldn't see him. "Then you can stay beside him."

She felt him looking down.

"Just shove over a bit, lady." Then the tweed-jacketed man was sitting beside her. She felt the warmth of his body pressed against hers. She remembered with indescribable pleasure the feel of his fingers on her arm.

Five minutes later, the lights came on. In the sudden illumination the tweed-jacketed man was revealed still holding the young man captive. The thin little arms looked like her husband Ralph's – puny inside the big fists.

"Well done!" She smiled her I-now-declare-the-Christmas-bazaar-open smile. She was Lady Marjorie again. "Thank you for your help Mr. . . . . er?"

"Cody. Bill Cody."

She laughed, girlishly doubtful. "Is that really your name?"
"Why not?"

"It sounds too good to be true."

"Well, Cody I was born with. Bill's a kind of nickname. Or is it the other way round?" He gave her that sardonic smile again. "I'm never quite sure."

She remembered thinking I would never know when he is serious and when he is teasing me. And then the train started to

28

move very slowly forward again, and there seemed no more reason or excuse to speak to him again.

The woman on his left seemed to trust him. Apprehensive as he was in the waiting darkness, Blake had found himself with a new and undeserved stature in another passenger's eyes.

When panic began to spread in the compartment, when the child screamed its lungs out, and some unidentifiable man in the next cubicle tried to open the door and get out it was his own voice he heard calling, "Stay where you are! There's a down train due!" And though it was other hands that held the man down, other feet that scraped and other breaths that panted, they did it because *he'd* said the word.

Nothing and no one could stop the child. "Really tears at you, that," the woman murmured.

"Have you any family?"

A long pause. "No." Another pause. "Unfortunately." Then politely, "Have you?"

"A boy and a girl."

"That must be marvellous."

Blake said that it was, though it seemed no more true to him than her opinion of her husband's artistic merit. Somewhere in the scheme of things that he probed in this limbo-land, his family fitted. They were part of the order of things that he accepted but didn't understand. He loved them therefore . . .

Suddenly the lights came on. Hastily he retrieved his arm from the woman's shoulder. He gazed down at her with the dis-believing curiosity of a figure materialised out of a dream. She was older than in his imagination. The sweet clean hair that had tickled his nose was brown and wavy but very lightly, at the temple, streaked with grey. The profile he had glimpsed was well-proportioned with a pointed chin and wide but furrowed forehead. The eyes were hazel, screwed up now against the dazzle of the light. These were clear with golden flecks in them, and the beauty was not so much diminished as made more poignant by the mesh of little lines around them. There were smile-lines round her mouth. Her skin was fine and she wore hardly any make-up. She could have been anything from thirty to forty.

And yet as she felt his eyes on her, that fine skin deepened in a blush like a girl's.

Outside on the track, between the train and the tunnel walls, lights bobbed. Shadows were flung on the glistening brickwork.

"Which is the older?" the woman suddenly asked him. "The boy or the girl?"

"The boy."

"That was very clever of you." She smiled. A small sweet smile. He was thinking that she must have been pretty when she was a girl, not unlike Sarah perhaps, when the train began to move.

There was a cheer from the compartment. Relief made everyone else talkative. The woman lapsed into silence.

As they clanked through the tunnel with stealthy slowness, she stared out at the damp mossy brickwork of the tunnel walls.

Just before Blake returned into his limbo-land, he noticed a place where the bricks had been eroded so that the water cascaded down in a miniature waterfall. It looked very pretty in the lights of the carriages. When he did return to his reverie, his mind kept turning on how he would have got the woman out if there had been a real emergency in the tunnel. They were all out in the sunshine and halfway to Croydon before he became aware that he still held both her hands.

They said nothing to each other for the rest of the journey to Victoria. He opened the door for her to get out of the carriage and on to the platform.

"We apologise," boomed the woman-on-the-Tannoy high above them, "for the late arrival of your train at Platform Twelve. This was due to maintenance work in the Blackwater Tunnel."

The 8.01 from Ocklington, twenty minutes late arriving into Victoria, turns itself about into the 9.43 to Parkfield, and leaves at ten o'clock.

Now the second carriage from the front is completely empty. There is no rush, no squeezing, shoving, talking, staring. No fears, no hopes, no plans, no joys, no loves, no hates – everything is peaceful. This is the time to have a good look at it.

30

Number 56324 runs on two sets of double bogies, sixteen wheels in all, and is painted dull British Rail blue. Built at Derby thirty-one years ago, it is separated into two compartments – one smoking, one non-smoking – joined by a narrow corridor in which there is a lavatory. The benchtype seats, eighty-four in each compartment, are arranged in banks of twelve, back to back, with an aisle in the middle. Some 1,921,063 different people have already travelled in this carriage, and the number increases by hundreds every day.

There is not much left of their brief occupation. Three telephone numbers pencilled on the woodwork of one of the doors – whose? A sum of amounts in pounds – household budget, income tax? A crude drawing of a woman and an even cruder drawing of a man. All the windows along the right side were broken by football fans nine months ago – you can see that they are newer than the others. A girl was strangled in the front compartment, and her body was wrapped in newspaper and arranged on that luggage rack. A couple had sexual intercourse on that seat in the non-smoker. Three bulbs in the smoker have been removed from their sockets. Someone has carefully cut into shreds the red and blue moquette of the end seat by the window on the right-hand side. High up on the white ceiling another has scratched a heart with F and R in the middle of it. On the window ledge below it is pencilled shakily *12.45 p.m. . . . in great pain*. On the end walls, there is a coloured photograph of Parkfield pier in one of the advertisement slots, next to another in which there is an outstretched arm and the words *get the whole strength of the insurance companies round you*. Over everything hangs a faint whiff of old cinema, sweat, scent, tobacco smoke and soot.

Of all those thousands of people, only a handful were directly affected by the electric train. To most of the others it remained throughout a means of transport – the connecting link between their home life and their work life – not unlike the corridor connecting the smoker and non-smoker compartments. In it they worried about mortgages, read newspapers, played chess or cards, stared out of the window, chatted inconsequentially to others, dreamed daydreams or went to sleep. During term time, there was an influx of schoolchildren doing their homework. Sick

31

people have gone up to London for appointments with specialists. People were made redundant or retired – and never rode the
train again.

But on those eight people travelling to Victoria on that particular morning, the electric train was to exert very much more
influence. It was to be a thread that was to be woven in the fabric
of their lives. That pretty Sheila Tate with the blue eyes and
fluffy curly hair would have laughed if you tried to point out the
likeness of the carriage to a fairy godmother's pumpkin coach.
Gordon Cunliffe, Chairman of the Passengers' Consultative
Committee and second-in-command at Nettleship and Hammond, property developers, would most certainly not have lik-
ened it to a bandwagon. Miss Price, 55, spinster, Primitive
Methodist, would not dream of it as a marriage bureau. Under
no conceivable circumstances would Lady Marjorie Mannering
regard the Blackwater Tunnel as an escape route, with a
bright light shining at its northern end. Bill Cody would not
have recognised it as the gateway to High Society. Edward
Blake, the man to whom things happened, would never have
conceived of anything materialising from his meeting with the
brown-haired woman. Only the white-faced youth with the
variegated hair whose name was Kevin Clarkeson would have
seen further possibilities in the electric train.

Nobody was there to see on its return journey that morning
through the Blackwater Tunnel, the water still streaming down
the early Victorian brickwork, glinting like a crystal veil, a rainbow in the reflected light, the blue-white sparks shooting up into
the colours like stars from a magic wand, hear the wheels chanting over the joins in the rails electric train, *electric train . . .*

On that journey, it caught up a little time, and arrived at the
coast only twelve minutes late. But throughout the rest of the
day, the engine and three carriages began inexorably to lose
more and more time, coming back through the tunnel twice more
to London, then out again to Parkfield so that by the evening the
returning commuters were still waiting at 6.30 p.m. on No. 16
platform at Victoria for it to arrive from the coast to turn into
the 5.55 East Croydon-Crowfield-Woosley-Ocklington-South-
over-Fordbridge-Parkfield train.

Even so, delayed by an endless meeting at the Treasury,

32

Blake did not catch it. Bill Cody caught it, but Lady Marjorie's presence was required at a Nurses' cocktail party at St Mary's Hospital. Gordon Cunliffe was immersed in the details of a big property deal involving Ocklington land and worked late. The woman with the brown hair did not catch it.

Sheila Tate and Miss Price also caught it. Sitting side by side in the non-smoker, they could not have looked less alike – the pretty girl in yellow, the long-faced spinster with the thick round glasses.

"Hello, Sheila."

"Hello Miss Price. Wasn't it *awful* this morning? That man . . ."

"It was shockin'!"

They knew each other slightly from their trips on the train, but their backgrounds were quite different. The Prices lived at 66 Bridgend, close to the gasworks, a terrace of houses built two hundred years ago for the workers in the iron-ponds – puddlers, charcoalmen and firers. Now an assortment lived there: a schoolmaster, four fitters at the car component factory, a shopkeeper, a bus driver, a manager, two gasmen, a stockbroker who used it as a country cottage, and the Prices – mother dead, father twenty years retired from the brewery, daughter Head of the Typing Pool at Peterson Brothers. The Tates had this neat little semi-detached house in Station Approach – father a cost clerk in a light machinery factory, mother always fussing over her only child, making her wear winter uniform when all the other girls were in their summer dresses, insisting on an extra thick woollen vest that was tickly and too warm against her chest, and, at the same time, ever so slightly scornful about her dearth of boy friends. So far, the only young man who had showed any interest in her was Tom Armitage, and all he had in the world was a dirty old motor-cycle. He was always ringing up, speaking in that slow common accent, asking her to go out with him. Now and again she went because there was no one else – but all in all she had as little time for him as her parents, who made no bones about the fact that he was "beneath her". Since the topic of unmarried girls was the subject of main interest in Ocklington, her parents were always being asked, "Is Sheila courting yet?" To which her mother would shake her head and say,

"Plenty of time yet." And if she happened to be in the room, "Sheila's very particular, aren't you, dear?" Shame-making, hateful, privacy-destroying – particularly as her mother had married when she was seventeen, and Sheila was aware that she really thought her (to use her mother's phrase) "a bit slow off the mark" – as though girls were greyhounds in little traps and they were in some awful race with the boys as electric hares. She had once seen a girl on the train with a badge on her arm like the sort of badges you won for needlework and first aid and tying knots in the Girl Guides on which was written *Where have all the young men gone?*

Disappeared – that was her view, or become indistinguishable from girls. In the old days they were brought to church and a girl could look them over. The friends of her parents produced few boys, and those too young or too awful. At the dances she attended, she hated having to sit with dozens of other girls – Ocklington was teeming with pretty girls – lined up against the wall, while the boys drank beer at the bar. Once her parents had taken her on a package holiday to Spain, and she had seen the boys and girls promenading up and down in the evening on the *ramblas*. The Ocklington girls had to go searching for them, turning over rocks and stones and looking up gullies and down holes. Not that *she* was allowed to – a nice girl didn't. According to her mother a nice girl sat, like a flower it seemed, ankles decorously crossed, clean hands clasped in her lap, skirt pulled well down over her knees, eyes downcast, waiting for "the right man" to come along.

Miss Edna Price had given up hoping for the right man to come along many years ago. She studied no advertisements, went to no hairdressers, wore rather long skirts and sensible flat shoes.

They talked politely and desultorily to each other in between reading the magazines open on their laps. Miss Price was half-way through the last instalment of the serial in *Woman's Weekly*, and Sheila's attention was mainly on the Problem Page in *Woman's Own*.

"That's a pretty coat, Sheila."

"Thank you, Miss Price."

"Still at the same job at the hospital?"

34

"Yes."

"Lab Assistant, isn't it?"

Sheila nodded. "How are Peterson Brothers, Miss Price?"

"Mustn't grumble."

It was no use talking to Sheila Tate about all her problems with temporary secretaries coming for easy jobs and leaving when they didn't get them, coming in late and leaving early, gossiping about boy friends, putting every penny they earned on their faces or their backs.

There appeared to be nothing else to say to each other. Silence fell between them in the Blackwater Tunnel. Sheila turned her attention from the Problem Page in *Woman's Own* to the astrology forecasts, particularly for those born under the sign of Taurus: *The most outstanding feature of this week will be an unexpected meeting . . .*

"Look, Sheila!" Miss Price broke through the honeyed sweet notes of "Some Enchanted Evening" thrumming in her ears.

Now they were out of the tunnel and through the grey mist of twilight could be seen a tall figure in a drenched yellow jacket standing on the embankment and waving.

"He was waving at you, Sheila!"

Sheila Tate looked quickly away.

"He's soaked through! I wonder what he's been up to?"

The damp figure disappeared behind them, still waving.

"What's his name, Sheila?"

"How should I know, Miss Price?"

The clicks of the wheels were getting fainter and slower, now they were coming in to Ocklington. Miss Price had closed *Woman's Weekly* and was packing it away neatly in a scuffed leather bag. Inside Sheila Tate, an invisible conductor was bringing the orchestra up to a crescendo, sweet and certain and deafening loud . . . some enchanted evening, you will see him standing, you will see him standing across a crowded room . . .

But not *him*.

THURSDAY   18 September

EDWARD BLAKE caught sight of the woman on the train several times after that introduction in the Blackwater Tunnel. He saw her hurrying down the platform at Victoria, a slight but not ungraceful figure, carrying a large holdall stuffed with what looked like paint brushes, or in the compartment, not always the same one, and not always the same seat, but always squeezed up to make room. Brown hair always looking as if it had just been washed, sometimes glinting in what pale sun penetrated the grimy greenhouse of Victoria. Always dressed in the same fawn, a complement to those fine clear eyes perhaps.

Those eyes did not see him. There was after all nothing to make him stand out from the others bunched in the mornings round the second Victorian lamp standard, or hurrying with hundreds like him for the 5.55.

He was, after all, so very ordinary. Quite unlike the smart city smoothness of Cunliffe, dwarfed by the earthy physique of the tweed-jacketed Bill Cody, stale and middle-aged beside the freshness of Sheila Tate, plebeian beside the patrician grandeur of Lady Marjorie Mannering.

Thursday for a change was sunny, and on his walk to the station it was as though everything he saw had been washed and rinsed, and sparkled. He could smell the sharp smell of nettles, the warm nutty smell of harvest, the haunting scent of autumn leaves.

In the booking hall, people were crowded round the stove, complaining about the cold wind but he had not noticed it. On the green baize board was another notice from the Chairman of the Passengers' Consultative Committee: *A reply has been received from British Rail regarding our complaint that either there are no First Class compartments or all the First Class seats are occupied by the time the 8.01 reaches Ocklington. Regret is*

36

expressed at this unsatisfactory situation which is unfortunately unavoidable due to shortage of rolling stock. Signed *Gordon Cunliffe (Chairman).*

"He does his best for us all," said Miss Price, who had never travelled First in her life. Bill Cody looked round and said, "Who does?"

"Mr Cunliffe . . . our Chairman."

Cody said nothing. It was one of the regular chess players who said, "Good man!"

The man in question arrived three minutes later, on foot as he always did. He addressed his flock, expressing the hope that the 8.01 would not be quite so late as on Tuesday.

The minutes ticked past. The commuters conducted a desultory hate session against the South East Region of British Rail, until one by one they followed each other out to take up their positions on the platform.

Blake waited with the others under the second Victorian lamp standard, vaguely wondering whether she would be on the train. When the 8.01 at last arrived, she wasn't – certainly not in the carriage next to the engine. He remembered feeling vaguely disappointed, and looked out for her at the other end, in the stream of people, going for the buses. But there was no sign of her. It had turned cold in London. The wind was blowing a crackling carpet of beech leaves before him as he walked through St James's Park, and up the twelve steps into Treasury Chambers.

Inside everything was grey, the marble plaque headed *The Band of Brothers*, naming those Treasury officials killed in the 1914–18 war, being the only decoration. No similar extravagance for the 1939–45 war. No pictures, not a statue. High-ceilinged empty corridors, grey-painted walls, grey-painted doors, a grey stone mosaic on the floor. It was like a museum from which all the exhibits had been stolen, and only the fire doors and the red fire hydrants had been left. All that he could hear were his own echoing footsteps as he passed room after room, each labelled with the occupant's name till finally he came to his own, a rectangle tipped on its end with the distance to the ceiling greater than the distance to the other wall, floored with grey linoleum and a faded grey carpet, furnished with a chipped wooden desk, a high-backed chair and in the corner a brand new grey steel security cabinet, on which was pasted a small poster with the message *A clear desk is a clear conscience*, and in red letters, the only piece of colour in the room, *Keep our secrets secret*. He considered himself fortunate to have this cupboard to himself instead of sharing. Its one window gave out on to a courtyard. Someone had once suggested that a swimming-pool should be built there – thus achieving eternity, for that was many years ago and was still remembered and laughed over. It was now a car park.

The messenger had left the morning's mail in his In-tray – a whole stack. Ever since the onset of the present economic and political crisis, he had been inundated with work. He began going through the letters. Halfway through the morning, he picked up one from the Department of the Environment, opened it, and began to read. ". . . you are aware that since the recent decision to make a further ten per cent reduction in public expenditure throughout Whitehall, British Rail are in considerable difficulties, particularly regarding certain sections of its network that have hitherto been uneconomic and for which grants-in-aid have been provided. The Board have made all the passenger and freight increases they are allowed, but due to the present inflation coupled with the cutback in public expenditure find themselves faced with no alternative but to close down the majority of these uneconomic lines – and this against a background not so long ago of well-publicised government intention to increase investment on the railways. While the Board will proceed with closing down these lines, it is considered that a strong case exists for preserving one of them particularly. I am, therefore, writing to ask whether you could see your way, in these special circumstances, to agree to the provision of further finance . . ."

Another begging letter – a real tear-jerker and getting worse the further one proceeded. At any rate, Aird would be pleased. Above all else, his Assistant Secretary loved flabby letters begging for public funds. You couldn't ask for money on the strength of past achievements, future hopes, employment, defence value and modernisation. You couldn't blame it all on the Victorians. He read on.

". . . the line in question is the Victoria-East Croydon-Woosley-Ocklington-Southover-Fordbridge-Parkfield. For some years, there has been evidence that turnover from both passenger and freight traffic is annually increasing, and in normal circumstances might be expected to break even within ten years – much sooner if the plans to make Ocklington one of the New Towns materializes. However, there are serious problems regarding the replacement of old rolling stock and the renewal of the line itself, while the bridges over the Dene and Aire, the Colebrook Viaduct and the Blackwater Tunnel are all in need of extensive repair and maintenance. These repairs and renewals are likely to be expensive – an estimate of £60 million has been obtained, much of which would be needed for repairs and reconstruction of the Blackwater Tunnel . . ."

He turned the matter over in his mind. The letter got better as it went along. He had had no idea that the Ocklington line was threatened. There had, of course, been many rumours at the time of Beeching, but that was years ago, and it was clearly evident, as the Department of the Environment pointed out, that there was now much more traffic on the line. Trained to think objectively, now he tried to do just that.

As regards himself, of course, any closure would have consequences. He would have to sell 19 Arlington Avenue. Daphne needed the car to ferry the children to their private schools at Warborough, so he could not drive up. Buses were far too slow, and anyway the nearest London route was eight miles away. Alternative transport would be provided, but as always would be totally inadequate. For him, a closure would mean the end of living in Ocklington.

He shifted his mind from his own private interests to those of the public in the present economic crisis. He had past experience of railway closure problems and knew of their capacity for emotive and volcanic backlash. He stared out into the courtyard – the one that someone had once suggested should be made into a swimming-pool – then sent the letter to the Registry to be returned on the file. After which he became immersed with other and totally different problems, working all through the lunch hour, until, just on five-thirty, the letter was brought back from the Registry on file R/372/54. He minuted to Aird. *On the face of it this seems reasonable, but in the present difficult circumstances is there finance available?*

That evening he was going out with Daphne to a dinner party to celebrate a twenty-fifth wedding anniversary at a neighbour's house, and it was imperative that he caught the 5.55. Even though he was lucky with a bus down Victoria Street, he nearly didn't. He ran to Platform 16. They were already closing the barrier as he came up to it.

Just then, a hand lightly touched his arm. Impatiently he glanced over his shoulder.

The brown-haired woman flushed at his frown. "I just wanted to say thank you," she murmured breathlessly, "for the other morning. You were so kind."

The whistle sounded. Blake wrenched open the first carriage door and bundled her unceremoniously inside.

It was a smoker. The air was already thick. With his hand under her elbow he guided her to the aisle. She held the upright as the train lurched forward. The top of her head just reached his shoulder. And though she made him feel as brawny as the tweed-coated man opposite, he was wearing his old mackintosh, and her eyes were just level with where the seam was coming away behind the arm.

"I've wanted to say thank you," she went on, "but I've never seemed quite able to catch up with you."

Blake murmured that it was absolutely nothing. "I enjoyed making your acquaintance."

He bowed slightly, feeling terribly stilted and old-fashioned.

"So did I. But I was extremely silly."

"I felt exactly the same. Quite terrified!"

"I don't believe you." She laughed. She had a trick of shaking her head when she did so, as if to shake the droplets of merriment from those expressive eyes. "And anyway, Dylan said I should have made it my business to thank you properly."

"Dylan's your husband?" He would have a name like that, he thought.

40

She nodded. He wanted to ask her if that was why she carried the bag stuffed with paint brushes, an unending supply for The Master, but that seemed altogether too forward.

"I told you he painted, didn't I?"

"Marvellous to be so talented."

"Isn't it?" She glanced up at Blake with such conviction that he knew it wasn't true.

"How long . . ." He was for some extraordinary reason going to ask, "have you been married?" Instead he finished, "has he been painting?"

"All his life. We met at art college. But I'm no artist . . ." The fine skin flushed again.

"What do you . . ." But without his noticing it, the train had screeched to a halt at East Croydon. Doors were flung open. A dozen travellers struggled out on to the platform to force their way through the incoming tide.

"A seat over there!" Cunliffe, ever the gentleman, pointed it out to her.

She was gone.

The East Croydon commuters pressed those standing hard against the windows on the other side of the compartment. The 5.55 rocked southwards through the beginnings of night.

He caught a glimpse of her bowed brown head in the light of the lamp above as they entered the Blackwater Tunnel. She was no doubt staring down at her paperback, hands tightly clenched. It would have been nice if he could have at least stood beside her.

It was dark when they emerged from the tunnel. He saw the evening star and a sliver of moon. Their beauty in the clear air of the country enchanted him.

The oil lamps were lit at Ocklington station. She didn't glance at him when he got up to leave. He last saw her face beautifully mirrored in the moving window. He hurried home with the inexplicable feeling of something about to happen. Relieved at catching the train perhaps. Looking forward for once to an evening out and dinner.

The lights were all on in 19 Arlington Avenue, the bedroom curtains drawn. Sarah and Peter were sitting in front of the television. There was a cold supper laid out for the children

41

in the kitchen. Automatically, he put his head round the door of the sitting-room.

"Done your homework?"

They didn't tear their eyes away. "Yep."

He went upstairs, two at a time. The bedroom door was open. Daphne was sitting at the dressing-table, her perfume spray in her hand. She was all ready. She looked very handsome. Her blue dress was low-cut, her back white and well-powdered. Her hair had been rinsed and sprayed with something that made every strand stand out, glittering like spun brown sugar.

He leaned forward to kiss her. She recoiled, but only with a kind of rallying reproach.

"Go away!" She squirted his jacket with her scent spray. "You've brought the smell of the train in with you!"

TEE-WHO – the klaxon again. Doors slammed. The whistle blew. Bill Cody called out "Half-time!" Gently as a falling hand at 8.19, the 8.01 from Ocklington began sliding away from the platform.

And then suddenly footsteps, running footsteps, becoming louder and louder. A grey shape blurred by speed was racing the accelerating train. An open coat flapped behind like broken wings, while long legs pounded down the platform.

Just before the end, the man stretched out his right hand, grasped the handle of the door of the carriage, and leapt on to the running-board. The platform disappeared. The train gathered speed. The background now was the council estate. Everyone in the compartment was watching the face outside the window.

For a full minute he made no attempt to move. Neither did the inhabitants inside the compartment. The stolid hostile stares from inside were met by the grinning face of the suppliant outside.

Peering through a maze of arms and legs and heads, Sheila Tate saw him – a young face with a jutting jaw. A flag of fair hair was being blown away from a high forehead by the slipstream of the train. Pale grey eyes, big red lips, now parted in a smile.

Some enchanted evening . . . what did a few hours early matter?

"Crazy idiot!" said a chess-player.

"Bloody dangerous!" said Gordon Cunliffe.

The man was struggling with the doorhandle. The train was accelerating. He had turned his head away from the cold sharpness of its speed.

Sheila Tate leaned over, took hold of the inside handle and turned it. The door swung open. Panting, the man hauled himself into the compartment.

All the men glowered at him. Cunliffe spoke for them all. "You'll kill yourself one of these days!"

"Would have killed myself today," the young man closed the door, flashed a smile at Sheila, "if it hadn't been for this young lady."

. . . you will see him standing. Who said horoscopes were a lot of nonsense?

He was still smiling at her. "Thank you very much."

. . . across a crowded room. Quite right! She was too full of emotion to smile back.

"Is there room for a little one?"

There was no room, but he inserted himself. "You are so slim." He gave Sheila a close-up of dazzling white teeth. "Hope I'm not squeezing you?"

All she could manage was a shake of the head and a blancmange of a smile.

"Of course," he continued in a confidential tone, "I never use these beastly trains as a rule . . . but I had an accident."

"Oh, dear!"

"Yesterday. Coming back from the Coughtons. You know the Roman bridge over the Nene?"

She nodded.

"Bit of bad luck. The Alfa went into it."

"Oh dear!"

"It'll take months to repair."

"Oh dear!"

The young man started to say something more, stopped, shrugged his shoulders and relapsed into silence. After such lukewarm response, clearly he had given up the conversation as hopeless. Tongue-tied, Sheila Tate sat with her knees together, clasping an Army and Navy carrier on her lap, in a kind of strawberry ice pudding of embarrassment. Drippy, that was how she had sounded – no doubt about that. Unable to think of anything to say but "Oh dear!"

Into the Blackwater Tunnel and out again. Woosley, East Croydon, Clapham Junction and still no further conversation. He had opened the *Financial Times* at the Property page.

Clack, clacketty-clack, clacketty-clack went the wheels . . . and you are getting older every *clack. At the third clack, you will*

44

be nineteen years, four months, three weeks, two days, nine hours, thirty minutes and forty seconds. At the third clack, you will be . . .

What is the matter with me, she thought? It was given to me on a plate, just as *Woman's Own* forecast. And what do I do? I muff it.

Just as I always muff everything.

Cl - aa - ck went the wheels in slow-motion agony. You're late, you're late, you're always too late, sighed the air wheel-brakes as the electric train crawled to a halt on Victoria Bridge. Stuck, that's what you are, that's what you always will be. Stuck with your parents, stuck with No. 6 Station Approach, Ockling-ton, stuck with your job at St Mary's Hospital, stuck with yourself. Here you sit, with your long black dress and your silver dancing-shoes in an Army and Navy carrier bag on your lap, like a bird in the wilderness. What's the point of going to the hospital dance tonight? What's the use of trying?

Stuck! There, it said so in the new *Woman's Own*. Taurus. *No skirmishes with danger for you this week. A dull period ahead with no excitement but do not despair.*

Despair? It was no use telling her not to despair! What girl wouldn't despair, stuck in the mud like she was? Not mud either, quicksand, and she was being slowly sucked under.

It was no use just sitting, waiting. These days, it didn't work.

She had heard girls talking about "catching" a man, then watched what happened. There was a game called Grandmother's Footsteps she used to play at school. You stood with your face to the wall while from the other end of the room the others came up stealthily to touch you. Every now and again, suddenly you turned and if you saw them move, back to the beginning they went. It was like that with boys. Once they saw you move for-ward, it wasn't just back to the beginning – they would run a mile. And in any case, she had never seen any boy – until now – that she *wanted* to move forward on, even if she had the nerve and the lack of shyness to do it. She had once carefully studied a piece in a women's magazine entitled "How to make the first move", but she had remained unenlightened.

How would she know the right man? How would he show

himself? How was she to attract him when he did appear? Was it colours – red and yellow catch a fellow? Was it scent? Was it clothes? Was it hair? Was it teeth? Was it boldness? Was it cheekiness? Was it goodness? Was it badness?

She was bombarded with advice from advertisements, articles, friends and relations – but she still did not know, and she lived in an aura of unease because those questions remained unanswered. Dilys Roberts, the other laboratory assistant at the hospital, had loads of boy friends. She also had her own room in London which she had tried to get Sheila to share – unsuccessfully because her parents wouldn't let her and she had not wanted to have an out-and-out row with them. Dilys had not been pleased, "I'm Mammy's little girl from High School," – on being put out, Dilys had a habit of chanting old rhymes in high falsetto – "Clean hands, clean face, clean petticoat trimmed with lace. I'm Mammy's little girl from High School . . ."

Not now she wasn't. Not after that row at breakfast this morning.

The train was stuck on Victoria Bridge. The Houses of Parliament stood sentinel beside the twin towers of Westminster Abbey. Nothing moved. Everything was stuck – just like she was, sitting here in silence, hugging her Army and Navy carrier bag.

That bag had started the row at breakfast. Coming in from the kitchen with her father's bacon and egg, her mother had almost tripped over it.

"Sheila . . . you are careless! Just strew things all over the place!"

"Sorry, Mum," she had said automatically, putting lime marmalade on the second unbuttered Ryvita allowed under the Slimma Silhouette programme. "Just my long black and my silver shoes. It's the hospital dance tonight."

"You never told me."

"Mum, I did!"

"I don't remember."

"I told you last Friday. At supper. Dad, *you* remember?"

Behind the *Daily Mail*, her father had shaken his head in a vigorous negative.

"Is Tom Armitage taking you?"

"Course not!"

"You're going on your own?"

"Course not! Dilys and I are going together."

"And what train home are you catching, miss?"

"The one forty-five, Dad."

That was when the volcano had erupted, redder than the morning horizon, darker than the four shadows of the chimneys of Battersea Power Station, sinister as a battleship's guns lying across the stationary train, more powerful than the smoke pouring up into the sky, bigger and wetter than the Thames flowing past Millbank, Charing Cross and the Tower of London to the sea – the skin on her father's face puce as a plum, her mother crying into a minute handkerchief, shouts, yells, pounding fists, the smell of toast burning, the rattling of plates and the slamming of doors.

The train was moving again – very slowly forward. *Cl . . . aa . . . aa . . . ck* went the wheels in a long-drawn-out howl of derision. Off the bridge, past the sewage works, shuddering to a stop at the platform. The molecules disengaged themselves. The tight compact pie of human beings burst out of the crust of the compartment and, as if to dissociate themselves each from the other, set off isolated again, each having a little area around them that was not to be trespassed upon.

Out on the platform, Sheila paused to get a better grip on the carrier bag, turned right towards the ticket barrier, the row with her parents still ringing in her ears.

"You'll come back on the ten forty-five."

"I most certainly won't!"

"You most certainly will!"

"I most certainly won't!"

"You'll do as you're told!"

"You can't make me!"

"Oh, yes, we can!"

"I'd like to see you try!"

"Don't try my patience too far, miss!"

"I'm not a child. I'll come home when I want."

"You'll come home on the ten forty-five. Miss . . . I'm warning you!"

47

"Sheila, your father's warning you!"

The sound of her mother's voice, tinny with irritation, merged with the Tannoy apologising for the late arrival of their train. Sheila was conscious that she would be *very* late for morning briefing in the radiography office and that Mr Hart who was in charge might be cross. She could not bear to have another row on top of the breakfast eruption, and now she began to run for the 10.15 bus to St Mary's thinking even as she did so what an undignified sight she must look – a girl in high heels carrying a carrier bag pelting down the platform like a panic-stricken Cinderella, threading her way through the commuters like a skier in a slalom race.

She had passed the newspaper kiosk, was on the last twenty yards with her season ticket in her hand, when she heard the sound of running behind her.

"You're in a hurry, too, then?"

She turned her head and saw the young man on the running-board. Face to face, he was even better-looking – grey eyes and smiling.

She suddenly realised that Destiny was going to do what Destiny was never supposed to do. It was giving her another chance.

She slowed. He slowed.

"I'm late for an appointment."

"And so am I."

Both showed their tickets at the barrier at the same time. Now they were outside in the little lane where chauffeurs with Rolls-Royces and Bentleys waited for the rich and the elderly, the privileged or the powerful.

"After your help this morning," he said, "the very least I can do is to offer you a lift."

She was not quite sure what he meant. "I go by bus."

"We'll get you there quicker. Where to?"

"St Mary's Hospital, but please don't bother –"

"Absolutely on my way, I promise you."

They walked down a line of glittering vehicles, till a chauffeur in dark green uniform stepped out and said, "Good morning, Mr Mannering," and opened the door of a silver Rolls-Royce.

48

Then she was inside, and there was the smell of leather and the soft purr of the engine as the Rolls slipped through the traffic.

He looked at his watch. "Precisely five minutes ago, I was seeing the Managing Director of Nettleship and Hammond. What about your appointment?"

"Oh, it was nothing very important."

"Train was very late."

"Always are these days."

"Typical British inefficiency." He paused. "Oh, by the way, the name's Mannering . . . Crispin Mannering."

"That's a nice name." She went pink at her own boldness. "I'm Sheila Tate."

"That's a nice name, too. And what do you do at the hospital?"

"I'm in the laboratory."

"Sounds very scientific. I'm in Peterson Brothers. You know, the big property people."

She nodded.

"We've got a big deal on with Nettleship and Hammond. Six thousand acres."

"Where?" She had asked only to keep the conversation going but he became immediately very cloak-and-dagger and whispered, "In the Ocklington area actually." He put his finger on her lips. "Very hush-hush! So now, you and I have got a secret!"

The chauffeur knew the side streets, and too quickly the ugly red brick of St Mary's loomed ahead. Moving quickly to open the door for her, his right leg kicked the carrier bag, toppled it sideways. The immediacy with which she leant down to pick it up made him say, "I'm sorry . . . hope I haven't broken anything?"

"There's nothing to break." She stepped out on to the pavement outside the porter's lodge. "Well, thank you . . . and goodbye."

"I hope not. Goodbye, I mean. I thought we might have dinner, together."

"Oh, yes . . ." She must not make the same mistake twice. "When?"

49

"What about tonight?"

"Tonight would be fine."

"Six-thirty suit you?"

She was too overwhelmed to do anything else but nod.

"I'll pick you up here then."

One more smile, the soft sound of thick tyres and the silver Rolls had gone. Standing there under the frowning windows of blackened Victorian houses, she seemed to be in a dream. A rich young man, a Rolls and a dinner date – it was straight out of fairyland. The smell of disinfectant and floor-polish in the corridor tried to expunge the memory from her mind.

As she came into the laboratory, Dilys Roberts began chanting, "Strawberry, raspberry, gooseberry jam, what is the name of your young man?"

"I don't know what you mean."

"Or is it an *old* man?"

"Dilys, whatever . . . ?"

"Sheila, I *saw* you. *Flagrante delicto*. Rolls and all!"

Sheila slipped into her white coat. "I'm terribly late. Hope Mr Hart hasn't –"

"He has and he's furious!"

Just before she went out of the door again, Sheila said with elaborate casualness, "Oh, by the way, I won't be coming to the dance tonight, after all."

"There was a young lady of Niger," chanted Dilys spitefully, "who went for a ride on a tiger . . ."

So it was that Sheila Tate did after all catch the ten forty-five train back to Ocklington and arrived home just before midnight, after an enchanted evening. Not that it exactly lived up to the silver Rolls, but Sheila didn't mind. He came on foot. They took a taxi to a pub, then went to a Lyons at Marble Arch, after which it was time to return to Victoria station. Crispin had talked animatedly about sailing in the Mediterranean, skiing in Switzerland, his big job in property development, the problems of the business, particularly with politics and the Labour party. She had listened, saying very little. On the train in the Blackwater Tunnel, he had kissed her much more ardently and passionately than Tom Armitage did.

At Ocklington station, he apologised for not having "the

50

Alfa," but said that of course he would walk her home. He seemed a little taken aback by the vehemence with which she said he wasn't to bother, it was out of his way and it wasn't far anyway. She could not bear him to see 6 Station Approach or to risk her parents possibly catching sight of him with her.

"See you on Monday on the 8.01 then," he said.

Dawdling down Station Approach, she watched him turn up through the short cut to north Ocklington before opening the garden gate of No. 6.

All that evening, the house had rocked with her mother's upbraiding her father for not being firm enough, for not leading the family, and her father retaliating with accusations of spoiling and the need for discipline. The pink rose-papered walls had echoed with stories of drugs, sleeping around, pregnancies, abortions, assaults, fatal accidents, and the fact that they still hadn't found the chap who raped and murdered that girl on the electric train two years ago. When meekly at the time appointed, Sheila made her appearance in the sitting-room, she was immediately welcomed, fussed over, cosseted and asked, "Did you have a nice time, dear?"

"Lovely." Further questions were forestalled by, "But I'm a bit tired now, Mum."

"Of course you are, dear! Into bed with you, and I'll bring up a nice hot cup of chocolate."

Later that night, just before she put the light out in their own room, her mother had said to her father. "She's a good girl, really."

"You worry too much, that's your trouble," said her father. "Worry, worry, worry . . . and in the end, what was there to worry about?"

EDWARD BLAKE came back from his Sunday afternoon walk
with the family and hung up his old mackintosh. Daphne hadn't
noticed the seam under the arm, and for some reason now he
didn't want to draw her attention to it. He stood in the small
shadowy hall staring at it – shabby, empty sleeves, lopsided,
awkward, self-effacing. Like him. As if it were his sleeping body
he'd sloughed off and which some more exciting inner self was
looking down upon. And then he looked in the mirror, and his
own hound-dog face stared back at him. How, he wondered,
following his family into the living-room, could anyone get a
heart-quickening impulse from him?

"Something on toast in front of the fire?" Daphne suggested,
briskly rubbing her hands together. She worked hard in the
house. Her palms made a faint rasping sound, nerve-twanging as
chalk on blackboard.

"If we can take it in front of the telly," Peter said.

"And if you don't drop anything on the carpet." Daphne eyed
her son indulgently. Her favourite without a doubt. A glow to
the eye that never quite reached *him*, Edward thought, and was
immediately ashamed.

"Like me to help you stick those leaves in your scrapbook?"
Edward asked Sarah.

She looked over her shoulder at him, blue eyes wide with
surprise. She shook her head. Her hair shimmered in the firelight. No heartbeat quickened there either.

"You don't usually," she pointed out, as if some of his sense
of exclusion penetrated even her eleven-year-old mind.

"Well, *do* you?" Irritably, when he didn't answer.

"I suppose not."

He leaned forward and tried to rumple her hair the way he
used to when she was very small. She eluded him, stared at him
as if he had gone mad. He suddenly thought he had never seen

52

his children's eyes light up at the sight of him. Never been watched out for and greeted at the end of the day, "Daddy's home!" – like the corny films and television advertisements. Never thrown their arms round him. Never tried to cajole or captivate him. Did real live children still do that these days? Was it just him? Didn't he communicate as a father? He bred them and fed them, was that it? They needed him, of course. Loved him in their own undemonstrative way. Would miss him if he wasn't there. But did he give to their lives any special quality unique to him? Did he to Daphne?

He opened the *Observer*. With relief, it seemed, Peter turned on the television. Sarah carefully aligned a gold-brown oak leaf on the first page of her autumn scrapbook. And Daphne went through into the kitchen.

For some unfathomable reason, he saw the face of the woman on the train superimposed on the newspaper text and the advertisements and the clever pictures.

In the background was the sound of eggs being whisked and the smell of toast.

He skimmed through an article on the power of the subconscious.

"I am a happy man," he told himself five minutes later through mouthfuls of scrambled egg. "I have a fine wife, two healthy children, a happy home, a safe and surprisingly interesting job, not too large a mortgage, no debts."

Why then did he feel that all this was simply marking time, waiting for something to happen? Because he was that sort of person? The sort of person that events happened to?

"Tired?" Daphne asked, perfunctorily solicitous, taking his plate from him.

"Not really. Fresh air always makes me sleepy."

And being sleepy is an excuse for not making an effort to talk. He didn't even dry the dishes with Daphne. Ostensibly he still read the paper. Peter and Sarah watched the television. Sunday night film. Another cowboy. Another Wells Fargo. Gunfire punctured his half-waking dream. The sound of the old-fashioned train ...

The train. He must have dozed off. He was travelling somewhere. He was no longer alone. He was conscious of an almost heartbreaking sweetness. The sound of the train swelled loud and shrill. Then abruptly cut off. He was suffocated in darkness. A tiny light flickered at the end of a long tunnel. Something pressed on his face. He couldn't breathe. He was struggling to get out. Voices shouted.

He woke to a darkened room. His newspaper covered his face. He could hear Peter jumping up and down, his voice shrill with irritation.

"What's up? What's happened?" His own voice came muffled with sleep, unnaturally worried.

"Power cut." Daphne's voice. "Yet again."

Peter swore.

"Now then, young man," Daphne said sharply.

"Well, right in the middle like that!" Peter's face was caught in the dim glow of the fire's remains. "Nearly gave poor old Dad a heart attack."

Edward folded up the offending paper. He felt very old.

"Bedtime anyway, you two," Daphne returned with candles. Her face up-shadowed in the pale light looked like a stranger's.

She kissed them both, rumpled Peter's hair, and said again, indulgently reproving, "And watch your language, young man!"

She returned to the theme, as Edward and she undressed by candlelight.

"He picks it up on the school bus, you know."

"What?"

"Swearing."

"Oh!"

"You don't sound very interested."

"They all do."

"But did you hear what he actually said?"

Edward watched his candlelight shadow on the ceiling shake its head.

Daphne stepped into her nightdress and repeated the offending word. Twice.

"Just an old-fashioned Anglo-Saxon word," Edward murmured. He had actually heard one of his colleagues at the Treasury say it.

Daphne looked at him strangely. He thought at first she was

54

going to object. The candlelit face, the stranger's face was less real to him tonight than the dream face.

Instead he heard Daphne laugh. "You still have the power to surprise me, Edward." She pulled back the covers, and sat in the bed with her hands clasped round her drawn-up knees.

"Nice surprise?" he asked her with matching archness.

"Sometimes." She put her hand on his shoulder. She leaned close to him. He smelled her freshly applied perfume. He felt a kind of superior pity for her clumsiness. But before she drew him down to her, she blew out the candles. He was in a suffocating tunnel of darkness again. He knew his body had to work, to thrust and drive. He was afraid of failing her. And he knew with a timeless echoing terror that in this particular darkness, there was something much worse of which he had to be afraid.

"GO ON IN then, Dad!"

The old man's foot wavered over the running board as the 8.01 quivered impatiently at Ocklington platform. From behind, Miss Edna Price gave her father a cross between a push and a helping hand. The compartment was packed. The grey-green trilby hat, the worn woollen overcoat and the bright red muffler over a framework of skin and bone made no progress as a battering ram. The high tide from behind carried him forward like a piece of flotsam, deposited him and his daughter in the far end top corner, flattened them both against the weeping window.

The doors slammed. They began moving slowly north.

Kept upright by the press around him, the old man managed a watery smile and his daughter held his hand and said, "At least you can see out, Dad. Look now . . . there's our house!"

He gave no indication of being able to see anything.

"You all right, Dad?"

He nodded at her, opened his mouth like a baby bird, but before he could say anything, there was a pushing and a struggling, and a large man with a smooth round white turnip of a head, with one long strand of hair upright in the centre of it like a root, got to his feet and indicated the few inches of red and blue moquette on which he had been sitting, now vacant.

"Oh, you are kind! Go on then, Dad! The gentleman's offered you his seat."

Like a piece of a jigsaw, the old man was turned, twisted, pushed and pulled till he fitted in a treat.

"Say thank you."

"Thank you, Edna."

"Not to me, silly! To the kind gentleman."

"Thank you, sir."

Face to face now, squeezed hard against each other, Miss Price wrinkled her nose apologetically at the plump man and explained, "It's his outlet day . . . wouldn't bring him otherwise . . . not on a commuter train."

"His *outlet* day?"

"His sort of holiday . . . his bit of entertainment. There's just the two of us, you see, and it's so lonely and dull for him when I'm out. So once a month, I take him with me when I go to the office. We have coffee and a cake in a café. Then I take him to a cinema for the morning, and I tell him to meet me outside at one o'clock. We have a Cornish pasty and a pint of bitter. Oh, he does like his beer . . . and for the afternoon, I pop him into another cinema and pick him up again to catch the 5.55 home."

"He must enjoy that."

"Oh, he does! It's his treat. Mind you, it's got to be a cinema close to the office." She gave an embarrassed little giggle. "He sees some shockers!"

"He must do . . . from what I've seen." The train shrieked into the Blackwater Tunnel. "On the posters outside, of course."

"Oh, I wouldn't go in *myself*," said Miss Price.

"I wouldn't call myself a cinema-goer either."

"Shockin'!"

"One of these days they'll put their foot down!"

"But the films don't affect *him*. He doesn't hear very well. And he never remembers."

The organ notes of the clicks on the rails echoed and re-echoed in a crescendo around them as a southbound came rushing past them.

"You all right, Dad?"

The lights of the passing train gave an old-fashioned flickering cinematograph effect to the old man's unmoving face.

"Where are you taking him this morning?"

"To the Astoria."

"Then he'll see *The Naughty Nun* . . . if my memory serves me. I pass it on my way to Campion's."

"You work there?"

He nodded. Campion's was a small store in the Buckingham Palace Road. She looked at him with new respect.

"Perhaps I'd better introduce myself." He passed her a card and in the light reflected from the walls of the tunnel she read *Mr Henry Osborne, Campion's Store. Furniture Department.*

"I'm Miss Price . . . Peterson Brothers."

"The property developers?"

"That's right."

The train shrieked back into the daylight. Her eyes flitted over his face, at the moist full mouth and the dewlaps of fat like a napkin round his neck.

"And where will he go in the afternoon?"

"The Cameo."

"He'll see *Daughter of Dracula* there."

"Ooh!" She gave a surprisingly girlish shudder. "But *he* won't mind. It gets him out of the house. You can understand, can't you? Look at him now, sitting so quiet. But at home, would you believe it, he's never still a minute! Clump, clump, clump up the stairs, in and out the doors, poking in the cupboards, opening drawers. 'Have you lost something, Dad?' I ask him a dozen times a day. 'What are you looking for?' I don't know what it is. He shakes his head and I lead him back and sit him by the fire again, and I say 'You've found it now, Dad. You're all right. You can watch the telly now.' But next minute, he's up again . . . looking, looking, *looking* . . ."

He shook his head sympathetically. "It must be difficult for you."

"It isn't easy. But he's been better, since I've been giving him his outlet. Something to look forward to, see. He could be terrible before. Never sleep. And there was that awful night . . . that's when all this outlet business started. In the middle of the night, I heard this noise. And he wasn't anywhere to be found! He had unbolted the door and gone out into the street and way over the bridge . . . a little old man at two in the morning. And I went after him and caught him up, and he didn't recognise me and he said, 'Who are you?' 'Dad,' I said, 'what are you doing?' 'I'm trying to find an outlet,' he said, whatever that may mean. So I said 'Let's find it together.' Then he recognised me and said 'I've been waiting for you a long time, Edna. Wherever have you been?' So I said, 'Let's go back home, Dad, and have a nice cup of tea.'"

Battersea Power Station, over the Thames, past blocks of flats into the outstretched arms of the waiting platform.

"Victoria already!" she said. "The time *has* gone quickly! Come on, Dad! We're here!"

Obediently he struggled to his feet, only to be knocked back into his seat as the commuters exploded out of the train.

"No manners these days!" said the gentleman from Campion's as they waited for the compartment to empty. "No regard for others."

"It's shockin'!"

"The young people . . . they're the worst.'

"No respect for authority."

"No respect for anything."

Slowly the three of them walked to the ticket barrier, with the old man in the middle.

"No discipline," said Mr Osborne.

"None! It's shockin'!"

"A little old-fashioned discipline, that's what's needed."

"That's what they're asking for!"

"You may think me old-fashioned, Miss Price . . . but I'm a firm believer in the stick."

"I'm old-fashioned . . . very old-fashioned."

"A taste of the stick . . ."

"It's shockin'."

As they reached the barrier, another train had arrived at the same platform, disgorged a further swarm who came rushing up behind them. Miss Price produced the two tickets, aimed her father for the opening.

"Go on out then, Dad!"

Walled in alive in the middle of the compartment, Gordon Cunliffe was delayed even further by his fellow-commuters. He struggled to the doorway, only to find it blocked by a rag-and-bone man, a flagpole of a woman and a fat oaf carrying an out-size briefcase labelled "Henry Osborne, Campion's Store."

Cunliffe cursed them to hell.

He had a habit of this, unusual in one of so respectable an outside appearance – dark blue suit, short cavalry-style overcoat, bowler hat – of muttering oaths and obscenities aloud, but not usually loud enough for anyone to hear him. At last out on the platform, he repeated the performance, this time for the benefit of the woman on the Tannoy who was quavering tinnily, "We apologise for the late arrival of your train on Platform Three. This was due . . ."

"Bloody bitch . . . always apologising!"

He was late – late *again*, and he had particularly wanted to be early today because Franklin had said he would like to have a word at ten, and now he wasn't going to make it, and that had got him into one of his states. Though his hands were tightly clenched, they shook. A curious sick feeling had come into his stomach. His rather short legs pounded like pistons as he made for the barrier, his mind obsessed – White-Rabbit-like – with one single thought . . . I'm late, *I'm late.*

Nobody would have guessed at what was going on inside him. The negro porter who checked his ticket saw a calm, purposeful looking man with a warm smile on his lips. Whatever his emotions, he always appeared good-tempered. He exuded confidence. "Cuddly" was what the girls in the office of Nettleship and Hammond privately called him. "Dedicated" was the Board's view. "Efficient", "highly qualified", "well-educated" were frequently expressed (Franklin, of course, never gave an opinion) by his business associates.

Actually he had left school when he was fifteen, a fact that he had successfully concealed from everyone, even from Alice, his wife. He had no business training and no qualifications. He had worked hard to cultivate a veneer of culture. He had regularly jumped from one job to another slightly higher, so that his experience appeared, when suitably window-dressed and exaggeratedly labelled, both comprehensive and impressive. He was a public-relations man, a real professional, and he himself was his principal promotion. His eyes were upturned to the stars, always he searched for higher and higher things. Never did he do anything or say anything that was not designed to help him personally, nor did he let slide any opportunity to advance himself. But his confident smile hid the fear that was always with him – that one day he would be found out for what he was.

Even his hurry he controlled. He moved swiftly towards the

Underground without giving the appearance of effort. Alice used to say that it was no use firing at him, no one could possibly hit him because he was never still. He had had another "do" – row was the wrong word as she would never fight but simply retreat to her bed – with Alice this morning, which had made initial inroads, even before the delays, into his peace of mind. He had touched her on her sore spot – Blakeneys. Ever since the court-case after the car accident and since Alice didn't drive, he had had to walk to and from the station over a mile and half away, and on foggy autumn mornings like today what with the mud in the lane from the rains over the weekend it was no picnic and he had made noises that really Blakeneys was too inconvenient – and that had been enough to send her bedwards.

He had never liked the place anyway. Tucked up in that unmade lane, isolated, hidden away under bramble and bracken on heavy Weald clay, the thatch full of insects and the oak beams riddled with woodworm – it had been Alice's fairy-story cottage, saturated with what she called atmosphere, and it was she who had insisted. Not that the view was much either, though Alice raved about it – the back end of Ocklington, the ragstone church, that stretch of heath called Terrible Down rimmed by the river with the railway running through the middle of it. What he had liked was the name – Blakeneys promised a gracious Georgian mansion, not a tumble-down Tudor cottage – the price (for they had very little money) and the fact that it was far enough away from London and so inaccessible that neither Franklin nor anyone else important was ever likely to find it. When they had bought it, of course, he could use the car. And Alice was pleased because she said that after years of living in city smoke, at last here she could breathe.

He had met his wife at the wedding of a business acquaintance eighteen years ago. She was a thin girl, with aristocratically high cheekbones, a long sculptured neck and huge luminous eyes. She had a far better education than he had – girls' public school and Cambridge – and was given to wearing very long gowns with big patterns, wooden beads, her fair hair sculpted over exquisite chiselled ears. He had been impressed by her beauty, and even though her family were penniless, they had obscure connections

61

with the nobility. Perhaps it was because they were such opposites that they had been well-matched to help each other in a partnership. She had uncanny intuition, had at first not been demanding. He was capable and could organise her disorganised life. She had been teaching music at a girls' school which she hated, so that perhaps even his completely unmusical approach to life was an asset in a prospective husband. For the first few years, when they had lived in Chelsea, the marriage had been reasonably successful. It was only after she began having this chest trouble, which perhaps added to the nervousness innate in her personality, that things became difficult. She had developed an almost neurotic fear of people. Her beauty had withered, she had become haggard, withdrawn, a positive hindrance to any business entertaining he might have to do at home.

Down here at Blakeneys she had certainly improved. She loved birds and wild life, lay awake for hours in the early morning, identifying tits and warblers and thrushes and peewits, and there was great excitement one night last year when she had heard the nightingale. Domestic animals she pitied, ranting against what she called their "imprisonment" almost as much as she did against fox-hunting and blood-sports. She was interested in all sorts of exotic plants and cacti and had even tried to grow orchids in the back kitchen. She had planted a eucalyptus tree which had grown at a great rate and now towered like a flagpole above the thatch, twinkling with coin-shaped blue-green leaves – as incongruous as herself, he often thought, beside the bulky oaks and elms and beeches of Kent. She became a vegetarian. She spun. She produced folk-weave on a handloom. She read a great deal – solitary pursuits. She had this fanatical passion for freedom – she would often say that in Blakeneys she felt *free*. Perhaps, he thought, this had something to do with her claustrophobia. She could not bear to be shut in, hated locked doors, had once become hysterical when she had got herself accidentally locked up in the ancient wall-cupboard by the fifteenth-century chimney. She explained it by saying that we were incarcerated enough in our own flesh and blood without adding to the walls around us. Night she feared as being another black wall: night imprisoned us, night made us blind. She hated being on her own at night, being buried alive in sleep. Certainly it was lonely at Blakeneys, but that was her choice, and her insistence on his presence there every night was as inconsistent as it was inconvenient.

He had arrived on the Underground platform just as a train was leaving. There was an interminable wait for the next one. When it came, the clock said 10.02, and even so it stood there throbbing while another Tannoy voice as high as Alice's called out mechanically "Mind the doors . . . mind the doors, please!"

"Bloody bitch!"

He strap-hung to Threadneedle Street. He was squeezed along with the others up the toothpaste-thin stairs into the hurrying grey open. He had to wait to cross the congested road to the cement skyscraper in which Nettleship and Hammond were lodged.

The clock at the top of the tower said 10.16.

He had to wait for the lift, wait at all fifteen floors until he was finally discharged into his own corridor. There opposite him was his name in bold black letters, *G. K. Cunliffe, Company Secretary. All visitors to Miss D. S. Leigh in Room 1608.*

He took the Yale key out of his pocket. He opened the door. He hurried through. He took off his hat and overcoat and hung them on the peg behind the door before closing it. Then he looked up at his own clock as though hoping for a reprieve.

10.23.

And then he saw the neat little typewritten note on the blue leather top of his massive desk.

Mr Cunliffe, I told Mr Franklin's P.A. that you were calling at Peterson Brothers on your way to the office so that you would not be able to make your 10 a.m. appointment with him. Debbie.

He had hardly sat down when the telephone rang.

"I heard you come in, Mr Cunliffe. Did you see my note?"

"Yes, thank you, Miss Leigh."

"When you hadn't come in by nine forty-five, I guessed your train was running late again, so I phoned Mr Franklin."

"Thank you, Miss Leigh. I'll go along and see him now."

"Yes, Mr Cunliffe."

As he put down the receiver, he was aware of the slightest

63

reproachful disappointment in her voice. He called his secretary three names – Miss Leigh for official occasions, or when he was reproving her or when other people were present, Deborah for normal workaday routine, when there were just the two of them together, and the diminutive, Debbie, very rarely and only when he was well pleased with her. She might have felt that this was just such an occasion, which was why purposely he had gone to the other end of the spectrum. It was necessary to keep people firmly in their place. Give them an inch, a foot through the door, and they were in. A touch of the whip was necessary to preserve the hierarchy. You must never get under an obligation to anyone. If people do help you, don't make a fuss of it, play it down, bring up some good turn from the past that you did them. Alternatively, if you do help other people, *make* a fuss about it until you are justly rewarded. He owed his present position in the property firm of Nettleship and Hammond to this simple technique. From a considerably more humble position in Cameron and Company, he had steered a valuable contract into their hands. The gentlest but most persistent reminders of un-redeemed past favours to people in powerful places had been amongst his most effective appliances in scaling his ladder – the others being his skill at dressing up his qualifications, his soft slow voice and his outwardly confident manner.

If something has to be done, do it *now* – that was another of his maxims, and without even sitting down at his desk, he was off again down the corridor to Franklin's first outer office in which sat two junior typists. In the office beyond, there was an older woman, Millicent Smith, Franklin's Personal Assistant, in charge of them – quick, efficient, angular, ginger hair and glasses.

"Good morning, sir."

"Good morning, sir."

"Good morning, Mr Cunliffe. Do go right in. H.F. is free."

This office was larger than his own, panelled in a red African wood. The carpet was thicker, the desk was bigger. Only the man behind it was smaller, not nearly as thick-set, built like a whippet with the same bright glistening eyes. Younger too, more elegantly dressed, sleek black hair, movements quick and nervous.

"Morning, Gordon."

He spoke quickly too, clipped and crackling. Hugh Franklin had built this company from almost nothing. He lived and breathed it and expected his employees – particularly his senior employees – to do likewise. He came into the office at eight every morning, and insisted on everyone else being in at least by nine thirty. It was one of Cunliffe's many duties to see that this was enforced, which at present, what with the vagaries of British Rail, was proving embarrassingly difficult. Franklin paid salaries well over the odds and demanded an equivalent return in work, efficiency and loyalty. Nobody knew what had happened to Nettleship and Hammond, but the speculation throughout the company was that either they had never existed or that H.F. had eaten them.

"Good morning, H.F."

"You popped in to Peterson Brothers, I hear?"

"That's right, H.F." Cunliffe sat down in an armchair on the left-hand side of the desk and unhurriedly crossed his legs. "Hope you didn't mind."

"Why should I mind?"

"Well, there was this appointment . . ."

"Your girl rang my woman."

"She told me."

"On the ball. Smart little thing. Pretty, too. What's its name again?"

"Leigh."

"What sort of Leigh?"

"Deborah Leigh."

"Suits it. How old?"

"Twenty-eight."

"Nice age."

"Yes."

"Odd it's not married. Or is it married to its job?"

"Well, I know she likes it very much, H.F."

"Good, good! And how were Peterson Brothers? I hope you kicked some slumbrous arses?"

"I did, H.F. I did."

"And when are we going to receive the actual contract for the Ocklington land?"

65

"By the end of the month." If it didn't turn up then, he could always blame it either on the lawyers or on Peterson's.

"Question . . . how much do they know about the plans for making Ocklington a New Town?"

"Well, of course, they're vaguely aware of them, H.F."

"Question . . . *how* vaguely?"

"They know of it only as an outside possibility."

"Question . . . how definite *are* the plans for Ocklington New Town?"

"Well, H.F. . . . . in this life there's nothing definite."

"Give it to me as a percentage probability."

"Eighty per cent."

"Good enough for me." Franklin grunted. "Question . . . if Peterson Brothers reckoned on this degree of probability, what would happen to their asking price?"

"Twice as much."

"Question . . . if there weren't this threat from the Labour Party on development land and nationalisation, what effect would that have on the price?"

"Treble it."

"And yet the Labour record on compensation isn't all that bad." Franklin smiled. "You tell me what I want to hear, Gordon, you have put my mind at rest." The Managing Director paused. "You see, I had a character from Peterson Brothers in to see me last Friday morning."

Cunliffe's heart lurched. It was at the root of all his business philosophy that the various protagonists did not meet, that he alone was the go-between, negotiator, peace-maker extraordinary. "Who was that?"

"Oh, just some young underling, nobody important. They tried to dress him up big by sending him over in Peterson's Rolls."

"What did they want?"

"Higher price."

Cunliffe put a puzzled expression on his face. "Odd that they didn't mention it to me this morning."

"Not really. Sent him off with a flea in his ear. They were just trying it on." He paused, "Well, the sooner we get the contract, the better. Right?"

"Right!"

"We're one of the few property firms with no liquidity problems. Right?"

"Right!"

"So we buy at the bottom. Right?"

"Right!"

"You'll go on pushing Peterson Brothers. Right?"

"Right!"

"Good! Then I can depend on you to see it through. Right?"

"Right!"

"We're lucky, having you on the spot in your country place at Ocklington, keeping your ear to the ground. I won't forget that, Gordon."

"Thank you, H.F." Sensing the end of the meeting, mindful that Franklin had his time carefully costed, Cunliffe had risen to his feet. "Well, if that's all . . ."

"One other thing."

Cunliffe was already moving towards the door. "Yes, H.F.?"

"This boy from Peterson Brothers. He was late. That was how I knew about the Rolls. I was at the window, waiting, and I saw him arrive." Franklin paused. "His excuse was that the train was late." Franklin paused again. "The Ocklington train."

"Friday." Cunliffe closed his eyes as though trying to remember. "Yes, I believe it was."

"He was . . . *very* late."

"All trains are very late now and again. Particularly at this time of year. And what with these go-slows on all lines . . ."

"Question . . . everything's all right with the Ocklington line, isn't it?"

"Well, we have our fair share of troubles, H.F."

"You're a pretty important chap . . . I mean, Chairman of all sorts of things down there, dealing direct with British Rail. Question . . . you'd be the first to hear if anything was in the wind?"

"I think so, H.F."

"And you've heard nothing?"

"I hear all sorts of things."

"Nothing about the line closing?"

For a fraction of a second, Cunliffe hesitated. There *had*

67

indeed been something – something about expense, something about maintenance and repairs, but very hush-hush, though as always Sir Ralph Mannering had heard about it. "Nothing," he said emphatically.

"That's all I wanted to know. Thank you, Gordon."

Cunliffe's hands were tightly clenched again as he walked down the corridor. He could feel his heart hammering, and his mouth had gone dry. He was aware that he had been in a state of high tension pretty well from the time he had left Ocklington station. Did Franklin suspect anything? He knew no one in Peterson Brothers who lived in Ocklington. What exactly had this boy said? Who was he anyway?

Again he opened the door of his office. He went across the blue carpet, and sat down in the plump comfort of his padded chair, still breathing deeply as his eyes went round the room. He looked at the eighteenth-century prints of London. He looked at the nude calendar on the wall. He looked across the massive altar of his desk, on the leather top of which was a steaming hot cup of coffee and a little plate of biscuits and in front, so low it was almost kneeling – spindly, steel-framed, frugal – the empty secretary's stool.

Miss Leigh had brought in his opened mail and relevant files, laid them to the right of the desk for his eventual attention. She would have gone round fastidiously with her little duster, cleaning up after the cleaners. Now she would be sitting just beyond that closed door to the outer office, the electric typewriter in front of her, her pencil lying in the spine of her open notepad, her hands folded in her lap – waiting.

It pleased him to think of her sitting there. It pleased him to keep her sitting there. He took up his round ivory ruler, rolled it in the palms of both his hands, feeling the tension beginning to drain out of his skin. He took up the coffee and began to drink. Then he leaned to the right, put out his forefinger, touched the button, picked up the receiver.

"Yes, Mr Cunliffe?"

"Would you come in for dictation please, Miss Leigh?"

"Yes, Mr Cunliffe."

He put down the receiver, kept his eyes on the blue leather of his desk as though deep in concentration. He heard the door open, the soft sound of her high heels in the thick pile of the carpet.

Then he looked up and saw her momentarily framed in the doorway, head bowed, carrying her notebook and pencil. She had a helmet of black hair cut in a fringe over her forehead, a small pink shrimp of a mouth, a neat pointed little chin, and a Chelsea china shepherdess neck. She wore a grey dress beautifully matching the colour scheme of the room. She came forward, smoothed her skirt tight against her hips, sat herself down on the little secretary's stool, opened her pad, lifted her pencil.

"H.F. is being awkward, Deborah."

"*Again*, Mr Cunliffe?"

"And Peterson Brothers are being tiresome."

"After all you've done for them, Mr Cunliffe!"

"Address the letter to Garside." He paused. "In regard to the Ocklington contract, it is with some concern –"

Her pencil hurried and scurried over the paper, lest she miss one syllable. He felt the sentences flow out of his mouth spontaneously, rhythmically, confidently. Now her head was bowed even more, almost in an attitude of prayer. She had a small straight parting on the top of her head, neat and clean, the black hair shining on either side. Peeping from under her skirt, he saw the lace frill of a brilliant white petticoat.

"That's telling the bastard, Debbie!"

"You've put it beautifully, Mr Cunliffe."

"And as for that bloody man, Franklin . . ." His words trickled into silence.

She looked up. His brown eyes met her grey blue ones. A faint flush came up into her cheeks, now delicately pink like apples ripening in front of his eyes.

"Bumped-up little fart! Fucking sonofabitch . . . two-faced bleeding bugger . . ."

The relief was delicious as the obscenities streamed from his lips.

"MRS QUINTON on the telephone, m'lady."

Wanting a donation for her distressed gentlefolk's home.

Five minutes later. "Miss Patrick on the telephone, m'lady."

Wanting a subscription for her university scholarship fund for the disabled.

That was the trouble, Marjorie Mannering thought – hearing in their voices and seeing in their eyes that they wanted something you had got, could give them, make them happy. The continued askings preceding the simulated surprise when she yet again said she would.

"You're a glutton for punishment," her husband said when she resumed her seat. "Why don't you tell them to go to hell?"

That's what he did – except every now and then he did give something – something small . . . and what a grateful fuss they made of him then! She had once suggested to him that they should turn Ocklington Park into a sort of international orphanage – for children from all the trouble-spots of the world, Vietnam, the Middle East, Ireland, India, Africa. He simply wouldn't take it seriously. Then seeing that she did, told her the Foreign Office would never allow it.

"Mrs Robb on the telephone, m'lady." Most people in her position had an excuse all ready that came tripping out slick and sweet and virgin white. Yet when she tried, the words got stuck on her tongue as though something had put a half-nelson on them, and they came out muffled, stiff with untruth, black.

"People have only to open their mouths," her husband said, "and you give them what they ask."

Except you, she thought – and perhaps that was at the root of her guilt – I can't give you what it is *you* most want.

"And you even go up to town so that you can prolong the agony. It's one of your London days today, isn't it?"

He knew perfectly well that it was – every Tuesday for her

charities and committees. He regarded her trips to London as unnecessary and undignified. He ran his own multifarious international business and property enterprises from here – his secret eyrie at Ocklington Park. People came to see *him*.

"It is. St Mary's Hospital Committee. And I'll have to hurry if I'm going to catch my train."

"Can't understand why you don't get Robbins to drive you up."

"Because with all this traffic, it would take too long."

"No longer than British Rail."

"I don't like having Robbins hanging round doing nothing, waiting for me."

"It's what he's paid for."

"Anyway," she pushed back the Hepplewhite chair, started to get up. "I happen to *prefer* the train."

He raised his eyebrow – not in the sort of grand sardonic manner that Bill Cody would have done, but quizzical, amused. She had told him briefly about the stop in the tunnel, the jazzy haired young man who had opened the door and tried to get out. His intention had been thwarted by a big chap in a tweed jacket. Ralph's pronouncement on the episode then was that if she *would* go slumming, she must expect such adventures. Now all he said was, "You have queer tastes, Marjorie."

"I know."

"Enjoy them while you can is all I can say."

Halfway to the door, she spun round to look at him. "What d'you mean, Ralph?"

"They're closing the Line."

"But they can't!"

"Oh yes they can!"

"It's doing so well."

"If that's what you call running at a loss for thirty years . . ."

"Aren't you going to make an official complaint?"

"Why?"

"They're your constituents. Closing the line would hit Ocklington hard."

"Still only a rumour."

"But from your usual well-informed sources?"

"I keep my ears to the ground. In my business, you have to."

71

"What about the Ocklington New Town Plan?"

"Shelved." He got up, walked over to open the door and give her a light kiss on the cheek. "Look after yourself."

"I will. See you this evening."

"Don't let them wheedle any more money out of you."

The door closed, she walked over the polished parquet floor of the hall to where the butler was ready with her coat and bag. She was surprised by the vehemence of her own feelings. Was it simply that she resisted change, was shocked by the decay of any thing – human beings, old churches, railways? Or was it that just for a little while, disguised as a commuter, she had a different role, enjoyed seeing different faces, such as Bill Cody's, who were oblivious of her existence as m'lady?

She considered whether he would be on the train today. Whether he was in fact a commuter. Probably not, she thought, as the warm chrysanthemum scent of the domed hall gave way to the sharp moist smell of a September morning. It is unlikely I shall ever see him again. We walk on different paths: pity, really. Now the hug of the car's inside, the soft leather upholstery, the mohair rug being tucked over her knees.

"Comfortable, m'lady?"

"Yes thank you, Robbins."

M'lady – that's what she was, that's what they had all been, all those Mannering women stretching back all those years. Every minute of their day occupied with the management of the great house, the servants, the tenants' wives, St George's Church, the village school, entertaining neighbouring families and politicians – not a second left to think and probably a very good thing too. M'lady, she thought, watching the gracious Queen Anne red-brick façade growing smaller and smaller in the driving mirror – to be aware all your waking life of people *wanting* something from you, hinting at it, brazening it out, being too embarrassed to bring it up. Never thinking that *she* might want something. For heaven's sake, what could she want? She had everything in the world, married to a charming, educated, civilised, gallant man, a Member of Parliament and the owner of a fair slice of Kent.

The Rolls slipping out of the lodge gates now, turning left towards the station, passing on the right the Norman stone church with the tall cedar-tiled steeple. They were all there, those other m'ladies, carved in alabaster, lying dutifully beside their soldier husbands, with their children like little dogs below their feet. M'lady – the mother-goddess to be sucked from by all, symbol of the eternal order of things, dispenser of hospitality, generous supporter of the poor and needy, comforter to the sick – separately and affectionately identified by their Christian names, whether or not they were earls' daughters. Lady Ursula, Lady Anne, Lady Caroline, Lady Amelia – Ralph's first wife, killed in a plane crash with their only child, a son – even the naughty Lady Elizabeth who broke her neck on this sharp corner, riding to her lover.

Over the bridge now, into the square. Down Station Approach, already peppered with people.

The Rolls stopped. Robbins opened the door.

Just very faintly, as she stepped out of the car, her heartbeat quickened.

"I shall definitely come back on the 5.55, Robbins."

"I shall be waiting, m'lady."

She avoided looking at her own reflection in the polished bonnet. She was, she knew, looking as pretty as, at her age, she could look. She was wearing a finely fitting suit of a very becoming shade of grey. It had a small mink collar and with it she wore the same blue mink hat as last time. She was an animal-lover and she had a vague conscience about wearing fur. Sometime she intended to ban it from her wardrobe. But, she thought with real sadness, like so many things she had a conscience about, she hung it about herself like a jockey carrying weights rather than actually *doing* anything. Besides, she thought, a quick glimpse in the glass of the booking-hall door, mink *did* something for a woman.

And today, dear Lord, she wanted something. Many things perhaps. But what? To be herself? Or rather, for all her separate selves to come together. To make one smooth whole as convincing and becoming as her outer self. For I am now what I seem, she wanted to cry aloud. I am not the fertile goddess, the dispenser of plenty. This motherly bosom suckles no child, no grandchildren will lisp their silly nursery rhymes round this knee. Pink and white and powdered skin, pretty eyes and soft

73

wavy hair. I contain inside, like the thin man within the fat struggling to get out, a dark-visaged rebel, a real Northumbrian, a young girl. I would like to be this pert-faced nineteen-year-old with the skinny legs and the short short skirt queuing in front of me.

She waited, smiling with abstracted patience, while Sheila Tate renewed her season ticket. The clerk nodded to Lady Marjorie obsequiously. But to the majority of commuters she was blessedly unknown. Commuters tended to mix little with country life, treating Ocklington as a dormitory town. Because it was cold and damp this morning, most of them were huddled inside the booking-hall round a coke stove. Lady Marjorie cleaved her way through and on to the upline platform.

A few people paced up and down the windswept platform. The man in the tweed jacket was standing quite still facing the entrance, legs slightly apart, hands on his hips. He wore a thick polo-necked sweater underneath the old tweed jacket. He looked relaxed and yet watchful. He was a little younger than she remembered him, and for some reason her heart sank. Yet he looked as if he had been waiting for some person to come through that door behind her. And with a tremulous fearful pleasure, she knew it was herself.

"Hello." He smiled, walking the couple of paces up to her.

"Good morning."

"You forgot something the other day." He towered above her. His eyes looked a dark blue, the colour of the jumper.

"I did?"

"Yes. You forgot to tell me your name. I told you mine."

"Cody," she repeated smiling. "Bill Cody." Out of the corner of her eye, she could see the commuters pacing up and down the platform had paused in their perambulations and were taking up their action stations. She could hear the faint clicketty-click of the oncoming train.

"You remembered it."

"Only because it was easy."

"Naturally. And yours?"

"Mannering."

Tee-whooo. Now the train was racketing round the curve. A yellow two-eyed face.

74

Bill Cody's smile shut off. He stared down at her oddly. Not exactly hostilely. Not exactly calculatingly. Not exactly disappointedly. But something of all three.

"Relation to?" He threw the question over his shoulder, turning to glance at the oncoming train.

She almost answered, "Afraid so," and then bit off her disloyal words.

"I'm Marjorie Mannering." She put out her right hand. She did it badly, condescendingly, as if she were going to bestow his certificate with the other.

He ignored it.

"Mrs or Miss?"

And when she didn't answer, he raised his thick black brows and pulled down the corners of his mouth. Sulky. Wry. Despising. As if he were the very epitome of her other self. The rebel self. The self that thought what bloody nonsense all this was. And, ironically, she found all her other separate selves reacting, united in quite Ralph-like indignation.

What right had he to despise *her* title, *her* possessions, Ocklington Park or anything else for that matter?

She gathered herself up, allowed herself to be cut off from him by the flood of commuters bursting out of the booking hall. Held her eyes away from his dark sardonic face, and stared at the seven slowing carriages willing there to be a First Class amongst them. The God of Ocklington's rich church and all wealthy communicants naturally heard her. Answered her prayer and more. The First Class compartment stopped immediately in front of Lady Marjorie.

She got in without saying goodbye, found herself an empty compartment, and slid the door firmly shut behind her, subsided into its corner seat with mingled irritation and relief.

Bill Cody opened it. "D'you mind if I come in?"

"It's your right," she said, flushing. And then with inspiration, "So long as you've a ticket."

He smiled a slow derisive smile, and sat down opposite her, his hands hanging loosely between his knees.

"I have a ticket."

"Good."

"Of sorts."

She smiled without meaning to. "Of sorts won't do."

"It's worth risking. So long that is as *you* don't object."

"Why should I?" She shook her head. "You were most helpful before." The whistle sounded. Lady Marjorie held her breath a moment. No one else got into this First Class compartment. There were advantages to riches. Marjorie Mannering's heartbeat quickened in time to the clicks of the wheels.

"Did I say something to offend you back there?" He jerked his dark head at where Ocklington station lay behind them.

"Not really." She smiled. "Offend is the wrong word. You rather *looked* . . . how can I say it?"

"How?"

"As if I were something archaic, some anachronism." Why did she go on so, rallying and railing? Skittish, even. She would never have talked thus even to a friend.

He raised one eyebrow and smiled unkindly.

"There, that's what I mean," she said, half amused, half angry. "You made me feel like some brontosaurus."

"Wrong." Held up both large hands, waved them protestingly, humorously. "An *anachronism* maybe. In a way, you are. But brontosaurus, no. Certainly no. You are quite unlike any brontosaurus I've ever met."

She said nothing.

"Relieved?" he asked her, leaning his head back and eyeing her derisively from under half-lowered lids.

"Of course!" She smiled playfully. "But why that look?"

He shrugged. "I was alarmed, you might say, to find the lady was a Lady."

"Ah!"

"Yes, and something else." He sat up straight. He looked out for a moment abstractedly at the flashing fields, the bare woods, the tarnished iron ponds.

Lady Marjorie had a sudden romantic idea he was going to say, "And the lady's married," and was asking herself exactly how she should reply, when Bill Cody finished slowly.

"The lady's husband is my landlord."

"Ralph! Is he really? How?"

"Applegarth Cottage. I am the tenant thereof." He gave her that slow hostile smile that already she hated. "You don't even know it, do you?" Softly, yet terribly angrily. "You have so many, eh? Isn't that it?"

"Only about seventy," she declared roundly, lapsing into the real Lady Marjorie again.

"Shame! Damned shame! Only seventy!" He patted his deep broad chest and sighed.

She tried to freeze him with her stare. But he simply stared back with a loutish insolence.

"The roof leaks by the way," he said deliberately to provoke her.

"Then find accommodation elsewhere, Mr Cody."

She glanced outside as if the conversation were now definitely over, and she was interested only in the beauties of the autumn countryside. But they were already slowing for the tunnel. Her own face looked back at her from the glistening brickwork. She was flushed, she looked youthfully pretty.

"Not a hope at the price, alas, Lady M. Peppercorn rent."

"Ah, there, you see." Softened by the reassurance of her own reflection, she turned on him almost gaily. "We're not such bad landlords."

He looked as if he might have said something different. He seemed surprised by her sudden change into gaiety, matching it with an exaggeratedly reproachful expression. "I was merely complaining that you didn't know of my existence."

"But you didn't know me." Again that younger rallying tone. What, a voice cried to her, was she beginning. How would it end?

"I've only been here a fortnight."

Surreptitiously she looked at the big hands spread out on his knees. "Do you live alone, Mr Cody?"

He smiled. "Mostly."

She smiled back. "You haven't a wife to look after you?"

"As far as I can tell, they don't do much of that these days."

"Of what, Mr Cody?"

"Of looking after, Lady M." But he didn't actually say he wasn't married and for some reason though the answer seemed important to her, she didn't like to press him.

77

"And where did you come from?"

"Here and there." He shrugged. "I'm a rolling stone."

"But you've taken root at Applegarth Cottage?" she laughed. It was the sort of remark the real Lady Marjorie would have made and it sounded like the traditional singing of "Jerusalem" on a Women's Institute Monday . . . and did those feet in ancient time . . .

He didn't deign to answer it. He changed the subject.

He frowned down at his boots. "That young bastard sitting next to you last time . . ."

"The one that tried to open the door? Yes. What about him?" He sounds almost jealous, she thought, smiling inwardly.

"I saw him the other day. He asked me who you were."

"So you were finding out for him?"

"Not entirely. He said you had a kind face."

"How depressing," she sighed, self-mockingly.

"Now if I said it wasn't true, you wouldn't like it." Mr Cody stretched out a hand and quite unselfconsciously patted her knee. "And if I said it was, that would be wrong too."

"You've learned a lot in your short life, Mr Cody?" she asked as they burst out of the tunnel and into half-hearted sunlight.

"Not that short, alas."

"How old are you?"

"Thirty-eight." An insolent smile. Deserved, she thought. "And you?"

She was saved the indignity of refusing to answer or, worse, the self-revelation of a lie. The corridor door was shoved open.

"Tickets, please." The ticket collector was old and sour. He had been on this line as long as Lady Marjorie could remember. He knew her of course.

He took her ticket with deference, clipped it as if it had human nerves, handed it back to her. Then turned, judgment suspended, to Cody.

Bill Cody smiled at her across the man's vinegary profile. He handed him his ticket.

"Second only, sir." He glanced apologetically over his shoulder at Lady Marjorie as if she might in some way have become infected by the interloper's presence. Or even *involved*.

Bill Cody dipped his hand into his trouser pocket and brought out a small handful of loose change. Some other telling voice inside Lady Marjorie's newly sensitised being told her this was all the money he had. No Diner's card. No stuffed wallet, no hateful purse like Ralph. Nothing.

"I'll pay the difference," Cody said airily, sorting through his handful of coins.

"The lot, sir, if you please. The *whole* first class fare," the collector replied with pleasure. He brought out his little flimsy pad and began pencilling furiously on it. "Two pounds ninety-five, sir."

"Rubbish! Robbery!"

"No sir, that is the exact amount."

"I'll pay the difference. I owe you ninety pence."

"Two ninety-five. Bye-law 23." The train gathered speed. The ticket collector swayed like a bantam cock in front of a big black peevish panther.

"Look here," Lady Marjorie put her authoritative hand on his arm. "I invited this gentleman in here." She raised her well-bred voice ringingly. "To talk some business over. *I* shall pay." She opened her leather bag. "*I* insist."

"No, you damned well don't!" Cody leaned over and put a great capacious hand on her wrist. "No, lady." His fingers bit into her soft flesh. She struggled for the pleasure of feeling them dig deep.

"Now then, sir, please! None of that!"

"Ninety pence, one hundred." Bill Cody was counting fast with his other hand. "One pound, you sharks! Fifty! *One* fifty! Two pounds. And fifty. Bloodsuckers, British Rail!"

Finally he produced everything. But to get rid of the man quickly, to smooth the incident over, Lady Marjorie pressed a fifty pence piece into the ticket collector's hand. After all, she had her bag open.

"Why the hell did you do that? You think that's how it's done, don't you?"

"No, I don't."

"Of course you do!" With a beastly coarse black-visaged face.

"Damn you, then why not!"

"If you don't know, then I can't tell you!"

79

They sat for the rest of those wasted minutes of privacy, in their own corners, glowering at one another. Horrible insolent man, she thought. East Croydon's outer wastelands came up. Early morning washing flapped in the narrow terrace backyards. She was enveloped in depression. Slowly they clicked over the points, past the car park and into the blackened concrete of the station. People swarmed in. Mr Cody and she were hemmed in their isolation and their displeasure with one another by a godly band of bowler-hatted bespoke-suited manifest first-class ticket-holders, spiky with umbrellas. Custom-built tailor's dummies to contrast with Mr Cody's aggressive masculinity.

At Clapham Junction, it was she who leaned forward to make the first move. He came part-way to meet her.

"I'm sorry," she smiled tentatively.

"Then come and have lunch with me."

"I can't today. I'm lunching with the Committee." Regretfully she rubbed her wrist. This was the end of it surely. He couldn't expect . . . this was, after all, no way to behave. Lady Marjorie Mannering, wife mark you, of Ralph, must never . . . could never . . . He didn't press her. He watched her thoughtfully, nevertheless.

"I shall however be coming up next week. And it so happens that I'm free for lunch."

She expected him to jibe at her effort at condescension. But instead he smiled for the first time with such a genuine sweetness and delight that she wondered why she hadn't ditched the whole damned hospital committee today and gone.

Just as he had said, on Monday Sheila Tate had looked out for Crispin Mannering on the 8.01. She had again looked out for him on this Tuesday, but there had still been no sign of him. No sign either of his white Alfa Romeo, modern equivalent of the prancing white horse of Kent.

Had he died? Killed himself? Gone abroad?

In fact, none of these things had happened. He had had a touch of migraine and his mother had felt that he should stay at home. At the same time on the Tuesday evening that Sheila Tate was getting into the 5.55 at Victoria, Mrs Mannering entered the lounge at Falklands and inquired of the figure sprawled on the sofa, "Well, Crispin . . . and how did things go this afternoon?"

There were no lights on in the room, only the fire that flickered over oak panelling that lined the walls from floor to ceiling. The impression given was of a wardroom of a ship, which indeed was the intention. For Falklands had been built by a sea captain, who had fought in the 1915 battle. It was the one action in which he had been involved, and he had commemorated it with this house, built of grey stone with a slate roof above a low third-floor glass-fronted projection that was constructed as a ship's bridge from which on a *very* clear day you could actually see the sea. The whole appearance was that of a warship stranded on sandbanks north of Ocklington.

Her son simply shrugged his shoulders and said nothing. An air of gloom hung over him, matching the afternoon.

Victoria Mannering reconnoitred the room for clues to answer her question. There appeared to be none. The only hint that a girl had been inside here was the faintest hint of Arpège sweetening the scent of the chrysanthemums.

"Jane comes from sea-faring stock, too."

"I can believe it."

"She's Admiral Villiers' daughter." She paused. "What did you think of her?"

"She's seaworthy, Mother."

"Crispin!"

"Shipshape and Bristol fashion . . ."

In looks, Victoria Mannering was not unlike a ship herself, but a sailing ship, square-rigged with a great pointed clipper bow of a chin. Bright unwinking eyes – one starboard green, one not exactly port pink but certainly reddish brown – kept watch through the sounding of all ships' bells. Energetic, never still, always talking, she was the captain of every company – the W.I., the Darby and Joan, the British Legion, Meals-on-Wheels, distressed gentlefolk in hospital, Guides, St John's Ambulance, the School Committee, the Parish Council, the Church Parochial Council – giving everyone their orders and untiringly driving them in the Rover up to the school to vote Conservative on polling days. Her husband had been one of the youngest

81

commanders in the Navy. Seeing three Japanese battleships while escorting a convoy to the Philippines, he had unhesitatingly turned to attack in his unaccompanied light cruiser. His widow would have done the same. As for his son, his only child – Victoria Mannering looked down at him with eyes brimming over.

He looked so vulnerable, so boyish – much younger than his years, lying there, his long legs stretched out before him, one foot over the other, his socks hanging slackly over the tops of his shoes, his long fair hair turbanning his head. The face now half-turned towards her was as long-chinned as her own, but thinner and sharper so that the effect was beaky rather than prow-shaped.

Even so, it was good-looking. There was no indication there of his succession of illnesses culminating in a bad attack of rheumatic fever which might (no two specialists could ever agree) have affected his heart, except a certain down-turned petulance about the mouth which to the detached observer might indicate a spoiled invalid.

But to his mother he was perfect. Her everything. Indeed, he had to be everything, because he was, apart from Falklands, all she had. The fact that she had to live on a Navy pension supplemented by only a small investment income, she kept a secret even from her son. No relations from her side of the family were ever produced. Who her forebears were and where they sprang from was not known. One day towards the end of the last war, the Commander had turned up at Ocklington Park with a pregnant wife. There had not been time then for his elder brother to make inquiries, and after his death, it seemed prudent not to. It also seemed prudent not to make too many inquiries into his sister-in-law's finances. She had never asked him for a penny. She appeared to manage remarkably well – that house, the white Alfa. He paid for his only nephew's education at Marlborough, and when he showed neither the ability nor the inclination to go on to the university had got him a job in Peterson Brothers, one of the many companies of which he was the *éminence grise*. After which, he considered his duty done.

To Crispin's mother, it was never done. She cherished him, cosseted him, protected him, equipped him for the high position in life which she was always telling him one day he would rightly assume. "Possessive" was the adjective most often used by the ladies of the church, but it was one she would hotly deny. Certainly she had initially kept girls at bay, because Crispin was such a late developer. But after the Betty Jones affair, and when his high prospects became more and more evident, and now that he was almost thirty, she could not have been more anxious to get him married – to a suitable girl, of course, who would be able to carry on the high tradition of the Mannering mistresses at Ocklington Park. To this end was the expense of the white Alfa, symbol of the dashing young man about town with great prospects, her lunch and dinner parties *à trois* for suitable prospects, with her discreetly disappearing after the meal – as she had done this afternoon leaving her son and Jane Villiers side by side on the sofa.

"How did she like you, Crispin?"

"Mother, how do I know?"

"What did you do?"

"Nothing."

Like fog, her son's mood came up to engulf her, but resolutely she fought it back. All her little efforts in the marriage matter seemed to end like this. Did the girls sense behind the carefully luxurious façade of the room the whiff of poverty, a hint of family connections well down from the top drawer, despite the Mannering prospects, see the ghost of Betty Jones? Surely it could have nothing to do with Crispin himself? There were people who said you lived as you drove. But surely as far as Crispin was concerned, he was too shy, backward rather than forward? Perhaps that was it, he was altogether too tongue-tied, they had not had enough to talk about. Though at the lunch table he had been very animated, and the girl had seemed quite amused.

"Why didn't you go for a spin?"

He winced at the 1930s word.

"She would have *loved* to have seen Ocklington Park."

"In *her* car?"

"Did you suggest meeting again?"

"I asked her to come to a theatre on Thursday."

"Good!"

83

"But she said," there was the slightest emphasis on the word, "she had a date."

"Did you suggest another day?"

He shook his head. "I didn't pursue the matter."

Not a pursuer, Crispin. Too readily took no for an answer. Didn't think enough of himself. Too submissive, not enough cheek, fight, spunk, electric spark.

Ah well! But it was to herself she sighed. Outwardly she remained the same bustling, organising, efficient gentlewoman bustling with life. As she walked over to the window, she was turning over the need for haste, for results. Ralph was very strait-laced. One more Betty Jones episode, and in spite of his blood lineage preoccupations, he might arrange matters so that there never *was* a Sir Crispin Mannering, Bart, of Ocklington Park.

She loved her son with a selfless passion. It was his happiness alone she lived for. To that end she would fight to the death, feared nothing and nobody. Her life was over anyway – it was his preservation that was paramount. And if she had to lose him to another woman, she was going to make quite sure that the girl deserved him.

She went over to the window and began to draw the curtains. Through the smudgy darkness of the valley came winking the bright lights of Ocklington Park.

"Beginning to clear up," she said cheerfully.

As she went out of the lounge to bring his medicine, mentally she had put a cross over Jane Villiers and buried her beside Lady Felicity Forsythe, the Honourable Anne Lowell and all the others. Now she began thinking of a piece of information that she had garnered at the Church bazaar. In a week's time the Plunketts were going to Madeira on a cruise that included a fortnight on the island – expensive of course but in the circumstances worth it, for the family were merchant bankers, and there was Marcelle Plunkett, *such* a pretty girl. She rode, of course, attended all the hunt meets. Mrs Mannering had never been keen on Crispin riding since the time in his teens when he had been bucked off and half killed.

But perhaps the time had come, now he was bigger and stronger, when there would no longer be any danger . . .

WHEN a stream of work is fed into the machine as it is at the Treasury, there is usually not time to do anything else but man the production line. Blake had been conscious that file R/372/54 containing the letter about the closing of the Ocklington line on which he had minuted to Aird two weeks ago had not yet come back to him – but there could be lots of reasons for that. Aird might have sent the file on to someone for his opinion, and that someone might have sent it on to someone else, and that someone else might . . .

In any case, Aird was absolutely snowed under with work, and this particular matter was after all only one small item amongst a complicated mass of others. Blake did not like to trouble his Assistant Secretary with reminders. Aird's priorities were his own.

But on that particular Friday, the telephone rang at 11.30 a.m.

"Blake."

"Williams." The name meant nothing till "Department of the Environment" was added.

"Oh, yes."

"I wrote to you a fortnight ago. About the Ocklington Line."

"I remember."

'When do you think it might be possible to receive a reply?'

"Well, it's all rather complicated."

Politely: "We do realise that."

"We're trying our best to help."

"Oh, good!"

"It's all a matter of whether we've got the money."

"This we understand."

"I put it up to my Assistant Secretary."

"I apologise for troubling you . . . but the engineering side of British Rail are becoming a trifle concerned. Obviously, we all want to keep the Line open if the money is available. And then there's this matter of Ocklington New Town which our planners are naturally becoming more doubtful about unless –"

"I understand. Look, I'll have a word with him."

"If you would be so kind."

"I'll go straightaway."

Aird's room was larger than his own, but furnished with the same austerity, a cross between a monk's cell and a schoolmaster's study. On the wall, a Victorian oil painting so cracked and dark it was difficult to see that it was the portrait of a woman. A modern water-colour over the empty fireplace, and a few personal pieces of Aird's – a chunk of coral now used as a paperweight, a cut-glass inkstand, a photograph of his wife flanked by two identically smiling daughters.

Sitting beside the desk was another Assistant Secretary in deep conversation and Blake was about to withdraw when Aird signalled him to stay. There was about the office an air of subdued concentration that Blake recognised as a sort of trance into which Civil Servants sank when they were really faced with a particularly difficult problem, and he tiptoed to the vacant chair lest he break the spell.

It was in fact surprising the power that these men held. In the Treasury directory, their names were laconically linked to British Waterways, Civil Aviation, Defence Expenditure, Mining, the Environment, heavy industries, overseas commitments – every sort of money-producing or money-spending activity was someone's responsibility, and in the course of a few minutes' persuasive argument between comparatively young men millions of pounds affecting the working lives of thousands of people could be lopped off or added on to some particular enterprise. The Treasury were the aristocrats of the Civil Service. They had first pick of the new recruits. Those Whitehall whizz-kids destined for high places were usually hatched in these cold corridors. The Treasury recognised the Foreign and Commonwealth Office as a relation, a sort of Australian cousin, and sat next to it at meetings, but considered all other Government Departments (with the exception of the Civil Service Department whose meteoric rise after the Fulton Report it had bitterly resented) as being born on the wrong side of the blanket. The Treasury was small. The Treasury was élite. The Treasury was clever. It was quite divorced from the actual *happenings* of life: the new factories, decayed mines, the building of motor-cars, the flying of aeroplanes, the going up and down of electric trains. That these things occurred, the Treasury recognised in terms of money. Money was its business, money was beauty, money was art, money was ethics, money was morals, money was religion, money was food and clothing and heat and shelter and defence, money was civilisation, money was power – and the Treasury held on to its power jealously. As a result, it was painfully overworked, but that too was a matter of pride and tradition. It was right and proper that MPs coming out of the Houses of Parliament just across the road after a late session should see through the darkness the office lights burning bright in Treasury Chambers. Certainly some power was delegated, but grudgingly, and every day all over Whitehall Civil Servants were writing to the Treasury, for authority to spend sometimes a few pounds, sometimes millions, as though to some rich and cranky aunt – servilely, almost guiltily – only to receive eventually the sharp rap and the initial negative that was again a Treasury tradition. The Treasury was many things – not least an exclusive club in which Christian names were the order of the day, regardless of rank, and in which to raise your voice or show emotion or talk out of turn or contradict was shocking bad form. If your work wasn't up to it or your face didn't fit you were quietly decanted to less exalted crannies amongst the rocks and crags of White-hall. It was hard to get into the Treasury, but easy to get out. The very words "I am going to the Treasury" conjured up a vision of gold coffers, crown jewels, and the Holy Grail. Decisions on weighty matters from such a place must surely be inspired out of the ground like oracles by hordes of wise old men with long grey beards. It was inconceivable that they could emanate from a man like Aird, in his early forties, with bright eyes, a white face and rather long red hair, whose lunch invariably consisted of a cheese sandwich at his desk since he never had the time to leave his office.

The Assistant Secretaries were, in fact, talking about the railways, but in the wider context of the huge and invading deficit in the balance of payments, the economic crisis and inflation.

"British Rail deficits," Aird was saying, "are likely to increase

87

to £220 million this year even if pay increases are held down to a reasonable level, unless drastic economies are made immediately. As you know, it was a Cabinet decision that all industries must stand on their own feet. The 1968 Railways Act gave a once-and-for-all capital hand-out on which thereafter British Rail said they could manage. If we go on giving money away to the mines, to the railways, to the power stations, to newspapers, to motor-cycle firms, where are we going to end up?"

In the silence while the other Assistant Secretary looked into the icy crystal ball, Aird turned to Blake. "Yes, Edward?"

"Sorry to trouble you, but it's about that file I put up to you, R/372/54 . . ."

Aird indicated a mass of files spilling out of his security cupboard and over his desk. "It'll be in my compost-heap somewhere."

"There's a letter asking for further finance to stop a railway closure."

"I'll take a look at it."

Blake said apologetically, "The D of E are pressing . . ."

"Then I'll take a look at it *now*."

Aird rifled through his files, found R/372/54 and opened it at the D of E letter. Aird read it rapidly and expertly, crinkled up his fastidious nose at the poor English and inadequate arguments, passed it over to the other Assistant Secretary, saying, "Where do they think the money's coming from?"

"British Rail's share of passenger and freight traffic has fallen fifty per cent in twenty years and is still falling," the other Assistant Secretary said. "The White Paper calls for 6,700 miles of track, half of what we have now. And by Act of Parliament, British Rail must only do what is profitable. There is a growing lobby that railways haven't basically altered for a hundred and and twenty years, are outdated and should be scrapped. And if you ask me, they're right."

"What do you think, Edward?"

It would not have occurred to Aird that Blake might have private and personal reasons for keeping the Ocklington Line open. More than any profession, most Civil Servants kept their private lives apart. Few knew where their colleagues lived, let alone visited them at home. Up they turned in the morning, and away they went at night. That they went *somewhere* was appreciated, but where was immaterial. There was little social mixing. Even at lunchtime, people usually ate alone. Of an introverted character, Civil Servants kept themselves to themselves, being almost fearful of having their privacy invaded. As a rule, nobody knew and nobody had the time to know their colleagues' joys, interests, ideas, difficulties or problems. It would have been bad form to bring up one's own affairs or gossip about those of others. That there were hearts ticking away in the tombs of the Whitehall catacombs was appreciated as a physiological fact. Provided the right quantity of space and oxygen (dependent on rank) was allocated according to Civil Service rules, there was no reason why these hearts should not go on pumping blood through the body and into the brain sufficient for the carrying out of the government's business efficiently without further attention until retiring age.

"It's a difficult one," Blake said. "There are so many other factors involved."

"Yes." Aird considered the other side gloomily. "Juggernaut lorries on the roads. Then there's that pro-rail pressure group . . . Transport 2000, isn't it called? Not to mention the super-trains scheduled for the Channel Tunnel, if it materialises."

"If you're not careful," said the other Assistant Secretary, "it will go to Ministers."

Going to Ministers for a decision was the last thing Civil Servants liked. It implied they could not cope with an issue that then became a political football match played before an excited and emotional audience, while the government quietly worked out the equation of cost against numbers of votes lost.

"If the line is closed," the other Assistant Secretary said, "there's bound to be an outcry. Parliamentary Questions, I shouldn't wonder."

"And if the line is kept open," Aird said, going back to his original unanswered question, "where do they think the money's coming from?"

It remained unanswered. Nobody said anything. Aird sighed, took up the file and tossed it on top of his In-tray. "Leave it with me, Edward. I'd like to have another think about it."

Returning to his own room Blake worked through the lunch

hour. Round four o'clock, he had a cup of tea. At ten past five, file R/372/54 came back from Aird. On it, the Assistant Secretary had written: *Mr Blake. I agree with you that this is a difficult one. Clearly there are numerous factors involved. I find myself a trifle pressed, so would you kindly pursue, keeping me informed?*

It looked as though the Victoria-Ocklington Line would continue to totter along, as it and the British people had done for years.

Holding his pen just above the letter, Blake momentarily turned his eyes away and looked through the turret slit of his window out into the court, the one once proposed as a swimming-pool, now a car park. The evening sun rimmed with light the top ramparts of Edwardian stone, but down below the whole circle was filled with violet shadow. And there, mirrored and magnified as though in dark water, the face of the brown-haired girl, insubstantial as the last time he had seen it that morning fragile and shimmering, reflected in the last carriage window of the electric train just before the ticket barrier.

Then he brought his eyes back to his desk, and began to compose a letter to the Department of Education and Science, asking for their views on the transportation problems of children to and from school in that area of Kent if the Ocklington Line was closed.

"Mr Cunliffe . . . ?"

"Yes, Miss Leigh?"

"Could I come in for a moment, Mr Cunliffe?"

"Miss Leigh . . . I *am* rather busy."

"But it's important, Mr Cunliffe."

"Miss Leigh –"

He had very nearly sworn at her – something he had never done. He had had a trying business lunch. Alice was difficult. Franklin was impossible. He had said ungraciously well, all right, and had given his secretary a jaundiced look when she came in, which she had returned with a bright smile.

Then she had laid an envelope on the desk in front of him. "Mr Cunliffe . . . the Peterson Brothers' contract!"

"Deborah, this is excellent!"

He had not been expecting it yet. Deftly he went through it for snags. But there were none. Everything was in order – signed, sealed and delivered. Even the price was right.

It was in moments of extremes – triumph or despair – that he would especially expand with her. He would let off steam, that's how to himself he described it. When H.F.'s rumbles really disturbed him, when Alice's high note really grated on his nerves, he found relief simply in her presence, prettily sitting there, softly saying sympathetic syllables. When he was victorious, he would re-live the campaign (in which after all she had actively shared) with her.

"I wasn't sure I'd be able to bring it off, Debbie."

"I was never in any doubt, Mr Cunliffe."

"There's some very clever characters about."

"But you're more than a match for them."

"You've got to keep your eyes open. They dig elephant traps, that's what they do, and cover them over with green leaves. Then along comes little Johnny-Head-in-Air and –." He let his open hand expressively and noisily fall on to the top of his desk.

"You always keep your eyes open, Mr Cunliffe."

"It's a jungle, that's what the world is. And in the jungle . . . tread softly and carry a big stick."

"What *you* do, Mr Cunliffe."

"Keep your mouth shut. Listen but say nothing. Always one jump ahead of your man."

"That's right, Mr Cunliffe."

"And when you spread your bread upon the waters, that is when you do something for anyone, don't let them forget it. See that your harvest is seventy times seven."

It was times like that when Cunliffe would relapse into the Biblical language of the Chapel which he attended as a child, as though giving thanks to God. "But when blessings are given, we must rejoice!"

"Yes, Mr Cunliffe."

"Debbie, we shall kill the fatted calf!"

"The fatted calf, Mr Cunliffe?"

"In other words, we shall celebrate!"

"At Frascati's, Mr Cunliffe?"

Frascati's was where he took all his most important clients.

It was in Germain Street, at the top of the cul-de-sac. The outside was unobtrusive, a flat façade carved like a Grecian temple with wooden grapes, painted green and peeling, and a large frosted-glass window, sooty and starred.

But the inside was sumptuous.

A thick red carpet led up the stairs from the little bar at the bottom. On the walls, oil paintings of sylvan scenes, and in the main dining-room discreet little tables in alcoves lit by naked beeswax candles. The wallpaper furry and velvet and dark scarlet and looking as though it was two hundred years old, but unmarked by age, eternal, everlasting. The atmosphere was redolent of thousands of sumptuous meals, rich roast beefs, turkeys, lobsters thermidor, spare ribs of pork and sauerkraut, oysters, trifles and gâteaux in a sauce of Moulin Bernadotte, crusted port, burgundy, claret and brandy so that the air itself was enough, a meal in itself: to breathe deeply was to feel satisfied. Frascati's was Cunliffe's temple, perhaps because it symbolised the opposite of himself and was a sepulchre of secrets. Where did *his* red carpet lead to? A poor man, no education, no background, no medals, nothing after his name. Perhaps it was an unconscious feeling in him that with sufficient immersion in Frascati's such diseases could be cured, the warts would disappear, the scabs fade away, and grandeur and prestige and breeding would somehow rub off on him – and he would be reborn.

"Frascati's?" Cunliffe turned the word over on his tongue. It was expensive – in this world, you get what the firm pays for. But in fact a meal with Miss Leigh would be a fitting end to the whole thing, a business expense of a deal which had started at Frascati's where, three months ago, he had entertained Sir Ralph Mannering, the *éminence grise* behind Peterson Brothers, to lunch on one of his rare trips to London. After all she'd been through with him, she deserved to be fed the Queen's Jelly. "Frascati's, yes, of course!"

"That would be lovely, Mr Cunliffe! What date shall I book?"

WHY DO I bother? Why do I wait? Why don't I just get up, make my excuses and leave?

Lady Marjorie Mannering looked down this time at the polished oval pool of the mahogany table in which were reflected the committee members of the Trust for Research and Development.

A fairly typical bunch of narcissi heads clustered round that pool. The grey one of the knighted Chairman, an industrialist hoping to be called a Lord before he was called to his humble Maker. The black narrow aristocratic head of public-school headmaster Dr Basil Temple, a couple of hereditary peers, the expensive hair-dos of half a dozen well-to-do women with not enough to do, then the straight no-nonsense bob of Lady Symons, widow of a Vice-Chancellor of Nantwich University, and the flyaway pepper-and-salt frizz of ex-headmistress Dame Dorothy Braine, casting adoring glances at the Chairman, and coming full circle, directly opposite, a bored prim-lipped Civil Servant keeping absolutely silent.

No one was listening to anything that was said, though the Civil Servant was taking it all down. Everyone was simply wanting to unload their own observations, and to receive from the Chairman a metaphorical pat on the back.

"That is a very important point, Dame Dorothy."

"I rather think so too, Sir Robert." She wriggled with delight as if she were back in the first form at her old school.

They were discussing secondary education in Ranjibad and the vital need to investigate it. The whole idea was the inspiration of Professor Poll of Nantwich University and three of his postgraduate students and Lady Symons was pushing it for all she was worth.

Another crackpot scheme, Lady Marjorie told herself, another handout of public and private money. About as valuable as loincloths to Sumatrans. This generation, these days, the educationists were taking over where the missionaries of yesteryear left off, dispatching to the aboriginals *Under the Greenwood Tree* instead of Bibles. She transferred her eyes to the fine brass clock elegantly moving the time along for them.

Past noon. Soon the Chairman would dip his grandfatherly fingers into his waistcoat pocket and produce his own heavy gold watch, which would stop short never to go again if it had any sense, long before the old man died. And with a benign expression of surprise, he would exclaim on the lateness of the hour, and how all these valuable meetings went so fast. He would suggest a little sherry wine before they went on their ways rejoicing. Even the Civil Servant would open those lips, the same colour as his confidential file, and imbibe. And then at last Lady Marjorie would fly away, free as air.

Frascati's, Bill Cody had said. She never knew when he was joking. He'd laughed at the doubtful expression on her face. Christ Almighty, not *that* Frascati's! Nothing like it. His was right t'other end of town. He'd spread those big hands. He was a working man. True. What was wrong with *that*? He was proud of it. Besides she'd like this place much better. No nonsense. And they knew how to cook. Been on the go elephant's years before that clip-joint set up.

"The whole idea then it seems," Dr Temple's head inclined kindly to Lady Symons, "and a very valuable one if I may say so, is to spark off further interest?"

Isn't that the idea of most things, Lady Marjorie thought? To spark off further interest. Ah, yes. She doodled on her blotting pad, and felt blissfully young and schoolgirlish and defiant under the Civil Servant's disapproving stare.

What would you say, she looked up and asked them one by one but silently, if you knew I had what Nanny used to call an assignation? Shake bored shoulders, no doubt. Everyone did it to some extent these days. Ah, but if you knew it was with Bill Cody, Working Man Extraordinary? That would be different.

"Gradually build up a connection," Lady Symons nodded sagely.

"From small seeds mighty oaks are made? Ah, yes!"

94

"And what do *you* think, Lady Marjorie?"

That all over the country there would be cosy gatherings like this. That was what she was thinking. Where people were trying to manipulate others. And all under the different cloaks of Charity or Efficiency, or Art or Economy or Usefulness. Now the whole of this wintry but tremulously fair morning was being spent on arranging a vacation swan for Professor Poll and his minions.

"Is this the sort of nebulous project one should spend our money on?" she asked, not wanting to demur, but unable tamely to let it go.

The Chairman smiled with restraint. "An important point and one which can easily be cleared up by referring to our Memorandum and Articles of Association." He turned to the Civil Servant.

Oh, why did she ask? Why didn't she let them get on with it? Now she had to wait, admiring the silver lacquer on her nails while the Civil Servant opened his file, read very quickly through a list of objectives, finally slowing down to pronounce with emphasis, "Experimental educational schemes, particularly in the East."

"So there you have it," the Chairman smiled. "We are *quite* justified."

"The money's there," Lady Symons pointed out.

"Yet why is it," Lady Marjorie demanded rebelliously, suddenly pierced by thoughts of British Rail and the news of the Ocklington Line, "that the money's never there for something that's *really* wanted?"

"But this *is* really wanted."

"By whom?"

"The Ranjibadians."

"I doubt if they know anything about it."

"Professor Poll will soon put them in the picture. He will work wonders."

Why should she argue? Did it matter anyway? In ten minutes' time she would be in her taxi and away. At most committee meetings, justice wasn't so much seen to be done, as injustice slipped under the table.

"Are we all agreed then? Or shall we put it to the vote?"

Not even another minute would she spend on a vote. Lady Marjorie smiled graciously, giving in.

All the narcissi nodded their heads.

The Chairman took out his watch, and exclaimed on the lateness of the hour. "Shall we partake of a little sherry wine before going on our separate ways rejoicing?"

"Would you excuse me, Sir Robert? I have to meet one of my husband's constituents."

Oh Lord, how sweet was the lying truth! Lady Marjorie, tireless in the service of others, from one charitably spent morning to a charitably donated lunch. She clicked on her elegant high-heeled shoes out of the room to the murmur of their approval.

Down the circular marble staircase and out into the wintry sunshine. It was half past twelve. She was late. She felt as excited and tremulous as Cinderella.

The commissionaire summoned her a taxi, opened the door and saluted her in.

"Baldwin Street," she said breathlessly to the driver. "Just off Shaftesbury Avenue."

She sat back and brought out her compact, tweaked her beautifully set hair more prettily round the same mink hat. Her lucky hat, she now thought of it. Her own smooth pink face looked back at her. Over the last week or so it had acquired a curious subdued radiance. It reminded her of a rejuvenating treatment she had read about, where they injected wax under ageing skin. Or how her face had first responded to the fertility drugs Dr Carleton had recommended. Whatever it was, she looked satisfactorily pretty. Her eyes clear, and picking up the subtle blue of her new Hartnell dress.

"Whereabouts in Baldwin Street, miss?"

Miss. It was all she needed.

"A little restaurant called Frascati's," she replied. "It's all right. I think it's just here. I can see my friend waiting outside."

"I thought I was to be stood up," he said, when she'd paid off the taxi.

"Why? Am I as late as that?"

"Late enough."

96

He put a hand on each of her arms and held her lightly away from him. "You look super. Really beautiful."

"And this looks a nice place," she replied, quite overcome not so much by the compliment as the tone in which he said it.

In fact, Frascati's was nothing more remarkable than a double-fronted shop, whose interior was withheld from view by pink and orange slatted blinds. There was a faded pink and orange awning over the doorway furled for the British winter and Frascati's in the same colour scheme on a hanging sign.

"Well, it'll be a new experience, if nothing more." He still held her arm. "We'll go straight in before it fills up. It's not the sort of place where you order a table, Lady M."

He opened the door and propelled her in. A fat woman behind the cash desk beamed at Cody and nodded. There were three rows of white-clothed tables, mostly filled. But an empty one by the corner formed by the hat rack almost at the far end.

"This do?" He held out a chair for her.

"Fine. Couldn't be nicer."

"Don't overdo it," he grinned at her. "Maybe you'd better take that hat off, too. Otherwise they'll charge me extra."

He caught her hand, imprisoning it as it was half upraised to do his bidding.

"I'm teasing, silly!"

She sighed. "I never know." She unbuttoned her matching coat and hung it over the back of her chair. "I never know when you're joking and when you're serious."

"There's only one thing now that I am serious about." He took the menu from the waitress.

"And what is that?"

He looked at her thoughtfully for a moment, his eyes dark and serious. Then he smiled. "Food!" He transferred his gaze to the little waitress. They had a brief laughing exchange on what Momma and she recommended, finally settling on lamb in bay leaves with a side plate of green salad for Lady Marjorie.

"Slimming?" he asked her mockingly.

"Sort of."

"Bloody silly."

"Why?"

97

"Just is. Anyway, you'll have to eat it all up today. Pudding and all."

"Why?"

"Because it's *all in*. I pay regardless. Think of that."

She smiled. "And you've already thrown enough good money away on me."

"Exactly!"

She laughed. I am beginning to know when you tease and when you don't, she thought with pleasure. She felt immeasurably warmed and comforted. As if in some odd way that knowledge armed her against any further loneliness.

The food when it came was hot and delicious. "I wouldn't want to leave it anyway." She forked it into her mouth.

"You eat very delicately, Lady M," he said, watching her.

"I am a very delicate person," she smiled.

"No, you're not. You're lusty and gutsy and brave. You're timid. You're malicious and gentle. You're my kind of person."

She said nothing. She looked down at her food, her face flushing. We are going too fast, she thought, much too fast. It's as though we're on a train, and it's accelerating. The brakes are off. And there's nothing now we can do about it.

"You don't really know anything about me. And *I* don't know anything about you."

"We don't know the *details*, no." His mouth set, as if disappointed in her.

"I don't even know what you do for a living," she said, sounding condescending and frightful.

"Lady Barnett, let the next challenger sign in for What's My Line!"

"You know what I mean."

"I do." He nodded gravely. "You wish to know what I do for a living. I'm a labourer."

"Good," she exclaimed, meaning "God!"

Not that she despised him for his work. Not that it made any difference. Just that it made everything more difficult. Less likely of any resolution. An affair (for already she recognised it would be) of unending furtiveness.

"Where do you do this labouring?"

"Victoria Tunnel. Digging out the extension."

98

"It must be very hard work." She spoke in her Lady Marjorie prize-presenting voice again. He raised his wicked black brows scornfully.

"I don't exactly wield the shovel. Though I have done it in my time, I can tell you. I'm on the boring machine. The mole."

"Isn't this your job then? What you've always done?"

He shook his head. "No. I don't believe in that crap. *Your* job, your line, what are you, anyway. I'm me. I've knocked around. Been in the Navy. Farmed. Done skin-diving. Worked on an oil rig."

He glared at her with a kind of haughty exasperation. "Now you're Mr Mole," she said, gently touching his hand with her finger tips, "and you live in a Hole."

He laughed, catching on to her fingers, his anger dissolving. "I am the tenant of Applegarth Cottage I would remind you."

"Is that why you live there? A breath of country air?"

"That's why I *went* to live there, yes. Why I *continue* to stay is a different matter." His smile faded. His eyes darkened into a disconcerting gravity.

"Shall you always stay there?" she asked, baffled by the expression in his eyes.

"I'm a rolling stone," he said, cupping her hand in his. "So that rather depends."

"On whom?" she asked shyly, suddenly wanting him to say herself.

"On me, of course. Who else?"

The fact that the 5.55 had no First Class carriages was the only bit of luck Kevin Clarkeson had had for days. He saw the handsome woman, in the fur hat, the same one who had sat next to him the day he'd nearly got out of the train in the tunnel, go into an ordinary compartment and he nipped in quick as knife after her and slid himself into the next seat.

She glanced at him abstractedly but without recognition, seeing only a small dapper young man with brassy blond hair. She sat with her gloved hands holding her soft leather bag, like a woman in a dream. In a way, she was just that to him. A figure in one of his many dreams. The only difference between her and the other inhabitants of his dream world was that she actually existed.

For, especially in the last few years, Kevin Clarkeson hardly bothered at all with people who really lived. His dreams encroached more and more on reality. Except for himself, he was hardly aware that anyone else was alive. He knew the dreadful bunch in the warehouse office where he worked in North London were alive, because they tormented him (teased, they called it). He knew his landlady was alive. Her whining and her slatternliness obtruded on his own obsessive neatness and cleanliness. She grumbled that he changed his shirt, his pants, his socks every day, and spent what money he had on experimenting with his hair and eyebrows. She could not understand, as indeed the middle-aged men and women in the warehouse office couldn't understand, why he needed to.

He always had this odd conviction that if only he could jump as it were *through* himself, discover some secret recipe, he would find a newer, better life. He couldn't remember any part of his life other than his dreams that he'd really enjoyed. His childhood he had somehow forgotten, and at twenty-five he already felt as old as the hills. His mother had been unmarried. He could remember vague reluctant stays with even more reluctant grandparents, very young uncles, and horrifying child-minders. When he was fifteen, he got a job living in as a hotel bellhop. And on his first day off, he found his mother had disappeared.

He never saw her again. Some days he had the urge to look for her. He reminded himself that he would be as difficult to trace as she would be. In one of his favourite dreams, he had her looking for him. A kinder, warmer, more frankly prosperous woman than he remembered, someone vaguely like the handsome woman now beside him, holding out her loving arms to him. But even he knew it was an unlikely dream. How would this long-lost mother ever get on to him? He'd changed his name, his work, his habitat almost as often as he'd changed the colour of his eyebrows. So these days, the arms were becoming much more synonymous with the arms of death.

In the last three years, not counting his effort in the tunnel three weeks ago, he had made eight suicide attempts, six of them resulting in a hospital stay. Whether they were wholly serious or not no one, least of all himself, seemed certain. He usually left a note, or made a phone call or even made the attempt in public. And really it was the look of horror on people's faces or the shock in their voices that gave him the biggest kick of all.

His last attempt had been at the Regent's Park Zoo. It was within walking distance of his awful office. He used to like to watch the quite pretty little monkeys burrow deep deep deep inside the stinky furry bodies of their ugly mothers. And just two weeks ago, while a party of children gaped with him and giggled (for they were rude disgusting creatures as well as pretty when they were young) he had tapped the teacher on the shoulder and shown her his empty Valium bottle. The result had been very exciting. But as usual his stay in hospital was far too brief. They hadn't really cared. The psychiatrist had been as black as the ace of spades and had been no more intelligible than the father monkey whom he had most strikingly resembled.

Kevin Clarkeson had been disgusted. The last few days he'd been miserable, without even a decent dream to indulge in except the vague look-out for the fur-hatted dame. Now he had her. He could smell her sweet expensive perfume. He could even, he swore to himself, feel some soft friendly emanation from her body.

Surreptitiously his curious froggy eyes travelled over her, drinking in every detail – her expensive high-heeled shoes, her well-turned ankles, strong calves, the lovely dizzy blue colour of her dress and coat. For some reason, as he devoured her sideways, she took off the fur hat, ran her fingers through her hair, and then tucked the hat down carelessly on the seat beside her between him and her.

Then just before the whistle blew, as always, a whole crowd of last-minute commuters rushed in. Kevin Clarkeson had a very lovely experience. He had to move up to let an old man squeeze in next to him. That way he was close enough to feel as if he burrowed deep, deep inside the soft, soft wool and fur of the motherly woman next to him.

We all need someone to kiss away our tears.
Stonily Sheila Tate read the message printed on the T-shirt

of the buxom teenage girl sitting opposite her on the 5.55 that took her home again that Tuesday. She was already coming to the conclusion that the someone to kiss *her* tears away might not be Crispin Mannering after all.

Beside her, Miss Price jolted up and down as the electric train sped southwards. She had left her left palm open and was staring into it like a mirror with intense myopic concentration.

Devotee of all such arts, Sheila knew what she was doing. She put her own finger into the middle of those myriad lines that criss-crossed over the worn white skin and ran her finger along a groove across the hand.

"You've got ever such a good Line of Head, Miss Price." She opened her own hand. "*Much* better than mine."

Miss Price studied the pink-and-white flesh offered for her inspection without enthusiasm.

"And *look* at your Line of Fortune! Miss Price, you're going to be rich!"

Miss Price appeared similarly unmoved by the prospect.

"But what's happened to your Line of Life, Miss Price? It stops ever so suddenly."

Miss Price seemed neither surprised nor alarmed. All her attention was focused on a faint indistinct wrinkle descending transversely from her middle finger. She cupped her hand, as though trying to bring it into focus.

"My Line of the Heart isn't much."

"Oh I wouldn't say that, Miss Price."

"Yours is longer, Sheila." She said it wistfully, and then suddenly she closed her hand firmly and said, "It's a lot of nonsense anyway! Doesn't mean any more than that rail map!" She jerked her head to the intricate cobweb of the South Eastern region of British Rail on the advertisement hoarding opposite. "Might just as well read our fortunes from that!"

Perhaps she might – perhaps they all might. That something would happen all those eight were aware because things *did* happen in the course of the days passing. But what and how and whom and why they none of them thought about.

Edward Blake had now seen the brown-haired woman often, had made a catalogue of what clothes she wore, the expressions on her face, the few words they exchanged as a boy might collect stamps. In the middle of family birthdays, his wedding anniversary, planning for the annual holiday, he would think about her. Perhaps simply thinking about her would end. He could not see how it would be otherwise.

Lady Marjorie did not really believe that anything further would develop in her relationship with Bill Cody. Indeed she was faintly surprised at herself that they had come this far.

Gordon Cunliffe was totally preoccupied with the Ocklington land contract, obtaining praise while it lasted, making his discreet and hidden preparations in the event of a backlash. That his secretary appeared to be just as totally preoccupied with Frascati's escaped his notice. As he had so frequently demonstrated to Alice, he had the greatest power of single-minded concentration.

Kevin Clarkeson at least had his fate and fortune in his pocket. He would often hold it in his hand, fingering it lovingly – his bottle of Valium. When next and where?

To and fro, northbound and southbound into the Blackwater Tunnel and out again, carrying them all went the electric train. A dark rushing shape in rain, a long sparkler on a frosty night, a bright blue lozenge in sunshine. Chattering comfortably over the joins in the rails past the stubble fields and the tinted trees, howling in cuttings, playing a deafening organ crescendo in tunnels, murmuring into country stations, crackling with electric life – unpredictable, mysterious, changeable as its passengers, sweet and quiet, beautiful and ugly, menacing and angry. Always different and yet always the same.

Line of life, symbol of life – kicking and breathing and hooting *tee-who tee-who tee-who* – alive, *alive*, ALIVE.

ON the news-sellers' hoardings all down Whitehall – POWER
CRISIS AFFECTS TRAINS.

Edward Blake took the warning and left the Treasury at 5.15.
Even so, he was too late. By the time he reached Victoria, the
station was quite dark. A strange stillness hung over everything.
Hundreds of people jammed tight, but not speaking. Just the
soft sounds of breathing, the shuffle of shoes.

As usual, in such cases, all officials had gone to ground. Only
suddenly that same woman on the Tannoy announcing, "We
apologise for the inconvenience caused. All electric trains in the
south-eastern area have been cancelled. Passengers are advised
to seek alternative means of transport home."

Muttering started. Cody called, "Three cheers for British
Rail!" To Blake's right, a match flared to the tip of a cigarette,
flickered over Cunliffe's face. Staccato sentences like small arms
fire came out with the puffs of smoke. "Criminal inefficiency . . .
rot at the top . . . last straw . . ."

A whiff of Diorissima above the smell of onions, dust, oil,
damp raincoats, sweat. An elegant voice saying, "What are we
going to do?"

Lady Marjorie Mannering appealing for help.

"Pray," said Cody.

"Give them a chance," said Mr Osborne, producing a torch
from his large briefcase. The light illuminated a small crack in
the midst of the pushing swaying blackness – they were the
regulars from under the second Victorian lamp standard. The
woman from Fordbridge was there, too, over on the fringe.

"Real Boy Scout you are, Mr Osborne."

"Be Prepared, Miss Price . . . that's my motto."

"Got a rope in there too, then?" Cody asked.

"That's right, boy!" shouted a disembodied voice, "Hang
'em!"

"Tonight can hardly be blamed on British Rail." Blake murmured with the fairness of the Civil Servant who saw both sides of the situation, and was immediately ashamed that the brown-haired woman should hear him say such a pompous little sentence, till Cody put the record straight with "Bugger British Rail!"

"The Station Manager," Cunliffe said briskly. "That's the chap to go for! It's his duty to get us home. And by God, he's going to do it!"

There was a murmur of assent, admiring whispers of "Chairman of the Passengers' Committee." Led by Cunliffe and in the light of Osborne's torch, the little group began to struggle through the crowd.

"This way!"

Blake found himself pushed forward from behind. Out of the corner of his left eye, he could see her right at the back. But of the same company. Alarmingly, his heartbeat quickened. He was possessed by a feeling of inevitability, of being carried on by a force not of the crowd. More powerful, more inexorable. Now we are about to meet again, he thought. Something is about to begin in this vast catacomb, fighting through swarming humanity. The two of us, stranded, waiting to be rescued. Perhaps from many things.

"Only way to get on in this world," Cunliffe fumed into the night. "Thump the bloody table!"

"Exactly," said Blake, hoping that the crispness of his voice would carry to the back, anxious to erase that goody-goody impression.

"Where's the bastard's office?" asked Cody, almost breaking into an angry trot. The pace of their collective footfall quickened. Commuters in lynching mood, Blake thought, conscious now in himself of a high expectancy.

"Up these stairs." A breath of warmer, even staler air. "At the far end of the corridor. I've had dealings with this character before . . ."

Behind, among the tramp of shoes, the click of precisely placed high heels. Hers? Or Lady Marjorie's? Heavy breathing amongst some of the older ones. Now down a murky corridor to a glass door flickered by candlelights.

The Chairman of the Passengers' Committee turned. "You wait outside. Best if I do this on my own."

"Shout out if you need any help," Blake said, smiling tentatively at the woman. She didn't smile back. Candlelight sculpted her face. He wondered if other people would call her beautiful.

"Just say the word and we'll throw the bastard out of the window," said Cody. "Justifiable homicide."

The glass door flung a small shower of reflected candlelight over them and slammed shut. Almost immediately from behind came the sound of raised voices. Everyone outside listened. Breaths held, eyes lowered, disclaimingly, pressed close together. "Disgraceful service at the best of times . . . lamentable lack of efficiency . . . I am the Chairman . . . I will not be spoken to . . . Member of Parliament . . . The Minister, Public Opinion . . ." Then the sound of telephone calls.

Once when Blake looked up, he saw her eyes on him. She smiled faintly.

Five minutes later Cunliffe emerged, smiling. The Station Manager's head on an invisible charger. "He's diverting the Hastings diesel all round by Warborough to Ocklington and beyond."

There was a sigh of relief.

"You really have saved the situation," Lady Marjorie declared, rising to the occasion.

Cunliffe gave an obsequious little nod. "Thank you, Lady Marjorie."

Back down the corridor again. Cautious haste down the stairs. Blake neither hurried nor dawdled. The stream carried them side by side across the crowded station, through the barrier down the platform, past the throbbing and juddering of the waiting dark train. It was already full. Their group began wrenching open the doors, fearful of the last chance to get home being snatched away by the whistle.

Blake opened a carriage door, turned to let her get in. But she had already melted into the darkness. He held everyone back for a moment. Then, pushed and pummelled from behind, he got in, fought his way over protesting feet, through into the crowded corridor at the other side.

A match flared. In its brief illumination, he saw that she was just a few feet down the corridor from him. He shoved and shouldered till he stood beside her.

It might be still dark in the tunnel again.

In fact, they didn't go through the Blackwater Tunnel at all on that ride home. None of them cared really which way they went so long as they were moving. They had all squeezed in, their little rebel band, like multi-coloured toothpaste through the carriage doors into this same corridor.

Cunliffe, their triumphant captain, as was proper, brought up the rear, closed the door and called out peremptorily to the faceless ones, the dark unknown shapes milling and swaying outside, "No more room."

"We're all right," Blake said to the brown-haired woman. "We're lucky."

"Very."

"Don't worry about the dark."

"I'm not doing." He heard her voice smile. "But it was nice of you to remember."

"We're bound to have lights soon."

Almost immediately, the whistle sounded. The train moved forward and the lights came on.

"You're a prophet," she said, smiling up at him. Her eyes looked magnified and bright in the sudden glare.

The train began moving out of Victoria. The lights thrown from the compartments reflected on a sea of faces.

"Awful to be stranded," she said. "Families worrying at home."

He made a sympathetic sound with his voice. Actually the sight of people waiting when he was safely on the move gave him a regrettable sense of triumph. But he felt that it would not do to say so to the woman beside him. He felt he wanted to show himself in his best and most noble light. Almost as if he were trying to sell himself. I am not the middle-aged civil servant that you see. Underneath this shabby mackintosh, behind these unemotional eyes, beneath this no-colour hair is this unique me. Blake was reminded of a turbanned Indian hawker who had come to his mother's house when he was five. Out of a shabby Gladstone bag he had produced bangles and necklaces, lace and sari silk, at the same time working himself up to a hopeful sad ecstasy.

"Dylan always worries if I'm late."

Dylan would, Blake thought, ashamed that he should take such an inordinate dislike to a name.

"Would you have been stranded?" asked Blake.

"If they hadn't put us on to this, oh, yes absolutely. There's no bus from London goes our way. I suppose you're the same?"

They commiserated on the lack of transport. The weight of bodies on either side of them pressed them to each other. The train was slipping now over the dark Thames, gathering speed into the night.

Whither? He saw her eyes rest on the glimmering surface of the ebb tide as if asking herself the same question.

"Perhaps he'd have driven up to get you?" Blake asked when he'd given up the mental search for a more memorable remark.

"Dylan? Oh, no. He hates London."

"Don't blame him." He sighed, blaming Dylan, despising him.

"Besides, it's a long drive from Fordbridge."

"How do you like living there?"

"Quite well." He watched her unfocused eyes moving with the darkened landscape whipping past outside. "Every place has its drawbacks." She wasn't talking to him. She had forgotten him.

The train gathered its rocketing speed, swayed dangerously from side to side. He was pressed against her, pulled away. The bogies thumped under the soles of his feet. Far ahead at the front, the engine hooted angrily.

"I don't like diesels," he exclaimed.

"Nor do I."

"Give me an electric train any day."

"Yes, *electric*. I like the word too. Electric. You can almost see the sparks in it."

"And the clicks on the rails." He smiled. "How do you see diesel?"

"A slurp of oil?" The hazel eyes danced.

"The sizzle of a hot engine."

"Horrid!" she said. They both laughed. He beamed down on her. He felt quite inordinately pleased that she saw words in pictures as he did. At a single discovery she became a friend. A fellow enthusiast. Familiar. The known unknown.

"Horrid," she repeated, like a connoisseur. "It looks like its meaning, doesn't it?"

"So it does."

"Words do, somehow."

"How about joy? Joyfully? There's a word for you! Fairly kicks up its heels."

She narrowed those clear eyes. "Too enthusiastic. Too angular. Runs away with you."

Like the train, he thought, running away with this journey. Or a horse. Or many things.

"Galloping?" he asked her.

"Not as good as trot."

"Neat little horse. Neat little girl."

My daughter, he thought. He was pierced by an undeserved guilt. He saw the woman read the shadow that crossed his face. If they had been sitting side by side, she would undoubtedly have pulled out her paperback. As it was, she was stuck with him.

"Binstead," he announced suddenly, peering out. "They're routing us half-way round Kent."

She shrugged but said nothing. Through darkened stations they rocketed, through unfamiliar towns. A little oil lamp under a sign, Aston. Then a tunnel – not nearly as long as Blackwater – fast through and the wheels ringing and clashing like cymbals. He felt her eyes on his face studying him carefully. Over on his right, he could hear Cody chatting up Lady Marjorie, Cunliffe recounting what he said to the Station Manager. The man didn't appear to have got a look in.

Seventrees. And still no word from her. Tillingham.

The lights had come on everywhere now. Red, blue, green – a whole slanting kaleidoscope of colours from curtained houses and shop windows. It had started to rain. Strings of silver beads hung between them and the blackness of the night. The train was going faster than ever now, screaming with speed, slamming over level crossings and bridges on the outskirts of Gatley.

He suddenly thought he had never seen the reflected colours on the pavements look so beautiful.

"Like an artist's palette," she murmured following his eyes.

"More like a spill of oil," he corrected. To hell with Dylan. "Are you an artist too, then?"

She shook her head, smiled teasingly. "Are you in oil?"

"In that my Masters own about half of British Petroleum, I might be said to be in oil."

"The government?"

He bowed. "That much-maligned Aunt Sally, the Treasury."

"I'm a distant connection as well. To Art. I restore pictures."

"It sounds exciting."

"Not really. Nothing like painting your own."

"Nor is mine anything like having your own money to spend. So we're birds of a feather. Where do you do your restoring?"

"At the Victoria and Albert."

He wished he had some pertinent comment now to make on Art. To cement their camaraderie. It was no more than that. He spent several precise minutes rifling through the Gladstone bag of his memories of duty visits to the National Gallery and the Tate with Daphne and the progeny. Shame should have nipped his fingers. Perhaps it did. He came out of the process empty-handed.

It was she who discovered something. She peered out of the window. Unnoticed, by him, familiar ground was streaking past outside. The train was decelerating.

Barrington Hill slid past, pricked with a few lights. The brakes squealed. The curve at the junction to Warborough. The big signal box. A glimpse as they passed of the glowing red blobs on the meshed map. Row after row of familiar houses. The brickworks. The bridge.

"Ocklington," said Sheila Tate.

"Already?" said Blake.

"At last!" said Cunliffe.

The beginnings of the platform sliced alongside like the blade of a chopper.

"How will you get home?" she asked, eyes following the rivulets of rain.

"The way I came. Walk."

"Even in the rain?"

"I'm well protected." He unhooked his umbrella. "The civil servant's sceptre."

She smiled at his rueful almost apologetic expression. "I like walking in the rain," she said.

When the train came to a halt, he waited till the others squeezed out. He was last on to the platform.

Just before he closed the door, he said to her, "They're not so bad."

"What aren't?"

"Diesels."

The guard's whistle shrilled impatiently twice. He stood in the wet alone on the platform till the train disappeared and the smudge of the rear light was erased by the night.

Then he walked over the bridge, his footsteps echoing with a curious significance that matched his mood. He paused before he walked up Station Approach to unfurl his umbrella, conscious that a different Edward Blake had closed it. He hardly noticed the rain on his mile walk home.

Ahead of him, the chintz curtains glowed pink and cheerful as he came up the garden path. As he let himself in through the front door, Daphne came out of the sitting-room. She looked at him with astonishment. Resentment even.

"Edward . . . what a surprise! We saw on the News that the trains were all cancelled. Nothing out of Victoria this way." Now she smiled, rushed over to him and planted a perfunctory kiss on his cheek. "We decided you'd stay up at the Treasury in the emergency beds. We've all been eating in front of the telly."

He hung up his mackintosh. "Cunliffe did his stuff. Got a train diverted. But we were routed all round the houses. I feel as if I've been halfway to the moon." He put his arm on her shoulder. "Still, it's nice to get home." What I am really saying he thought is "I have been a long way from you. Claim me back."

She eluded him kindly but firmly. "You're wet through to your jacket! Go and change while I whip up an omelette. Peter, the greedy one, ate up your supper in your absence."

"WHAT are you doing, Gordon?"

"Measuring up, Alice."

He wound up the tape measure, stood up and gave his wife a smile. She was standing at the bottom of the stairs, still in her dressing-gown, in a pool of pink sunlight shining through the eastern lattice window.

"What for?"

"Ah!" He put his finger to the side of his nose. "That would be telling!"

He implied that his efforts had been directed towards the purchase of fitted carpets, something she had been asking for ever since they came to Blakeneys.

She seemed pleased. "I'd have thought after last night you'd have taken it easy this morning."

"No, no. Got to catch the 8.01."

"You mustn't overstrain yourself."

He smiled wryly but to himself. Alice didn't know the meaning of hard work. Always flitting from one thing to the other, dropping everything to shoo the cat away from the birds, starting reading a novel in the middle of baking a cake, never even being able to get his breakfast of a boiled egg and bread and butter without several interruptions.

"That shocking business last night. I can tell you the Ocklington commuters wouldn't have got home but for me."

"They owe you a lot, Gordon."

"Sometimes wonder why I bother. Nobody really thanks you."

"I'm sure they're grateful, all the same."

"I do my duty."

In fact, that day they appeared to be grateful. Several people, including that Civil Servant chap who lived in Arlington Avenue, came up and thanked him for his efforts. He was

113

gratified, assured them that he was going to have a "real go" at British Rail now, "pulling no punches", "no holds barred", and that "last night had taught him a real lesson".

The exact nature of that lesson, however, he kept to himself. It was that, quite apart from the chaos caused by the power cut, British Rail had not the money, nor the staff, nor the equipment to keep the Ocklington Line open. What with the Blackwater Tunnel, the bridge over the Nene, the Colebrook viaduct and track just as obsolete, there wasn't a hope in hell that the line could last, particularly in the context of the economic and political crisis and the perpetual strikes and go-slows. Sir Ralph Mannering had given it till August, but Cunliffe was now convinced that it would be much sooner. The autumn wasn't the best time to sell a house, but it was better than the middle of the winter and with the commuter line closed down. Even as he accepted his fellow commuters' praise, he was composing an advertisement for the Estate Agent . . . *beautiful sixteenth-century thatched cottage in the Garden of England and only fifty-nine minutes from London.*

In fact, that day it did take fifty-nine minutes, as though somehow a compensation for the travails of last night. He related his adventures to his secretary.

"You commandeered a train, Mr Cunliffe?"

"Well, you could say that, yes, Debbie."

He spent most of that morning dictating a long letter to British Rail, letting them know in no uncertain terms, as he had promised, that the commuters were at the end of their tether, and that they could no longer treat human beings in this way.

"There should be a Society for the Prevention of Cruelty to Human Beings, Debbie."

"They'd make you Chairman of it, Mr Cunliffe."

The afternoon he spent, also with his secretary, making up slogans for posters and car stickers demanding a better Ocklington Line train service, and organising the printing of them.

Just before leaving to catch the 5.55, he put a telephone call to a firm of London Estate Agents who publicised the fact that they had a mailing list of customers for "period properties" telling them the dimensions of the rooms and his idea of an advertisement. They appeared reasonably interested but seemed dubious about the price he was asking. He made a point to them that all appointments to view must be made through him at Nettleship and Hammond.

"Are you giving Blakeneys away then, Mr Cunliffe?", she asked as she brought him in the letters to sign at the end of the day.

"What do you mean, Miss Leigh?"

"Thirty-five thousand seems very low."

"Property market isn't as good as it was, Miss Leigh."

"All the same, a lovely place like Blakeneys . . ."

He had rather thought she listened in to all his telephone calls. Now he knew for certain. But on reflection, why not? She was his trusted personal assistant. There could be no secrets between him and her. Showed she was keen to keep abreast of all his affairs, to continue to work at his side, to join him in all his enterprises in fighting the good fight.

"Well, thank you." He finished the last signature with a flourish. "Goodnight, Debbie."

"Goodnight, Mr Cunliffe."

Just before she went through the door into her own tiny office, she said "Oh, Mr Cunliffe . . . ?"

He was already shouldering his way into his overcoat. "Yes?"

"About Frascati's . . . you remember, Mr Cunliffe?"

"Of course, of course!"

"What day shall I book, Mr Cunliffe?"

"So many things." He collected his bowler hat off the peg. "So many things . . ."

"It's over a fortnight ago, Mr Cunliffe."

"Frascati's won't run away, Miss Leigh."

"But Mr Cunliffe, you promised . . ."

"One of these days, one of these days." He picked up his briefcase and opened the door. "Goodnight, Miss Leigh."

"Goodnight, Mr Cunliffe."

That night on the notice board at Ocklington station, he pinned a copy of his letter to British Rail, and underneath the car sticker slogan, beautifully set out in Letraset by Miss Deborah Leigh: WE ARE WINNING.

THE following Friday, Blake discovered an alarming pheno-
menon. Some unrisen antennae deep within his primeval skull
knew when the brown-haired woman was near. It was a fine
evening. There was a long violet city dusk. He'd got a seat on the
5.55, and had subsided into it when he felt this sudden certainty
that she was close by.

He was at the end of an open compartment with his back to
the engine. He surveyed the seven solemn-faced commuters
opposite, the fat stockbroker type beside him, the hand-holding
couple on the other side of the aisle. He listened for the sound of
her voice amongst the murmur behind him. Then he gave up and
opened his paper with a self-admonitory sigh.

Just before the whistle went, a shopper in a fur coat and red
hat, bristling with Marks & Spencer's bags, struggled in through
the second door. A veritable camel barely managing the needle's
eye. She hailed the invisible passenger seated back-to-back with
Blake. "It's Celia Mortimer! How are you?"

The brown-haired woman's voice, recognisable anywhere,
returned the greeting. "Let me take some of those parcels."

There was some protesting, followed by the rustle of much
unburdening. The brown-haired woman must have squeezed
herself up in her habitual manner again. "Room for a little one,
eh?" The red hat disappeared from Blake's vision. "Ah, that's
better!" He felt the invasion of a determined bottom from the
other side of the upholstery. Intermittently all the way home he
heard Red Hat's voice, and occasionally, Mrs Mortimer's
answering.

Only a word here and there, undrowned by the rhythm of the
train, floated back to him. *Husband.* The ubiquitous Dylan was
with them. *Everyone in Fordbridge* had been worried about
something. *Such a pity, so disappointing.*

Two hundred yards before the tunnel, the train slowed to a

crawl. In the quiet, and in reply to her companion's question, Mrs Mortimer gave her quick little laugh. "I eat in the Park. Sandwiches. Then I cook for us both when I get home."

At Ocklington, a sliver of moon had risen above the station buildings. The sky was dappled with small pale clouds. Her face was in profile as he passed her lit window. She didn't turn. She was wearing a brown suède jacket with a scarf tucked in the neck. He could imagine her sitting in the Park, wherever it was, with the wind ruffling that clean brown hair.

Over the week-end, that vision intermittently returned. Daphne was manning the Tombola stall at the Convent Bazaar. Sarah was in the Dancing Display. Peter was playing football. Blake swept up the leaves on the path, saved the perfect ones for Sarah's Nature Table. For some reason, he saw the woman stirring her neat brown court shoes in them like a child dipping in water.

He worked hard all Monday. He hadn't time to stop when the coffee trolley came trundling down the corridor outside his cell. It was half past one before he looked up from his files. His stomach revolted at the crisped-up kept-warm food, the stale civil service faces in the restaurant on the top floor. Besides, beyond the shadowed rectangle of the courtyard a blue sky glistened as beguilingly as some distant sea. He locked his filing cabinet, deposited his key, and with a feeling of high days and holidays went out into the cold autumn air.

His feet led him to a small sandwich shop round the corner of Petty France. He queued with youngsters for the privilege of buying himself a ham roll and (a favourite of his boyhood) a custard tart. Then he walked into St James's Park.

She was not there, of course. His antennae warned him. He hadn't really expected her to be. Nor was his brief essay into the unusual wholly successful. He found the corner of a bench to perch himself on. But it was shared by three girls who obviously did not welcome his presence. He spread his handkerchief on his knees and ate with clumsiness and haste. He was further discomfited by seeing Watkins, the Deputy Secretary, stroll past. Watkins smiled with amused condescension.

It came to Blake in the middle of the tunnel a couple of days later that, of course, Hyde Park would be the nearest to the

117

Victoria and Albert Museum. He left for lunch punctually at one that day. He bought his sandwiches with greater care and a more lavish hand. Then clutching his paper bag he caught the bus to Hyde Park and walked briskly down the macadam path towards the Serpentine.

He knew he would find her by the water. She was sitting alone on the first seat past the little hump-backed Chinese-looking bridge. She had finished her lunch and was crumbling the remains, tossing them to the ducks. She looked infinitely more touching than his imagination had dreamed up. He walked towards her not stealthily, but slowly. Savouring the moment.

She looked up as his shadow stopped. There was a moment of quick recognition, immediately painted out by a polite but formal smile.

"Hello."

"Hello, Mrs Mortimer." She didn't seem surprised he knew her name. "May I sit down?" He lifted his bag, his passport, proof of his integrity.

"Of course." She moved up. When would he teach her not to do that? "I'd finished. I was just going." She looked at her watch.

"Please don't." He put his hand on her arm. And in explanation of his vehemence, "I hate eating alone."

She smiled gently. "Like I hate tunnels?"

"Something like that."

"But don't you usually?" She pointed to his bag. Then she laughed suddenly, "Or do you chance your arm?"

"On whom I meet?" He felt scandalised. "Of course not. I've just taken to this. Time, you know," he added vaguely. "Saves time."

"Are you very pressed for it at the moment?"

He unwrapped a ham roll and nodded vigorously.

"Looking after the national wealth?" she asked, her eyes bright with laughter.

"What's left of it." He smiled back wryly.

"Helping in the ruthless cuts in government spending?" She nodded towards a *Daily Telegraph* lying abandoned on the seat opposite.

118

He returned her smile less surely.

"I suppose you wouldn't have anything to do with grants to uneconomic railways?"

"Telepathy." He sighed. "I am plagued by day and night by requests for uneconomic railways."

"But apparently you resist?"

"The Treasury *always* resists. Obfuscate and resist, the Treasury's watchwords." He swallowed his roll. The ducks sidled nearer hopefully. Pigeons descended out of a cool blue sky, held off on angelic vertical wings. The sunshine was warm as May. "Since I have sat at this desk, it has been an invariable rule –"

He began guying himself and his situation. Immediately she caught his mood and laughed.

"Civil Service talk?"

"I fear so."

"Do you always have to talk like that?"

He nodded.

"Go on."

"I am a trifle surprised at your statement."

"What does that mean?"

"What the hell d'you think you're saying?"

"The mailed hand in the Regency glove, eh? Well, I suppose the hand that holds the coffers rocks the world."

"And how it rocks it!" He offered her a custard tart. She accepted it with a slight and curiously beguiling blush.

"I used to like them as a boy."

"I make them sometimes." She looked as if she might have gone on to say she'd make some for him, then thought better of it. "What other strange expressions do our civil masters use?" she asked.

"I would point out with respect . . . that means are you blind? I would point out with great respect . . . you *are* blind."

She laughed.

"I would point out with the greatest respect . . . you are deaf, dumb *and* blind. And the most famous of all, when you're in a cleft stick, of course, and there's no more money in the bank, *I agree.*"

119

"That's what we all do, isn't it?" she said gently. "In the end. If there's nothing we can do about it?"

"There's always something really we can do." He didn't look at her. He fixed his eyes on the bare slender tracery of a birch as fragile and perfect as the skeleton of a leaf he had found for Sarah.

Beyond the trees and the park the skyline of London glowed pale and clean in the unexpected bonus of this fine day. He watched a pintail dive. He smelled water and cut grass, a mixture of late flowers – chrysanthemums and Michaelmas daisies. He thought London had never looked so impermanent and yet so beautiful.

"It's time I went," she said, standing up and looking at her watch. She let out an exclamation. "Time goes so quickly. And you're in a hurry." Deftly she packed the plastic box and stowed it in her holdall.

"Don't go yet." He put his hand on her arm. "Let's walk on the bridge. Throw this stuff to the ducks." He was offering her a childish bribe to stay. She might have been Sarah.

"All right. Then I really must dash."

He put his hand lightly under her elbow as they walked. The sun flung their shadows sideways on the grass. A man with a red beard lay with his face turned upwards like a ragged sunflower. Sparrows and pigeons pecked around their feet, flew up no farther than autumn leaves. He felt at one. But with what he didn't know. He felt himself.

Then they were on the bridge, leaning over, beset by a multitude of wings. Far away and high above London a jet drew four white silk threads across the glass of the sky. The sun was behind them. It flung their two shadows on the water like the two lovers on the blue Willow Pattern plates. The china-coloured sky, even the pendant birds, he thought.

He shivered. He felt conscious of some inner chord of anguish lightly but surely touched. Yet of what had he to be afraid?

"Time," Mrs Mortimer said. "We really must go."

"Time," he echoed. Nothing more to trouble about than that. The time it would take to wait for the bus again. The time the journey would take. His civil-service self resurged. Already the afternoon tempo of work would be under way. The messengers

120

would be around with yet more files. His tray would be filling up. His cup running over. With work. Only with work. The wind was already whipping the clouds as he walked briskly away, as if the jet's white silk threads had actually cracked open the blue glass of the sky.

It dawned on him that he had never felt quite so close to anyone as the slight brown-haired woman he had just left, and yet because he was as he was, they had not even exchanged Christian names.

Back at the Treasury, another letter had come in from Williams at the Department of the Environment:

I am sorry to have to press you for a reply to my letter of 15 September about the Ocklington Line, and you will remember that I also telephoned you on 30 September about the same matter.

We do appreciate your difficulties and are very grateful for your view that further finance might be made available in order to keep the Line running. However numerous meetings have been held by British Rail on operational problems that are involved. The Blackwater Tunnel particularly is giving cause for concern. There is apparently damp behind the arching, and this combined with the exceptionally wet autumn has caused the facing of the bricks to weep. British Rail are taking such precautions as are possible, particularly against vibration. They have already imposed a speed limit of ten miles an hour through the Tunnel, and will now not allow two trains in the Tunnel together. British Rail are also about to impose a drastic reduction on the number of trains on this Line, so that at least some repair work can be started. Inevitably there will be further delays and discomforts and inconvenience to passengers, and this may lead to further demonstrations and probably representations to Members of Parliament, but . . .

Blake called for the file and saw that a reply had not yet been received from the Department of Education and Science. He picked up his pen and wrote *I regret that it has not been possible yet to reply to your letter of 15 September, but you will appreciate that reactions regarding possible closure of the Ocklington Line are necessary from other Departments, and these have not yet been forthcoming. I confirm that further finance may be available, and as soon as I have anything of substance to report I will let you know* . . .

He spent the rest of the afternoon writing to the Department of Trade and Industry, the Coal Board, the Electricity Board and Kent County Council. Then he marked File R/372/54 back to the Registry with the words *Put by: Bring up in two weeks.*

AT the wet mouth of the Blackwater Tunnel, the 8.01 seemed to hesitate. Slowed to a crawl, it poked its head reluctantly into the round black hole – then half way through, stopped dead.

All the lights went off.

There was a loud groan in the compartment. A voice – Bill Cody's – called out "Encore!" Sheila Tate pleaded, "Please, hasn't anyone got a light?" People started rooting round in pockets for matches and lighters. Mr Osborne whispered into Miss Price's ear, "Will he be all right?"

It was her father's outlet day, and just after leaving Ocklington he had gone along to the lavatory.

"He should be."

"He won't be frightened of the dark?"

"Oh no! Nothing like that. He isn't like that."

"Perhaps I'd better pop along and see."

He opened the baggy brown briefcase on his knee, and began rooting around inside. Almost everything that anyone could ever want was in that bag – the morning's paper, a stick of chocolate, matches, a screwdriver, a novel (a light romantic one such as ladies love), a packet of cigarettes and a tin of tobacco (though he did not smoke), a plastic hood, an umbrella that folded to unbelievably small proportions, a packet of ham and tomato sandwiches, a banana, a pear, a bottle of bitter lemon and a miniature flask of brandy, paper handkerchiefs, ruled paper, a rubber, a pair of Victorian opera glasses, a tiny camera, a toothbrush, a corkscrew-cum-bottleopener, and a torch. He picked out the last, switched it on, stood up, began elbowing people out of the way, saying "Excuse me" till he reached the glass door with Toilet on it and the indicator reading "Engaged".

"Dad," he called out.

There was no answer.

Mr Osborne began rapping on the glass. "Dad . . . can you hear me?"

Nothing.

Now he began turning the handle, twisting it this way and that. Then he put his shoulder to the door, pushed hard – but it would not give.

The people in the corridor watched him silently. Every now and then, under the dark train, there was a rattle and a thump that then died away. Osborne threaded his way back to the compartment.

"I can't make him hear, Miss Price."

"He's very deaf."

"I shouted."

"Sometimes I think he doesn't hear on purpose."

"I banged hard on the door."

"Oh, he is a nuisance! He'll have locked himself in and can't get out."

"That's what it'll be."

"He won't be able to see."

"Not a thing."

"Oh, I'm sorry! I *am* sorry to put you to all this trouble, Mr Osborne."

"No trouble."

"He is such a *nuisance*!"

"Don't worry . . . it'll be all right."

"But what are you going to do?"

Mr Osborne had begun rummaging again into his briefcase, finally produced a screwdriver. "We can't have him in there, locked in the dark. I'll open the door from the outside, that's what I'll do."

"It's ever so good of you . . ."

The torchlight flickered over her pinched white face.

"You stay here, Miss Price."

"Oh, Dad is a nuisance! He really is! Why did he have to go *now*? Before I left the house, I said 'Now Dad, you've been?' And he said yes, yes, he had. Three times. Oh, he is too bad, putting people out like this . . ."

He went back to the toilet door, called softly through, then

124

louder, then started banging with all his might, shouting
"*Dad!*"

Nothing. Not the shuffle of a sole. Not a stir. Not a breath.
He carefully undid the screws on the indicator, took away the
casing, managed to get the screwdriver in through the opening
and worked the lock back.

Then he pushed open the door, went inside – the torchlight
fingering the way ahead.

The old man was sitting on the toilet, his trousers round his
ankles, his head slumped between his knees. The torch flickered
over the faded velvet on his coat collar, the muffler round his
neck, the staring eyes, the open mouth.

"No," Mr Osborne said as others tried to come in. "It's all
right. I can manage."

The torchlight flickered over the dirty bin, filled with soiled
tissues, the single sliver of soap puffy with bubbles on the wash-
basin, the notices *Passengers are requested not to use the toilet
when the train is standing at a station* and *Gentlemen lift the seat.*
Like a yellow bat round this tiny cream-painted cell up to the
ceiling and on to the bright red chain. *Pull down to stop the train
. . . penalty for improper use £25.*

He put his hand on the old man's face. It was cold and very
slightly damp. He put his finger on the old man's wrist, but there
was no pulse. He took a mirror out of his inside jacket pocket
and held it in front of the old man's mouth. A sharp reflection
back at him illuminated the grey spikes on the old man's chin,
the thin bloodless mouth.

"No! Please close the door!"

A high nervous voice. "But I want to come in!"

"You can't!" He pushed the bolt across the door. He put the
plug in the basin, pushed the tap for warm water, pulled out a
handful of tissues. Then he picked up the old man in his arms
and wiped him clean, sprinkled water on his face and hands.
Through the oval window of crystallised glass, every now and
then in the torchlight there was a muzzy glimpse of the black
wet brickwork of the tunnel wall.

He tucked in the old man's shirt, pulled up his trousers, but-
toned them, combed his hair, flushed the toilet and closed the

lid, put the old man down propped in the corner with his head on his chest.

Then he switched off the torch and stayed in the darkness, making his plans. He would stay with the old man, ask a British Rail official at Victoria to get an ambulance to take them to Ocklington, where he would arrange matters with the undertakers.

He heard the hiss of air brakes, the grinding sound of wheels turning. The train was moving forward again. Slowly, very slowly, they were clanking through the tunnel .

The blackness turned to grey, then to white. A shaft of sunshine now through the crystallised oval. Mr Osborne pulled back the bolt, opened the door into the corridor. He told the man standing just outside that there had been an accident. Nobody was to go inside. Then he went into the compartment and sat beside Miss Price.

"Oh, I'm sorry . . . putting you to all this trouble . . . really . . ."

He said nothing. He put his arm around her and held her close. After a little while, very quietly and softly, she began to cry. She had lowered her head so that nobody would see.

Tee-who – the electric train was trying to make up for lost time, rattling over the rails – *tee-who, tee-who, tee-who,* lonely as a seagull's cry over the wet grey roofs of Croydon.

It was now over a month ago that Tom Armitage had dropped the letter to Sheila Tate into 6 Station Approach and, wet through, had waved to her at the Blackwater Tunnel entrance and been ignored. He had received no answer and no explanation. Six times he had rung to propose a date. Five times he had got her mother. The sixth time he had got her and she had said no.

That Friday, he tried again.

"Ocklington 631."

"Sheila . . . this is Tom."

Coldly: "Yes?"

"Would you come to the dance?"

"What dance?"

"One at Woosley on Guy Fawkes night."

"Oh, *that* one."

"Should be good, love."

There was a long pause.

"Well?"

"Well, what?"

"Are you going to come?"

There was an even longer pause.

"*Not* on the back of your motorbike again, that's for certain!"

"We'll go by train then."

Sheila Tate considered her situation. Her continued vigil had still produced no results. After such a promising beginning there had been not the slightest sight or sound of Crispin Mannering. Perhaps after all the Alfa had been repaired, and no longer did he ride the electric train. Perhaps she would never see him again. Perhaps he, too, had joined that place where all the young men have gone.

"All right then," she said generously. "All right . . . I'll come."

SATURDAY–TUESDAY
25 October–4 November

THEY met only on Marjorie's London days – every Tuesday, on the 8.01 going up to London and the 5.55 coming back.

They talked about all sorts of things – her childhood up in Northumberland, the walks and rides over the hills, the cold chill of bathes in the North Sea, what she hoped to do – but never succeeded in doing – and of her committee work. He spoke very little about his past.

"You're a mystery man," she said, gently teasing, coming out of the Blackwater Tunnel in late October and clattering towards the lights of Ocklington.

"Not really." He shrugged his shoulders. "It's *your* past I like listening to. You wouldn't be interested in the adventures of Sinbad the Sailor."

"You're so wrong! You've probably been to many more countries than I have, even though Ralph and I do go abroad for a holiday together every summer."

"I doubt it."

"Where *do* you go for your holidays?"

It was then that she suddenly noticed the book on his lap, *A Guide Book to West Australia.*

"Never have the time."

"What's *this* then?" She patted the bright-coloured jacket.

"Australia."

That was the first time, she was to remember later, that he had ever said the word *Australia* – coming into Ocklington station that frosty evening, getting up from his seat and making as if there wasn't time to say anything else. "I couldn't possibly afford to go for a *holiday* there."

A certain stoicism had developed on the Ocklington Line. Rumours of closing both the station and the railway had filtered through to the commuters, and though largely discounted as nonsense had had a diminishing effect on the numbers of complaints. Possibilities of greatly reduced trade, property values, facilities and convenience had sent a tremor through the community. Champions like Mr Osborne said They would never allow it. Most others argued that it was evident that passenger and freight receipts had increased enormously in the past three years. People pointed to the possibility of Ocklington becoming the next New Town. And though there were pessimists like Tom Armitage, these were routed particularly by the staunch attitude of the Chairman of the Passengers' Consultative Committee who denied the remotest possibility of the Line closing down and denounced those who even spoke in this way as traitors to the cause.

Meanwhile to and fro, into the Blackwater Tunnel and out again went the electric trains. No longer was the late arrival of the 8.01 greeted with howls of derision. No longer were there vociferous grumbles when there were only three carriages on the 5.55, and everyone was packed in tighter than sardines. When the train again stopped in the tunnel on Wednesday, the atmosphere was more of dumb endurance and suffering silence. Gordon Cunliffe, Bill Cody, Celia Mortimer, Miss Price and Mr Osborne had all been on it – and so had four Salvation Army lassies with the words "Blood and Fire" and the metal S on their high collars, wearing their black straw bonnets and their black stockings and their black high-heeled shoes. One of them had a guitar with "Chislett, Yvonne" on a yellow tag attached to it on which was also written "Smile Jesus Loves You", and written on her handbag "Jesus Is and Lives Today". "Why was I called Yvonne?" she had been saying. "My father says he had a girl friend called Yvonne when he was five years old . . ."

And all together, softly they began singing to Chislett, Yvonne's guitar: "I'm glad I have salvation. I'm glad I have salvation. I'm glad I *have salvation*" – high now and confident and loud – "by trusting in the Lord".

Slowly the wheels started turning. Gradually the electric train emerged from the Blackwater Tunnel. Dark skeletons of birch trees, the beginnings of houses.

And now again, the electric train was slowing, and a porter's voice shouting through the darkness, welcoming them all in "Ocklington, Ocklington . . . this is *Ocklington*!"

That Wednesday morning, Mrs Mortimer saved him a seat. Her carriage stopped beside the second Victorian lamp standard, and she squeezed herself up when she saw him, to make room.

"That was a bit of luck," Blake said, blowing out his cheeks with the cold. The upholstery felt warm where she'd been sitting, and hot dry air came from the heaters by his feet.

"Yes, wasn't it?" She smiled. Her fine skin was rosy with the frost. The little white threads by her temples looked touching and unreal, like a girl playing at being an older woman. He felt cosseted, warmed, comfortable – possessed again of that sense of inexplicable well-being.

"It was jolly cold out there," he said, as the train drew out of the platform. The unsheltering lamp standards fell behind, the factories and houses of Ocklington disappeared like the background of a dream. "First frost of the season."

"Beautiful," she murmured, her eyes on the whitened fields. He had never before noticed the green glimmer of the autumn grass through waves of frosted tussocks. It gave the feeling of lightness and delicacy, at one with his mood. A petrified sea. The petrified woods. Bare trees, breathlessly still, a floor of brown beech leaves, crunchy with sugary white. The sun not visible, but the sky a distant Arctic blue. The iron wheels as they raced the journey away, sparking and snapping with the frost.

"It would be lovely in the Park on a day like this," he said wistfully. A pause. Diffidently, "Shall you be lunching there?"

She shook her head. "I've got to collect a miniature from a private gallery."

"Pity. To miss weather like this, I mean."

She nodded, her eyes now reflected back at him from the tunnel walls. Her hands lay calmly on her lap, close to his own.

"How about you?" she asked after a moment. "Shall you be feeding the ducks on ham rolls?"

He shook his head. "I am somewhat pressed." He paused. "At present, anyway. But towards the end of the week . . . perhaps Friday?"

"Friday," she nodded as they burst out of the tunnel into horizontal sunlight. Little puffs of white frost cascaded down from the frozen brambles at the tunnel mouth. The countryside had never looked so dazzlingly beautiful.

Two rows of seats farther down he could hear Miss Price exclaiming about her chilblains, Mr Osborne mourning that he hadn't brought in his geraniums. The *Daily Telegraph,* the *Mirror,* the *Guardian, The Times* were full of strikes and shortages, wars and disasters. He felt ashamed of this undeserved spring of well-being inside himself, water in a world of drought, good food in famine.

That Friday was still cold, but there was no frost. The sky was heavy with rain clouds. The park swept by a north-west wind, the surface of the Serpentine tossed into miniature white caps.

They watched the mallards breasting the little waves, remarked on the way the females' brown feathers merged with the last of the leaves, while the drakes' blue heads caught the light of the sky. Children were trundling a Guy on an orange-box with wheels, their faces scorched with the cold. She said they were like something out of Breughel, and he gave them a fifty pence piece to show off to her.

Whenever he could spare the time now – which was rarely enough – he went along to the Park and sat and ate his sandwiches with her. In the evenings now he left the Treasury in good time to catch the 5.55. He searched the tide of commuters sweeping into Victoria for a glimpse of her brisk slight figure. He was inordinately disappointed if he didn't manage to catch her before they passed through the barrier.

On the way home, they discussed the day's doings. He found himself possessed of a hitherto-unrecognised skill as a raconteur. The Treasury became suddenly full of amusing characters. Or maybe she was simply a good listener. Her name was Celia. She had been married for eighteen years.

"You must have been young?" he said gallantly.

"Not specially. Twenty."

"Happily married?"

"Very. And you?"

"Oh, yes. I've been very lucky."

There was nothing between them but friendship and a most

131

unusual companionship. They found it easy to exchange ideas, to communicate, he supposed the pundits would call it. He saw things the better for her being there. As if before life had been a photograph, and now it had assumed its three-dimensional reality.

Once or twice he even mentioned her name at home. There was no reason not to. To Sarah, struggling with the History of Art. "I met a nice little woman on the train who spends her time touching up priceless old pictures and tapestries."

"How deadly," Sarah murmured.

"Has she ever discovered a fake?" Peter asked, but lost interest when his father shook his head.

"Only me," Blake said to himself, and immediately stifled the thought.

On that Saturday, his family persuaded him to take them to the Ocklington Guy Fawkes Celebrations. He disliked crowds. He had enough of them every day. But he went with as good grace as possible, bought drinks and roasted chestnuts. And as if the crowds were a magnified version of commuter time at Victoria, he found himself searching the torchlit faces. Once as the masses gathered round the fire and the band played, and the hooligans threw their jumping jacks under people's feet, he thought he saw her. Standing beside a hefty red-faced black-bearded man. If it were she, she looked curiously diminished.

Oh, yes, she said on the Monday, she'd gone to the Bonfire. But not for long. They had left when it had begun to rain. Dylan had always been intrigued by the idea of painting the torchlit procession as it went over the river bridge.

They had talked about painting most of that week. Blake found himself an apt and willing pupil. He asked about Dylan. She said he was a genius.

It was Daphne who gave him the only piece of information on Dylan other than that. The Women's Institute in their constant gleaning for speakers had invited him to give a talk on Art.

"Never turned up," Daphne said, preparing supper still in her second best blue suit. "Does this apparently. Did the same at Fordbridge Women's Institute. Drinks like a fish. Even in the daytime. Nasty bit of work. He was only invited because the woman who talks on bee-keeping has got arthritis."

132

"I thought bee-stings were good for arthritis," Blake said, to cover his embarrassment.

"That I wouldn't know," Daphne replied. "One thing I do know though. Everyone was talking about the Line closing down."

"There's always been rumours of the Line closing down."

"Even so, it would make quite a problem for us if this time it's true. The progeny wouldn't be able to get to senior school. And the Treasury would fold up without you, wouldn't they?"

"Indeed, yes."

"I'd hate," she said, stirring the gravy, "to live in the suburbs again."

"Wimbledon wasn't so bad." The idea horrified him. But it would never happen. "Besides, if the worst comes to the worst, these things take years. I'll have retired by the time they get around to it."

He said the same to the brown-haired woman on the train. He couldn't think of her somehow as Celia. "In any case," she murmured, "things have a way of working out."

"DON'T KNOW WHY you bother."

"Got to earn my living, haven't I?"

"You've never liked the hospital."

"Who says?"

"Clever girl like you . . . there's lots of jobs in Ocklington."

"Such as?"

"The banks, they're always needing girls."

"Who wants to go into a bank?"

"Who wants to trail to London and back every day?"

"Better'n sticking in the mud. And you meet *people*."

"Lots of people in Ocklington."

"Not *those* sort of people, silly." Sheila Tate fastidiously smoothed the red skirt of her dance frock over her knees. "*Interesting* people."

"You got to be careful," Tom Armitage hinted darkly.

"Oh, I can look after myself."

"That you can't!"

The electric train gave its usual hiccup before entering the Blackwater Tunnel. It was the same old collection of carriages that made up the 8.01. Above the luggage racks, the same advertisements urged all passengers to get the whole strength of the insurance companies behind them. But instead of mackintoshed commuters, the carriage was filled with young people – boys in best suits and girls in long dresses, all going to the Guy Fawkes dance at Woosley, all except Tom Armitage in the highest spirits. The differing forms of gauntlets that his love had to run in the course of commuting to and working in that metropolitan den of iniquity was a matter on which he was always brooding.

"Then you could always get a job in Warborough."

"Oh, change the record!"

"What do you mean?"

"On and on! Do this, don't do that! You're as bad as my Mum!"

Sheila turned her head away from him and stared through the compartment window at the gathering darkness. At the back of her mind was a flicker of hope that Crispin Mannering would make his long-awaited reappearance tonight, nurtured by her horoscope for the week, *An old flame returns*. Nobody approaching him on the train, though. Really rather a rough crowd, shouting and giggling, now throwing fireworks out into the tunnel. A jumping jack banged just outside the glass. A rocket – all red and green stars – exploded in a bright magnesium flare, turning the tunnel into a crystal cave.

"Idiots!" Tom said.

"Oh, they're just having a bit of fun. Something you can't understand."

By the time they emerged from the tunnel and had reached Woosley station, they were hardly speaking to each other. They walked up the hill to the village hall in silence. Tom paid for the tickets, followed Sheila inside.

The place was half-empty. On a dais at the far end, a group of three long-haired boys and a fair-haired girl were strumming away on guitars, but no one was dancing.

"Drink?" he asked.

There was a bar in an alcove to one side. They sat, the only two, on high stools in silence. Sheila had chosen gin and lemon but left it untouched on the counter while she watched the door. Tom studiously drank a pint of beer.

Gradually the hall filled up. Two couples began dancing – weirdly swaying in front of each other, their feet hardly moving, their arms flailing the air like half-hearted windmills.

"Like to dance, Sheila?"

"Who with?"

"Me, of course."

"No."

She had given up watching the door. Now she turned her eyes to the boy who had brought her. She didn't like that brown suit and his shoes were so clod-hopping and big, not suède and slim. And his fingers, holding the handle of the tankard, were so big and red. And his manners, too, finishing off his

135

beer and wiping his mouth with the back of his hand. She shuddered.

"Cold, love?"

She shook her head.

"Dance now?"

She slid off her stool in answer, and he followed her on to the floor. Now she was feeling slightly ashamed of herself – after all, he had brought her – and now she tried to make up. The trouble was that his dancing was so bad, no rhythm to it, clumsy, and all the time a great big smile on his face that searched for an answering happiness on hers.

They danced on and off for an hour, till he trod heavily on her foot in semi-darkness while rotating lights coloured them all red, white and blue. She cursed him and hobbled back to the bar.

"Sorry, love."

"Why don't you *look* where you put your feet?"

"Couldn't see my feet." And then, "Is it hurting?"

"Course it is! Your feet weigh a ton. My toes are all crushed."

He knelt down and started to take off her shoes.

"Here, leave my shoes alone!"

"I was just going to massage your toes."

"You needn't bother."

"Sorry, love. Didn't mean to hurt you."

"You've said that before."

"Sorry, love."

"You're always saying sorry. Is that the only word you know?"

"No."

"Not the world's most inspiring conversationalist, are you?"

"Neither are you."

"If you were a gentleman, you'd have at least tried to make yourself interesting."

"But I'm not a gentleman."

"You don't have to tell me that. Nor my family. You should hear my Mum when you ring up. It's that navvy again for you, Sheila. That's what she says."

"Can't say she gives me a thrill either."

"You're in a dead end! Haven't you got any initiative?"

"That's a big word for a little girl."

"I get almost as much as you. You know, honest, I feel mean sometimes, letting you pay for me."

"Next time, just pay."

"If there *is* a next time!"

She could feel him getting angrier. His left hand reached over into her lap and took her fingers one by one and turned and twisted them as though wringing their necks. But he said nothing, just sat there, his head hunched over his chest, staring at the floor, while the music became louder and more strident, the walls vibrating to the stamping of feet, and high to the roof now the wail of a flute, sharp and sweet above the twanging guitar-strings.

"Hello there!"

Sheila turned her head – and there he was, the flag of yellow hair waving over the bright grey eyes, tall and elegant in a dark blue suit, Crispin Mannering risen as though from the dead.

She made an attempt at indifference. "Long time no see."

"Been away. On a cruise."

"That must have been lovely."

"Fabulous. Care for a dance?"

"Thank you, Crispin."

Tom watched the pair of them go, merge with the crowd, become another ever-changing jiggling reflective surface under the flickering of kaleidoscopic colours. Yet all the time, he could identify her, did not lose her amongst all those blobs, kept his eyes on that tossing head as it sank below the waves of the sea around it, rose, inclined sideways, looked up, looked down, and even in the darkness of the forest of legs and feet, like a jungle on the move, he could see the twinkling white stockings and the red-heeled shoes.

That Crispin was a good dancer. There were glimpses of him now and again when some invisible wind blew aside the other quivering foliage and allowed a sudden glimpse of his body moving rhythmically, gracefully, all his limbs in tune with each other as though dancing was what they were born to do – the easiest and most natural thing in the world.

Sheila was enjoying herself, there was no doubt about that. Laughing, her eyes bright and mesmerised as though she was

137

under the influence of some double-acting drug that sent her body into a frenzy, and her mind to sleep and sweet dreams. So long as she's safe and having fun, Tom said to himself, buying another beer for himself in order to try by such artificial means to keep in step with her mood.

The time passed, and she did not come back. The head bobbing up and down in the swell had suddenly disappeared. There was no sign of either of them. Tom had another beer, looked at his watch, saw it was five to twelve. Time to go if they were to catch the last train home.

He got up. He moved to the other side of the hall. Behind a clump of potted palms, beside a notice announcing a Sale of Work to be opened by Lady Mannering, he found the two of them sitting on a bench.

"We're just resting," Sheila said.

"It's time to go."

Crispin rose. "But we're in the middle of this dance!"

"You've got to come now, Sheila."

"It's early!"

"Last train leaves in ten minutes."

"Doesn't!"

"Does now . . . with the cutback." He held out his hands. "Come on, love."

"Don't be so daft."

"I'll see you home," Crispin said. "Still haven't got the Alfa back . . . but we can get a taxi."

"I brought her here and I'm taking her home!"

"She does what she wants to do."

Tom Armitage leaned forward and took the girl by the wrists. "Sheila, we'll have to hurry!"

He was just pulling her to her feet, protesting, when Crispin put his right foot between Tom's legs and gave him a push in the small of his back. Off-balance, he stumbled forward, tried to recover, rocked back on his heels, then fell heavily to the floor. There was laughter, a short nervous giggle, the sound of feet scurrying away.

But not far – Tom was up before they reached the dance floor. He caught them up, grabbed Crispin's collar.

"Let me go!"

138

"Leave us alone!"

The yellow flag of hair waved furiously. Half strangled by Tom's grip of his neck, Crispin's face had gone purply red. He began swinging his arms.

"Don't try anything, mate!"

"Tom Armitage! Who do you think you are?"

"A bum, that's all he is, Sheila. Take no notice of him."

"Come on, love. Be good and come quietly."

"I'll look after you, Sheila." Crispin had managed to turn his shoulder round. "Can't you see you're not wanted? Push off! Go away, you little –"

"What?"

"Or I'll really –"

"Really *what*?"

A blue arm, blurred by speed, swung right round over Tom's shoulder. A fist connected against the side of his face. He staggered backwards, then pulled himself forward by his hold on Crispin's collar. He swept round, smacked Crispin hard on the cheek, then gave him an uppercut to the jaw that sent him reeling backwards. The next moment his head had gone clean through a stained-glass memorial window. There was a tinkle of glass. Abruptly the music stopped. Someone shouted "Order!", and a crowd formed round the two of them to watch the fight.

But there was no movement from the body on the floor.

"You've *killed* him," Sheila hissed.

"Don't be so daft!" Tom mimicked her words of three minutes ago, "He's just resting." He put his toe into the body. "Come on, *up*!"

Slowly Crispin staggered to his feet, his face had gone ghastly white, his cheeks painted into two clownish daubs of red blood. There were cuts under his eye, his lips were swollen and he was gulping for breath.

"There you are, you see! He can stand." Tom took hold of Crispin's tie and pulled it hard. "Now behave if you want to stay vertical!" He grabbed Sheila's arm and began propelling her towards the door, "You and I have a date with a train!"

Outside, it was colder than ever, but crystal-clear in moonlight. You could see half Kent turned Chinese yellow, to the south the street lamps of Ocklington sparking like fireflies, and to the north the horizon stained red from the lights of London. Tom began running now, down the hill to the station, dragging Sheila behind him as though he was one of those steam engines that used to run on the Ocklington line pulling a coal tender behind, his arm the coupling between them.

"Quickly!"

The air was filled with the thump of his feet and the click of her heels. Panting and breathless, they reached the darkness of Woosley station, only to find it deserted.

"We've missed it." Sheila leaned against the empty booking office window. "Now what are you going to do?"

Tom banged at the locked stationmaster's office. He walked down to the shunting line, the engine shed – everything deserted. He came back to her, still leaning against the booking office, ankles crossed.

"Well?" she said. "Well? Last train to San Fernando." She began singing, tapping loudly to the rhythm of the tune.

"We'll wait."

"But I'm cold!"

He left her and walked down the platform slope to the emergency signal just south of the station which had been set up as a safeguard against the possibility of two trains being in the Blackwater Tunnel at the same time. He moved the manual lever down. There was a *clunk* as the arm moved. The green light slid to red.

He returned to her and said, "There's a relief engine that goes down to Southover about this time. Not always. But there's a chance."

They waited for another quarter of an hour.

"I'm freezing to death!"

"Give him a few minutes more."

"Then what will you do?"

But Tom was spared the need to reply. *Tee-who* came hooting from far up the line, and then the clanging of slowing wheels. Tom went to the edge of the platform, waving his arms into the beam from the spotlight.

There was a screech of brakes and the engine stopped. It was Jack Gow, a driver he knew. The two of them bundled in beside him. Slowly forward now, stopping so that Tom could put the

140

signal back to green, then moving towards the Blackwater Tunnel.

"What a big round black mouth it's got!" Sheila was mollified now, warmer, basking in a privileged position. She was not displeased to have two men fighting over her, and she was rather enjoying this ride through the tunnel. Electric sparks crackled in the blackness. The headlight speared the dark wet dome ahead. "Isn't it beautiful? Just like the Crystal Palace!"

"You should have been through Blackwater in steam!" said the driver. "Could hardly breathe! Smoke and cinders fair suffocated you. And you'd come out with your face black as a nigger's."

They went through the tunnel faster than usual. The sound though smaller was sweeter and echoed round the brickwork, rising and falling like organ music.

"All the same, the steamers . . . that's where my heart is! Uncomfortable, dirty, hard work, but the thrill of it! Electric trains . . . no, not for me! Not through the Blackwater! Too damp, been too damp for years. I get a cough in the winter and feverish turns, Blackwater fever, that's what my missus calls it!"

With a whoosh they emerged into the starlit night, flanked now by the white glaciers of the embankment. Ocklington ahead, its lights twinkling over frosted fields. The engine slowed, came to a stop.

"Thanks, Jack."

"Any time."

Ocklington station was eerie in its emptiness. Nobody here – nothing but the advertisements gummed on the hoardings. Three silent ghost girls beckoned towards the hovercraft. A shadowy man silently read *The Times. Convent Capers* (X) at the Roxy. The Samaritans were always available, telephone Ocklington 468. *Trust ye in the Lord,* Isaiah xxvi 4.

Hand in hand, Tom and Sheila moved down the platform. No lights – the ironclad shadows lying flat on the pavement as though part of the Victorian lamp standards had fallen down in the moonshine.

This was theirs – theirs alone – the twin platforms joined like a catamaran by the steel-gantried bridge, the station alight and alive like clouds of frosty breath that seemed to puff through the windows and doors. The tiles on the roof had turned to silver, giving a Chinese-palace effect, pagoda-like, to the whole structure, scenery for an Aladdin pantomime.

Sheila stood quite still. "Beautiful!"

It was as though the ice-cold air had intoxicated her. She felt airy, light, snowflake-size. Hands tightly at her sides, now she began dancing, a Principal Girl teetering on the tips of her toes as Miss Allison at ballet class had taught her and then at the end of the platform, as though it was a stage, turning and curtsying to him, her eyes brimming over with laughter, the moonlight frosting her face.

"Don't you see?" she called out to him. "All this is ours!"

He was infected with that same intoxication. As she came back to him with tiny steps, he took hold of her, lifted her off the ground, threw her up in the air, caught her as she came down, put her back on her feet.

"You're in the wrong pantomime," she said, "you're King Kong."

"Me? I'm Tarzan!"

"Right!"

He ran lightly up the stairs of the bridge, climbing on to the girders at the top, balanced like a tightrope walker from one end to the other. Then at the far end, he jumped over to the other side, balanced his way back. Quickly now, a somersault in the air, then upside down, walking on his hands back along the girder, his legs tight together, like a moving spire, the moonlight glinting on the soles of his shoes.

She clapped her hands. "Encore!"

And this time, light as a gymnast, he somersaulted right way up, straightened, jumped, caught the bottom girder of the bridge, swung high above the line, making his way back to her, his feet swinging and swaying in the empty air.

"What about that then? How's that for Tarzan?"

"No," she called back at him. "No! That's kid's stuff. Peter Pan!"

He was breathless now and panting, his shadow long over the track. He let go his right hand. Now he was hanging by his left arm, twisting and turning. "How's that then?"

"Jump!" she demanded.

"Right!"

"Go on then!"

"You see where I am? I'm right over the live! Jumping . . ."

She had forgotten the live electric line. "Don't! Tom . . . *don't!*"

". . . *now!*"

He jumped suddenly through the air, a falling ghost, landing on both the live and the dead rail.

She shrieked.

He took no notice, balancing now on the glistening silver of the live rail, walking north towards Blackwater, the frost brushing from his shoes like sparks. Then he turned and came back to her, standing there with her hands over her face.

"It's all right. Current's turned off now at one!"

"Tom Armitage, you –"

He jumped on to the platform reaching out his hands to get her. But she was in full flight. Now it was her turn to pelt up the stairs of the bridge, with him following.

Laughing, her hair streaming, she jumped down to the other platform, dashed behind a luggage carrier, twisted round three crates, caught the second Victorian lamp standard, where in daytime she waited for the 8.01, in her left hand, and swung round it like a maypole. He caught hold of her skirt but she pulled away – over by the broken fence now, slipping under the bridge, dashed across to the gate to Station Approach and was struggling to get it open when he caught her, held her tight in his arms, his face cold against her skin, but his lips warm and wet against hers.

They stood there with their arms round each other, hugging and laughing and kissing.

Then she pulled away from him, glanced at her watch, "Look at the time!"

"It's not over yet."

"What isn't?"

"The pantomime. You've forgotten the last scene."

"What's that?"

"Principal Girl marries Principal Boy. And before the curtain comes down!"

143

I AM the sweet-scented vision in filmy chiffon about to go to the ball, mistily observed by the sleepy child in the cot and carried over into his dreams, Lady Marjorie thought, coming back in the Rolls from opening the church bazaar. A permanent smile, a permanent soft voice, a permanent interest in their knitted socks and elderberry wine. She felt that they actually ached to touch her – not in a kind of must-touch-flesh way, but as an almost healing contact, a momentary helping hand through the coming night. I am not really any different from that alabaster sisterhood lying in the church. I am doing the same things they did. It is simply my turn now, that's all.

And any day, any night it would be somebody else's – this aye day, this aye night every night and all, fire and sleet and candle-light and God receive my soul. Here comes a chopper to chop off your head – if only you could see it, have a chance to take avoiding action, it wouldn't be so bad! Poor Sir James and Lady Jane Mannering who had so carefully and lovingly planned and built the great house, they could scarcely have imagined for a moment that friendship with a king would end so suddenly with their heads on spikes side by side on Tower Bridge!

Life is transitory, it's later than you think – you were always being told that, but what were you supposed to do about it? Everybody is so insecure, everybody wants to believe that there *is* such a thing as security, actually to see it, to touch, to hold it in their hands. Do your duty, and you will be looked after – that was the password. Back in her Northumbrian childhood, her nursery governess croaking through the lavatory door "Have you done your duty?" Here she was now, having done her duty in seeing others did their duty. Lady Marjorie Mannering, the Irish brogue of Eamonn Andrews whispered to her, *This is your life.*

Turning past the lodge now, into the drive, slipping between

144

elm trees breathing mist, the lights on in the library, muzzy promises that Ralph would be waiting with the drinks laid out and the roses in the Queen Anne bowl, the *Financial Times* ostentatiously out of sight, soft Chopin Preludes, which she loved, leaking from the hi-fi. Ralph, too, making his little preparations to do his duty.

She often wondered whether the mood came on him by chance, or whether he noted it down in his appointments book, as he did all his other duties. He planned his courtship like a military campaign – as indeed he planned everything in his life, including all his business ventures, which probably explained why he was so very successful in keeping the wealth that he had inherited and, in these tax-ridden times, actually increasing it by diversifying and making his interests world-wide. His politics, too, were naturally the Siamese twin to this obsession to *preserve*. He had to preserve everything – this vast old house kept in a perfect state. It was the same with all the property he owned, the farms, the factories, the fields, the buildings, the antiques. It was the same with his rather small body, kept remarkably fit and wiry by hunting, shooting, massage, exercises, and by what he would call temperate living.

The Rolls softly stopped. A sudden smell of autumn leaves and cold clay. Stepping out now. "Thank you, Robbins. Goodnight."

"Goodnight, m'lady."

The warm hug of the hall. Ralph had been listening for the car, was at the top of the stairs, coming down towards her.

"Hello, darling." He gave her his loving kiss. "How did the bazaar go?"

"Well, it went."

"How much did they make?"

"Two hundred and three pounds."

"Good going!"

Sherry in the library. The firelight flickering on the Gainsborough and the two Constables. Ralph continuing with his courtship. "You're looking very beautiful tonight, my dear."

"I don't feel it."

"You're tired, poor darling. Come on, put your feet up on the sofa."

145

Ralph's view of abandoned living – the servants seeing m'lady with her feet up on the sofa.

"I like that dress, darling."

He took an inordinate interest in her clothes. Particularly he liked tight-waisted dresses with wide flared skirts – like this blue wool one, emphasising what he would call her child-bearing hips and Bill Cody would call her beautiful bottom.

"Feeling better?" Just a trifle anxiously. It would never do, now the wheels had been set in motion, for her to go to sleep. "Here, have another sherry!"

The evening proceeded, identical to other such evenings before it. Conscientious in everything, perhaps he had read some-where – his mother, the Lady Veronica, would certainly never have mentioned it, and his father was never off his office chair sufficiently long to get around to the subject – that a woman must be courted all evening, and doggedly that was what he did. Short and often amusing stories – about people, never about business, which he did not trouble her with. He would never mention to her even on other less dedicated occasions than this, his business and political problems. Apart from the park and its surroundings, she had no idea of what he owned, of how many companies he was chairman or a director. Vast wealth, huge difficulties, enormous worries she knew he must have, but you would never think it. He would have thought it bad manners to discuss such matters with women. He was old-fashioned enough to believe the sexes had their separate roles, and he would never have wanted to trouble her with his business problems. Never irritable, only put out, he was always equable – amusing even, for he was a good mimic and could produce acid take-offs of the Opposition. Miserly, people said he was, but she had seen none of it. He was careful with his money, certainly, but then he had to be. Brave and chivalrous, rich as Croesus, still handsome even if he did dye his dark hair, what more in a husband could a woman want?

Dinner now – French vegetable soup. He was complimenting her as though she had made it. The lazy, often witty, chit-chat, a game of verbal ping-pong, always careful on these nights to see that she won the point.

Venison, cooked to a turn, with petit pois and sauté potatoes –

146

he was talking now about some alterations he intended doing on a Scottish castle he owned, asking her advice, flattering her with exclamations about her good taste, taking note – actually putting them down on the back of an envelope – of all her suggestions.

Watching his shining pink cheeks, his bright blue eyes, she thought that if he was himself getting some satisfaction out of all this elaborate lead-up, it wouldn't be so bad. If, in fact, he was extending the period of titillation, elasticising the sexual act over a period, obtaining pleasure from seeing her as the final culmination of succulence, she might herself have obtained some excitement from this long-drawn-out ritual. But it was nothing like that – no. He was simply going through his Before Take Off Check List, as though she was an aeroplane he was about to fly, a personification of those suggestive airline advertisements – *I'm Lady Marjorie, fly me to* (where, she wondered?).

And he always somehow saw her as Lady Marjorie. Almost he said those two words to her as he brought her creamy coffee. In the bedroom, as in the drawing-room, she would not be allowed to escape that role. Talking about films now, leaning forward on the sofa, reaching for her hand. He was politely asking questions about *Far From the Madding Crowd*, which she had seen for the third time.

Ah, Sergeant Troy! Courting a lady with your sword! Yet Ralph was twice as brave and a hundred times more sensible.

Discussing *Tom Jones* now – that gourmandising greasy gluttonous scene between the man and the girl, eating each other up!

"How about an After Eight, darling?" Chocolate-covered mint time.

Books – it was surprising the way he managed to find time to keep up with what he would call culture. Analysing a recent biography which they both had read.

Liqueurs – two Napoleon brandies.

Warm on her stomach, cosy and reassuring as the firelight. All the lights out, the conversation now on art, some painting he was thinking of purchasing.

"A nude, darling. Eighteenth-century. After the style of Rubens."

147

He would love that. A big plump bare lady with big plump bare hips – a real breeder. That's what he really wanted. That's why he chose me. The itch to preserve: the name, the house, these estates, this wealth carefully sequestered all over the world. An heir must always have been his number one priority. Still was – these occasions were, she noticed, carefully timed. And this elaborate courtship, was it a sort of pre-incubation preparation to get exactly the right temperature, blood pressure, chemical secretions, the best physiological and psychological environment to produce the perfect child? What a disappointment she must be to him that he must satisfy himself with painted substitutes!

The fire was very low now – the logs grey and flaked like so much cigar-ash. The servants had gone to bed. Almost complete darkness – just little fireflies of light.

His hand on her knee, softly caressing. No talking now – a reverent silence. The only sound, the slither of wool skirt moving up over silk stockings.

"Ralph . . . ?"

He did not answer at first.

"Did you know there's a strong rumour that British Rail are going to close the Ocklington Line?"

The programme had been interrupted irreverently and irrelevantly. He spoke at last – equably enough but with the short slur of the slightly disorganised. "Yes, I did know."

"It's caused a big shock."

"Naturally."

"At the bazaar, people were talking about a petition, organising a protest meeting."

"That would accord with the normal British pattern of behaviour."

"They sounded very militant."

"They always do."

"Have you had any letters?"

"One or two."

"Aren't you going to do something about it?"

"Such as?"

"Asking a Parliamentary Question."

"Perhaps."

148

"Don't you think it's a *scandal*?"

"As a commuter" – an affectionately derisive smile – "you will know more about it than I do."

"And I think it *is* a scandal and you should table a Question."

The smile ever so slightly tinged with irritation. "One of the many things I love about you, Marjorie, is that everything you take up" – her charities, her committees, her bazaars, little bits of nonsense like this Rail business was what he meant – "you do so whole-heartedly, give your life and soul to it."

"Then you will?"

"Sweet," he kissed her cheek, slid his mouth round to her lips, "your wish is my command."

Hand in hand, they went up the dark stairs. Through the windows, moonlight frosted the green carpet. He went into his dressing-room to undress. She slipped off her things in their bedroom, put on a pink silk nightdress with puffed-out sleeves that he liked, awaited him in the canopied Tudor bed.

His short red dressing-gown, scarlet pyjamas, red leather slippers. The smell of toothpaste, tobacco and pine after-shave lotion. He knelt down at the foot of the bed. What did he pray for? Forgiveness? The downfall of the Labour Party? Or an heir?

I come unto my courtship as my prayer. Prayers almost over now. The soft touch of his cold hand.

"Darling . . . I *worship* you."

The goddess Lady Marjorie up there on her pedestal. All those others in the church – Lady Amelia, Lady Ursula, Lady Caroline, Lady Anne – they would all have lain in this bed as she was lying now, for better or better, for richer or richer.

Afterwards – now there was a word! She turned it over in her mouth as if it was a chocolate, trying to suck some sweetness out of it. Beside her, Ralph's head on the pillow – five minutes of endearments completed, eyes closed, gently sleeping, menu over. She lay on her back, staring up at the dark ceiling. It was very quiet now, silent as the grave. Only in her mind, dry and splintery as that old lavatory door, like a conscience, the croak of her nursery governess: "Lady Marjorie . . have you done your duty?"

IT WAS as though now he could see things clearer and in their true perspective. That was her effect on him, Blake thought. No longer did he sit in the train in his dream limbo-land. Now he noticed people, the colour of the sky, the greens and browns of the wintering Weald. And always he saw in her eyes that she had seen them at the same time. It was as though their thoughts and feelings were unified in one enveloping aura.

Looking back at the train standing at the curve of Woosley station, he saw how like a crescent of houses the sixth of a circle of carriages was, and he saw that she had seen it too, had formed the same simile. He saw her watching a girl with long hair putting up her right hand on it as though it was a piece of foliage that she was clinging to to save her from drowning, tugging on it, hanging on to it for dear life, and it was the same thoughts that passed through his mind.

He saw her looking at the live rail running along beside the two dead ones, and knew that she was thinking that was where the spark was, the vitality: no one knew what electricity was any more than they knew what life was.

And getting out of the train at Victoria that Wednesday with her, walking towards the ticket collector at Victoria, looking towards the next platform, he saw a whole string of people joined like a daisy-chain, old people mostly, though there were some young ones, men and women, pretty ones, plump ones, thin ones, white-haired ones, dressed in an assortment of clothes, all holding on to the shoulder of the next one in front of them, all laughing and talking, some of them wearing funny hats and carrying bright-coloured baskets. And then he saw the white sticks that each of them carried, and he saw superimposed over them that Great War picture by Singer Sargent of the blinded men walking across the zigzag path above the shellholes of a battlefield – and he saw the same concern in her eyes that they were so close to the edge of the platform.

With her, I am alive, he thought. I can see! The walk through St James's Park seemed that much more elevating, the chrysanthemum beds that much more brilliant and beautiful. Even the Treasury in the autumn sunshine looked softened and benign, and he almost welcomed file R/372/54 there on the top of his In-tray like a long-lost friend.

These days the Ocklington file was constantly on the move and was never in the Registry. The matter of the Ocklington Line was discussed at various levels, though it was basically at Blake's level that the business was done. Concern had been voiced in the corridors about the possible repercussions and quite apart from Sir Ralph Mannering, other MPs were beginning to take an active interest. Several Ministers had also had something to say.

It was Blake's view that the matter would go on – as these things do go on – indefinitely. If it was also his wish, he kept that submerged in his subconscious mind. He would have been surprised if anyone had suggested that perhaps matters had been rather slower than usual. He was doing what he should do – consulting other Departments. The vagaries of political and economic life he was well aware of. Any day now there might be another election. The economic situation might improve with a dramatic fall in commodity prices. Further large oil finds in the North Sea might alter the balance of payments picture. The decision should not be taken lightly.

He opened the file and read the minutes, summarised them and added a number of comments of his own.

Then he minuted on to Mr Grange in the Economists' Department.

It had not come back two days later when his telephone rang. It was Williams again from the Department of the Environment.

"I'm sorry to have to tell you that British Rail are issuing notice to close the Ocklington Line on the first of December."

"But we are still trying to find you the money!"

"I know that. That's what I've told British Rail." A pause. "You're still hopeful then?"

"Of course. The Economists are working on it now."

151

"The trouble is, the Engineering Department are pressing them. Something about repair and maintenance."

"They might have let us know."

"Yes, I'm sorry . . ."

"They seem to have jumped the gun."

"Yes."

"There'll be every sort of protest. Public meetings, Questions in the House. It will certainly go to Ministers."

"I know. That's what I keep telling them. But they're in a cleft stick between you and their Engineering Department."

"Well, you can tell them from us, we're *still* trying to find the money."

After the old man's death, it became Mr Osborne's habit always to sit in the second carriage of the 8.01 and look out for Miss Price – always with a big smile on his big turnip face, always either keeping a seat for her beside him or, if that was not possible, getting up and giving her his own and standing beside her. In the evening, he would wait at the barrier of the 5.55 for her to arrive and travel with her. It was never quite so full on the return journey. Bill Cody was working overtime ("for the money" he told Marjorie), except on Tuesdays when he caught the train so as to be with her. It was only about once or twice a week that Edward Blake managed to get away from the Treasury in time to catch it. Sheila Tate often went on the earlier train. Crispin Mannering had not made a reappearance – perhaps he was still recovering from Tom Armitage's attentions at the Guy Fawkes Dance. Cunliffe was busier than ever these days. What with the selling of Blakeneys, the need to quieten certain unwelcome suspicions on the part of Franklin about the Ocklington land contract (now signed, sealed, delivered and the money paid over), and a certain amount of a problem with Miss Deborah Leigh who kept reminding him of his promise of a date to sup the Queen's Jelly at Frascati's, just reward for services rendered, never mind his toings and froings with British Rail and his visits to Sir Ralph at Ocklington Park, now almost never did he manage to get the 5.55, arriving home late, hungry and tired to the high tune of Alice's reproaches.

So it was these days only Miss Price and Mr Osborne among the regulars on the 8.01 who could also be called regulars on the 5.55. They chatted to each other continuously on both the journey up and the journey down. In return, Miss Price would retail the latest disasters in the typing pool of Peterson Brothers – how Joan, Connie, Sylvia and Maude had arrived two hours late or never turned up at all, of a continual string of painted faces clumping up from the Bureau on six-inch wedge shoes to sit at their typewriters.

"If I had my way, Mr Osborne . . . I'd give them their cards!"

"They must be a great trial, Miss Price."

"And so rude! It isn't as if they're just lazy. Why the other day, you'd never believe it, Mr Osborne, but that Freda Forsyth, who thinks she's Lady Knobs, said to me . . ."

Mr Osborne's brows would darken. He would express his horror at such behaviour.

"It's shockin'."

"No discipline, that's the trouble, Miss Price."

"But what can you *do*, Mr Osborne?"

"A taste of the stick . . ."

He lived at Southover in a little bungalow near the Station. He used to work locally, but when his wife died last year, he felt that he wanted to get away during the day, if Miss Price saw what he meant. So he had got this job at Campion's, a firm that was "going places, Miss Price" and offered a hard-working man a real future. He had gone over to Ocklington last Saturday, and had tea with Miss Price and then had a walk over Terrible Down beside the banks of the river before returning to the terrace house near the gasworks for supper.

Every weekday was chimed with Mr Osborne's "Good morning, Miss Price" and Miss Price's everlasting shy surprised "Why, it's Mr Osborne!"

And when they parted, they never said goodbye or goodnight. They said, "See you on the 5.55, Mr Osborne," or, "See you on the 8.01, Miss Price."

153

It was now normal for the electric train to hesitate at the entrance to the Blackwater Tunnel – first moving forward, then stopping too abruptly with the clanging of buffers, then moving back to the same musical accompaniment, then moving forward again so that the electric train's progression was like a herd of chained elephants dancing the minuet to the music of the cymbals of the gods. Everyone knew that the reason for this was the prohibition on two trains being in the tunnel together at the same time. Most people had seen the sheen of water that now and again covered portions of the brickwork, and had felt the wheels slithering on the wet leaves on the rails. "One of those things," they said, shrugging their shoulders and accepting the inconvenience and the discomfort. "An Act of God," they said when an oak tree blew on to the line just north of Woosley. "Gremlins," they said when ice froze the points at Clapham Junction. An engine broke down between Woosley and Nutover, and they said that now and again all mechanical things failed. There were several militant dissenting groups who blamed the present misfortunes of the Line on a number of different *bêtes-noires* – the Unions, the Permissive Society, the Government, the Board of British Rail, God – but these were now less in the ascendant.

The commuters took a deep breath, closed their eyes and for the most part held their tongues.

So the announcement in all the national newspapers on Saturday came as a shock and a spark to a situation that was more explosive in that tensions had been kept tightly under control and passions had been restrained.

It was brief. It simply said

NOTICE OF LINE CLOSURE

The Board of British Rail hereby give notice that on 1 December that portion of the Victoria-Parkfield Line beyond

154

Woosley, including the stations of Ocklington, Southover and Fordbridge shall be closed. Alternative transport arrangements will be announced.

The second carriage next Monday on the 8.01, No. 56324, rocked with fury all the way to Victoria. The only person who evinced no surprise was Mr Osborne.

"All that grumbling and those letters! Told you. They wouldn't put up with it much longer, Miss Price."

"We asked for it, Mr Osborne."

"A rail service is a privilege, not a right."

"A sharp lesson was needed."

"It has been necessary for Them to give us a taste of the stick, Miss Price."

"But they won't *really* close the Line . . . ?"

"No, no. It's just that They must make sure that we learn our lesson."

The most vociferous of the passengers, as one would expect from a Chairman of a Passengers' Consultative Committee, was Cunliffe, who acted as a totem-pole round whom the others rallied. More than anyone else except Blake, he would be aware of the meetings, minutes, letters, telephone calls, power struggles, different factions of economists, engineers, administrators, managers, unions, politicians, experts that must have gone on behind the scenes behind that short stark announcement. In fact, Cunliffe had been informed by telephone of the probable outcome of all this human activity, necessitated by what was tersely described as an "operational decision".

But Cunliffe's vociferousness was as nothing to what awaited him in the office of the present Managing Director of Nettleship and Hammond.

Franklin had been away for a fortnight in New York, so that the late arrivals of the 8.01 and Cunliffe had passed unnoticed. By ill luck on that Monday, the succession of late arrivals had continued and it was almost ten o'clock when Cunliffe had managed to slip into his office.

"Mr Cunliffe . . ."

"Yes, Debbie?"

"H.F. has been asking for you."

"I'll go and have a word with him straight away."

He had in fact been expecting an outburst – but nothing like this. Franklin was not sitting at his desk, but was standing by the window reading Saturday's *Times*. Immediately Cunliffe came in, he advanced towards him as though he was going to strike him with it. His face was even whiter than usual, the only colour being in his eyes which were very bright and steely blue.

"Cunliffe . . ." H.F. was famous for his rages. He had eaten people in the past. He could hardly get the words out. But it was at moments like this that Cunliffe really came into his own. He had mastered the art of disguising his emotions, controlling his voice, not giving an indication of what he was thinking or feeling. He even managed a smile on his face and an almost jaunty air of warmth and confidence and well-being.

"Don't tell me, H.F.!" His voice was smooth and slow and soothing. "I *know*."

"*Cunliffe* . . ." It was like a half-strangled cry.

"Came as a complete surprise."

"Cunliffe." With an effort, Franklin managed to get himself under control. "Where have you been?"

"*Been*, H.F.?"

"Look at the time!"

Cunliffe's face was a blank.

"Twice I've been into your office. That girl of yours told me you were at Peterson Brothers. Were you?"

"Well, this morning –"

"You seem to spend most of your mornings at Peterson Brothers."

"Of course the Ocklington contract . . ."

"I rang them. No one had set eyes on you there for weeks."

"Sorry, H.F. Debbie must have got it a bit wrong. The train –"

"– was late."

"I've told you, H.F., now and again –"

"*As usual!*"

"H.F., we'll *fight*."

"Are you trying to tell me, Cunliffe," Franklin's voice sounded dry and cracked, "that you had no idea of this?"

156

"As I've told you, H.F., closures are always possibilities."

"You *must* have been consulted! You *must* have known there were difficulties."

"I never tried to keep it from you that there were difficulties."

"And you said the New Town at Ocklington was a certainty!"

"That I did *not* say, H.F. Nothing is certain in this life."

"But the Ocklington contract!" A vein stood out, blue and big, on Franklin's forehead. "What do you think the land's worth *now*? A half, a third of what we paid? How many millions do you think we've lost? What's the Board going to say on Wednesday?"

The storm lasted force eight for an hour and a half. When he turned the doorknob to go out of the office, Cunliffe's hand was slightly shaking, but there was no other visible sign of what he was feeling.

Back in his own office, he pressed his bell.

"Yes, Mr Cunliffe."

"Could you come in for a moment, Miss Leigh?"

In she came and sat on the penitent's stool in front of his desk – head down, eyes lowered, dark fringe over white forehead, pretty shoes at attention.

"Miss Leigh."

"Yes, Mr Cunliffe?"

"Why did you tell Mr Franklin that I was at Peterson Brothers?"

"But I thought –"

"You knew perfectly well I wasn't."

The head raised. Two round patches appeared painted on her cheeks.

"I've always known you weren't, Mr Cunliffe."

"Miss Leigh, use your common sense!"

"I was only trying to help, Mr Cunliffe."

"Haven't you any imagination? Don't you realise that you must have sounded like a cracked record? He telephoned Peterson's and *I wasn't there*. Can't you see what he would think? Are you dim?"

"But Mr Cunliffe –"

157

"Every time in the past you'd told him I was at Peterson's, now he'll have jumped to the conclusion that the train had been late."

"But Mr Cunliffe, that's what –"

"Miss Leigh, you bloody fartarsing little . . ."

It all came out then – obscenities, swearwords, incoherences. She had heard them all before from him, of course – but always at other people, never at herself.

Head still up, she sat there on her little stool, watching him and listening.

"FELLOW sufferers –"

That produced a laugh, brought down the temperature a trifle. The Board Member of British Rail stopped staring at the carafe of water on the green baize-covered table, and turned his eyes gratefully up towards the composed impassive face of Gordon Cunliffe. He had been told by the Chairman of British Rail (all good clean fun, of course) to prepare his neck for the noose. What with the publicity in the papers, the posters he saw everywhere, the people in the foyer distributing rosettes and pamphlets and car stickers with the words "Keep the Ocklington Line Alive", he had begun to think that his last hour might indeed be imminent, and was actually relieved to see that what was awaiting him on the platform of the Warborough Town Hall was simply a cane-bottomed chair and not a gallows.

The iron pillars of the hall (not unlike the second Victorian lamp standard on Ocklington station and manufactured about the same time) held a creamy canopy of ceiling above the assembled multitude. Not only were the regulars there – Bill Cody at the back, Kevin Clarkeson fiddling with his pillbox in the front row, Sheila Tate side by side with Tom Armitage, on the left of the aisle Miss Price and Mr Osborne – but people had come from as far away as Southover and Parkfield. Cunliffe had been gratified to find that Lady Marjorie intended to be present and had prevailed upon her to sit on the platform next to the Mayor of Warborough.

"... these terrible times we are living through ..." Cunliffe's port-wine voice reverberated round the walls "... wars, violence, corruption, oil crises, power crises, economic crises, inflation – you name it, we've got it! But I think I can say as your Chairman to Mr Lovell, who so kindly accepted my invitation to come and hear our views, that all these we on the Ocklington Line have borne with traditional British stoicism and good

159

humour." Cunliffe, paused for a full ten seconds, softly continued: "Until now . . ."

Sitting halfway down the hall, Edward Blake knew somehow for certain that Celia was in the hall, but at first he couldn't find where. Then he caught sight of her a couple of rows behind and across the aisle. She smiled and nodded in response to his upraised hand. He had been in two minds whether he should attend this protest meeting. He reasoned it out with himself. Could it really be said that the fact that the Line came marginally into his schedule was prohibitive to the involvement in any sort of activity connected to it? It would take place whether he went or not, and it could be argued (already he had formulated the words) that coming along tonight could be useful (a Civil Service word) constituting as it did in effect a watching brief (a Civil Service phrase), provided, of course, his role was low profile (a real Civil Service favourite). In the end, it was Daphne who had given him the final impetus to attend. Sarah was so well settled at school, and Peter had so many friends here, the last thing they wanted to do was to move – *of course* he should go.

". . . we've had late trains, jam-packed compartments, dirty compartments, power strikes, points frozen up, stoppages in the Blackwater Tunnel, engines failing, go-slows, working to rule. And now, after patiently and quietly enduring all that, we're told we're not going to have any trains at all!"

In the ensuing uproar, Marjorie Mannering caught Cody's eye – quizzical, half closed, underlined by the white crescent grin on his face. They had met at a pub a few minutes before the meeting. She would have preferred to have made it longer, perhaps had a meal, but he said he was working (he normally worked on Saturdays she found) and wouldn't be able to make it in time. She missed him most over the weekends – that terrible gap between Friday and Tuesday. Looking down at him, trying to be dispassionate, against a background of Cunliffe's swaying body and smooth words, she tried to work out why it was she found him attractive. An ugly big bastard – certainly there was sufficient outside evidence to merit a description such as her husband's friends would give him. Infatuation? Not altogether, because she could really be quite rational about him, saw perfectly clearly his faults and absurdities. The attraction of opposites? On the face of it, quite probable, but why did she have this feeling that deep down they were very much alike? The intrigue of a mystery man? Possibly – since certainly there was some story behind him, that she didn't know and he was careful to conceal. Last Sunday afternoon she had gone along to the tile-hung cottage by the ironpond in which he lived. Perhaps she expected to find some further clue about him – a wife and children, you never knew. The garden was beautifully kept, with late white chrysanthemums and roses, and in the vegetable plot Brussels sprouts and broccoli.

She knocked at the door, but he did not appear to be in. Peering through the window, she saw him engrossed in a book – a textbook on sheep-farming, she could see photographs of different sorts of sheep. He looked quite startled when she knocked on the latticed pane, had come loping towards her, not even offering her a cup of tea.

". . . gentlemanly behaviour is clearly being regarded as weakness! Endurance is taken as sheep-like conformity! Sympathetic understanding of British Rail difficulties is simply taken advantage of . . ."

There was a wise injunction, he had told her, when she had taxed him with his unwelcoming behaviour on the train on Tuesday, regarding own doorsteps with which he was heartily in agreement. M'lady had a role to play in Ocklington. Think of the scandal if there was the least hint of a liaison! She didn't want to assume the mantle of Lady Elizabeth, now did she? He was, he said, a great believer in discreet darkness. What no one sees never happens. They met for lunch in a Wimpy Bar and continued the argument. They had continued it when they had met this evening. "You don't want to become further involved with me," she had said. "You don't want to become further involved with me," he had simply repeated back at her. And there was nothing more that could be said, because it was the truth. And yet it wasn't *quite* the truth. She *did* want to become more involved, but in a different life, going on at the same time as her own historical life, like an X film accompanying a perfectly respectable U-certificate. It would make hardly any difference to her if the Line was closed, he had said. Why was she fighting so passionately to keep it open? Why was he coming to the meeting, she had retorted. Because, he replied, the rent was peppercorn, he could live on next to nothing, and the Kent countryside was a green balm on his spirit, after being entombed underground. He liked wide open spaces. "Like Australia?" she had asked, and suddenly she had seen him hesitate.

"Australia?" he had said, as though playing for time to think. And that was the second time she had heard him say the word. What was behind it? Was he going to emigrate? Behind so much of Bill Cody there was so much she didn't know, yet for some reason she was too diffident to probe further.

". . . that's all anyone ever does to the great British public. Kick it around! And I tell you this, Mr Lovell, and I speak for everyone in this hall, indeed every commuter and every passenger on the Ocklington Line, our patience is exhausted! We're not putting up with it any longer!"

So this is the great British public, she thought, looking round the faces in the hall – all different, all arranged in rows like chocolates, giving little indication of the filling inside except a certain shape and a certain squiggle on the top, and even then you had to have the key on the inside of the box before you could interpret. That woman right at the front, with the long white horse face under a black witch's hat, fiddling with the huge wooden beads of the necklace round her neck: why was she looking so worried, hanging on every word that Cunliffe said? That brown-haired man in the mackintosh who was vaguely familiar: why did he keep turning his head round? Why was that boy with his arm round that pretty girl she sometimes saw on Ocklington station looking as though any moment he would vomit?

". . . I say this, we all say this to British Rail, Mr Lovell, keep the Ocklington Line *alive!*"

Cunliffe sat down to a storm of clapping hands and stamping feet. In his place, Mr Lovell reluctantly rose.

"We apologise," Cody called out, "for the late arrival of your train. This was due to –"

"The driver not having finished his tea-break."

"Someone switching off the electric current."

"Bloody inefficient management!" roared the whole back row.

Mr Lovell opened his mouth, but not a word could be heard. Cunliffe had to get up again, holding up his hands for peace, calling out, "Fair's fair."

"What I want us to try to do," Lovell's voice eventually came croaking to the surface, "is to get this whole thing *in perspective . . .*"

"Double-speak!"

"Blind 'em with science!"

"Wool over eyes!"

". . . and it has *nothing to do with the Board.*"

"Praise the Lord and pass the buck!"

"It's money," Lovell persisted doggedly. "The country hasn't got the money. Look at the big expenses the government has . . . the big motorways, the Concorde, the oil deficit –"

"Stuff 'em all!"

"Sheer extravagance!"

"But keep the Ocklington Line alive!"

"That's just it, the Board have big plans for the Ocklington Line. I don't have to tell you that the carriages are old, bridges, viaducts, tunnels . . . all are old and need repair. And that costs money, a *lot* of money. Oh, I know receipts have been getting better. That's what we keep reminding the Department of the Environment, and they in their turn keep reminding the Treasury. All grants have been cut. We keep on asking for more finance, but none materialises. We haven't got the staff. Yet we have all this reconstruction and maintenance to do. We've been taking certain precautions, speed limits and so on. But we can't go on. We've got to call a halt. We simply haven't got the money. It's as simple as that. *That's* why we're closing the Line on the first of December."

There was a full minute of silence. Then Cody called out, "It *isn't* as simple as that. It's a matter of priorities. The Ocklington Line must be too low on someone's priorities."

"That's right! Why the Ocklington Line? Why not the North-end Line?"

"The Government told us to move out of London. It's up to the Government to get us to work."

"There aren't enough schools in Ocklington. How are our children to get to school?"

163

"What about the value of our house if the Line closes? Will the Board pay compensation?"

Mr Lovell stirred uneasily. "I'm very sympathetic. The Board is very sympathetic . . ."

"We don't want sympathy! We want action!"

"The Ocklington Line is our Lifeline."

"What perhaps Mr Lovell doesn't realise," in the front row, Alice Cunliffe frantically fingered her big wooden beads as she spoke, "is that the Ocklington Line runs through bluebell woods and orchards and primrose banks and it's the most beautiful railway in England!"

"Keep the Ocklington Line alive!"

"But you don't understand," Mr Lovell raised his voice. "We, the Chairman, the Board, British Rail, *want* to keep the Ocklington Line open. But we haven't got the money."

"Then the money must be found." Marjorie Mannering could no longer restrain herself from speaking. "Kent County Council should make a contribution from the rates."

"I'm sure we are all obliged to Lady Marjorie," Cunliffe said smoothly, "for that very sensible suggestion. It should certainly be explored."

"But all this takes *time*," Mr Lovell pointed out uneasily.

"My husband is the Member of Parliament for this constituency." Even as she pronounced the words she caught sight of Bill Cody's grin widening. "And he intends to table a Parliamentary Question *demanding* that the Line shall be kept open."

"That's right, Lady Marjorie." Cunliffe was quick to jump on the bandwagon which now he saw was actually moving. "Everybody write to their MPs. Write to the papers. Fight the good fight with all your might!"

It was at this moment of explosion, when the hall was again in uproar, that Tom Armitage chose to make his unfortunate interruption. Without consulting Sheila, without giving her an inkling of what was on his mind, he stood up on his feet and said stolidly, "I say close it."

The surprise throughout the hall was immediate. There was a sharp and concerted intake of breath, followed by muttering of "What's he saying?"

"I say close the Ocklington Line *now*!"

"What do you know about it, sonny?"

"I work on the Line, and, unless more maintenance and repairs and –"

"Siddown! Siddown!"

"I'm telling you we can't get the staff. We can't –"

A small white hand had got hold of the tail of his coat and was
pulling him hard down. Sheila's face was crimson. Keeping her
eyes down on the floor, she was hissing at him through her small
white teeth.

"I say to our young friend this." Henry Osborne had risen to
his feet. "Like all the youth of today, he forgets that They know
what They are doing. And I am quite sure that in the fullness of
time, They will contrive the means to keep the trains running.
Let us trust in Them."

Beside him, Miss Price closed her gloved hands three times
together in a little clap of applause.

"Keep the Ocklington Line alive!"

"And now," Cunliffe had risen to his feet to bring the
meeting to its climax, "I'm sure Mr Lovell has got the message
on how strongly we all feel. In our turn, we understand and
appreciate the difficulties of British Rail. We don't want to be
difficult. We are not thinking selfishly of ourselves. We are thinking of those who went before us, who made this *beautiful*," he
smiled down at Alice, "railway and bequeathed it to us to use,
to manage, to enjoy and then to pass on intact to those that
come after us. Are we going to go down in history as squanderers
of our inheritance?"

"*No!*"

"Keep the Ocklington Line alive!"

"Shall we have a show of hands?"

Edward Blake had listened intently to all that had been said,
watched people he saw on the electric train get up and express
themselves. It was a strange sight, he thought, all those figures
leaning forward, the faces turned upwards, the hands raised like a
forest of headless trees, illuminated in the sharp light thrown from
the platform. The moment was something to paint, to preserve
before it disintegrated and the hall again became empty, dark
and dusty, just brick and stone, brass memorials and row upon

row of vacant chairs. But as far as he was concerned, faced with a vote, should he not really opt out? Caught between his public and private roles, should he not really declare himself now, as judges and politicians and councillors are supposed to do? Then turning his head, he saw that she was smiling at him, holding up her right hand, and quite instinctively and naturally, moved by himself as a person, quite forgetting roles and rules and etiquette and expected behaviour, he raised his own hand up and smiled back at her.

"Those against?"

A solitary hand outstretched.

"Then that's unanimous." Cunliffe simply ignored Tom's arm, which in any case was being pulled down by the embarrassed girl beside him. "As you see, Mr Lovell, we are united. And now, sir, what action can we expect from British Rail?"

Lovell glassily surveyed the sea of faces in front of him. "Well, I shall certainly report to the Board your strong feelings."

"But with respect, they know them already."

"I'm sure, in the light of what I tell them, that they will see whether any avenue has been left unexplored."

"That's not good enough!" the back row shouted.

"Of course, I can't speak for the Board –"

"We know that, sir, but what will you recommend?"

Lovell hesitated. "Well, I think perhaps we should reconsider the situation."

"What does that mean exactly? The Line is supposed to close on December the first."

A dead silence fell over the hall. All eyes were on Lovell's face. All ears were waiting for his next words.

"Well," he said reluctantly, "I suppose there might be a postponement. I can't promise anything, of course, but in view of the circumstances, perhaps a delay of execution –"

Immediately the hall reverberated to a shout of triumph. Hands clapped. Feet hammered the floor. This was regarded as a victory. Thanks to their efforts, the electric trains would continue to run. A reprieve had been granted.

There was a vote of thanks to Lovell. There was a vote of solidarity in the fight for the future. Congratulations were show-

166

ered on Cunliffe as the hero of the occasion. An air of jubilation and confidence exuded throughout the hall.

Even Blake was caught up in it as along with the others he was carried along in the stream to the door. In the foyer, she slowed her pace, waited for him the way any friend would have done.

"What did you make of that?" she asked as they were spilled out into Warborough's meagrely lit main street.

There was a cold wind from the north. She huddled inside her camel coat. Their breaths fanned out in front of them.

"He was cornered."

"You mean, he had to make a show of doing something?"

"Yes." He smiled at her. "If he was going to get out of the hall alive."

"So you think the Line will close then?" Her voice was edged with sadness.

"Possibly when the Channel Tunnel electric line replaces it."

"Hasn't the Channel Tunnel been cancelled?"

"It'll be brought back. Eventually."

"So we've got years and years . . ."

". . . and years."

They walked slowly along the High Street.

"Why are you so certain?"

"Two things I've learned in the Civil Service, Celia. One, it takes ages to start anything new up."

"And the second?"

"It takes ages and *ages* to stop anything once it's started."

They both laughed. "That's a comfort," she said.

"You see, at heart we're all like you . . . conservationists."

"It's all done for Art's sake?"

"Governments are devoted to Art," he said gravely. "And to hobbies. And to the floating voters of the 8.01."

She laughed. "For the next election?"

"Governments come and governments go."

"Only the Civil Service never dies?"

"We soldier on," he said. "Well, that's my car over there." He pointed to the green Cortina. "Can I give you a lift home?"

"Oh no, thank you very much." Dylan wouldn't like that. She didn't say so, but somehow it was explicit. "I got a return on the bus."

"What about the other end?"

"It's only a step."

"But *dark*." He felt immediately protective.

"I'm not frightened of the *country* dark. I like it. Only the dark of tunnels." She smiled up at him. "And that not so much. Not now."

He knew what she meant to say. She was less frightened because of him. He could not have received a sweeter compliment. He felt quite choked up with emotion.

"Well, what time's your bus?"

"Nine-fifty."

"That gives us half an hour. Let's go and have a drink."

She hesitated.

"You do imbibe, don't you?" He took her elbow, sounding heavily jocular.

"Not very often." She allowed him to guide her across the road, down the pavement on the opposite side and into the saloon bar of the *Warborough Arms*.

He found a small table in the corner near the fireplace. A small coke fire glowed. He had that strange feeling again of warmth and well-being, as though already some strong spirits infused his blood stream. "How shall we celebrate the defeat of British Rail?" he asked, bending over her proprietorially. "What shall it be?"

"Could I have a soft drink?" Her eyes were clear and wide. Her skin coloured darkly with embarrassment.

"Have exactly what you want." For some reason, he was disappointed. What had he expected her to say – champagne?

"A ginger ale, please, if you don't mind."

He returned a couple of minutes later with her drink and a pint of beer for himself, and sat down opposite her.

"Though I did no public speaking whatsoever, I'm remarkably thirsty." He nodded towards his drink, chatting to cover his disappointment. For some reason, inexplicable to him, this had seemed an occasion in their friendship, a sort of celebration. Obviously she did not thus regard it.

He raised his glass. "Cheers!"

She clinked glasses with him. "Cheers!" Her smile deepened. "Don't think I'm being unsociable."

"Nothing was further from my thoughts, Celia."

"Yes, it was." She laughed. "You can't fool me. I know what you're thinking." Then she became serious again. "It's just that Dylan can't do with drink." She didn't elaborate. And something in the set of her lips discouraged any further questioning. She took a sip of her ginger ale, and changed the subject back to the meeting.

"The Chairman takes his job very seriously."

"Cunliffe? Yes, doesn't he?"

"I suppose we should be grateful."

"If only he wouldn't preach –"

"And suck his words like sweets."

"He makes me feel such a poor sinner."

". . . lovest thou me?"

"Next hymn is Number Forty-Two in *Ancient and Modern.*"

"But he had to make his point."

"Which he did." He dipped his nose into his tankard. "Ah, that's better! All in all, it wasn't a bad meeting." He felt somehow and in some strange way almost jealous of Cunliffe, as though the Chairman had done all the fighting while he had simply sat there, a non-participant on the sidelines. "You don't think I ought to have got up on my hind legs?"

"No."

"It's just that," he actually reached across the table and caught the tips of her fingers with his, "as a Civil Servant, I can't."

"I understand."

"There are rigid rules."

"Not in any way to disparage you," she smiled, "but I don't think it would have made the slightest difference if you had spoken."

He said wryly "True. All the same –"

She was still smiling at him.

"I might have ventured to suggest . . ."

"What?"

He was aware that he was guying himself, speaking civil-servicese. "That it would be helpful if the electric trains didn't stop in the Blackwater Tunnel."

"At least Cunliffe got them going again."

"Yes," he said. "Yes. Good old Cunliffe!" He downed his beer sadly. "Here's to Cunliffe!"

"You put up your hand," she pointed out.

"Only because you put up yours."

"In any case," she said softly, not looking at him, "it's as if we're all on some invisible train. The wheels are in motion. No matter what anyone says or does, nothing is really going to change it."

"I agree." He was aware even as he said the words that he was giving the Civil Service Benediction – *and now to God the Father, God the Son:* "I agree."

Sheila Tate stood alone by the bus stop, the ribboned rosette which she had collected in the foyer of the hall still pinned to the lapel of her coat. Above her, the illuminated round face of the church clock ticked away the minutes and there was still no sign of a 61.

She could hardly speak to Tom Armitage after the meeting. He had made such a fool of himself, standing up like that and pretending to know everything. As they went out of the hall people kept their distance away from him as though he might be infectious. She went on ahead out into the street, disowning any connection with him, having made it quite clear that she had not the slightest intention of being taken home on the back of his motorbike. He had pleaded with her, wheeling the thing as she walked up the road, stayed and argued as she waited, told her that the buses were as bad as the trains and she'd be lucky to get home that night. Throughout she had stared fixedly ahead, not saying a word, taking not the slightest notice – till finally he shrugged his shoulders and left her.

It was cold. A wind had sprung up. She shivered, feeling abandoned and apprehensive. There was in her not exactly a religious faith (though she went to the parish church with her parents on Sunday) but a curious kind of belief in a being with a face like a Pre-Raphaelite Christ and a body like Cinderella's fairy godmother who watched over her and protected her and who spoke through the oracle of the horoscope in *Woman's Own*

170

and had this week announced that *a surprise was just around the corner.*

She stared down the empty street – and still there was nothing. And then suddenly, slowly as a coach and six white horses, a gleaming white car preceded by the lances of two enormous headlights turned into the kerb and a man's voice, "Want a lift? Why, it's *you* . . ."

The Alfa and Crispin Mannering in person.

"Where have you been hiding, Sheila?"

"Oh . . . nowhere in particular."

"Haven't seen you for weeks."

"Were you at the meeting too?"

"What meeting?"

He knew nothing about it. No, no – he wouldn't have gone anyway. He'd simply come in to Warborough to collect the Alfa. They had finally managed to repair her. Wasn't she a beauty?

Sheila admired the car as it accelerated out of the town. Then she said, "I was wondering what had happened to you."

"Truth is, Sheila . . . I haven't been at all well. Something I picked up on the Madeira cruise perhaps. Then that lout –"

Her immediate concern rather touched him.

"Oh, I'm all right again now . . ."

In the slight light from the dashboard, he saw the gleam of her hair against the pink and whiteness of her skin, the big dark eyes. He smelled the rather sharp tang of her perfume. She really was a *very* pretty girl. Reminded him of someone . . . who was it now . . . yes, Betty Jones!

The headlights spilled their yellow juice on the blackness of the country lane ahead.

"On the train . . . I looked out for you."

"I missed you, Sheila."

"I missed you, too."

"Lucky I came along."

She nodded happily. "I was getting so cold." Her face clouded. "But I suppose now . . . you'll be going to London by car?"

"Oh yes." He reached over and took her hand. "But that doesn't mean we won't be seeing each other, I hope. I'll give you a ring and fix a date. Only this time, we'll make it Frascati's!"

171

MONDAY–MONDAY

24 November– 1 December

VICTORY FOR THE COMMUTERS – that was how the local Kentish papers headlined the meeting at Warborough. The battle was reported in detail, complete with photographs, and there was no doubt that its villain was the mild-mannered Mr Lovell and its hero was Gordon Cunliffe. The story was picked up by the National Press – permutations of the St George and Dragon legend have always been popular with the British, and the little man-against-Bureaucracy is one of the favourites – and reading of the reprieve and their sudden fame throughout the nation was sufficient solace, for those who waited under the second Victorian lamp standard on Ocklington station, to make up for the fact that on Monday the 8.01 was a record three-quarters of an hour late.

"See you've got yourself into the papers."

Franklin had been waiting in Cunliffe's office. On this occasion, however, no excuse for his lateness was required. From the way the Press reported the chaos on the Ocklington Line, he was lucky to arrive at all.

"Haven't seen it, H.F., but I believe there is some small piece about our Warborough meeting." He had, in fact, avidly read the accounts in three papers during the trip up to Victoria.

"You seem to have clobbered them, Gordon."

It was Miss Leigh's Peterson Brothers excuse that had introduced the acid into their relations. It was not so much the fib that Franklin had feared as what might lie behind it. He had always lived in London, always within walking distance of the office. Never having experienced them, he did not understand the problems of commuters, regarded their fights and trials in much the same light as he regarded the situation in Northern Ireland – "the troubles", in fact, perennially in the news – which he hoped and prayed would one day be sorted out.

172

He had no idea how the Ocklington Line troubles would be sorted out, and he sometimes woke up in a cold sweat, dreaming of the unimaginable things that might be behind them. Few property firms had the liquidity of Nettleship and Hammond. Most had bankers breathing down their necks. These liquid assets had very largely disappeared in this one gamble on Ocklington land. The Board had been very scathing at their private meeting last Wednesday, confronting him with notices issued by British Rail on the closure of the Line. Where was his precious New Town now? What did he think the value of the land was now? How much did he think they had lost – in millions? Whatever had *possessed* him?

Franklin was not a man to pass the buck. He had not said, "Cunliffe had always given me to understand that the Line was safe, and he was in a position to know." In truth, Cunliffe hadn't done so, not in so many *definite* words, though the overall impression had certainly been there. He had hedged his remarks as though they were bets, at the same time in Franklin's view leading him powerfully on. For the last six weeks, ever since the signing of the contract, he had felt a deep distrust of Cunliffe, though he had no actual evidence to go on. At least the man appeared to have put up a genuinely good show against the closing of the Line, and had clearly won a reprieve which would spike the Board's guns – at least for a time.

"So you think the trains will continue to run, Gordon?"

"*Now* I do, H.F."

"And the New Town?"

"Where else but Ocklington could they put it?"

Cunliffe had been aware of the souring of his relations with Franklin. He had the sensitivity of a seismograph on such variations of human behaviour. He was what is called an operator, and needed such antennae equipment. He was, at present, in a strong position – he could hardly lose, since Sir Ralph Mannering had practically promised, the last time they had met in Ocklington Park, that he would be "looked after" in Peterson Brothers. In the unlikely event of the Line being kept open and the New Town being built, it should be easy, particularly now, to divert the credit in his direction for his further advancement in Nettleship and Hammond. At the same time, he needed to keep control of the timing. An out-and-out row with H.F. would be unfortunate. For the next fifteen minutes in his smoothest and most conciliatory voice, he worked hard at healing the breach, and before Franklin left, he said, "Oh by the way, H.F., I'm finally taking your advice."

"What d'you mean?"

"I'm moving up to London."

"You're not saying now," Franklin had turned sharply round on him, "that the Line *will* close."

"Oh no, no, H.F. I'm finding it tiring. And inevitably these days, trains run late . . ."

He managed to imply that by this move he would be first in to the office in the morning, last out at night. Franklin appeared to accept the reason and to be pleased with it.

The situation between them, to Cunliffe's satisfaction, appeared to have normalised.

When she brought in his letters to sign at five past five that evening, Miss Deborah Leigh said, "Oh by the by, Mr Cunliffe, have you heard the news?"

"What news, Miss Leigh?" Since his brush with her on that rather tactless handling of the Peterson Brothers excuse, he had been formal and very correct.

"Millicent's leaving."

"Millicent?"

"Millicent Smith, H.F.'s Personal Assistant."

"No, I hadn't heard. Is she retiring?"

"Not exactly. She's got a sort of silver handshake."

"But she's got the business at her fingertips!"

"H.F. wants someone younger, Mr Cunliffe."

"He'll find it difficult to replace her."

"I suppose they'll advertise, Mr Cunliffe?"

"Oh yes, in all the papers. Is that the last letter, Miss Leigh? Good!"

Just before she went back into her own office, she said, "Oh, Mr Cunliffe . . . ?"

"Yes, Miss Leigh?"

"About Frascati's . . . you remember . . ."

"Yes, yes!"

174

"What day shall I book?"

"Later, Miss Leigh, later."

"What are you looking at?"

Marjorie Mannering pulled at Bill Cody's sleeve. His head was turned right round on his neck, staring backwards.

"Nothing . . ."

"You were!"

The head turned to face her. She saw that the calm grey of his eyes had been slightly ruffled.

"Just that brickwork."

"That brickwork?"

"Of the tunnel."

"Professional interest?"

Jaunty now. "You could call it that."

"Well executed?"

"Difficult to tell today."

"We went through too fast?"

"For a change."

"But you were looking for something," she persisted.

He said, almost apologetically, "That water."

"You're not still worrying about that, are you?"

"It seemed a lot."

"But last week it rained buckets!"

"Even so –"

"You should see some of the walls inside the Park! They're sopping."

All that same week, during the whole day Blake never left his desk, trying to keep up with the files that kept pouring into his In-tray.

Among them was R/372/54. Replies had been received from the Department of Education and Science to say that alternative transport arrangements could be made for schoolchildren if the Ocklington Line closed down. The Department of Trade and Industry were not so definite – factories were starting up in the area that looked like expanding. The Coal Board wrote to say

175

that road deliveries could be arranged. But Kent Council and the Roads Department of the Department of the Environment were concerned about the resulting great increase in traffic on the roads, for which there were no plans for widening or improving.

And then on Friday, the telephone rang and it was Williams from the Department of the Environment. Had Blake seen the Parliamentary Question that had been tabled? To be answered orally on Thursday: Sir Ralph Mannering (Warborough): *to ask the Minister of Transport whether further finance will be guaranteed to keep the Victoria-Ocklington-Parkfield Line open and will he make a statement.*

"No," Blake said. "I haven't."

"We think here that basically it is for you to answer."

"I wouldn't see it that way myself."

"Well, it would be helpful to know whether further finance *is* going to be forthcoming."

"No decision has been taken."

"Are you in a position to say when it will be taken?"

"At the present time, no."

"You appreciate that it may well go to Ministers?"

"I appreciate that. And you will appreciate the need for consultations with other Departments."

"With respect, some answer will need to be forthcoming for Sir Ralph."

"I would venture to suggest that you simply say that the matter is under the most urgent consideration."

"I doubt whether Sir Ralph will be satisfied with that."

"We can do no more at this stage."

"But he will certainly ask as a supplementary when a definite statement can be expected."

"And you can say 'At the earliest possible opportunity'."

There was a pause at the other end of the line. Then, "Well, I see." Another pause. "We are having problems."

"I do appreciate that."

"Are you hopeful that the money will eventually be forthcoming from some goatbag?"

"Very hopeful."

176

"Good." The voice sounded relieved. "So long as I've got something to keep them happy."

"We'll do our best."

"Thank you. Thank you very much. I'm sorry to trouble you, but there *is* some urgency . . ."

TUESDAY   2 *December*

At 5.15 p.m., when she brought in his typed letters to sign
(including another one to British Rail), Deborah Leigh said,
"Looks like snow, Mr Cunliffe."

He turned his head to look out of the window. A typical
December London evening, it appeared to him – oil-black clouds
tinged with the red and yellow lights of the city so that the whole
sky looked like a smouldering coal.

"And I see from the paper I bought to read with my lunch
that there's a threat of a lightning strike by the engine-drivers."

"God help this country!"

"Are you still going to try for the 5.55, Mr Cunliffe?"

He sighed and said, "I shall have to."

"Might be even worse than the time there was that power cut."

"Alice has invited guests to dinner. The Misses Fotheringham
and an Indian."

"You might miss dinner."

"No alternative but to try."

She looked at the carpet, drew thoughtful little doodles on her
shorthand pad. Head down like that, each separate hair of her
fringe exquisitely lacquered on to the ivory of her forehead,
there was a statuesque quality about her, a serenity and yet a
youthfulness. For a full minute, neither of them spoke. Then he
said "Hell, Miss Leigh! For Christ's sake . . . why am I always
trying to kill myself for other people? Get me Mrs Cunliffe on the
telephone!"

There followed an uncomfortable five minutes. He very rarely
stayed up at his club. Alice never liked being alone at night. As
he put down the receiver, he was left with an echo of ache ringing in his ears from the other end of the line which he smothered
by shouting through the open door. "Well, we've got to eat, I
suppose, Debbie . . . so you better book a table."

"At Frascati's, Mr Cunliffe?"

178

He hesitated. He had been fully aware in the past weeks of an air of ever so slightly injured innocence, of grievance bravely borne emanating from Miss Deborah Leigh. Every now and then, he had made feelers towards repairing the relationship, but their reception had been cool. She kept on bringing up the subject of Frascati's interlaced with the preparations that all the girls were making for Millicent Smith's, H.F.'s Personal Assistant's, imminent departure. Cunliffe never liked any sort of tension in his personal relations. Friendship was an absolute essential in his scheme of things. As he watched her sitting there so prettily, he thought to himself that here and now was presenting itself an ideal opportunity to heal the wound. And after all, a gentleman always kept his word. He would meet no one of his acquaintance at Frascati's at this time. And it was only five minutes' walk from the office.

"What time shall I book, Mr Cunliffe?"

"Let's make it eight o'clock . . . then we can get some work done before we go."

Leaving at seven forty-five, seeing the light on, Franklin looked in, seemed pleased and grateful to find the Company's business still being pursued. "Couple of keen types, eh? Goodnight, Gordon."

"Goodnight, H.F."

They arrived at the restaurant just before eight, and immediately they were enveloped in its warm perfumed womb. As he followed her up the stairs, he saw just in front of him the swing of her skirt, heard the soft hissing sound of her heels in the deep silky pile of the carpet. It was the first time he had ever been to Frascati's in the evening, and now there was another quality to it – conspiratorial, a hint of wickedness, just the slightest suggestion that behind those red furry walls were girls in red velvet swings, the rustle of can-can petticoats, the soft sound of clothes descending, the glimmer of marble baths and the splash of water against bare flesh. The candles on the tables sketched on the scented dusk the almond shapes of women's eyes. Is this, he thought, the next step up – your business friends to lunch, but your girl friends to dinner?

The Head Waiter led them to a table in the corner.

"Like it?"

"Fabulous!"

"What are you going to eat?"

She was hidden by the enormous menu. "I'm completely lost. You order for me."

He ordered cream of pumpkin soup, sole au vin blanc, pigeon à la catalane, finishing with a strawberry sorbet.

"And what about wine? Shall we have a martini to start with, and then a white wine with the pigeon?"

"That would be lovely."

He discussed with the wine waiter, finally settled on a Montrachet. And when the martinis came, "Cheers, Debbie! Good health and a long life!"

"And you, Mr Cunliffe."

This was an evening of pleasure, and it was with pleasure that he looked at her, sitting very still, very upright, hands in her lap, eyes looking at him, large and dark, having in each iris, miniaturised, a tiny candleflame.

During the soup, they spoke of her. He knew a fair amount about her – a doctor's daughter, almost went to university, preferred what she called "making my own way in the world". She shared a Bloomsbury flat with two other secretaries which they had recently been decorating. It was of the experiments, adventures, triumphs and disasters of this exercise that he now learned.

"I hope you like the pigeon, Debbie?"

"Mr Cunliffe, it's delicious!"

He fingered the stem of his wine glass. "I don't honestly see, Debbie, that you need to keep up this Mr Cunliffe. Reminds me too much of Nettleship and Hammond. After all, we're not here on *business*. We simply can't have you drinking Montrachet '28 in candlelight, and calling me Mr Cunliffe. Try Gordon for size!"

"Gordon," she said, putting her hands up and cupping her chin. "I've always liked the name Gordon."

"Deborah is a nice name."

She inclined her head, "I prefer Debbie."

He had made a great fuss over the petit pois – cooked in parsley and butter with just the slightest hint of garlic and mint. He had been ever so slightly doubtful about the Montrachet, until he had been reassured that she loved it. The candles were burning low. The talk in the restaurant had died down to a muted softness as they finished the sorbet.

"Fabulous," she said, putting her napkin to her small pink mouth. "Fabulous . . . I *did* enjoy it, Gordon."

"Cigarette?"

"Thank you."

He passed his silver case over to her. In doing so, his fingers touched hers. He flared his lighter, holding her hand so as to keep her cigarette steady.

"This has been a lovely evening, Debbie." He made a moue at her. "Not what I expected at all."

"Will it be over now . . . at Blakeneys?"

"I expect so. The Misses Fotheringham fortunately leave early."

"The Misses Fotheringham are not to your taste then?"

He gave an exaggerated shudder. "Long-faced, high-voiced, big wooden beads."

"How do you like your women, Gordon?"

He smiled mysteriously. He had, in fact, never been a womaniser at all – he had never had the time. He had always considered women to be somehow one of the big prizes at the top of the tree – something delicious he would find when he ascended to the topmost stair of Frascati's. Only Alice – poor Alice! Cryptically he said, "I like my steaks rare. It's only then that you get the flavour."

The dinner was progressing to its tranquil end with coffee and Turkish Delight and Chateauneuf brandy. The candles were guttering out, one by one. The atmosphere now was both drowsy and intoxicating – the rustle of silk, whispers, an electric tingling lighting the dream, making it come alive. Then suddenly she said, "Oddly enough, I was in Ocklington over the week-end. In a friend's car."

"You should have come to Blakeneys."

"I did."

In an immediate stereo flash, he saw Blakeneys both as she would expect and as she had seen it – shabby, small, the thatch needing repair, the unmade road muddy, the gate off its hinges.

181

"You should have called."

"Oh, we didn't want to impose." She paused. "What's that funny little tree near the gate with the blue-green leaves?"

"Oh, that's Alice's eucalyptus."

"Looks queer."

"Unusual, I agree."

"What did you say you were asking for it?"

"Thirty-five thousand."

"Mmm!"

So now she knew. Another little false façade to be added to the others – the white lies about Peterson Brothers, his role as double agent in the Ocklington property deal, his communications with Sir Ralph Mannering, the two faces of the Chairman of the Passengers' Consultative Committee. Another defence had gone. How much more had she guessed? How many more twos had she put on twos to make four? But then a confidential secretary *did* know everything. That was what she was there for – to know all the secrets about her boss – nobody pretends to be whiter than white – and protect him.

But little confidential secretaries weren't as clever as their bosses. He said triumphantly, "And I got it."

"I'm surprised."

Indeed perhaps so – for he had not heard over the telephone, but had personally been along to the estate agents. He had shown two lots of people round Blakeneys on successive Saturday afternoons when Alice had gone shopping and then out to tea with her friends. The wife of the last couple had fallen in love with it – but she must have possession before Christmas. There was talk of a family party of relatives from America.

"Have you told your wife?"

"Not yet."

"When are you going to tell her?"

He shifted uneasily. "Soon."

"Where are you going to live?"

"In London somewhere. I'm a trifle tired of commuting."

"They'll miss you on the Passengers' Committee."

"Maybe. But they'll just have to manage without me."

"I've often wondered, Gordon, why you don't drive up."

"I haven't a car."

She wrinkled her small nose. "Isn't that a bit odd, considering?"

"Well, the roads are so packed . . . hardly worth it."

"Better than go-slows, strikes, being stranded." She laughed. "And thinking up new excuses for H.F."

There was hardly a candle left alight now. The red tips of cigarettes, the red furry walls were smudging into a smoky grey. Frascati's had turned into a cosy confessional. Now was the time for confidences, for easings of mind, for sympathy.

"I'll tell you something, Debbie, something I haven't told anybody. But I know I can trust you."

"You can trust me, Gordon."

"Just after I came to this firm, I had an unfortunate accident. It wasn't my fault, truly, Debbie."

"I'm sure it wasn't, Gordon."

"A woman on a pedestrian crossing. She died."

"That must have been awful for you!"

"Oh, God, Debbie . . . *you* can understand." He took hold of her hand in the darkness and held it hard. "The police . . . they more or less told me it was my bad luck. Exemplary sentence. Disqualified from driving. *Me!*"

"How unfair!"

"Fortunately, it wasn't in the papers."

"That was something."

"Debbie, now you understand the position. *Fully* understand it. Alice was so fond of Blakeneys. I didn't want to drag her back to London. That's really why I worked so hard at the Consultative Committee – trying to get a decent service. But now I recognise it's been a losing battle all along."

"You think the Ocklington Line will close, after all?"

"I'm *sure* it will." He paused and gave her a wry smile. "So you see, circumstances have been too strong for me. Fate has simply stepped in. The gods have had their sport with me and Alice."

"It's cruel, Gordon!"

"Now I shall have to try to find some place quickly."

It was her turn to pause. "Gordon –"

"Yes, Debbie?"

"There's a house I saw the other day. Number 17, Marlborough Square."

"Where's Marlborough Square?"

"Well, it's in Islington. Not far from Peterson Brothers."

"Sounds as though it might be convenient."

"It's on the big side . . . but so cheap! An executor's sale, unsold at auction. It'll go for a song . . . and Gordon, it's *lovely*! White-painted façade, portico, real Georgian. Are you interested?"

"I certainly am."

"Shall I get the particulars?"

"Do that, Debbie." He leaned across the table so his forehead made contact with hers. "Most kind of you, taking my problems on board. I'm touched."

"It would be far better, living in London. All that time wasted in the train. Alice will see far more of you."

"I hope I can make her understand."

"I'm sure you will be able to."

They sat there, the last in the restaurant, with the waiter waiting in the gloaming with the bill. Cunliffe suddenly saw the phosphorescent hands on her tiny wristwatch.

"Good God . . . look at the time!"

He signed the bill, helped Debbie on with her coat. Back down the red-carpeted stairs outside into the cold.

It was snowing – snowing hard. On the news-stand, the Evening Standard poster CHAOS AT EAST CROYDON.

Debbie pointed it out. "I was right, Gordon."

"You were right, Debbie."

"Where are you going to spend the night?"

"At my club. I should have given them a ring."

"But you'll never get a taxi."

"Oh, I'll manage somehow."

They began walking along the snowy pavement. "Well, in an emergency like this," she said, "there's always my flat. It's just round the corner. So long as you don't mind the couch in the living-room."

"That's awfully sweet of you, Debbie."

They turned left out of Germain Street, walked under a sheltering wall for a further five minutes. Then she led the way up three steps.

"Oh, by the way," she said, as she turned the key in the

184

door, "Mary and Kate are away, staying with Mary's aunt in Exeter."

In spite of the central heating, the flat was just slightly on the chilly side and smelled of fresh new paint. She lit the gas-fire, took him into her bedroom to hang up his coat. A small neat bedroom, chintz curtains at the window, pink quilted coverlet on the bed, a Chinese print of a horse on the wall.

He helped her take off her coat. He kissed her cheek, then moved round to her lips. The small trim body fitted nicely into his large arms.

"Miss Leigh –?"

"Yes, Mr Cunliffe?"

He stood with her at the far end of the platform, looking up to the north along the dark empty line, waiting.

It was like being on the prow of a ship here, tapering to a point and exposed, away from the superstructure of the station behind – waiting-rooms and refreshment-rooms and the steps up to the street. On either side were the tall thin rectangular blocks of East Croydon, like giant dominoes with their lights the illuminated dots.

The wind felt fresh on Blake's face. He was exhilarated, simply being with her. He had put his arm round her, and she had put her head sideways on top of his shoulder, so that now, joined together, it was as though they were a combined figure-head here at the front of this cold concrete ship.

The 5.55 had deposited them here – along with others from the second Victorian lamp standard, Lady Marjorie Mannering and Bill Cody, Sheila Tate, Miss Price and Mr Osborne and those unidentified blobs that waited farther down Ocklington platform. Some authoritative voice had called "Everybody out!" and when the train was empty, it had simply disappeared. Standing there all crowded together, a choir by the waiting-room had started singing "Why are we waiting?"

"I don't know," a railwayman had told them. "Because there'll be no more trains tonight. Lightning strike of all drivers till the milk train tomorrow." Railwaymen were often wrong.

The singing had turned to groaning – but still they waited.

185

Here there was a serenity, a stillness. Nothing moved but the snow softly falling.

One by one, on those giant crossword puzzles of offices, the lights went out, the darkening city merging with the night. This was eternity to him, feeling her against his cheek. This moment he had captured then, wrapped up, tucked away, safe in his little bag of things everlasting. It was impossible that there could be a time when they were *not* here – it was unthinkable.

But it was he who said, "If we wait here much longer you'll be turning into an ice maiden! That chap looks like being right. No more trains tonight."

Others were moving away now too. They walked up the stairs. Blake had queued at the telephone box, had eventually got through to Daphne. The car? Thick snow in Ocklington she said. Couldn't see a yard. No, of course, she wasn't to try, he said. He'd try for a taxi or else get some sort of accommodation in East Croydon, she was not to worry.

But after a number of inquiries it soon became clear that, with the snow getting thicker, no taxis were interested in going as far away as Ocklington. Celia then came up with this friend of hers – a neighbour, Phyl Jefferson, whose flat was less than half a mile away.

As together they walked through the unnaturally deserted streets, thicker and faster the snow came down.

The flat was halfway up one of those magnetic illuminated dominoes. A woman of about sixty with a big motherly bosom, and protuberant myopic eyes, opened the door. She peered at them for a moment in surprise. Blake obviously puzzled her. She stared at him blankly as if she ought to know him but didn't. Then Celia spoke and the woman's face cleared.

"Celia! Great heavens – is it you? Come on! I didn't recognise you for a moment. This *is* a nice surprise." She shivered at the cold air coming in from the corridor. "What a helluva night! Snow! *Ugh!*"

"Sorry to burst in on you like this," Celia said when they were inside the little hall, giving a brief account of the events of the last two hours. "But we're literally –"

"Orphans of the storm. Well, I'm glad you came. Great heavens yes! I'd've been monstrously hurt if you hadn't." She led

186

the way into a minute kitchen with white-tiled walls and a bright neon light. An electric clock said nine thirty-five. The woman switched on a coffee percolator. "Have you eaten? No, silly question. Don't answer it. Of course you haven't. Bacon and eggs do? No, Celia, don't argue! You know me. Stubborn as you are sometimes. I'm delighted to have you. Great heavens, yes!"

She knelt down at the fridge, speaking into it. "Now where am I going to put you. Celia, you can have my bed. Your friend . . ."

"I'm so sorry," Celia said, recovering herself. "Phyl, this is Edward Blake. Phyl Jefferson. As I told you we're old friends. Neighbours for years."

"Held each other's hands in numerous crises, eh?" Phyl peeled off some bacon rashers from a plastic pack. "Glad to meet you, Edward. It *is* Edward, isn't it? Not Ted, or Ed or anything?"

"Edward."

"Thought so." She dropped the bacon into a pan and slid it on to the stove. "And where do you fit into the picture, Edward?" she asked frankly, her protuberant eyes fixed on his face.

"Just a fellow-commuter."

Phyl's eyes expressed disbelief but she said nothing.

"His wife," Celia spoke clearly and with emphasis, "couldn't fetch him. They live at Ocklington, and there's quite a heavy fall there."

"Pity," Phyl said. Blake was sure she was not altogether referring to the snow.

"And I'm *not* taking your bed," Celia said, setting her mouth firmly. "Somewhere warm to sit will be absolute bliss, won't it, Edward? They're promising us the milk train in the morning. And it's that or nothing."

Phyl looked as if she was going to protest. Her eyes flickered from one to the other of them. Then she shrugged and appeared to give in. She broke a couple of eggs into the pan and basted them in silence.

"How's James?" Celia asked.

"Marvellous, thanks. James is my married son, Edward. Flourishing like the green bay. And multiplying like a bunny-rabbit."

187

"How many now?" Celia smiled. "He'd just started college when we left."

"Four, and one on the way."

"Bliss," Celia murmured.

Phyl turned off the gas under the pan with a smart snap. "How's Dylan?" she asked in a different tone.

"Fine."

"Really keeping," a pause, "fit?"

"Very fit, thanks."

"Well, come on you two." Phyl slipped the eggs and bacon on to two warm plates. "If you want to wash up first, you know where it is, Celia. Men can wash in the kitchen, my old man used to say."

And when Celia had gone, "I take it you haven't met Dylan?"

He felt her eyes on his face searchingly as he soaped his hands. "No."

She handed him a towel, "Then you have a treat in store, Edward."

"She seems very fond of him."

"Does she?"

She set out some mats and cutlery on the breakfast bar.

"In fact, she tells me he's a genius."

"I am disappointed in you, Edward," the woman said, gently enough. He didn't ask her why.

In any case there was the sound of the bathroom door opening. Just before Celia appeared, the woman touched his arm, and said, "Be good to her, Edward. It's time somebody was."

The smell of bacon and eggs and coffee still lingered in the sitting-room when Phyl had gone to bed. A large gas-fire hissed in the stone fireplace. There was a sheepskin rug in front of it, and two comfortable armchairs. Phyl had given them a stack of cushions, and Celia sat on the hearth-rug, with her hands clasped round her knees, and her back resting against the chair opposite to him. She had taken off her shoes and was curling her toes in the fur of the rug. The food and warmth made him sleepy. He was lapped again with that delusory feeling of absolute well-being. On the stone mantel a brass clock ticked. Towards midnight, the already muffled traffic from far below died away to a snowy silence. He had a childish desire to look out from a warm room at the snowflakes falling and, as if in response to his unspoken thought, Celia got up agilely, and drew back the curtains from the big modern window. Immediately it became a picture of steel sky and whirling flakes, with far away and blurred the bright colours of the other tall buildings, the shop lights and the neon signs.

"Like an artist's palette," she said, recalling him to their first real conversation together.

"Or oil spilled on a wet pavement?"

"Are you in oil then?" She came and sat at his feet.

"In so far as my masters . . ." he began just to show that he remembered every word of it. Then he broke off and laughed. He rumpled her brown hair, and sat twisting the silky waves of it round his fingers. It was as soothing as trailing his hands in water. They talked about Phyl and the days when they were neighbours. The V and A, the Treasury, what might happen if the line closed, the countryside round Ocklington and Fordbridge.

After a while, they turned out the reading lamp and sat in the glow of the gas-fire, the better to watch the whirling hypnotic flakes. The better to savour that feeling high up here of absolute cut-off from the rest of the world.

"If you look at them long enough they seem to fall in exorable patterns," he said.

"Like sparrows?" she asked dryly. "Do you reckon that not one falleth without our Lord . . . ?"

"Alas, no. I would like to think so. But my civil-service mind finds the contingency highly unlikely."

"Yet," she clasped her knees. Her delicate skin was flushed, her eyes bright. In the soft red glow she looked very young and vulnerable. "Yet there *is* a pattern. The structure patterns of the snowflake are often similar to the florets of elderberry and cow parsley."

"That I didn't know." He was suddenly possessed of a feeling of how little he did know. Of a world of experience pressing from outside, whose most shallow periphery he had not yet begun to explore.

"So there *might* be a pattern in other things. It's just possible."

"All things are possible." He put his hand on her shoulder. All things seemed possible when he was with her.

About midnight, though he wanted most desperately to stay awake, he kept drifting off to sleep. He was in and out of the dream. Then the dream became continuous. Waking and sleeping, it was the same. The dream was this room, this place. The ultimate reality was that he loved her as he had never loved anyone before. And waking was the nightmare beginning.

Some sound roused him about five-thirty. When he opened his eyes, the room was stiflingly hot. Celia was lying curled up on the hearth-rug, her hair lying like Silas Marner's scattering of gold. Her arms were folded over her chest, cradling herself.

She woke as soon as he touched her arm. He stretched himself and walked over to the window. The sky was of clear indigo darkness. It had stopped snowing.

And far below in the city streets, the patterned flakes had melted away.

Tucked in tight, two of the first in the dimly lit waiting-room, Mr Osborne and Miss Price sat in the corner close against each other, perfectly comfortable in spite of the hard wooden bench. The stove was not on, but within a few minutes the place was so crowded that sufficient human heat was generated to be warm enough. There was a smell of dampness and too many bodies and the far away smoky smell that lurks round railway stations everywhere – perhaps the dying breath of ghostly steam engines long since departed on their last excursion. They were too near the telephone boxes – they who had no one to phone – so that for the first two hours around them was a continuous pushing and shoving, the sound of coins being pressed in slots, a succession of different-coloured voices – exasperated, practical, frantic, humorous, tender, frustrated – illuminating their predicament to their homes.

"Where's Mr Cunliffe?" Miss Price asked. "Did you see him, Mr Osborne?"

"I don't think he was on the train."

190

"Pity. *He'd* have done something."

"Oh, Mr Cunliffe would have got things moving."

Beyond the grimy glass windows, the black night had become polka-dotted with white spots, increasing as they talked.

"Sooner in here than out there, Miss Price."

"Will we be here all night, Mr Osborne?"

"Oh, They will get something organised eventually, Miss Price. Give Them a chance."

In the centre of the waiting-room, people were still standing, leaning against each other for support, sporadically muttering amongst themselves. Now and again a match flared to add another glowing cigarette-end to the dozen other red stars in the semi-darkness. No trains ran, no footsteps now on the platform. They were too far away from the roads to hear the cars, and in any case, East Croydon now had become muffled in snow. They were all pressed together as they were in the moving carriages each day, a cross-section of the good-humoured, long-suffering British public caught in this sooty preserving-jar, doing nothing, patiently waiting, expecting – what?

"Comfy, Miss Price?"

"Not too bad, considering."

"You don't look too warm to me." He began to remove his overcoat. "Peaky."

"I'm all right. Truly, Mr Osborne."

But he insisted on spreading his coat like an eiderdown over them, tucking it right up to their chins.

"I'm a bit worried about you, Miss Price."

"You shouldn't be, Mr Osborne."

"You've looked so white. How have you been sleeping?"

"Well, you know, it's a bit lonely."

"And I'm sure you're not eating."

"Oh, I do myself well."

"Sandwiches and stuff. Not proper meals."

"Well, it's so much trouble cooking for one."

"Just what I thought! And it's not good enough. You'll make yourself ill." His hands came out of the overcoat and opened his big briefcase. "I've been thinking, Miss Price, what you need is *sun.*"

Out of the briefcase, like a magician out of a hat, he produced

191

holiday brochure after holiday brochure, their brilliant covers gay and sparkling in the gloom of the waiting-room.

"You and I are going to go for a holiday."

"Oh, I couldn't, Mr Osborne!"

"No couldn't about it." He flipped through pages and pages of coloured photographs of glamorous places – Tunisia, Athens, Cyprus, Madeira, Istanbul. "The only questions to be decided are where, and when."

"But they're so expensive!"

"Not for what you get."

"And I'd never fly."

"Why not?"

"Oh, Mr Osborne, they say it's so awful. Going up and coming down."

"Once you're up, you'd enjoy it."

"I'd be too scared."

"You'll be all right, Miss Price. I'll be with you." He spread two glittering pages in front of her. "Look at this one! Christmas in Morocco. Includes a gala Christmas Eve Dinner party with wines, cabaret and a present from Worldspan. What about that, eh?"

"Oh, Mr Osborne . . . it *does* look lovely!"

They turned over the pages, comparing the merits of almond-blossom time in the Algarve with the wine festival in the Rhine valley. All around them now, the packed community had settled down. Voices became muted, then died down altogether. A woman was humming a lullaby half under her breath in rhythm to the soft sounds of breathing.

Gradually the voices of Miss Price and Mr Osborne became slower and slurred as though they had sucked enough hot milk for tonight. Their eyes closed. Off they dropped to sleep simultaneously, their arms round each other, their heads together. In the sudden flash of a match from a sleepless smoker, under the brown woollen overcoat they looked like babes in the wood covered by autumn leaves.

Like that, they slept. Like that, the hours ticked by till the darkness outside turned smudgy grey. Then suddenly there was a clanking of wheels, a shudder of speed and a flickering of lighted window-frames.

Miss Price woke up with a start. "What's that?"

"It's all right, Miss Price," Mr Osborne said soothingly. "It's the relief of Mafeking. They have got the trains working again. Just as I said They would!"

Snow – early December and already it was snowing. Lady Marjorie Mannering stood with her gloved hands thrust deep in the pockets of her mink coat, blinking her eyes, entranced by the steadily falling flakes. She could feel Bill Cody's hand holding her elbow, feel the light press of his arm against hers. Snow hushed the diminished traffic and quietened the streets. She was held in a moment of suspended magic.

Together with the others, they had been ejected from the warm. But unlike the rest they hadn't waited for long on the platform.

"We'll be hanging around here all night," Bill Cody had said.

"At least, let's try to *do* something!" The cry of the rich and the spoiled. She had sounded, to her own regret, exactly like Ralph.

Yet what could they do? A lightning strike, and no more trains. Only snow, and more snow. Faster and faster. Snow gusting in under the inadequate awning. Snow resting, as if they were lines of lost and dying sheep, on the silent, patient taxi queue at the other end of the approach.

A large feathery flake landed on Marjorie's cheek, at the side of her mouth. She put out her tongue and caught it. Delicious and cold. Redolent of childhood.

Long-distant childhood, she told herself firmly. Time passed faster than the whirling flakes. It could not be caught or held. Or if you tried to it melted between your lips. Already as they stood there, the polka-dotted pavement had become a thin white carpet.

"What do you suggest we do?" Bill asked her, watching her face. "Apart from making a snowman."

"Oh, that would be super, wouldn't it?" She was going to ask him if he ever wanted to be young again. To build a snowman, run barefoot in the dewy grass, swim naked . . . she stopped her erring mind. She couldn't ask him that. He was a man and still young.

"Say the word, and we'll make one now."

This trick of answering her unspoken question, reassuring her innermost need. She shook her head. Then she stretched out the tip of her brown suède boot, pressed it down and made a footprint in the virgin white.

Symbolic, she thought. Though none of this is of *my* doing. It is not my fault if the train does not run and the snow falls. These are Acts of God. *Your* doing, Lord.

"I must telephone Ralph," she said suddenly straightening with resolution. She pulled the collar of her coat up round her cheeks.

"Of course you must." Bill Cody watched her with a neutral uncommitted expression.

"He might send Robbins up for me."

Bill Cody nodded.

"Though the road'll be hell."

"Well, let's find a box where there isn't a ten-mile queue." He pulled her towards the booking hall behind. Through the half-misted doorway they could see long dejected queues.

"There are bound to be others," he said.

"If one just knew where?" she looked up at him, her eyes very clear and wide. For the first time, she thought we are both dissembling with one another. Not because we want to deceive or explain. But for exactly the opposite. We both want to be sure that the other feels the same. That what is about to happen is what the other wants also.

"Most hotels have telephones," Bill Cody said as she silently asked him to say.

"But the big hotels will probably be busy."

"Then we must find a small one. I suppose," he said after a moment, "we could always try getting a taxi to take us to Ocklington."

"Down Dead Man's Hill in this stuff? Not a hope."

"And that blasted taxi queue hasn't moved since we've been here."

"Come on, let's walk and see what we find. That taxi queue hasn't moved for the simple reason there hasn't been a single taxi along." She put her hand through his arm. "Let's walk and see what we find. We're marooned, Mr Cody. Praise be and Alleluia!"

"Amen, to that," he said. "Amen."

"What did he say?" Bill Cody was waiting for her outside the single telephone box in the foyer of the small hotel. The foyer was warm and clean. There was a red patterned carpet on the floor, a table covered in magazines and a coke fire burning in the fireplace.

"Ralph?" she shrugged. "He was very concerned, of course."

"Of course."

"He'd been in touch with British Rail and the A.A. Parker had heard of the weather conditions on the television so Ralph had been busy."

"How about Robbins?" Bill Cody looked down at her upturned face, his expression blank.

"We *both* preferred that Robbins didn't risk it." She took off her hat, and shook the drops of snow from it. "He's old. Probably give him a heart attack if he got stuck on the hill."

"So . . . ?" He put his hands on her shoulders.

"There's nothing we can do about it," she whispered. It is like walking through dream obstacles, she thought. Put out a hand and they vanish.

Five years ago, she had launched a ship for one of Ralph's subsidiary companies. She had marvelled at the way the holds that barred the ship's progress to its element should, one by one, drop away at the crack of the bottle and the press of the button.

"Except book rooms," he said, standing now with his back to the fire, his hands thrust into his trouser pockets, swinging himself backwards and forwards on his heels.

"*A* room," she corrected.

"No." He shook his head.

She came and stood close to him, eyes wide. Pleading gave way to embarrassment. Embarrassment to anger. He put his hand on her arm. She shook it off. "I wish I'd told Robbins to come. And to hell with him."

195

"Were you thinking of Robbins?"

"No, damn you!"

He smiled down at her shaking his head. "You've never done this before."

"Of course I haven't. No doubt *you have!*"

"Perhaps. On the other hand perhaps *not.*"

"Revealing as always," she snapped, her anger subsiding all the same.

"What worries me is this . . ." he put his finger under her chin and tilted up her face. "You might change your mind."

"Of course I won't."

"I don't mean *tonight*. Or *tomorrow*. But after that. You may want Bill Cody and all his works" – he pulled his finger across his throat – "forgotten."

"I doubt it. But make your point."

"Just supposing, *ever*, your husband decided to check on you. Oh, don't say he wouldn't. You never know what anyone is capable of. He could easily do it. You're not exactly an undistinguished-looking person. If he did, the evidence would be there to hand."

She sighed and smiled, letting him turn her round and walk towards the reception desk. Should Ralph ever wish to get rid of a barren faithless wife? As Bill said, one never knew. But if he did, she would want to go.

"We could book in as Smith," she smiled as he pressed the bell for attention.

"I'm booking in as *us*."

"So you really are Bill Cody.'

"It would seem so."

"Are you not making it unnecessarily difficult?"

Their conversation was cut short by the arrival of the receptionist. A middle-aged woman with pink hair and big split almond teeth. "Sorry to keep you, ducks. But I'm having to double up in the bar. The usual girl's got stuck with the snow. Well, what can I do for you?"

"Two singles if you've got them, please."

"For *tonight*?" She sucked her teeth, and cautiously scratched her scalp with a pencil.

"Yes, we've also been stuck with the snow."

"British Rail," Marjorie put in, throwing the receptionist a victim.

"Oh, don't mention *them* to *me*! They make me wild. Yes, ducks. I think I can just do it. One single for the gentleman. Have to put *you* in a *double* if you don't mind, madam. Cost a little extra. But there's a bathroom too. It's all very snug. And it's all we've got."

The receptionist peered at them over the top of the counter, with jaded curiosity. What did she make of the pair of them, Marjorie wondered as they signed the register.

"No baggage, I s'ppose, if you've been stranded?"

Marjorie shook her head.

"Just as well. The porter didn't turn up either. If I give you your keys you can see yourselves up, can't you? You're both on the second floor."

The last dream obstacle was falling away. She knew she was launching herself at gathering speed into unknown waters of perilously unknown depth.

"So this is it," Marjorie thought, as they stood in the doorway of the double room. Bill Cody had paid no more lip-service to his single room than to fetch the towels and the soap.

"Do for you?" he asked, holding the door open and propelling her in.

"Fine."

"You sound not over-sure." He walked over to the window and pulled the floral curtains.

"I'm sure of the room," she smiled.

"But not sure of me?"

"Perhaps." She sat on the edge of the double bed and he came over and unbuttoned her coat. "Remember the first time we met, you said I was a bit of an anachronism?"

"That was the second time we met."

He hung her coat up in the wardrobe, glanced at himself somewhat dejectedly in the mirror, came back and stood over her. He began to take off her dress.

"Was it? Yes, so it was."

"But go on. I remember saying it. Thinking it too." He

197

pulled her to her feet while he slid her dress round her ankles. Then her waist slip, then her bra.

"Well, it's you that's the anachronism."

"Really! How do you make that out?"

"You never seem to ask anyone for anything."

"Not true."

"Not me. You don't ask me like other people do."

"I ask." He kissed her bare shoulder. "I do ask, lovie." His big warm hands slid down to the top of her pants. "I want *you*, damn you! I don't want what you've got. Or anything else, you can hand out. I just want *you*." He straightened up and shouldered his way out of his jacket, pulled at his tie. Lifted his shirt over his head. The room was chilly, and she draped one of his towels round her naked shoulders.

He snatched it off. "I want to see you," he said peremptorily. He leaned over and kissed the skin between her breasts. His chest was deep and strongly muscled, the tanned skin covered with thick black hair.

"Haven't you ever seen a man undress before?" he asked, suddenly.

"No," she shook her head in perfect truth, vehemently.

"What about your husband?"

"He goes into his dressing-room."

"Christ!"

"Come on!" He pulled her to her feet. "Ever bath together?"

"Never."

He ran the water while she brushed her hair with a little hand-bag brush. Then he sat behind her in the bath with his thick strong legs on either side of her, soaping her back.

She averted her eyes like a young girl from his desire made powerfully manifest, and put herself in the bed, sheets drawn up to her chin as soon as he had towelled her dry.

She was suddenly acutely aware of how woefully inexperienced she was. A bride at twenty-two, then a coming of age of marriage. Twenty-one years of Ralph's courtship and passion. Would Ralph's painstaking manipulations of her body, even his courteous fair play – some pleasure for you, some pleasure for me, like the gardener they'd had who used to scatter three handfuls of seeds, one for the birds, one for the worms, and one for

198

me – be any preparation for *now*? The young girl quaked inside the calm middle-aged woman.

Bill came out of the bathroom, switched out the light and drew back the curtains. It was snowing heavily. He stood for a moment watching the whirling flakes. Light from the neon strips in the street below cast a pink and muffled incandescence. It sculpted his huge handsome body. She felt no longer frightened, but weak and boneless in her desire for him.

Before he pulled back the bedclothes, he cupped her face in one hand, trailing the fingers of his other over its features, as if learning them like a blind man.

Then he was in beside her. She felt the shock of warm tense flesh. His hands moved over her skin – touching, trailing, melting. When he penetrated her body, she felt an almost unbearable anguish. Then their bodies found each other, moved together, in a breathless furious gallop. Their climax came together. The breaking of a huge engulfing wave inside her, sending spontaneous little tremors of vitality through her whole body.

She fell asleep with her head on his chest. She woke about three. Somewhere a clock chimed. Bill Cody lay as still as an effigy in Ocklington Church. It was snowing harder than ever. The faint glow in the room from the neon lights was blanched by the white pall on the opposite roofs. Everything was very still. She suddenly thought with uncanny certainty, tonight of all nights I have conceived.

It had already begun to snow heavily when Tom Armitage left the railway line, loped his long legs over the wire and set off home over the short-cut across Terrible Down. He had heard from his mates that both Unions, ASLEF and the NUR, had called a lightning strike, and there would be no more trains south of East Croydon that night.

Inside the living-room of 3 Railway Cottages, his supper was on the table. A big blue tin pot of tea, a hunk of Cheddar cheese and two kippers congealing on a plate beside the bread and butter. His father was watching television by the fire, and the movements of his mother and the sound of the radio could be heard in the little kitchen at the end of the passage.

"Snowing, eh?" his father asked.

"Yes."

"Going to get worse, that's the forecast."

Tom took off his yellow jacket, sat down and bolted his food in silence. Then he got up again, and collected his helmet, goggles and oilskin leggings and cape.

"Where are you going then?" his father asked.

"Out."

"Where are you going, Tom?" his mother asked as he passed her in the kitchen on the way to the shed at the back where he kept his motor bicycle.

"Out."

The Norton started from cold first kick. The powerful headlight picked up the face of a whitening deserted Ocklington. Coming out of the square, he turned right and opened up the throttle, heading north over the Downs through Woosley and Bramfield. He knew that the 5.55 had left Victoria – Sheila would certainly be stranded on East Croydon. And since everything that went wrong with British Rail she blamed on him, he had no doubt that this lightning strike of engine drivers would be laid at his door. But that was nothing – what he was most concerned about was her being stuck on her own up there on the icy station, probably all night surrounded by strangers.

He moved the lever up to full throttle, racing now through the soft flurries of snow, weaving in and out of cars hurrying home before it got worse. He dipped down into East Croydon, skimmed over the icy roads at sixty, screamed up to the station.

She wasn't in the waiting-room. There appeared no sign of her on the platform. He was beginning to think that she had stayed up in London with that girl-friend at the hospital, when he found her more or less where the 5.55 had dropped her, behind a pile of waiting boxes and unmanned trolleys.

"Tom! I'm *freezing*!"

"Sorry about that, love. Why didn't you go into the waiting-room?"

"Because it was full."

"Did you phone your mother?"

"Couldn't. Too much of a queue."

"Well, I've got the Norton here. Soon have you home."

She allowed herself to be led through the crowd.

"Honestly, this is the limit!" She was railing blackly through chattering teeth against British Rail. "Disgrace! You lot never think of other people."

"There's not enough staff to run the line, love."

"Then you should get more."

"We can't, love. That's the trouble. That's what the strikes are about."

"You shouldn't sell tickets if they give no service."

"We don't want to, love. We want to close the line."

"You mean *you* do!"

Outside the station, he slipped off his helmet and put it over her hair.

"Careful! I've just had it done."

He fastened the strap round her chin, put his cape over her coat.

"Up on the pillion then . . . that's right!" The Norton's engine blared, the headlamps fingering the blanched walls and windows of East Croydon's shops. Tilting forty degrees, he skidded round the corner of the High Street, and dodging two lorries, roared south.

Muzzy haloes in the cold mist, one by one the street lamps lengthened behind them, then gave out altogether. As they climbed, the snow became worse. The black night had turned white – blinding, dazzling white, glittering back into Tom's eyes. He could hardly see beyond the spurt of frozen grit thrown off the front wheel. The wind was stronger too, blowing hard against them, as houses and trees gave way to bleak fields on the bald top of the Downs. Half blinded, through the opaqueness ahead he watched for each gleaming diamond reflector on the strips of white line. There was no traffic now – just the two of them on the Norton rocketing through the swirling snowfilled night. It was as though the roof of the sky was now one vast igloo that was disintegrating in icy fragments on top of them.

His face felt frozen stiff. Every few seconds, he had to wipe the snow from his goggles. He could feel her arms round his waist, her body hard against his, her face curled into the nape of his neck, using his head as a shield against the wind and the biting bullets of hail and frozen snow. Twice the Norton skidded badly, the wheels wobbling and shuddering as he frantically fought to right the machine. He nearly lost himself, almost taking the wrong fork. Then civilisation showing up bleakly with the shadows of Woosley, and they started dipping down into the Weald.

Dark Ocklington now – a ghost town buried in a white shrouding sheet, the road ahead a virgin carpet of snow, the tyres crunching and sliding as he turned left into Station Approach, stopped outside Number 6.

A rectangle of blurred yellow.

"*Sheila* . . . is that you, Sheila?"

"Yes, Mother. And I'm *frozen!*"

"Come on in, poor darling . . . before you catch your death! Who's that you're with?" A plump grey silhouette advanced to the garden gate. A pair of spectacles peered through the snow. "Oh, I might have guessed! Whatever possessed you, Tom Armitage, taking our Sheila out pillion on a night like this?"

"HAVE you told your wife about Number Seventeen, Gordon?"

"Not yet, Debbie."

The particulars of 17 Marlborough Square had been obtained. Together they had gone along to view, and the visit had been a success. The house was in good repair and, considering all things, not too expensive to heat and maintain. The rooms, apart from a large drawing-room that would be ideal for business entertaining, were moderately sized and beautifully proportioned. It was an elegant and impressive establishment, and as she had said, the price was rock-bottom. Immediate cash was what was wanted, and quite apart from the fact that the money from the sale of Blakeneys would be paid as soon as vacant possession had been given, a bridging loan would be easy to arrange from Nettleship and Hammond. "Do you think your wife will like it?" Debbie had asked him. "Oh, I'm sure she will," he had replied.

She would hate it – there was no doubt about that. Not even a railinged bit of lawn, not a flower, not a tree. A paved court only and battlements of grey roofs.

"When are you going to tell her, Gordon?"

"One of these days."

"It'll have to be soon, won't it?"

"I'm waiting for the right moment. She doesn't like change."

There was a pause. Cunliffe searched around his desk for a different subject of conversation. She had been needling him on this one for days. "Oh, by the way, this letter from the lawyers –"

"I like a change."

He looked up. There were two red spots on the pink and white cheeks and her eyes were very bright.

"Millicent Smith goes next week."

His forehead wrinkled. He did not understand this drift of the conversation.

"H.F. asked me to take on her job."

He looked at her, horrified – he who kept his feelings and emotions under tight control behind a smooth façade. With her only had he let the mask drop. Only she had been allowed to suck his secrets. All sorts of confidences about home life, business, his struggles with British Rail, his ambitions, his philosophy of success, his black and white lies were contained in that neat little bosom. And in any case, with her now, he had a special relationship. There had been no further repetition of the Frascati adventure, but nevertheless he felt there had been between them a drawing-together, a trusted familiarity. Only on the most public of occasions now did he call her anything but Debbie.

"You're not going to do it!"

"Well, I said I'd think about it."

"What's there to think about?"

She extended four small fingers with crimson tips, and ticked them off one by one. "Promotion, more pay, more holiday, business trips abroad." She paused. "And H.F. is such a dynamo!"

"But, Debbie, you wouldn't *leave* me!"

"Why not?"

What had got into her? Why was there all this fuss about telling Alice? What business had it to do with her? What business had Franklin to trespass on his property? Was he suspicious of him or something? It was not right that Franklin should have this key to his nakedness. It was underhand, peeping-Tom, and if there wasn't a law against it, there should be. Some definite coercion, a sort of chastity belt for confidential personal assistants – they should never be allowed to leave their boss, and when he died they should be walled up in his tomb.

"Is that all, Mr Cunliffe?"

Her head had bowed again. The red spots had disappeared from view. The small neat figure was very still and quiet. He ached to pulverise that pink and white flesh and the chicken bones into fragments. Anger and irritation mounted inside him. Perhaps, he thought, feeling the thundering of his heart and the blood rising to his face, there's a murderer in each one of us.

"That is all, Miss Leigh."

And yet even as he watched her go through the door, arms by her sides, neat skirt primly swaying, nice little legs on their pretty little shoes, he was aware that he would be lost without her. The quietness and tranquillity she brought was ointment to his rough red spirit one skin below his smooth surface. He had a sort of ache when the door closed behind her, and he was left alone behind the big mahogany desk, looking at the empty three-legged stool.

When he arrived home that evening on the 5.55, Alice was out in the garden, flashing a torch over the rubbish dump and calling to the cat.

"Gordon, I haven't seen him all day."

"He'll be all right."

"You don't think a fox could have got him?"

"Not him!"

All the same, she stayed outside calling him while Cunliffe went inside. Eventually a dark shape materialised from behind the eucalyptus tree and was immediately chided and caressed at the same time. There was no sign of supper; Alice had been too occupied, looking for the cat.

"It won't be long, I promise."

"I'm not very hungry, Alice."

"You're feeling all right, Gordon?"

"Oh yes, yes. It's just that –"

All the same, he waited until they had finished the soup and fruit and cheese she now prepared. He poured himself a stiff whisky and soda. She sat on the sofa in front of the fire, occupied half with watching the television and half with stitching away on embroidery round a cloak. The cat sat purring at her feet.

"Alice, these days I do get home feeling so *very* very tired."

"Oh you poor dear! Why don't you pop up to bed and I'll bring you a hot drink?"

"You have no idea what that damned Ocklington Line is like."

"But as Chairman of the Committee, Gordon, you've –"

"I've done what I can, Alice. All I can."

"Surely after the Warborough meeting, hasn't there been an improvement?"

"Alice, that Line needs *millions* spent on it. And British Rail haven't got the staff. They can't *get* the staff."

"But you got them to promise!"

"They haven't promised anything. They've only postponed the date of closing the Line down."

"I thought the County was going to contribute?"

"They daren't put the rates up any more." He turned his whisky glass round and round in his fingers. "So I'm afraid –"

She got up from the sofa, clutching her embroidery in both her hands. She looked at him over the top of her spectacles, alarm in her eyes, "You're not saying that after all, they'll close the Line!"

"In my opinion, yes."

"You've been so confident!"

"I had to be."

"Even if it did close down, they'd have to make alternative arrangements."

"Buses . . . few and far between, uncomfortable, taking even longer than now."

"But, Gordon –" The full implication of what he was saying, dawned on her. "You're not thinking of selling Blakeneys?"

There was no point in beating about the bush. When it came to the eventual crunch, naked truth was kindest. "I have already sold it."

The storm broke then. Cunliffe had known that it would be impossible to avoid, but he had hoped that it would not be quite so hysterical. What she called her glass menagerie – dogs and rabbits and lions – on the shelf behind the ingle-nook shook to the high wailing of her voice. Tears coursed down her cheeks. The cat, disturbed, turned bright green eyes up to the long white face, then slunk into the kitchen.

"All this measuring up! A fitted carpet? Oh, why didn't you *tell* me? Why did you deceive me?"

"Alice, I had to move fast. And I got a very good price."

"That's no answer, Gordon!" She had fallen back on the sofa and was sobbing now. Incoherent words, something about the birds and the trees, then babble about walls and prison and freedom came choking out in spasms from her lips. "When do we have to go?"

"We'll have Christmas here. Don't worry about that."

"*When* do we have to go?"

"Possession on the 28th of December."

"But we'll have no home! Where are we going to go?"

"We'll get another place easily enough."

"But where?"

"In London."

She closed her eyes and her head collapsed on her lap. "*London!*"

"There," he said. "There, there, there."

He tried to explain, but she would not listen. She couldn't go, she wouldn't go. Wild horses wouldn't drag her. She liked this place. This was the only place in the world where she could breathe. She'd suffocate, that was what would happen to her.

"Alice," he went on saying patiently. "Alice . . . Alice . . . Alice."

When she went on thrashing around in paroxysms of weeping, he reached for her handbag on the window-sill, produced her tranquillisers. "Here . . . take a couple, there's a good girl. Dr Dean would be cross with you if he saw you like this."

"What are you trying to do?" She shrieked at him, slapping at his hand so that the tablets spilled and began running like little white wheels all over the floor. "*Kill* me?"

He said nothing for a while. Gradually the sobs quietened. The room became suddenly still – only the crackling of the wood in the fire, the tiny scrape of the cat's claws in the kitchen as it looked for food. Then he said very quietly, the calm back in his voice, "If I went on commuting much longer, Alice, it would kill *me*. Four businessmen have given up. Couldn't take it any longer. A man the other day. Died in the lavatory. But I've *got* to go on, working hard, providing for us both."

She reached out then and took his hands. "Poor Gordon . . . it must have been awful . . . all those cold journeys day after day. I have been very selfish."

207

That was all she said. They went up to bed shortly afterwards. Twice in the night, he awoke and saw her there, her head very still, her eyes wide open staring at the dark ceiling.

Almost the first thing he said when he reached the office next day was, "I have told Alice about the sale of Blakeneys, Debbie."

She looked up from the pad on her lap. "Have you told her about Number Seventeen, Mr Cunliffe?"

"Who is she, Crispin?"

"Just a girl, Mother."

"That much I have deduced. But who are her family?"

"The Tates."

"Where do they come from?"

"Ocklington."

"*Tate*, you say?"

"Yes, mother."

"I don't know them."

"You don't know everybody, Mother."

"I've never even *heard* of them. They must have come here *very* recently."

"I don't know when they came."

"Where do they live?"

"Near the station, I believe."

"What does her father do?"

"He's in engineering, I think."

"You don't seem to know very much about her, if I may say so, Crispin."

"Mother, I was only fixing up a date."

Crispin Mannering had already had one date with Sheila Tate – and very satisfactory, in his view. He had met her outside the church in his Alfa late one Saturday afternoon, and they had driven down to a dance at a Parkfield hotel overlooking the sea. They had returned rather late, and there had been some problems awaiting her at home, but with the help of her mother she had managed to circumvent them. She had let it be known that her date had an Alfa and not a motorcycle – and that in itself to her mother was enough reason for a girl to come in late.

Sheila had rung Crispin three times at Falklands, getting Mrs Mannering twice. Crispin had rung Sheila four times at 6 Station Approach, getting Mrs Tate three times. "Ever such a nice voice," was her mother's comment to her father.

It was on this second date over which his mother had taxed him, again to Parkfield, that he had enquired whether she had known a girl called Betty Jones.

She shook her head.

"Nice girl. Terribly good fun."

She received the information in silence.

"Took her to Frascati's. You'll have heard of Frascati's?"

She nodded.

"Went to a club afterwards. Have you been to La Vie Parisienne?"

She shook her head.

"Of course it was far too late to drive back home. So we stayed in town. Do you know the Wentworth Hotel?"

"Vaguely."

"I was thinking –" He hesitated. "One night . . . if you'd like to, of course . . . I might try . . . well, a sort of encore. Only this time with *you*."

She was under no doubts as to what he meant. He had kissed her particularly passionately in Applegarth Woods. She had some idea which direction this particular acquaintance would have to take, if it was to blossom further.

"Well, Sheila, what d'you say?"

"Sounds fabulous," she said.

"Raining again," Daphne said, handing Blake his umbrella. "Not to worry! Soon the year will be on the turn."

She kissed him goodbye perfunctorily on the cheek, and then closed the door quickly behind him because the progeny were complaining about the draught.

There was a wind too. Great trundling rain clouds added their darkness to the remnants of night.

Blake walked briskly down the path and shut the gate with finality behind him. The time had now passed when he used these walks to and from the station as a kind of civil-service

209

dialogue between himself and himself. He now admitted that reprehensible and disloyal as it might be, the fact remained that Celia Mortimer represented to him the most important part of his life. That he would find life singularly diminished, not to say almost valueless, if he could not look forward to these brief meetings with her. He no longer asked himself how this foolish, yes, ridiculous, relationship might develop. He no longer asked himself what Daphne would say nor how the children would feel.

Nor was it that he didn't care. In a way, he cared as much as he had ever done, but it was as if his family and he now lived on different planes of existence. Or as if he was inside some unreachable decontamination area and they were contained in another.

Nor did he any longer hurl at himself such outdated and outmoded terms of derision as "No fool like an old fool."

He accepted his love for and need of Celia Mortimer with a kind of awed docility which he would probably have found distasteful, not to say hypocritical, in anyone else. And in accepting it, somehow he gave himself up to living.

Living began the moment he shut the gate behind him. Living was in the moist earthy smell of the December morning, the feel of the wind, the moan of it down the Weald, the way the tyres of passing cars hissed on the damp road, the headlights fingered outlines of the bare trees and sparkled on the dew-dropped webs that hung along the hedgerows. Living quickened with his accelerated heartbeat as he waited under the second Victorian lamp standard, waiting for the train to clank to a halt. Quickened almost unbearably with the first sight of her profile as the driver pulled the 8.01 farther up this morning to allow for the two extra carriages.

He had to sprint twenty yards, and even so he was almost pipped to the seat beside her by the hysterical laddie with the dyed eyebrows.

As it was, the young man in question got himself perched immediately opposite and sat staring at them with a fixed, unblinking concentration that Blake found most disconcerting.

"Did you have a pleasant week-end?" Blake asked Celia Mortimer politely, wondering why words were ever considered necessary. He could have talked Chinese or Hindustani to her and she would have understood. What he really was saying was, "Thank God the week-end is over and we are together again."

"Very pleasant thank you. Did you?"

"Pretty good."

The conversation went on to garden topics and Tom Thumb fuschias. The train accelerated towards the North Downs. The heavy clouds allowed a glimmer of first light through.

The young man opposite never blinked.

Kevin Clarkeson was in his own way as stilted up as Edward Blake. A high and desperate excitement coursed in his veins. Already his mouth felt dry.

Like Edward Blake, he had now abandoned any dialogue with himself. He no longer told himself why he wanted to die. He only knew now that he would die and die dramatically. As Edward Blake hoarded to himself the moments with Mrs Mortimer, so Kevin Clarkeson anticipated and savoured the looks of horror on their faces.

The last time he was in hospital, he had been visited by a psychiatrist and a social worker. He had listened to them because he had no option. He was in bed and they came one at a time to sit beside him. When he himself talked, they had taken down what he said eagerly and with approval. He would like to have stayed in that little white envelope for ever, occasionally telling them a few things which they would take down and *react* over. But just as he was feeling at home, happy in a way . . . *out*! They didn't want to talk to him or to listen. Their forms were filled in. There were other people who had taken overdoses now occupying his throne-like little bed. *Their* words were being taken down. He was a nothing.

Back to his miserable digs, back to his miserable landlady, back to his miserable job. He had stuck it for a week. Then he'd gone to the doctor. The bottle of Valium – full, untouched and all powerful was in his pocket. He fingered it without taking his eyes off the couple sitting immediately opposite.

He knew them vaguely by sight. He wasn't interested in who they were or where they came from. Just interested in their faces.

He had in mind that when he did *it*, he wanted to do it in front of the woman in the fur hat. But she wasn't on the train all that often, and he couldn't wait.

As soon as the train entered the tunnel, Kevin brought out the bottle of Valium and shook two tablets into the palm of his hand. He still kept his eyes on the woman's face. He swallowed them in two quick frog-like gulps without her apparently noticing. The man certainly didn't notice. His eyes were on the woman, hanging on every word of hers like the psychiatrist and the social worker had done with him.

Two more tablets, then another two. The woman shot him a concerned apprehensive look, laid a hand lightly on the man's arm, but he didn't notice. Two more at Woosley station. Three gulps again as they slowed up for the signal. His stomach was beginning to object, sod it. That's what had happened once before. He crunched the next couple loud and clear. Crunch, crunch, crunch, all the way through the Kentish woodlands. Now the woman was really shooting him some agonised looks. Maybe he'd got himself a winner. Maybe she'd react better than the fur-hatted dame.

Just past Woosley, he began to feel a bit odd. His moment could no longer be postponed. He leaned forward holding the almost empty bottle delicately between his thumb and forefinger.

"Madam," he said with a slight involuntary smile, "I have just swallowed ninety tablets of Valium." He sounded drunk and boastful. "Six times the lethal dose."

He waved the bottle under her nose, drinking in their expressions of astounded horror.

He half-closed his strange hooded eyes. He felt himself continuing to smile emptily and foolishly. Then just as he was truly enjoying himself, as usual he passed out.

Edward Blake sat for a split second, petrified. What to do? Thoughts, theories, lines of possible action clamoured in his mind like the clamour and tumult of the rest of the people in the compartment.

"Stop the train! Get a doctor! Get him to hospital!" He didn't know if it was himself who shouted or someone else. He reached his hand towards the communication cord and then thought better of it.

"Better find out if there's a doctor on board," he said to Celia. "Get the guard."

He thrust his fingers down the young man's throat. The brilliant red eyebrows looked clown-like and infinitely pathetic against the white, white face. There was the stench of sick. Then a man was shouldering his way forward, followed by the guard.

"I'm a doctor."

Thankfully Blake got to his feet and handed over. They moved everyone out of the cubicle at the front of the compartment and put him on the long bench seat. They could see nothing of him now. There was a screen of standing passengers, dispossessed of their seats.

Celia was shaken and apprehensive.

The train was accelerating with unnatural speed. They sat in silence, listening to the frantic sound of the wheels. The landscape of a winter morning fled past in a blur of grey and brown.

Then the guard called out, "Next stop East Croydon! No, no stop before. We're getting this chap to hospital."

"Is he all right?" Celia asked as they rattled through the station at Riseley, hurtling past the platform momentarily showing up matchstick figures of waiting commuters frozen in gestures of astonishment and annoyance.

"Dunno," said the guard.

Tee-who went the klaxon – *tee-who, tee-who*, on they rattled over the rails.

They sat holding hands and in silence for the rest of the journey, willing the man with dyed eyebrows to stay alive. For the train to get him to whatever safety he had to be got to. It was rather less than common humanity, Blake thought. It was somehow an omen for his own newly discovered living.

When they stopped at East Croydon, Blake looked out of the window and watched Clarkeson being carried off on a stretcher.

His face was uncovered – he was still alive.

"Marjorie . . . we see so little of you these days . . ." A

213

pregnant pause at the other end of the line. ". . . except in church, of course."

The two of them never missed – Victoria Mannering dragged that son along with her to sit in the front pew on the opposite side of the aisle to the Ocklington Park pew, simply waiting to move in. The pair of them on their knees, praying to Almighty God for the continued barrenness of Lady Marjorie Mannering.

". . . indeed I can't remember the last time we came –"

Three months ago, to dinner. The four eyes, black as rooks', fastening on her waistline. The careful appraisal of the silver, the carpets, the paintings, the eighteenth-century furniture.

What was she after today?

"Crispin's *not* been well. You heard we went to Madeira? *Lovely* sun! Oh, yes, he's better now." Doubtfully, "And he's got the Alfa back. You heard about that little contretemps, on the bridge?" More cheerfully, "So he doesn't have to use that dreadful train any more. Improving you say? And about time, too!"

A pause – when was she going to come to the point?

Doubtfully again, "Of course, he does drive so fast and that worries me. And then fast cars go with *girls* –"

Another Betty Jones coming up over the horizon.

". . . I want him to have fun. Youth is the time to sow wild oats." That tinkly laugh like a Burmese temple bell. "Later on, it wouldn't –"

Do. Not at all. Not when he assumes the role, the baton of the Knight's sword handed on for him to do his sprint in the relay race.

"You know what girls are these days."

He might be caught. Oh please, God, *please*!

"He is a Mannering, after all."

And like all Mannerings, he must marry an only child with land. Preferably not in Northumberland. Preferably in London. Or New York. Or Paris. Insert "the centre of" in each case.

"I often wonder, Marjorie . . . with all the people you know and your good taste and wonderful judgment," adjudicating for years and years between Mrs Brown's and Mrs Smith's apple turnovers, "whether you might know some . . . well, *nice* girls . . ."

Front page of *Country Life*. Choose your successor.

". . . a dance . . . perhaps on St Valentine's day . . ."
Poor decapitated St Valentine!
". . . at Ocklington Park."
Christ, I can actually *feel* the pushing little fingers in the small of my back!
"Victoria . . . I'm sorry but I can hear Ralph . . ." Calling, fuming, ranting, coming, going, sneezing, coughing, fainting, dying – oh what could he possibly be doing that would take her away from the telephone? "But a dance sounds a good idea. I'll give you a ring."

"What about this one, Miss Price? Unparalleled beaches, majestic caves, mouthwatering food complemented by the local wines. Hear the haunting songs of Spain. Watch the sardanas in the square."
"Where's that, Mr Osborne?"
"Torremolinos, Miss Price. A fortnight for seventy-five pounds."
"Is that a sea-view?"
"Sea view *and* balcony."
"When does that go?"
"December the sixteenth."
"That's a *little* early, Mr Osborne."
"Then how about this: Tunisia, a night club, dancing, private bath . . . only sixty-five?"
"When's that, Mr Osborne?"
"December the thirty-first."
"What is the supplement for single rooms?"
"Five pounds."
"It's certainly a *possibility*, Mr Osborne."
During the passages north and south of carriage no. 56324, now Mr Osborne and Miss Price continually discussed and planned their holiday. Would it be Geneva, departing 18 December, or Copenhagen departing 15 December? Or Norway on 5 January? Mr Osborne's large briefcase contained a library full of brightly coloured brochures – hotels, beaches, girls, ships, palm trees and the glittering sea. They considered the pros and cons of every holiday carefully. "Price," Mr Osborne said, "let's

215

forget price, and that's no pun, Miss Price! Let's really have the holiday we want."

So every day, to and fro from London, it was, "What about Athens, departing seventeenth of December, Miss Price?"

"Or a Christmas cruise in the Mediterranean, Mr Osborne, sailing from Southampton on the twenty-first of December?"

"Or Gibraltar . . . two weeks from the thirty-first of December?"

"Or Casablanca . . . leaving December the twentieth?"

"That sounds very nice, Miss Price. There would be no trouble with Peterson Brothers, booking your holiday over Christmas?"

"Oh, no, Mr Osborne. But would it be all right with Campion's?"

"They're very good, they'll fit in with my plans. Shall we make it Casablanca, leaving the twentieth of December then, Miss Price?"

"That would be lovely, Mr Osborne!"

But on the next trip of the electric train, they would be thinking that perhaps on reflection Venice or Taormina or Majorca could be more attractive. Or shouldn't they really have Christmas at home and go for a fortnight in the early spring to Morocco, when it was warmer?

IT WAS STILL pouring when, halfway through lunch, she saw one of the estate Land-Rovers drive up to the house in a bow wave of water. Minutes later, the butler came in to say quietly to Ralph only, as though apologising for the inconvenience just as they were finishing their saddle of lamb, that Dawson had arrived with "the person".

"You haven't let him in?"

"Oh, no, sir."

"Well, we shall finish our lunch. Then I shall see him."

The meal had hitherto been punctuated by observations, or more aptly instructions, on the likes and dislikes and general foibles of the friends and business contacts whom Ralph was expecting for the Local Shoot tomorrow. And who would grace their table for a well-earned dinner on the Sunday evening. Never mention Gerald Warner's wife, there was that scandal three years ago. Don't forget Tony Lawson-Howard is a devout C. of E. and a trifle anti-Rome. Peter Pierce *is* copper, so keep off Rhodesia, my dear.

Now the meal continued in silence, while Marjorie tried to work out who the visitor was, standing in the drenching rain on the doorstep. Dawson was the gamekeeper who lived at Marlcliff Cottages with the rather superior wife who sang in the church choir and plaited the loaf for the Harvest Thanksgiving.

When she had finished her pear Condé, Ralph said, "You go into the drawing-room, darling. Have your coffee. I'll join you later."

"What's the trouble?"

"Dawson's caught a vandal."

"Serious?"

"To my thinking, very."

He wiped his lips as if taking the taste of the crime out of his mouth, threw down his napkin on the table and opened the door for her.

She preceded him into the hall but she did not do as he told her. The last week or so she had not felt herself. She was a prey to strange fears and fancies. A terrible impenitent guilt now informed her attitude, especially to Ralph. She had this heavy feeling she had to protect him, though basically she knew that the protection – if any – he needed was from herself.

Nevertheless, these days you never knew. Twice the Hall had been burgled, and on the last occasion, the thief, running away into the darkness, had fired a gun. Nobody and nothing had been hit – the bullet had harmlessly disappeared into the night. But what with kidnapping and ransoms, wars and disaster, violence and villainy, fact and fiction forever in the papers and on the television, it behoved everyone to be careful. She would never forgive herself if anything happened to him. And Ralph was getting on. His eyesight wasn't as good as it used to be. In spite of his exercises, his reflexes were slowing. Even on business shoots, where he purposely held off to flatter the skill of his sporting guests, Ralph's bag was smaller than it used to be. If this vandal character tried something violent –

As she followed him towards the entrance door, powerfully she smelled danger. Her husband appeared oblivious that she was there, that she kept between him and the main doors which now the butler opened wide.

It was sheeting with rain and the sky was heavy and pewter-grey with more to come. Already the day had given up to a winter evening. The only light seemed to be the green and ghostly fluorescent mould on the wet trunks of the oaks. It made their familiar strength somehow weird and malevolent, like trees in a fairy-tale forest.

There was no one there. The drive was empty. Then two soaked figures appeared from round the corner of the portico. She recognised him even before she recognised Dawson.

Bill Cody's big shoulders were hunched inside a leather jacket, his black hair was gummed with rain to the sides of his head. He wiped round his face with the palm of his hand, before shaking off Dawson's hand and walking up to the bottom of the steps. He stood with legs apart, defiantly.

Relief, the comfort of Bill Cody's presence no matter what the circumstances, made her feel extraordinarily light-hearted again. The situation, and Ralph with it, became absurd, of nothing but a passing and amusing consequence.

When Ralph drew in a deep breath and asked, "Did you actually find him *in flagrante*, Dawson?" she wanted to laugh. She had to turn her eyes to the flagged step, like a schoolgirl, cheeks flushing, swallowing a smile.

"I didn't find him right on doing the damage, no, sir, not exactly. But I did see the fellow distinct as you and me, leaving the 'atchery sir, with an axe in his hand, sir."

"What happened?" Marjorie put in.

Ralph didn't look in her direction. It was Dawson who answered. "Busted up the south hatchery, m'lady. Let out a whole flock of tomorrow's birds."

"We've got others. Don't fret yourself, my dear. But as for you, my man . . ." Ralph shook his finger.

"I'm not your man."

"*No*. No? Are you really not, my man? Aren't you . . ." Ralph came down two steps the better to peer through the miserable light into Cody's face. "Aren't you one of my tenants? Tenant of Applegarth Cottage?"

"Only temporarily."

"My God, *I* should say only temporarily! And you also abuse the privilege –"

"It's no bloody privilege, mate."

"The privilege, I said, you oaf, of living at a modest rent in *my* cottage. And you repay that by doing wilful damage to *my* property!"

"Listen." Cody jumped up a couple of steps so that he was level with Ralph's eyes as he stood on the one above him. Dawson came flapping up after him in his oilskins.

"It's all right, Dawson," Ralph said. "He won't harm me. I know his sort."

"And I know yours. Wilful bloody damage indeed. What the hell d'you call it to keep birds tame like that to be mangled by your half-drunk friends. I saw the last bloody shoot. And bloody it bloody well was. I had half a dozen in my garden."

"*My* garden."

"Shall I phone the police, Sir Ralph?" the butler asked, aghast witness, pale and fidgeting.

Ralph pursed his lips and hesitated. Marjorie Mannering standing on the top of the steps felt a second of dizzy suspense. Something momentous hung in the balance. Or perhaps it was merely physical, a passing vertigo, an underlining of that odd sense she'd had in East Croydon of physical certainty. She looked down towards Bill Cody, but his eyes still held and somehow challenged her husband's.

"I think I shall sleep on it. Take him out of my sight, Dawson."

"What dreadful doings there are these days, sir," the butler said piously, as they went inside and the double doors obliterated the wet scene outside.

"We are witnessing a decay of the standards that you and I were fortunate enough to be brought up by," Ralph replied. "We shall have our coffee now. And we shall for the moment forget this unpleasant episode."

"But how can we?" she asked him when he reiterated his last words as he drew his chair close to the drawing-room fire. "I would *hate* you to go to the police."

"But why? It would be for *your* protection that I should do so."

"For mine?" She over-reacted. Her cheeks flamed.

"Of course for you, darling. I don't like a violent character like that around."

"But he's not."

"How can you possibly know, darling?"

"I could see. He was simply sorry for the pheasants. Being cooped up. And then just let out to be killed."

Ralph laughed. "So he takes a great chopper and hacks down the run." He shook his head. "No, I think not, darling. Besides you don't know the full story."

"*Is* there a story?"

"The man's no good."

"In what way?"

"He's been inside."

"Do talk plain English, Ralph!"

"He's been in prison. The police told me. About a fortnight after I let him have the cottage."

Marjorie put down her coffee cup, and walked to the window. She stood for a moment watching the rain course down the long panes.

"Perhaps that's why he let the pheasants out?"

"And broke up my property with considerable violence into the bargain? No, he simply wanted a crack at someone like me. Besides those damned pheasants are far better off where they were. Well fed, well housed, in no danger."

Marjorie didn't argue. She hadn't really been thinking of the pheasants. Women tended to personify and identify, as Ralph often used to say.

And had Bill Cody really freed her? Did anyone ever really free anyone else?

"No," Bill Cody told her. "I'm not going to fight it."

He had already received his two weeks' notice. He had no intention of stringing it out until eventual legal eviction. That wasn't the way the cookie crumbled for him. What was over was over. As he said, he was a rolling stone. His plan had always been to emigrate to Australia. Now was as good a time as any. What was the point of staying in this bankrupt country? His words and his tone of voice had seemed to carry a finality beyond and deeper than immediate plans.

Prison? Oh, yes – two years ago. But how the hell had that come out? What for? Contempt of court. He had refused, how did they put it? . . . to purge his contempt. She hadn't questioned him as to how it came about. Nor had he volunteered the information.

"It figures," she said softly, "contempt."

"Does it?"

"Yes. Contempt is what you feel for most things, isn't it? Most people, come to that."

"Most. But not for you." He covered her hand. Oh, there was no doubt that he meant it. Just as he meant to go away. Just as he meant that what was over was over. "I have no contempt for you, my love." He said the last two words very slowly.

"In spite of everything?"

"Because of everything." He drew in a deep breath. "I have nothing but the most respectful love for you."

It was the morning for truth and meaningfulness, she thought bitterly. Truth when it was too late. Meaning when the whole meaning of life was about to be taken away from her.

"Then don't go!" she said. "Of course I can settle this Applegarth business. You can stay there as long as you like."

She refused to believe that he intended to go. That Tuesday,

222

on her return from another interminable Trust meeting on
Professor Poll's educational project in Ranjibad, she told Ralph
she didn't see why he should kick the tenant out of Applegarth
Cottages. It wasn't that he'd been in prison for anything violent
or anti-social. And anyway, if the man had had difficulties,
surely that should be reason enough to give him a chance and
let him stay?

He tried to laugh her out of it at first. Then he became
puzzled. Finally irritated. This do-gooding was all very well
but there was a limit.

"Can't have that sort of person near the estate. Got to protect
you."

"Oh, Lord, Ralph!" She paced up and down the drawing-
room, in frustration and unaccountable rage. "You don't know
the meaning of the word."

"But of course I do! I watch your interests all the time. The
person you most need protection from –"

"Is *myself*! Say it! Go on, *say* it!"

"– is the tax man."

"Investments. That is really all you ever think of."

"Of course it isn't, my dear." He came over and sat beside
her on the sofa. He took her hand and patted it. "But money is
the root of much good as well as evil. I want all good things for
you, Marjorie. And you have always been so happy."

What was there to say?

"You have always had everything."

She nodded.

"I have given you all you ever asked for."

His words seemed to reflect off the white walls, the larger-
than-life portraits staring reproachfully down at them. I-have-
given-you-all-you-ever-asked-for. Was there the slightest
emphasis on that first word? While *you* . . .

What would he say if here and now she told him her secret
mingled hope and terror? What she already knew in the marrow
of her bones was true? Ralph's dearest wish at the very eleventh
hour about to be realised. If she told him she was pregnant
he would give her anything she asked. A dozen Applegarth
Cottages, inhabited by whomsoever her justified feminine
whim desired.

She was aware that they were on the threshold of what they had never had in all their married life – a quarrel. A row now and again, an exchange of words – of no deep significance, always on the surface.

Lady Anne, Lady Caroline, Lady Ursula Mannering had all lined up behind Ralph, shock in their beautiful faces. Dismissal in their cold eyes.

She got up from her chair, saying nothing. In the end, outnumbered, it was she who had retreated. She walked away into the little semi-circular music alcove on the right of the Adam fireplace where there was a Bechstein grand, now hardly ever played. Here, smaller than the gargantuan lounge ladies, painted life-size were the portraits of Ralph's first wife Amelia and of herself – both painted by a White Russian artist who had settled in England.

Two odd portraits – strange that they should be painted by one artist. The style was so totally different. There sat Amelia, all strawberry-pink and white, under the mulberry tree in a frock of flowered silk with mutton-chop sleeves, a honey-blonde spaniel in her lap. And there *she* stood.

"You want the painting wiz dawg?" the Russian lady had asked her. "That way, your husband like, you like, everybody like. I not like, but I only artist. To artists all is fairy story anyway, so what harm in touching up truth a liddle, heh?" Oh God, how awful, she had thought, for that was ten years ago. How terrifying! How false and how frightful that people should *need* to look at life and love like that!

Now she stared in dismay at the unsmiling mouth, the aching eyes, the body half turned away, looking as though it was trying to escape, slide out of the golden frame. It had been a mistake. There was no doubt about that. It was too painful to bear.

She averted her eyes, slid them sideways to the portrait of Amelia. That was how she should have conducted herself. That was how she should have behaved. That was how she should have been painted – wiz dawg, *wiz dawg*.

"I have been thinking that it might be a little lonely for you at Christmas this year, Miss Price."

224

"Well, it won't be the same without Dad, Mr Osborne."

"And there *are* holidays specially designed as Christmas House Parties."

"That sounds lovely! But isn't it terribly expensive, Mr Osborne?"

"Of course, we'll have the sun." Mr Osborne took his eyes off the brochures to stare out at the winter sky exactly matching the wet grey of the morning roofs of Clapham. "Sicily, for instance, won't be so warm. But listen to this . . . ten-day holiday in Taormina departing London Airport twenty-third of December. Excursion up Etna on Christmas Eve. Then a special dinner and carnival dance. Bumper Christmas dinner with 'bubbly'. Boxing Day trip to see the ruins at Syracuse. Three sight-seeing trips of your choice. And all for sixty-six pounds!"

"When did you say it was leaving?"

"Twenty-third of December, afternoon flight."

"I've heard of Taormina," Miss Price said coyly. "It sounds . . . very nice, Mr Osborne."

They talked about it all that week. And then they had finally decided. Taormina . . . Zeta Tours Christmas House Party. Departing on the noon flight of 23 December. Efficient as always, Mr Osborne got the tickets next day, proudly showed them to Miss Price that evening, gave her the special labels for her luggage. Then they talked about their preparations for the holiday. Mr Osborne pointed out the convenience of the departure times at the Zeta Tours office.

"We'll go up on the 8.01 . . . just as though we were going to work. But instead of Peterson Brothers and Campion's . . . paradise, Miss Price!"

TUESDAY   16 December

THAT TUESDAY, Marjorie Mannering and Bill Cody travelled up together for the last time on the 8.01. The train was crowded. The morning was wet and dark as midnight. There were no First Class carriages again. They had no privacy. No comfort even of sitting side by side. Bill Cody had to stand a couple of arms' lengths away from her. She'd rather have stood herself. But a middle-aged man, in deference perhaps to her unnaturally sickly look, had given her his seat. She still felt sick. Sick at heart. Sick in her stomach. She had been unable even to drink a cup of coffee this morning.

There was everywhere in the compartment an overpowering smell of damp leather and wet mackintoshes. Spiky umbrellas and knobbly Christmas parcels obtruded. Oh, who was it said the world went out not with a bang but a whimper?

The 8.01 was late leaving Ocklington. She tried to catch Bill Cody's eye as the whistle went. Exasperated and sharp, like a referee's whistle. The end of the game. Was *that* how he saw it? Perhaps he didn't see it as anything at all. He was absorbed, apparently, in his paper. He didn't look up to salute his last glimpse of Ocklington, the wet and glimmering platform, the lights of the early risers in the High Street and the farms in the valley.

Did he even think of Applegarth Cottage, as the train accelerated, empty of all his things? It was part of his existence. An *important part* if she was to believe what he said in those dark intense moments of his. Did he not feel he was leaving something of himself behind?

Her mind skidded to a stop there. She clasped her gloved hands tightly and stared down at the tips of her grey suède boots. She was a middle-aged woman she told herself, prey at this period of her life to frets and fancies, delusions even. Her body had ached for a lover and a child. And now her body and her mind were singing some dangerous delusory siren song to her.

Bill Cody was leaving her. He was a rolling stone. She could fasten no strings to him, even had she wanted to do so. He could leave any place without a backward glance. Then as they entered the tunnel, she saw his face reflected in the mirror, made by the wet brickwork of the walls. He was watching her. His expression was grave, and infinitely tender. She turned her head quickly, and surprised him with her look. "Don't go," she formed the words silently with her lips. He shrugged, as if he didn't hear her.

They clanked slowly through the tunnel. British Rail seemed to be conspiring to draw this agonising journey out as long as possible. The train stopped inordinately long at every station while extra-heavy goods and Christmas mail sacks were loaded. At Woosley, a crowd of schoolboys got on with their baggage and their bubble-gum, and their pretentious uniforms. I would not make a good mother to one of them, she thought. I could not imagine . . . But then I am only *imagining*.

At Victoria, Bill Cody did not go immediately to work. He took her to a café round the corner and ordered coffee.

"What were you trying to say to me in the train?" he asked her. But the moment had gone. The look on his face was now one of friendly amusement.

"What day do you actually go?"

He raised his black brows humorously. "The twenty-third. I told you."

"Did you? I don't remember." She stirred her coffee. Already we are drifting apart, she thought. The inevitable end is reaching out to both of us. I cannot say to him the words I want to. Whatever is meaningful my lips seem to change.

"It couldn't have been very important, then."

His voice was sharp, pained even. The sharpness somehow breaking through her own inadequacy.

"It's more important than anything else," she replied softly. She pushed her cup away from her. "That's what I was really saying in the train. Don't go."

"At all?"

227

"Yes."

"I see."

She glanced across at him. His eyes were dark and inward-turning, his mouth set, sullen almost. Bloody minded. She wanted to grasp the collar of his leather jacket, shake him and shriek at him.

"It would be no good," he said after a moment in an oddly judicious ponderous manner, "you know that." And then in sudden rage, "What d'you want me as anyway, a sort of tame bloody cock pheasant?"

"Ah," she exclaimed, "that's really why you smashed them! It wasn't to let them out. It was me! Me you were smashing!"

"If you like."

"I don't damn well like." She lowered her voice. "I don't want you as anything. I just want to be with you." Bill Cody sat very still. "Can't you see?"

"I can see."

"But you still won't stay?"

"No."

"Do you want me to come too?"

He didn't answer. She rested her hand on the plastic top of the table. She willed him to cover it with his. But he sat with both hands in the pockets of his corduroy trousers.

"Well, would you?"

"I'd want you to give it a helluva lot of thought first."

"Oh, God," she laughed, half-hysterically. "You'd want me to give it thought first. You sound like Ralph." She grasped the edge of the table to steady herself.

"Because *you'd* be the one that was giving up everything."

"I'd be gaining everything. You're the only person that's never asked me for anything. Maybe," she felt weak and light-headed, "maybe because I've got nothing that you want."

He looked at her carefully.

"That's not true, lovie, you know that. I want you. Just you. All of you. Nothing less."

Nothing could have been in its own way more final. She saw his face huge and magnified by her own tears. Oh, she would try them too if they would work. But it was all too late. She felt utterly defeated. Her hand gripping the table felt cold and dead.

Bill reached out as if to cover and warm it, but all he did was to push her coffee cup nearer her.

The smell was disgusting. She had never till this morning hated the smell of coffee. She felt sick and dizzy. A cold sweat touched her forehead like a dead hand. The walls of the café shimmered. Darkness came over her like a curtain.

Something cold was pressing on her forehead. She heard Bill's voice, "She'll be all right in a moment." Felt his hand pressing her shoulder. Then gently whispering in her ear, "Keep your head down for a bit longer, lovie. You'll be all right in a couple of shakes. There you can sit up now! O.K.?"

She was still in the same chair at the same table in the same restaurant. Nothing had changed, except the proprietor hovered as if fearing a scene of some sort.

"You passed out, lovie!"

She smiled weakly, "It was the coffee."

"Ssh!" He put his fingers on her lips.

"How long was I out?"

"About one minute." He raised his brows ruefully.

"It felt much longer."

He said nothing more. He sat staring at her thoughtfully.

"Silly of me," she said. "I didn't eat any breakfast. That must have been it."

"Why didn't you eat any breakfast, lovie?"

"I didn't feel like it."

He clasped his hands and stared down at them. "Well, now I'm going to get you a taxi. I'd rather you didn't go to your meeting."

"I must. I'd rather, anyway."

"All right. But you go straight home afterwards."

He seemed so changed towards her now, so gentle and approachable, that she tried just this once more.

"I'm going to come out to Australia with you," she said.

"Yes," he said, "I know you are."

MONDAY   22 December

FRASCATI'S had been fixed for the evening of Monday 22 December.

There were a number of reasons why that date was the most suitable. Crispin had obtained two complimentary tickets in the stalls of Covent Garden. He also had an important business appointment for Peterson Brothers at 9.00 a.m. on Tuesday at Enfield for which even the Alfa, in view of the traffic on the roads, would be unlikely to deliver him on time. Sheila had that day off from the hospital, so she could have an appointment at Anton's to put her hair up, Edwardian-style, on the top of her head. She could catch the 5.35 from Ocklington which he would meet. A table was booked for late supper at Frascati's, and so was the Wentworth Hotel.

"What's playing then, Sheila?" her mother had asked over kippers at their tea–supper in the kitchen on Friday.

"The Russian Ballet, Mum."

"How nice!" Her mother had always professed interest in the ballet. "That's nice, isn't it, Dad?"

"What train are you catching back?"

"Well, with the cut-back in services, there's no longer a 12.45," she had said carefully, emphasising her independence in that if there had been that was the train she would have been on. "Last train now is 10.30 . . . wouldn't catch that. So I'm staying the night with Dilys Roberts."

"Who's she?"

"*You* know, Dad," her mother said for her. "The girl who works with Sheila at the hospital."

She had taken twenty pounds out of her Post Office Savings Bank on Saturday. Now she had enough for the blue dress in Swainswick's. She bought shoes, stockings, underwear. More perfume – the cross between lily of the valley and lavender which her parents had bought her for Christmas was quite unsuitable. The green coat would do, but she bought a very elegant overnight bag in matching green leatherette.

She had gone to church on Sunday, sitting between her parents holding the little white prayer book they had given her for her confirmation. Lady Marjorie Mannering was there. So was Mrs Mannering – but no sign of Crispin. That evening, she painted the nails on her fingers and her toes bright scarlet, before getting in to bed. She lay there, head on the pillow, staring up at the ceiling. It was hours before her eyes closed and she went to sleep.

Monday cracked open like the inside of an oyster shell cut clean by the sharp blade of the sunlight – soft pearly colours, blues, greys, delicate translucent whites. And then her horoscope in *Woman's Own* delivered that morning with her father's *Daily Mail* promised that the week would start well with lovers reaching a new understanding, and what better omen could there be than that?

The morning was well occupied at Anton's, having her hair swept up on the top of her head, showing the long neat line of her slender neck, but after that, she was impatient to be rid of the rest of the day. After a light lunch with her mother, she spent the early afternoon upstairs in her room, making final preparations and packing.

Lying half an hour later in warm foamy bathwater, her hair carefully enclosed in a plastic cap, she was aware only of a glowing anticipation, a sort of rosy romantic cotton wool around her. She was enclosed in a small magical cocoon of excited bliss – her feelings, her present, her future as pink and soft as her bath-warmed flesh peeping in various plateaux, beaches and hills above the green scented bubbles of the water. All the time, she was keeping her eye on her small square wrist-watch on the chair. Time passing – young as she was, she was conscious of that. Years ago, an aunt who kept a grocery shop had told her that a woman had a shelf-life, like those pastries and pies and processed meats on which were stamped *not to be sold after* . . . but when?

She got out of the bath with lots of time to spare, dried herself carefully, padded along the small corridor to her bedroom, where she sat at the dressing-table, powdering her face, putting her make-up on, painting her nails. Just after five she had a cup of tea with her mother, then picked up her overnight bag and started walking to the station.

There was no one she knew on the platform. The 5.35 arrived on time almost empty. She settled herself by the window. Minutes later, Ocklington dissolved in a bumpy huddle of shadows. Dark fields and bare woods under a black sky travelling past on the other side of the glass.

And then suddenly, in the cutting just before the Blackwater Tunnel, the train slowed to a funeral march – then stopped dead.

Used to delays and having made provision for them anyway in her preparations, she simply went on reading *Woman's Own*. Ten minutes past. Fifteen, twenty. She looked at her watch, sighed, smoothed her skirt over her knees.

Now she began to feel apprehensive. She opened the window, stared outside. There were dark shapes moving, men shouting.

Ten minutes later, they started to go slowly backwards. They continued backwards until they reached Ocklington station, where they were greeted by a porter shouting, "Everybody out!"

"What's happened?" she asked him.

"Maintenance and inspection in Blackwater Tunnel."

Panic flushed her cheeks. "When's the next train?"

"No more northbounds tonight."

She said furiously, "Why weren't we *told*?"

But he had already left her and was explaining the situation to other passengers. Outside the station, the single sheet of overcast had been ripped, and it had begun to rain. Puddles were already forming as panic-stricken she ran home.

Her mother had gone out. Her father had not returned from work. The time was six thirty-three. What was she to do?

In a frenzy, she rang Tom Armitage. She had not seen him since the East Croydon episode. But now his motorbike was necessary again – this time for a northbound trip.

But there was no reply. She tried ten minutes later. Still no reply. She tried two taxi firms – no cars available.

How long would Crispin wait? Certainly he would ask about the 5.35, be told no more northbound trains that night. She rang the Wentworth Hotel, but there was no sign of him. He had not arrived at Frascati's. She left a message that he should 'phone. But by 8.50, when first her father and then her mother arrived, there still had been no word from him.

Her mother was sympathetic, started fussing. Her father pointed to the rain sheeting down outside and gave as his opinion that it was just as well she was at home.

Gradually her panic changed to anger. Typical British Rail! No notice, nothing! As usual, nobody seemed to know what they were doing. Then tears filled her eyes. Her mother brought her in a hot cup of Ovaltine.

She managed to get hold of Tom Armitage at 9.35. She could hardly get the words out, she was so angry.

"I've been ringing since half past six! *Where* have you been?"

"Sorry, love. Been out with the boys."

"At the pub, I suppose?"

"Sheila . . . you're upset. What's the matter?"

"Why didn't you *tell* me that the 5.35 would be cancelled?"

"Was it? I didn't know."

"I was going to Covent Garden and I was so looking forward to it . . . and now," she started sobbing, "it's *ruined.*"

"Sorry, love . . . sorry."

"And then when I want you to run me up on your bike . . . you're not there! You've gone! Gone *drinking!*"

"Sorry, love."

"Sorry is the only thing you ever say, Tom Armitage! And I'm telling you, one of these days, you'll say sorry once too often!"

"Alice . . . I have some very good news!"

It was almost dark in the office. Thick clouds had combined with the beginning of evening to squeeze the last sparks of illumination out of the dying day, and Cunliffe (a great believer in saving the nation's resources) had not switched on the electric light. The shadow of Deborah Leigh stood by the window, now being turned into an artist's palette by raindrops tinted red, yellow and green by the streetlamps and neon signs of the extravagant outside.

"A house . . . yes, near to the office. Within walking distance. *Far* less tiring for me. It's in Marlborough Square. Number Seventeen. Very attractive and going for a song. A garden? Well, it's not very far from the park."

A pause.

"Of course I want you to see it. That's why I'm ringing. I want to make an appointment with the agents for tomorrow."

A longer pause.

"Talk it over this evening? No, that's just it, dear. I don't know what it's like in Ocklington, but here it's pouring. Started to rain, you say? I feel awful, knowing how you don't like being on your own . . . but Alice, I really do feel I can't face the journey. Not tonight."

A very much longer pause.

"Forked lightning just then. Can you hear the thunder? There'll be chaos on the Line."

A very short pause.

"*Of course* I'll look after myself. I'll stay at my club. Oh Alice, I am so sorry. Sweet of you to understand. And you'll come up to London tomorrow? Good! Now ring Sutton's for a taxi. Catch the 8.01. That's right, the train I get. Don't bother with the tube. Take another taxi to the office of Nettleship and Hammond, Fetter Street. Then we'll have a chat and some coffee, and toddle along to Marlborough Square. You will? Lovely! See you tomorrow, then."

One last pause.

"And you, Alice. Goodnight, dear. Goodnight."

The shadow moved from the window.

"Well, that's done. Now I suppose we'd better think of a table for supper."

"Pelting down."

"Better somewhere near then, Debbie?"

"Frascati's, Gordon? Shall I book a table for two at Frascati's?"

And now Marjorie Mannering had begun to count the days – six left, five left, four left, three left, two left.

They would be leaving on the evening plane of 23 December.

234

Tickets and all plans and formalities completed. Nothing to do but wait.

Ocklington had never looked so beautiful – because she was leaving it. Miss Quinton, the Vicar, Mrs Dawson, Mrs Thwaites took on new qualities hitherto not fully appreciated. She attended Christmas Carols at the Secondary Modern School, watched the Nativity Play put on at the Catholic Church. She went to three cocktail parties, and everybody was charming. All that week-end she was in a state of exaltation. The telephone went on ringing, but now it was:

". . . the prizegiving at St Hugh's . . . when did you say . . . January the eighteenth . . . I'm afraid it's impossible."

". . . dinner on Boxing Day, Victoria? We'd love to come, but I'll be away."

". . . the Charity Ball at Ocklington Park at Easter? Not this year, I'm sorry."

The world had suddenly righted itself because she was going away with Bill Cody.

Sitting in the front row of Ocklington Church beside Ralph at evensong, looking around at all those faces: Victoria Mannering, that pretty girl who commuted on the 8.01, Sheila Somebody-or-other, sitting between her parents, farmers, shopkeepers, clerks, businessmen, Dawson, Robbins, all the Estate servants and tenants looking dutiful and uncomfortable. Thinking with relief I shall never see them again. None of them will ask me for anything else. And what will they say when I'm suddenly gone? The scandal of it, such a sweetmeat for them to chew over, suck at and enjoy! So much to dissect and gossip about while they consider the possibility of a successor. Conjuring up certain looks, certain words and re-interpreting them, declaring that they always had known she was a wild one – real spirit sister to Lady Elizabeth, cracking her ghostly whip over her foaming six horses.

On Monday, Ralph had to go to Paris on business for Peterson Brothers. She spent it walking in the park, mostly in the rain, packing a bag, nothing elaborate. Telling the servants she would be away for a few days.

In the lounge, the last drop of coffee after dinner, the oak logs settling in the grate, listening to the nine o'clock news on

235

television – industrial unrest, wars, riots, disasters, economic chaos. And now the weather – the deep depression over southern England which had caused heavy rains and flooding to all parts of Kent and Sussex for the past week was still stationary and the outlook for Tuesday remained unsettled . . .

It would be summer in Australia: there would be the warmth and the sun. The promise of a new life. Up in her bedroom, opening the lattice window, staring out at the Park for the last time at the dark shadows of the trees torn by the wind and the rain, she saw them already as props of her past. Didn't some sect believe that you had to be reborn in order to live?

"What did you put on the file?" she asked.

"*I agree.*"

The Civil Servant's benediction, Edward Blake thought sadly to himself – the ultimate bending of the neck. File R/372/54 had come back to his desk this morning with an impressive number of adverse minutes from economists, and a minute from Aird to the effect that in the circumstances further finance to keep the Line open was hardly justifiable, and did Mr Blake agree. Williams from the Department of the Environment had rung up to say that for operational reasons British Rail were now concerned, and he relayed the news to him. Williams said that in that case he was quite sure that the notice to close the Line (which had never been rescinded, only postponed) would be implemented to take effect from the end of British Rail's financial year.

"Not much else I could do," he said to her.

He had told her about the decision to close the Line sitting on their usual bench by the pool in the Park.

"When?" she asked.

"Thirty-first of December."

"So soon?"

"It's not the end of the world," he said, "we'll go on seeing each other."

She looked away then. He knew what she was thinking. The end of the Line, the end of *our* meetings, the end of their brief encounter, the death of the electric train.

"Of course we will," he said.

Clouds had formed up again. The sun made an eye-shaped hole in the marbled sky. Blake looked up at the blind white pupil of that bloodlessly bloodshot orb. A splash of rain fell on his hand. He shivered.

"I must get back to the museum." Celia struggled to keep her voice steady. "I'm busier than ever just now."

He caught her arm. "Don't go yet."

"I must." She got up to leave. The expression of her eyes was shielded from him by her lowered lids, as she packed her things in the shopping bag. The picture, as something told him she intended it to be, of the suburban housewife.

"I love you, you know," he said, following her.

She shot him a sudden off-guard look of absolute sweetness. Then, "It's a much over-used word. It's said so often it loses its meaning."

"Not for me. I've *found* its meaning."

Again that unguarded look. "But you love your wife and family," she said after a moment.

"Yes. But in a different way."

"And you were quite happy."

"Till I met you, yes."

"And I was reasonably happy with Dylan."

"Was?"

"Was."

"Don't go back. It's almost Christmas. Everyone's easing off. They won't miss you yet. Just let's walk together."

"Where?"

"Anywhere. I feel as if I can't keep still. I feel I want to . . ." he broke off. "Oh, I can't tell you what I feel. But you know. When I'm with you, I'm complete. All things are possible."

They left the bench and walked down the empty path beside the pool.

"But all things are not possible, Edward," she said softly.

"At this moment they are." He threw the crumbs at the bottom of his paper bag towards a moorhen, watched it cut a perfect V-shaped wake. He watched the hovering flight feathers of the pigeons' wings, spotlit in the white light of the slanting sun.

Everything in that moment seemed remarkable, delicately fashioned, infinitely beautiful.

"Whenever anything doesn't seem possible, I shall come back here." He turned her round and kissed her on the mouth. She returned his kiss with a reluctant and yet unmistakable ardour.

"You see, that would not have seemed remotely possible a month ago, eh, Celia?"

"Oh, I know. And I'm grateful –"

"Grateful? Heavens!"

"For many things. For more than you know. Edward," she clasped his arm, "I'm not like you, I'm no good with words, what I feel doesn't make me eloquent. It strikes me dumb."

He rumpled her hair tenderly. "What a funny thing you are."

"One day I'll touch up a painting for you," she said.

"Or better still, do it." But that reminded them both of Dylan. They were silent for a few minutes. They threaded their way now between people on crowded pavements. They had somehow come without conscious direction towards the Thames. He could smell the water, feel the slightly damper air on his face.

"I'll get you a taxi back," he said, as he saw her glancing around like someone waking out of a dream. "I promise you. But don't go yet."

"We've come miles," she murmured breathlessly.

"Too far to go back."

"Don't say that, Edward."

He stepped off the kerb to avoid a man carrying a small wooden rocking-horse wrapped in brown paper. He was astonished that they still made the things. It seemed another existence ago that he'd done the same.

"But it happens to be true."

They walked down Edith Street and crossed the road to the Embankment parapet in silence. They leaned over the stone. He felt it pressing into his chest like an unbearable weight. A full river ebbed fast below. A chain of coal barges sent back a huge wash of scummy water. Neon signs coloured the grey sky across the water. A winter evening was closing in on early afternoon.

He was acutely conscious of the insubstantial nature of their relationship. He had a terrible premonition, shadowy but certain, that he was about to lose her. He sought immediately to exorcise it by giving her substance, a place in the order of things.

"Where did you live before you were married? Where were you born?"

"Bristol. Pembroke Road. Near the Downs. You could hear the zoo from there. And you could get a free view of the monkeys."

"Nice." He smiled back at her.

"My father used to work at Filton. On the Brabazon."

"Retired?"

"He died. Just before I went to Art College in London. Mother still lives down there. With an unmarried sister."

"D'you go and see her?"

"Naturally." She said it stonily as if she knew he was going to suggest he might take her down there sometime. He felt ashamed, and yet he excused himself. He had come late, as it were, and time was short.

"So you see," she smiled sweetly up at him again, "I've had a very *un*remarkable life. Nothing momentous has happened to me," she covered his hand on the stone parapet. "Till now."

Suddenly there was the sound of marching feet. Through the mizzling rain, escorted by mounted police, came a company of Grenadier Guards. The heavy beat of their blackened boots sent the pigeons creaking up to the ledges on flat windows. Crimson chests out, arms carried, badges and buttons glittering with zeal. Row after row of anonymous faces, marching mindless boots. Left, right, left, right. So straight you could pass a ruler down the lines.

Right opposite where they stood, the Sergeant-Major leading them made some unintelligible bark. And where before they had moved as one with machine-like precision, now their arms and legs became again individual – ragged, not in time.

"What's happened?" she asked.

"They're going over the bridge."

Already in half a rainbow they had wheeled on to the suspension bridge – elegant, Victorian, painted bright red and blue and yellow. He pointed to the notice *All soldiers must break step before crossing the bridge.*

"They have to break step," Blake said. "Otherwise they might bring the damned thing down."

She nodded. "The vibration, I suppose."

She watched the men move away down the bridge and disappear, her eyes thoughtful and inward turning. He felt that in some way the sight of them had hardened her in some wavering purpose.

"All the same, Edward," she said, as if she had been holding an unspoken conversation with him. "If we've come too far to go back, we still can't go forward."

"What d'you mean?"

"We can't go on, that's what I mean."

"But of course we can! We're not doing any harm. It's little enough," he added bitterly.

"It is enough. Enough to," she bit her lip, "do a lot of harm. If we go on like this in our own way we are going forward. There are a number of people involved with both of us. There's no future in us meeting. Oh, it may sound banal and ordinary. But it's true." Sadly she eyed the traffic coming over the bridge. "If we go on like this we could bring them all down. Better quickly and cleanly, now the closing of the Line is definite."

"What absolute nonsense!" he exclaimed.

"I don't think so."

"You won't do anything silly like giving up your job or moving house?"

She shook her head. "No."

"In fact, you won't do anything at all, will you?"

"I can't promise."

He put his hands on her shoulders and shook her. His mood had swung completely round. It was as if an hour ago he'd been drunk and now he'd sobered. He felt a chill coming off the hurrying water. It smelled of damp and decay. He was oppressed with the impossibility of their situation, of time and tide hurrying by.

"I must get back," she said, wriggling out of his grasp. "Please. You said you'd get a taxi."

He stood on the edge of the kerb with her, willing one not to come. But even that didn't work. He'd only time to say, "But

240

you won't do anything drastic?" when a taxi appeared with its yellow light on.

Celia stood on tip-toe and flagged it down.

"No," she gave him a quick smile, and a kiss on his cheek as she got in. "I love you, that's the only thing I can really promise."

He even wondered if she would be on the 5.55. He half-expected her deliberately to give it a miss, had fortified himself against disappointment by constant repetition of those final words. But after all, he saw her. She was in the same compartment, but not close enough to talk. They smiled to each other across the swaying commuters and weary lady Christmas shoppers. They had an extra bonus together. The southbound was even later than usual – work going on in the Blackwater Tunnel.

When he got out at Ocklington, he stood on the platform, watching the train slowly gather speed southwards, her face blur away from him. He walked slowly up the steps and over the bridge. Seeing the people load into their cars in the rainy darkness, he was suddenly ashamed that Christmas was upon him and he had bought nothing for anybody.

He went out of his way down into the Square, where a small antique shop plied an evening trade. They were open. There were bits of holly stuck into imitation cranberry glasses, and tinsel hanging from the beamed ceiling.

Quickly he chose a second-hand silver and cultured pearl necklace for Daphne. He didn't even enquire the price. As he wrote the modest cheque his eye was caught by a small gold bracelet, delicate and beautiful, which he could see somehow on Celia's wrist. He bought that, too.

It would always do for Sarah he thought, if he lacked the courage in the end.

TUSDAY

TUESDAY   23 December

IT RAINED all night, sheeting down continuously with occasional rolls of thunder, but that Tuesday morning when Edward Blake walked to the station, there ahead of him was the sun – white as magnesium, bursting out of a cumulo-nimbus cloud like a huge spark, turning the moss on the oak trees to verdigris and varnishing the soaked fields till they shone like jade. There was a rainbow exploding out of Applegarth Woods and coming to earth in the middle of Terrible Down. All the bare twigs were tipped by crystals. Snowdrops had come out round the gate of 19 Arlington Avenue, and already he could see yellow oozing out of the side of the crocuses. There was a permanence about the morning, vivid and mysterious, as though it had been painted years ago by Millais – a sketch perhaps for *The Blind Girl* – and now it had come back alive again, a Pre-Raphaelite resurrection.

The air was washed clean, and he could smell the promise of the sap of spring, so different from the mildewy scent of autumn. It was the turn of the year: the days would be getting longer. Not long now and the winter would be over – a warm wet one with only the odd day of snow and little frost. It was a reawakening sort of day, invigorating and promising – the sort of day to begin things, not to end them.

It would not be today. He knew it would not be today. Not yet. Not just before Christmas. Not this month. Not this year. In the summer perhaps, or even the autumn. Things moved slowly. And one never knew, something might turn up, something might happen so that parting need not take place at all. Lying awake last night beside Daphne, listening to the rain, he turned over and over in his mind what Celia had said beside the bridge. It would end – yes, as in their hearts they knew it must end.

But not yet. Not today.

Turning down Station Approach, his heart was hammering –

242

excitement he said to himself at seeing her again, not apprehension that she would not be on the train. He joined the commuter stream – the grey and blue suits, the gay winter coats. He was wearing the same old white mackintosh, and Daphne had still not had the time to get around to mending the split in the seam. He recognised one or two of the regulars – Sheila Tate wearing her coloured rosette *Keep the Ocklington Line Alive* on her camel-hair coat, struggling along on huge wedge-soled shoes, Lady Marjorie Mannering arriving in the red Rolls, the chauffeur accompanying her into the station carrying a suitcase.

Now he began walking faster, passing a number of brown walkers, as though the whole thing was a race and he would see her sooner if he hurried. He had to get another monthly return – up 10% since last time – and he had the money already in his hand. At the ticket office he inquired how late the 8.01 was running, and to his surprise was assured that it was on time. Next in the queue behind him was the young man with the variegated hair, the first time Blake had seen him since he had been carried off on a stretcher at East Croydon.

He glanced at the station clock over the stove before going on to the platform. Another six minutes to go. He was early. Even so, not nearly so many waiting as usual. No sign of that big burly Cody character. No sign of Cunliffe either. The Christmas holiday, of course, people would simply not be going in to work. Quite a number were carrying cases and were clearly off on holiday. The Treasury officially had tomorrow, Christmas Day, Boxing Day and a privilege day off, but he would go in at least two days over the holiday to attend to urgent business. At home, the Christmas preparations had been efficiently organised by Daphne – presents bought, turkey and all the trimmings ordered, cards out on the mantelpiece and the window sills, tinsel silver tree in the lounge, holly and ivy and paper streamers festooning the hall.

Alone under the second Victorian lamp standard, a woman was waiting – a pale, long face, thin, he could see the bones protruding through the skin of her wrists. Wearing a long grey coat, a muffler round her neck, flat laced-up shoes. Not a regular. No one he remembered seeing before. Her eyes, large

243

and luminous, were pointed in his direction, but were unfocused, seeing nothing.

Here was a regular now – little Miss Price. She had a suitcase too, brightly labelled "Zeta Tours". He nodded and said, "Nice morning."

"Very."

"But a wet night."

"Shockin'!"

Lady Marjorie in her mink, standing against the privet hedge, an expensive leather case beside her. She smiled at him, a warm smile, redolent of the aura of peace around her. Surprised and flattered, he hesitated before smiling back.

A man coming up now, someone he remembered vaguely seeing before – one of the blobs that usually inhabited the bottom end of the platform. Accompanied by wife, with small daughter jumping in circles around them, also carrying an attaché case, but clearly destined not on holiday but on business, for the tag read "C. R. Holland, c/o Webster and Company, Buenos Aires". Just over Christmas – the family putting on a brave face, the wife smiling but holding his hand tightly, thinking perhaps of kidnappings and Latin-American revolutions. They came and stood beside the man with the variegated hair.

"Excuse me." The thin strange woman. A thin strange voice. "Does one have to change?"

"Not on the 8.01."

"It *is* Victoria?"

"Yes, Victoria." He pointed far down the line where coming up over the horizon was the yellow half-moon. "On the front . . . 88. That's Victoria."

"I'm sorry to trouble you."

"That's all right."

"I almost never go to London."

"There you're lucky."

"Yes, yes, I agree. I hate London. But today, I'm meeting my husband . . ."

"Oh yes?"

"He has seen a house for sale in London he wants me to look at . . ."

He was aware of the tentative gropings towards him of the lonely and uncertain. Lead me, hold me, reassure me – there was such a lost look in her eyes. He smiled, nodded, all the time moving slightly away from her. He could not bear to have her companionship thrust upon him today.

"This commuting is *so* tiring for him . . ."

Nearer and nearer now – how the train moved! Effortlessly slithering, like a girl in a long dress walking with her arms tightly by her side. For you could not see the wheels; you could not see how it was done. Up the track it came, miraculously eating up the long liquorice sticks of rails to the platform. Slowing now, slower still. The engine cab and the first carriage, the second carriage stopping. Now the fifth window down was directly opposite him.

Stopped.

At first he thought he had counted wrong. This must be the third carriage. A new man might be driving and he had brought the train too far up the platform. But it was a short train again – only five carriages, all Second Class. The window was empty, like a frame with the glass there but no picture.

"Victoria train . . . Victoria train!"

He felt suddenly dizzy. He swayed a little, standing rooted where he was, unable to move.

"Are you all right?"

The thin strange woman, holding the door open for him.

"Aren't you coming?"

He moved then automatically as though her words were a command; she had thrown some switch which energised his legs. Not there, he said half aloud, getting into the half empty compartment, as the woman hovered over the seat by the window where Celia usually sat, don't sit down there.

The woman sat down there. He took his usual seat, the one beside her. The doors closed. The whistle blew.

"I thought you were going to miss it!"

He could not speak. He stared beyond the angular profile down Station Drive. Empty, moving away as the train began pulling out into another world, separated. The daughter of C. R. Holland, holding her father's hand out of the open window, was running along the platform, faster and faster till

245

she reached the down slope. A sort of yearning in her eyes –
Sarah had never looked at him like that, would never hang on
so tight to him. He watched the two clasped hands slacken,
unclench, slowly separate, the fingers stretch out and now only
widening air between. The girl's hand fell away, disappeared.
The father stood there, leaning out of the window, vigorously
waving his hand up and down against a background of the
suburbs of Ocklington.

"I trust we'll be on time. My husband tells me . . ."

He did not hear. He had begun to produce defence mechan-
isms: Dylan might be ill, something might have happened to
stop her coming. It could not be the end. There would be a
perfectly rational explanation. Yet all the time, her words kept
coming back to him – better quickly and cleanly, now that the
closing of the Line was definite. There had never really been
any future in their relationship. Now the end could be seen,
tangible and sharp as a knife. No long-drawn-out agonising,
counting the days getting fewer. *Now*, she had said, but he had
been so sure she had not meant it. They needed each other.
Better to hang on to each other surely, as the daughter of
C. R. Holland had tried to hang on to her father, till the last
possible moment.

". . . take a taxi to the office of Nettleship and Hammond, he
said . . ."

That faded red and blue upholstery, it was the same as she
had commented on, that day when she was trying to get the
exact colour of the sky through her misty window. In that
fisherman's net of luggage rack above them, she used to put her
carrier bag. He remembered that they had both commented on
that coloured photograph of Parkfield pier, likening it to a big
blob of candy floss on the end of a stick. Over in that opposite
corner where they had been squeezed together by the crowd
pushing in at East Croydon now sat Sheila Tate reading *Woman's
Own*. Opposite her, Lady Marjorie, elegant silk-covered legs
crossed, looking out of the window towards Applegarth Woods
and the beginnings of Blackwater Hill. In the next set of seats,
side by side near the aisle, where they had sat coming back on
the 5.55 after that first date in the park, were Miss Price and
Mr Osborne discussing whether or not they would have the

time for a coffee at Victoria before going to the Zeta Tours office for the coach to Luton Aerodrome. At the far end of the compartment, standing up between the two sets of seats, difficult to understand why when the compartment was half empty, was the white-faced young man with the variegated hair.

". . . getting so tired . . . only a few minutes' walk from his office . . ."

Now he was conscious of the whole carriage as a familiar background that had changed, become unrecognisable to him. The very fact that there were so many familiar bits still in it and yet it was so alien made the whole place seem somehow sinister. It was as though it had been an impersonator before, had been wearing a mask – it was not a sort of paradise, a place of release, a platform on which to try to touch eternity, but a shabby little prison, soiled and smelling of an elderly cinema, damp and dust, a mirror-image of what he really was. He felt stunned, numb, conscious only of a great hollow gaping emptiness inside him – hadn't someone said Hell was an eternal sense of loss? He was aware not so much of pain as being without feeling, beyond the capacity ever to feel again.

". . . don't want to be late for my husband . . . such a busy man . . . Chairman of the Passengers' Consultative Committee . . . perhaps you know him?"

"Oh, yes! Mr Cunliffe." But it did not really register. He was only conscious of the woman's mouth, wide open in front of him and moving. Like baby birds and small animals everywhere, all mouth and big staring frightened eyes. Feed me, protect me, tell me there's nothing to worry about, I'll be all right, won't I?

All the world frightened of themselves and of each other. What am I? What are they? What is he trying to do to me? What's behind it all? Are we just shades anyway, not fully self-sufficient human beings, the ingredients only two-thirds there, so that we must be fitted with a uniform like a corset to keep us all of a piece? Here you are, Blake – a dark suit, an umbrella and *The Times*. The play begins there, but the ending is uncertain. Here are your lines – you are a clerk at the Treasury, married with two children. A minor role, but there are advantages in that you have much less to memorise. You do not actually have to *do* anything, but remember at your cues to speak up loud enough for those at the back to hear, yet not too loud lest you draw the audience's attention away from the stars.

The level crossing, the cock on the spire of Marlcliff church, the wooden stile, and the footpath. Now the green blur of the embankment becoming distinctly grass, the naked elms on the beginnings of Blackwater Hill not running but walking statelily upstairs. The clicks of the wheels had separated into single sounds. They were slowing down.

The woman's wide open mouth seemed as big as the tunnel's. "Are we stopping?"

He shook his head. "We're just slowing down for the tunnel. That's what they always do now."

The daylight faded behind them. The sound of the wheels echoed and reverberated. The artificial light of the compartment flung their shadows like a twin silhouette against the old brickwork streaming with water. But he saw it as though he was a man already drowned.

"We'll be all right," he said.

By the window on the other side of the compartment with her back to the engine, Lady Marjorie Mannering sat in a little cocoon of peace. There had been such a finality about the last preparations. No note left – nothing so dramatic. Before the plane departed from London Airport, she would simply telephone Ralph at Peterson Brothers, Paris, and say she was going to Australia for a while. He was used to her vagueness and sudden enthusiasms. At the moment, she could not bear explanations. To track a logical account of her actions was beyond her. She had been filled with a passion to escape, to get away from the fat oversweet suffocation of it all to a new, leaner existence where she could *breathe*. Once the big decision was taken, all the thousands of other smaller decisions seemed to melt away. No longer would anyone be asking her for anything. No longer would she be a figurehead. No longer would she be required to mouth the same platitudes on countless occasions. Her time was her own. She could do as she liked. She would be in a new world where nobody knew her past and nobody cared.

She stared through the grime-speckled window at the faded winter grass of Kent without regret. The last time she would see the church, the cottages on the edge of Terrible Down, Falklands up there on the hill, the high railings enclosing the skeletons of oaks and elms inside Ocklington Park. Beautiful in the spring and summer, the scent of cow parsley along the lanes. Beautiful in the autumn when the woods caught fire. Beautiful now, pale, with all colours drained away. But the price was too high. She would not wish ever to come back. The future with Bill Cody and his child had laughter and warmth about it, a meaning, a strength of its own. Outside beyond the glass there was richness and luxuriance – but cold, cold as alabaster.

They were going slower now, as though the train wanted her to have a really good long look to take away with her for ever. Applegarth Woods, Marlcliff spire, the beginnings of Black-water Hill . . .

Slower, slower – almost stopping. Sunshine sliding down over the wet grass of the embankment. A last glimpse of moss and fern round the old brickwork of the tunnel – then daylight disappeared.

Marjorie transferred her eyes to inside the compartment. The girl opposite had abandoned her magazine, opened her handbag and at the same time as she rummaged inside for something was staring anxiously into the tiny mirror on the flap. She could hear in the seats backing on to her the pear-shaped man talking to Miss Price.

". . . a gala party. Christmas Eve. That's free. The excursions are a bit pricey, but Etna on Friday is a must . . . You'll have a funny feeling in your tum and a popping of the ears when we take off . . . but once above the clouds, it's smoother than a train . . ."

All at once, she became aware that a man was moving down the aisle. Looking up, she saw the white face and jazzy hair of the young man who had really started it all – the one bent on suicide whom Bill Cody had saved. She remembered seeing him vaguely since that day. In some strange way, it was as though they were back at the beginning again, they had come full circle. He looked better, certainly, but what was he doing, walking about in the middle of the tunnel? Warily, she kept her eyes on him, moved her legs right in front of the door.

And then suddenly, far away, there was a sound as though of marching men – soft at first and stealthy, then becoming louder and louder, rocking and echoing, now high as gunfire, shelling, screeching and whistling.

The young man shot across to the door on the other side. He had already begun wrenching with the handle, when there was an explosion of noise. Bullets of bright light screamed past, inches away from Marjorie Mannering.

A hurricane now – a roaring wind. The whole carriage flinched, swung over to the left. A sudden jarring scraping noise, and the compartment filled with a damp sooty smell. On the metal roof, a rattling like heavy hail. The door was wide open. There was a scuffle round the gaping blackness. A man shouted. Then the wheels started banging up and down. There was a clanging and ricocheting of buffers. Marjorie was flung hard against the glass. The lights disappeared southwards.

Sudden silence – the train stopped dead.

No sign of the white-faced boy. The man in the mackintosh getting out on the running board and shouting.

From the other side of the seats, Mr Osborne's voice "He was going some!"

"I thought two trains in the tunnel at the same time wasn't allowed."

"Neither it is. When They –" He had stood up, saw the open door in the other cubicle. "What's happened then?"

Blake had already jumped down on to the stones at the side of the track, squeezed his way forward between the train and the tunnel wall, called to the driver. "Man jumped out . . . ran this way." He pointed. "And the door . . . it's hit the brick-work . . ."

The guard came up. No, he had seen nobody. A hurried interchange between guard and driver. Torches flashing over the brickwork, down on to the dark wheels. And all the time, over the three of them a light scattering of dust and soot.

"Well, what'll we do then, Jack?"

"Sure he went Ocklington way?" asked the driver.

250

"Sure." Blake paused. "He tried it before . . . three months ago . . . same chap."

"Nut case," said the guard.

"Anyway, we won't hit him. Nothing we can do." The driver shrugged his shoulders. "We'll report at Woosley. Now sir, back on the train, please. Nobody else out! We'll be moving in a moment." He went back, climbed up the running board.

Two wide eyes, an open mouth. "What happened? *What's happened?*"

"What about that young man?" Lady Mannering's voice from the corner.

"Driver's going to report at Woosley."

"Don't you think . . .?"

The train noise started up again, pulsating and throbbing like frantic heartbeats under their feet. Blake swung the door to, saw that the whole of the top of it was crushed and broken where it had connected with the tunnel wall.

"Won't close, I'm afraid," he said. "We'll have to hold it."

"What are they *doing* to us?"

"It's all right, we'll be –"

The screech of wheels, turning, slipping, sliding. High, high, on edge and in pain – now the whole train seemed alive and straining, buffers clanging, carriage racks trembling, power roaring and reverberating —

And yet never moving.

"What's the matter now?"

"We'll be all right." Mechanically, the only words he could think of. More screeching wheels – now the carriage rocking backwards and forwards. Nobody saying anything. The face of the woman beside him ashen, her eyes huge glittering pools. Noise and throbbing continuing on and on and on – like a car refusing to start.

Then silence again.

The driver and the guard moving out on the track now, inspecting the bogies, talking amongst themselves. Hammering the wheels and the axles.

The driver's voice cheerfully, "We'll be getting going soon!"

Starting up again – more throbbing and the screeching of wheels. It was like that for over an hour – attempting to start

251

alternating with hammering at the wheels. And suddenly the sound of moving wheels echoing in the tunnel, and the guard shouting that it was another engine come to help them.

Standing at the far window by Marjorie Mannering, Blake reported to the others what was happening.

He had the torch – the one he now always carried – and he shone it to the rear of the train. The other engine was coupled to the guard's van. Then the throbbing and straining and screeching started up again – twice, three times as loud, but because clearly help had come, the outside world knew, they were no longer isolated and alone, inside the compartment spirits rose. People made jokes. Mr Osborne repeatedly kept on saying, "They will have us out in no time."

But the minutes went by, and nothing moved. Just a continuous shuddering and juddering as the wheels spun round without gripping. "Leaves on the wet lines, Miss Price," Mr Osborne explained. "Grit'll get us moving."

More men outside now. The cheerful driver saying, "Little problem with one of the wheels on your carriage. So we're uncoupling all carriages behind you, and taking them out. Then the engine's coming back again, and with just your carriage between two engines, soon be on our way!"

Blake watched the operation from his place by the window. Not unlike the little girl's hand going away at Ocklington Station, the carriages and all their blazing lights glittering on the dark shell over them broke away, moving effortlessly now farther and farther down the tunnel – fainter and fainter, a tiny spark, then darkness. The sound of the wheels died away into silence.

"It'll be our turn next," said Mr Osborne.

Blake was just bringing his head in when he felt a tiny cold drop on his face, then another, then another, like fine rain falling. Puzzled, he looked up. Seeing nothing, he began flashing his torch this way and that over the roof of the tunnel. Everything looked all right – a damp mouldiness over the bricks, that was all.

The next moment, it was as though a volcano had erupted.

A hurricane wind blew hard in his face. Inside the compartment, all the lights blinked twice, then went out.

And through the silence and the darkness, a high panic-stricken shriek: "We're shut in! We're trapped! *We're buried alive!*"

How long Alice Cunliffe screamed, Blake did not know. An eternity, it seemed, going on and on, the noise as sharp and painful as knife-wounds. He had gone back to his seat and sat beside her, aware of her body stiff and cold with terror. He had kept his torch on, so that they were in a little pool of illumination, and now he put out his hands and tried to hold hers, but frantically she pushed them away as though she was afraid of them. He tried to speak to her quietly at first and then louder to try to get above the high continuous shrieks. Marjorie Mannering had come over and sat opposite, also trying to quieten her.

"Quiet!" Mr Osborne's peremptory voice. "Quiet!"

And since the screaming went on, up he came from the other cubicle. He yelled, "It's all right! We're not trapped! They'll know what to do."

She stared at him in the torchlight, not seeing him, not hearing him. She was sobbing wild hysterical dry sobs, no tears, just gasping for breath, a rattling sound in her throat, a mad bird cry, eerie and frightening, all the time clawing the air in front of her as though trying to climb up the darkness.

"Stop it!"

A sudden flash, and Osborne's hand connected hard against her face. Once, twice, three times – slapping her cheeks, knocking her head this way and that till the shrieking turned into real sobs, then whimpers, then an exhausted silence.

"Had to do it," Mr Osborne shrugged his shoulders. "Only way."

He went back to Miss Price. Their duet continued. "Only way," "sad," "works you see, she's quiet now."

Marjorie had got up and Blake had moved to one side so that she could sit next to Mrs Cunliffe, putting her arms round her, holding her close as a child. The words now were coherent, mixed with sobs and tears, on and on, sucking relief from Lady Mannering, clinging to her for protection.

People in the smoking side of the carriage were calling out: "What's happened? Where's the driver?"

Blake had gone back to the far window. The torch beam showed no masonry fall, but it was not strong enough to penetrate very far north or south. As he stood there, the businessman came up to him, the one with the wife and daughter, C. R. Holland. They talked for a while, reassuring themselves that the engine would soon be returning to pull them out.

But the time passed, and nothing happened. What had happened to the engine-driver and the guard, Holland inquired. Shouldn't they be examining the situation, do a bit of exploring? Blake said that he would go along to the engine cab and find out what had happened.

"No. You went last time. My turn."

They argued for a little, then Holland simply smiled, opened the door and went out.

"They did say to stay in the carriage," Blake called after him. "Be careful!"

"I will!"

The torchlight flickered on his figure moving forward into the darkness.

"You're very quiet!"

It was two hours after Holland had left, and there was still no sign of him back. Of course he and the driver would probably have been exploring ahead, had probably located a way through, were leading a rescue team back. Water might be hampering the return of the other engine. There had been no further shifting of the tunnel wall. No further avalanche – no sounds of falling masonry. Quietness in the compartment, Lady Mannering still comforting the pale Mrs Cunliffe. Mr Osborne was telling Miss Price that though they had certainly missed their plane, in the circumstances They would arrange a second flight out for them. Turning away from the window, suddenly Blake's torch had lit up the face of Sheila Tate, sitting by herself two cubicles down.

He went over and sat beside her. "You all right?"

"Yes, thank you."

"We'll be all right, you know." They seemed to be the only six words he knew. He was aware how dry his mouth was, and added, "Bit thirsty like me, I expect."

"Not specially."

"They'll have us out soon."

"I know."

He saw how calm and composed she was in contrast to himself, and was immediately ashamed. While he pretended to be unworried and confident, that was exactly what she really was.

"They will know all about us now outside."

"Yes."

"They'll be organising things."

"My boy-friend, works on the railway."

He smiled at her. "Well, he'll be along soon then."

"He *always* comes along."

"Like a genie."

"A what?"

"Aladdin's helpmate. You remember. The ring that Aladdin used to rub."

"Oh yes . . . and then he would come!"

He nodded. "Useful sort of chap. Better rub your ring hard!"

"I haven't got one."

"Well, wish instead. Wishing is just as good."

He said it wistfully, remembering. The girl was so confident in him coming to her. Everything was possible because of his love for her. While in his love for Celia, nothing was possible. A beginning, a few hours together, an end. Here he was now, imprisoned in this small compartment where he had begun to make tentative steps beyond himself. He would not try to pretend that what he called his limbo-land between his roles at home and the Treasury was heaven, but here with her help he had begun to see. He had reached out and tried to capture a few sparks from the bonfire that glowed alive around him, before the wind blew them away. And now he was even more alone. It was as though he was surrounded by familiar mirrors, all reflecting back at him his own single image.

He tried to pretend that he was glad that she had not come.

255

At least she was not trapped. And yet, he was overwhelmed by a sense of loss because she was not with him. She who hated tunnels, hated darkness – how could he really wish her here? And yet he did. He wanted to hold her hand, feel the soft hair of her head on his shoulder, listen to the steady beat of her heart. Then he would be alive. Now all his feelings were numbed. He was sick, but not with fear for himself. He did not expect to be rescued – how could they be when the tunnel appeared blocked both ways – but for himself it hardly mattered, since he was already dead. Celia would be pierced when she heard. So in their own ways would Daphne and the children – their taken-for-granted security shattered, only uncertainty ahead of them.

He looked at his watch: four o'clock. Time had gone quickly and yet so slowly, as though there wasn't such a thing as time anyway. He wondered inconsequentially what would be happening at the Treasury. Nothing very much. The door of his office opening and as quickly closing. Files collecting in his In-tray. The odd person might ask . . . isn't Blake coming in today? Is he ill? On leave? The messengers would be inquiring whether to put all his stuff in the Confidential Cupboard. The children would be arriving for the tea Daphne would be preparing in the kitchen – and then the television news.

On the seats the other side of the cubicle, Miss Price and Mr Osborne – quite fearless, real Roundheads, still singing their queer little duet on the need for discipline. Patiently and courageously waiting, still putting their trust in Them.

He listened, envying them both their blind trust and their mutual identity.

"I've been thinking, Miss Price . . ."

"Yes, Mr Osborne?"

"We have known each other now for three months, Miss Price."

"Three months and *two days*, Mr Osborne."

"And we're going on holiday together, after all, Miss Price."

"Yes, Mr Osborne."

"So the time has come . . . don't you think, Miss Price . . . for me to call you Edna?"

"Why, Henry . . . yes, of course!"

256

Behind the partition of his seat, he could still hear the pale woman, going on and on to Lady Marjorie. I am the unwanted one here, he thought, the outsider, the loner.

He got up then and moved over to the window. Perhaps there with the help of his torch he could find some role, even though it was only that of a Greek chorus reporting happenings outside in a calm voice, "Everything the same."

For the next hour, he stood by the window, keeping a lookout for Holland, announcing any activity. A few loose chippings fell. He could smell dust and stagnant water. And then suddenly far ahead, hazy in the weak light of the torch, from a black hollow in the cathedral-like arch, a thin spidery thing started to descend.

At first, he thought it was part of the ceiling, wire or piping, and then he saw a bulge on it moving down to the ground, twisting and turning, "Something's coming down . . . from a ventilator, I think."

The next moment, a shadow was flung – tunnel-length tall – flat against the wet brick wall of the tunnel. The sound of splashing boots, a torch five times as powerful as his own reflected full in his face, blinding him. A cheerful voice, magnified by the megaphone of the tunnel, calling out "It's all right! We've come!"

Everyone crowded to the windows. Osborne pointed out the ropes and special gear that were coming down the ventilator. That was how They were going to haul them out of the tunnel on to Blackwater Hill.

There was activity all over the track now, shouts and commands and the flashing of many torches. The first man was going along with a big loping unhurried walk, what looked like a motorcyclist's silver-painted helmet on his head, searching each window, looking inside the compartments. He had almost come up level with Blake when he suddenly called out, "Ah, there you are, love!"

And the next moment, he had lifted one leg on to the running board, hauled himself up, opened the carriage door, pushed Blake to one side, past Henry Osborne and Edna Price to flash the full brilliance of his torch on Sheila Tate, sitting blinking and dazzled, cocooned in white light.

257

"You've been a long time," she said.

"Sorry, love."

Tom Armitage took hold of both her hands and pulled her up on her feet as though for a dance, and pushed her towards the still-open door. He stopped there just beside Blake, and taking off his helmet, he put it over her head and did up the straps.

"Latest fashion," he said and clenching his fist, gave her a light punch on the chin.

Then he leapt down on the track and holding out his arms caught her as she jumped, unceremoniously slinging her over his right shoulder and calling over his left, "I'll be back!", began sloshing over wet stones and sleepers to the front beyond the dark stationary engine to where now lights blazed and men were standing with ropes, calling out:

"Stay in the carriages!"

"Don't come on the track!"

"Wait your turn!"

"Any more children? Women now then. Come on, missus!"

Staying at the window, Blake reported it all. One by one, a harness round them, passengers rose from the ground, disappeared through the dark hole in the roof of the tunnel.

"And the next!"

Inside the compartment, the sideglow from the lights outside quivered on a photograph of Etna in the guide book upon Miss Price's lap.

"They have everything well organised, Edna."

"Discipline, Henry."

They had come for the women in their compartment now, the same railwayman, minus his helmet, his hair soaking wet with sweat, panting a little, calling out to Miss Price, "Your turn, ma'am!"

"No," she said, "no. I'm not going yet."

"Go on, Edna!"

"No, Henry. I'll wait with you. For *our* turn. Then we'll both go up together."

"Come on then," the railwayman was shouting at Marjorie.

"She'd better go now," Marjorie tried to get the pale-faced woman on her feet. But calm and composed now, Mrs Cunliffe still clung to her. "We'll wait, then, too," Lady Marjorie said. "Take our turn later."

"Right then!" Tom Armitage moved away to the smoking half of the carriage beyond the corridor, wiping the wet hair out of his eyes. "We'll be as quick as we can!"

Inside the compartment, everything was very quiet. All excitement and fear seemed to have exhausted itself. Nobody spoke. Nobody listened. Blake sat down by the window, not looking out – conscious of people hurrying outside, lights flashing, shouting and calling.

There were just the five of them in the compartment now, waiting for their turn.

Ten minutes passed. Strange, Blake thought, that so many things had happened inside this compartment. He had stood over there with Celia only last week. On this blue and red moquette cushion at the side of his face, she had once rested her cheek. Over there, on that dark window, she had traced a drawing with her fingernail on the frost. She had moved in here, talked, laughed, sat in silence, lived.

"How are they getting along?"

Henry Osborne's voice jerked him out of his half-dream. He got up and moved to the window.

"I'll just see."

Blake switched on his torch. It shone through the dark corridor of the tunnel towards the activity two hundred yards ahead. The ropes were still there. They were still sending people up, two women waiting. He was turning to bring his head back into the compartment to report when, ever so slightly, he felt a dew falling on his face – then drops of water as though it was raining. Surprised, he turned his torch beam upwards to the roof of the tunnel.

Right above the carriage a jagged saw-tooth scar had appeared on the brickwork. As he watched, it widened, bulged, began breaking up. The whole ceiling began turning into an enormous diamond chandelier. Then he heard the gushing of water and the rattle of falling bricks. He shouted to the others to get down on the floor under their seats. The roof began shaking. There was the sound of tearing metal and splintering wood. A thudding now, and banging. And then an explosion like a mine

259

going off – the reek of damp dust as the roof caved in and a waterfall of bricks and metal and wood and water came sluicing through.

In carriage 56324, now nothing moved. A quietness, a stillness. Only the sound of water oozing in through the holes and the cracks and the scars of the compartment and softly slithering over the floor.

EPILOGUE

THE Accident Report into the Blackwater Tunnel disaster ran to sixty-five pages, and laid the blame on what it called "a number of inter-related human factors".

'. . . the main cause was certainly the existence of an underground lake below the North Downs and only slightly to the west of the tunnel site. Why this expanse of water, which for three months had been replenished and was expanding from excessive amounts of precipitation that had fallen during the wettest autumn since 1897, had not been discovered earlier, is not known. Indications there had certainly been. During the building of the tunnel itself over a hundred years previously, part of the brick arch had collapsed, killing three men. Bombs jettisoned on Blackwater Hill during the last war certainly produced shock waves that had a weakening effect on the masonry. For some time previously, but especially during the last four months, the structure of the tunnel itself had given cause for concern. Weeping over the bricks had been noticed, but in old tunnels of this length in wet weather this is not uncommon. There had also been a dislodging of brick and a small escape of water on 16 September, but this had been repaired. There was not the slightest doubt that extensive repair and reconstruction work would be required *eventually*. The cost of this would be many millions and under inflationary pressure was rising monthly. The Ocklington Line had been running at a considerable (though lessening) loss for nineteen years on a grant-in-aid. In spite of the fact that plans for making Ocklington the next New Town would have to be shelved, on 6 August the Board of British Rail reluctantly decided, under pressure of a new wave of cuts in government expenditure triggered off by the summer financial crisis, that the Ocklington Line would have to be closed. All possible alternatives were discussed with the Department of the Environment, and an appeal to the Treasury for

261

additional funds for the specific purpose of keeping the Line open was agreed. After the summer recess, the Department of the Environment wrote to the Treasury requesting further finance. It was appreciated that there would be considerable public opposition to the closure – particularly from the commuters for whom it was recognised that no satisfactory alternative form of transport could be found. Advice was sought from a large number of government, quasi-government and voluntary organisations – the road transport authorities, the Department of Education and Science, various sub-departments in the Department of the Environment, the Department of Trade and Industry, the Coal Board, the Electricity Board, the Kent County Council, the Consultative Panel of Rail Passengers – since the initial response from the Treasury, though by no means definite, gave some indication that the necessary finance to keep the Line open could in the eventuality be found. Ministers were also consulted. For a period of nearly four months following British Rail's decision to close the Ocklington Line, its future remained hanging on a thread. Throughout this time, there were pressures from British Rail's engineering and maintenance departments to close the Line. It was argued that the Line would *have* to be closed eventually for a prolonged period of time to effect a thorough reconstruction of the Blackwater Tunnel. Instead of closing, however, various safety precautions were introduced. A speed limit of ten miles an hour for all trains was laid down, and only one train at a time was allowed in the tunnel. Eventually, when no further progress appeared to have been made on the provision of finance, the Board of British Rail gave notice, as required, that the Victoria-Ocklington-Parkfield Line would be closed on 1 December. Public opposition was immediate and was greater and better organised than had been expected. A vociferous public protest meeting was held. A large number of Members of Parliament received letters from their constituents. Business firms wrote to various government departments. A Parliamentary Question was asked. The Board of British Rail, while not giving way, granted as it were a stay of execution pending further inspection. This further inspection was carried out, particularly on the Blackwater Tunnel, and on the advice of their engineers, the Board finally decreed that the

Ocklington Line would definitely close at 00.00 hours on 31 December, the end of British Rail's financial year.

In retrospect, with the perspective of various facts not fully known or insufficiently recognised at the time, it was unfortunate that such an important decision should have been allowed to remain unresolved for such a long period of time when there were clear indications of danger. Even so, it should be recognised that the accident still would not have happened had there not also been additional and unforeseen human factors that undoubtedly contributed to it taking place.

Due to a shortage of staff, the 7.30 non-stop Victoria–Parkfield express was driven by a driver who had considerable experience of the route several years before. He knew nothing of the speed limit. He did not expect the signal (which was at red) just before the Blackwater Tunnel, which passed unnoticed at sixty miles an hour. Undoubtedly weakening vibrations were set up by this transition of the tunnel at speed.

The very fact that the northbound electric train in obedience to orders was going too slowly was yet another factor in the accident, in that it was not protected by its own slipstream and received the full blast of the southbound express at speed. The second carriage was rocked and tilted to the left. At the same time, a passenger, for some reason not established for certain but presumably from a sense of panic, opened one of the doors which then connected violently with the walls of the tunnel, scarring and weakening a structure that was already marginal, and bringing down brick and debris which derailed one of the rear bogie wheels on the carriage.

The northbound was brought to a stop one and a half miles from the north end of the Blackwater Tunnel. Attempts to move it were made, but failed.

Although communications were difficult, the staff of British Rail then acted with commendable promptitude. The fact that the southbound express had passed the red signal was known. Its speed through Ocklington was noted. When the northbound 8.01 failed to arrive at Woosley, an engine was sent from the depot at Warborough, and a second attempt using both engines was made. But the dragging bogie and the wet rails forestalled movement either backwards or forwards. The wheels simply skidded and could not grip. It was then decided to uncouple the three carriages behind the second one (No. 56324) and take them out of the tunnel, after which the engine on its own would return. It was believed that the two engines between them could move carriage 56324 even with the dragging bogie. The three rear carriages were shunted out without incident, but before the engine could return, the Blackwater Tunnel began to collapse at a number of points both north and south of the remaining two carriages, cutting them off completely.

All the passengers and crew in these two carriages might well have perished but for the ingenuity and resourcefulness of a British Rail gandy dancer or tracker who organised ropes and tackle and with others descended a ventilation shaft which gave into the tunnel only two hundred yards from the trapped carriages. Sixty-eight passengers were rescued through the ventilation shaft, but before all could be evacuated, a fissure developed and extended in the roof of the tunnel directly over the two carriages. Attempts at rescue were made by those at the ventilation shaft, but these had to be abandoned due to the rising level of the water. It is perhaps fortunate that considerably fewer people than usual because of the holiday were travelling in those two carriages, but even so twenty-six passengers and one staff member of British Rail lost their lives . . ."

They have not gone far away – those twenty-seven. As the crow flies, no more than a couple of miles. Here they are now, all together in two neat rows in the churchyard of St Michael's Church, Marlcliff, just below the graves of the three Irishmen and to one side of the nineteen schoolchildren. All except one – Lady Marjorie Mannering of course lies three miles farther south in Ocklington Church with the others in that alabaster sisterhood . . . *beloved wife of Ralph, mourned by all who knew her, mindful always of her duty to others, warmly loving and steadfast, generous to a fault* . . .

The other monuments are simpler – headstones of plain stone, all the same, with the name and the date and one short carved line:

William Streeter   – *husband of Diana*
Sandra Frith   – *wife of John*
Frederick Jordan – *son of James and Margaret,*
                     aged seventeen

Patrick Grosvenor, Leonard Leighton, Charles Parkinson –
the list of unknown names goes on. Were they the ones recognisable to Blake only as blobs at the other end of the platform?
Did they move up to the front just that day? Or did they come
up on that one morning, perhaps, to do Christmas shopping in
London?

Here on the left of this row are the familiar names, the regulars who waited under the second Victorian lamp standard:

Edna Price   – *aged 55*
Edward Blake   – *dear husband of Daphne, father of Sarah*
                  and Peter

Next, *Alice Cunliffe, devoted wife of Gordon, Christopher
Holland, sweet husband of Jane, adored father of Ruth*, and then
one of those who came up the Line from the south *Henry
Osborne, aged 63*. Finally . . . *in proud and loving memory of my
husband Jack Gow, engine driver for forty-two years.*

It is very quiet up here. The churchyard still slopes steeply
down, and the grass is still very green. Harebells grow here, and
heather and wild orchids. Over the years, people have come
into the churchyard, seen the three sets of graves – the Irish
navvies, the schoolchildren, these twenty-six – and asked what
occurred on those three days over a century apart and
why. What were these people like? What did they do? What
happened to Mrs Holland and her daughter and Daphne, Sarah
and Peter Blake? How did Mr Cunliffe manage without his
devoted wife? What about those who survived? Some of
them even make further inquiries, are curious enough to ask
questions.

There is not much they learn. Most of the facts and remem-
brances have been washed away like water, disappeared,
drowned. But there are one or two exceptions. The case of
Kevin Clarkeson – ten times attempted suicide who fought his
way through to a chink of light at the end of the tunnel and
escaped, never to attempt suicide again – attracted the attention
of psychiatrists and a paper was written. The new Chairman of

the Land Reform Programme was announced in the papers last week – Lord Ocklington of Nene, now over eighty-five but still as active as ever, and there was a short description of his life of business and public service: how he had taken over from Hugh Franklin and then merged Nettleship and Hammond with Peterson Brothers to form the biggest property company in Europe, Chairman of several hospital boards, a pillar of St Andrew's Church, one-time Lord Lieutenant of Kent, Chairman of numerous educational organisations, Chancellor of Canterbury University. Mention was also made of the activities of his wife, Deborah, for generous entertaining at their delightful Marlborough Square house: Lady Ocklington has given continuous and unstinting support for her husband's activities, particularly in the charitable field where her untiring efforts for the Trust for Research and Development, especially in their programme for the advancement of secondary education in Ranjibad, are widely known.

Daphne Blake still lives at 19 Arlington Avenue, but the children have gone. Sarah married a naval officer, and Peter followed his father into the Civil Service and is now an Assistant Secretary at the Home Office.

Sir Ralph Mannering married for the third time – a well-built young woman from a Scottish landed family whose father had interests in North Sea oil. He died only four years ago, but not before he had seen his eldest son Adrian married to a German industrialist's daughter, and had played cricket with his grandsons on the front lawn of Ocklington Park. His sister-in-law, Mrs Mannering, still lives at Falklands with Crispin, who never married and retired only last week from his position as manager of the New Town Project – for Ocklington has multiplied if not by seven times seven at least by one of those sevens. Stores, multi-level car parks, a theatre, a recreation centre, all modern amenities. Miss Price's terrace house near the gasworks is now a Chinese restaurant. You cannot see the traffic lights at Gallows Cross Roads, where that farmer was hanged for stealing a neighbour's land – capital punishment for grand larceny after all disappeared nearly a couple of hundred years ago and has now been replaced by the burden of honours and responsibilities – since they are blocked out by the eighteen-storey tenement block planned and put up by the Chairman of Nettleship, Hammond and Peterson Brothers, Lord Ocklington of Nene.

To her mother's disappointment, Sheila Tate married Tom Armitage, wearing white satin and carrying red roses in Ocklington Church. Before the wedding, her father took the bridegroom on one side for a little talk and told him that he was taking on "a handful", that he would need to "keep a tight rein on her" and see that he "kept her fully occupied". The Tates still live at 6 Station Approach. The Armitages live in a small Victorian house overflowing with children, since Sheila and Tom had five and now there are grandchildren too, so that the whole place resembles an overcrowded untidy nest. Tom is still with British Rail, a foreman – not perhaps as high as one would have expected of him, but railway work demands long irregular hours away from home of which Sheila is not enamoured.

There has been nothing from Australia, though it is known that Bill Cody is farming in Queensland. A gamekeeper occupies Applegarth Cottage. Five miles away at Southover, Henry Osborne's bungalow was empty for a long time, since no will was left and the surviving relatives could not agree. Before there was a settlement, it was demolished under a compulsory purchase order to make way for the new motorway to the Channel Tunnel.

And Celia? Nobody knows. The house at Fordbridge was sold to a retired Army couple, quite unlike her and her artist husband. The neighbours knew little of the Mortimers. They did not mix – she particularly, they said, seemed almost frightened of meeting people. Where had she gone? Did she go with Dylan or alone? Again they shake their heads. Letters addressed to her are returned *Gone away*. She went as she had come, suddenly, at the same time of year, too, springtime, the time of primroses and the first daffodils.

Why *those* twenty-six, some visitors to the graveyard ask. Why did *they* die? Some punishment perhaps, some God on His throne dictating pain and death to those who broke His laws? Or was it in their stars? Or in their hands? Or were they just helpless victims of the machine? Or were they, like Tess of the D'Urbervilles, just playthings of the Gods who had their sport with them? Or was it just luck – a throw of the

267

dice and their number came up? Or did they bring it upon themselves?

Nobody knows. Nobody has even tried to work it out, like the simple priest awarding points to those who died when the bridge broke at San Luis Rey. And it is much too late now. The memory of all of them has faded, like the memory of all those others who preceded them – the navvies who built the railway, the soldiers from twenty wars, the squires who governed, the parsons who preached, the girls who flirted, the doctors who healed, the poet who lived at the turn of the last century on Blackwater Hill, the m'ladies of Ocklington Park, the witch of Terrible Down.

For we are back at the beginning again – here on Blackwater Hill. Everything has come full circle. It is dark, as it was then. You cannot see anything yet, and it is all quite still.

Look! It is beginning to get light, as it did that day in the last millennium. It is again the sixteenth of September, and grey up here and cold.

What a change, that is your first reaction! For Ocklington covers much of the Weald now. A nuclear power station provides the electricity. Thousand-seater giants fly in to Matley Airport and the sky is alive with supersonic aircraft. After intense public opposition and protest meetings, the Channel Tunnel was built and the countryside has become a noughts-and-crosses board of four-lane highways and six-lane rail tracks. Skyscrapers have been built on Terrible Down. A reservoir has been constructed. The Nene has been dredged.

Here is the sun! Look again, now that it is lighter. No change at all, you see. Ocklington Park is exactly the same, the golden cock on Marlcliff spire still glitters. The bridge over the Nene where the woman left her husband, the scar on the oak tree made by the bullet that murdered the girl, the carving *Mary and Alan* on the granite rock, even the gap in the hedge where years ago that boy on the motor bicycle went through at eighty miles an hour and killed himself – they are all still here.

A few bits and pieces have been added since last time. A deep cut in the bridge masonry where an Alfa-Romeo connected, a small gold bracelet for sale in the window of the antique shop in the triangular square, broken wire and wood fouling a clearing in Applegarth Woods, a blue-green eucalyptus tree high above a thatched cottage, a strange outsider in this land of oaks and elms.

And at this moment, somewhere in those skyscraper flats a woman is leaving her husband, a man is scheming to get control of his neighbour's business, a committee is planning a protest to the government, in a semi-detached house on one of the new vast estates someone is crying, walking hand-in-hand on Blackwater Hill a boy and a girl are plighting their troth.

And the tunnel, that is still here. Sealed up of course, and mossed over, with its turrets sticking up above a green wilderness, mistaken by the short-sighted for a Roman fort. The embankment is still here, too, though the three rails have gone.

Everything has changed – nothing has changed. Human nature is the same as it always was in all its hopes, its foolishness, its ignorance, its ingenuity, its love, its treachery, its insecurity, its happiness, its blindness, its bravery and its pain. Down there is still the soft south-east of England. Still the County of Kent, still with its prancing white horse and its motto *Invicta* – unconquered.

And here it comes! See it now, see it . . . alive, alive! Moving out of Ocklington Station going to Victoria, through a wide modern tunnel to the west of Matley, brand-new engine, brand-new overhead wires, twisting like a snake, sparks glittering in the gloom, crackling and throbbing and pulsating and kicking and breathing and hooting *tee-who tee-who tee-who*, line of life, symbol of life – electric train, *electric train* . . .